Lydia of t

Lydia of the Pines

Honoré Willsie Morrow

ÆGYPAN PRESS

1917

Lydia of the Pines
A publication of
ÆGYPAN PRESS

www.aegypan.com

Chapter I

THE TOY BALLOON

"I am the last of my kind. This is the very peak of loneliness."
— *The Murmuring Pine*

*T*here is a State in the North Mississippi Valley unexcelled for its quiet beauty. To the casual traveler there may be a certain monotony in the unending miles of rolling green hills, stretching on and on into distant, pale skies. But the native of the State knows that the monotony is only seeming.

He knows that the green hills shelter in their gentle valleys many placid lakes. Some of them are shallow and bordered with wild rice. Some are couched deep in the hollow of curving bluffs. Some are carefully secreted in virgin pine woods. From the train these pines are little suspected. Fire and the ax have long since destroyed any trace of their growth along the railway.

Yet if the traveler but knew, those distant purple shadows against the sky-line are primeval pine woods, strange to find in a State so highly cultivated, so dotted with thriving towns.

In summer the whole great State is a wonderland of color. Wide wheat lands of a delicate yellowish green sweep mile on mile till brought to pause by the black green of the woods. Mighty acres of corn land, blue-green, march on the heels of the wheat. Great pastures riotous with early goldenrod are thick dotted with milk herds. White farmhouses with red barns and little towns with grey roofs and green shaded streets dot the State like flower beds.

An old State, as we measure things out of New England, settled by New Englanders during the first great emigration after the War of 1812. Its capital, Lake City, lays claim to almost a century of existence. Lying among the hills in the northern part of the State, it contains both the state capitol and the state university. Of its thirty thousand inhabitants, five thousand are students and another five thousand are state legislators and state employees.

The town is one of quiet loveliness. It lies in the curving shore of one of the most beautiful of the little inland lakes. The university campus lies at the northern end of the curve. The dome of the capitol rises from the trees at the southern end. Between, deep lawns stretch to the water's edge with fine old houses capping the gentle slope of the shore. Inland lies the business section of the town, with the less pretentious of the dwellings. The whole city is dotted with great elms and maples, planted three quarters of a century ago.

A quiet town, Lake City, with an atmosphere that might well belong to New England, — beauty, culture, leisure, are its hallmarks.

Fifteen years ago half a mile inland from the lake was an empty block that once had been a farm pasture. Three fine old oaks stood with tops together in the center of the block. The grass was still firm and green and thick in the ancient pasture except for narrow trails worn by children's feet. To the initiated each trail told its own story. There was a hollow square that formed the baseball diamond. There was a straight, short cut that led to the little cress-grown spring. There were the parallel lines for "Come-Come Pull Away," and there were numerous bald spots, the center of little radiating trails where, in the fall, each group of children had its complicated roasting oven in which potatoes and "weenies" were cooked.

On one August afternoon the pasture seemed deserted. It was circus day and the children of the surrounding blocks had all by one method or another won admission to the big tent on the hill east of the town.

Yet not quite all the children. For under one of the oak trees was a baby carriage in which a little girl of two lay fast asleep. And far above her, perched lightly but firmly in a swaying fork of the oak, was a long-legged little girl of twelve. She sat where she could peer easily down on her small sleeping sister, yet high enough to be completely hidden from casual view. She was a thin youngster, with short curling hair of a dusty yellow. The curly hair did not hide the fine square head, a noble head for so small a girl, set well on the little square shoulders. Her eyes were blue and black lashed, her nose nondescript, her mouth large, her chin square and her little jaw line long and pronounced. She wore a soiled sailor suit of blue galatea. Caught in the crotch of two opposite branches was a doll almost as large as the sleeping child below. It was a queer old-fashioned doll, with a huge china head, that displayed brilliant black hair and eyes as blue as those of her little mistress. The doll wore a clumsily made sailor suit of blue calico, which evidently had been washed recently, but not ironed. It is necessary to meet the doll properly, for she was an intimate and important member of the little girl's family. Her name was Florence Dombey.

A battered red book lay in Florence Dombey's lap. It was called, "With Clive in India." It was written by G. A. Henty and told of the marvelous and hair-breadth adventures of an English lad in an Indian campaign.

Florence Dombey's attention, however, was not on the book. It was riveted, hectically, on her mistress, who with her tongue caught between her lips was deftly whittling a cigar box cover into doll furniture, of a scale so tiny that even had Florence Dombey had a doll of her own, it could not have hoped to use the furniture.

It was very quiet in the oak tree. The little furniture-maker spoke softly to Florence Dombey occasionally, but otherwise crickets and locusts made the only sounds on the summer air.

Suddenly she closed the knife sharply. "Darn it! I've cut myself again," she said. She dropped the knife down the neck of her blouse and began to suck her finger. "Here, let me have Henty, Florence Dombey. Don't try to pig it, all the time. You know I don't get hardly any time to read."

The furniture and the remains of the cigar-box cover followed the knife into her blouse and she opened the book. But before she had begun to read there was a sleepy little call from below.

"Yes, baby!" called the child. "Here's Lydia, up in the tree! Watch me, dearie! See me come down. Here comes Florence Dombey first."

With some difficulty the book followed the knife and the furniture into the blouse. Florence Dombey, being hastily inverted, showed a length of light martin cord wrapped about her cotton legs.

"Here she comes, baby! Catch now for Lydia."

The baby below, a tiny plump replica of Lydia, sat up with a gurgle of delight and held up her arms as Florence Dombey, dangling unhappily, upside down, on the end of the marlin cord, was lowered carefully into the perambulator.

"And here I come. Watch me, baby!"

With a swing light and agile as a young monkey, Lydia let herself down, landing with a spring of which an acrobat might have boasted, beside the perambulator.

"There, sweetness!" — kissing the baby — "first we'll fix Florence Dombey, then we'll start for home."

"Florence, home wiv baby."

"Yes, it's getting near supper time." Lydia tucked the still hectically staring doll in beside her small sister, turned the perambulator around and ran it along one of the little paths to the sidewalk. She hoisted it to the sidewalk with some puffing and several "darn its," then started toward the block of houses, north of the pasture.

At the crossing she met a small girl of her own age, who carried a toy balloon, and a popcorn ball.

"Hello, Lydia!" she cried. "It was a perfectly lovely circus!"

"Was it?" said Lydia, with an indifferent voice that something in her blue eyes denied. "Well, I had to take care of little Patience!"

"Huh!" shrilled the little girl, "old Lizzie would have done that! I think your father's mean not to give you the money."

Lydia's red cheeks went still redder. "My father's got plenty of money," she began fiercely. Here the baby interrupted.

"Baby love pritty — Baby love —" she held out two beseeching dimpled hands toward the red balloon.

"Patience, you can't have it," cried Lydia. "It — it'll make your tummy ache. I'll buy you one when you're older."

The black-eyed child, holding the red balloon, suddenly kissed little Patience, who was the pet of all the children in the neighborhood, and put the string of her balloon into the dimpled hand. "I had the circus — you can have the balloon," she said.

Lydia jerked the string away and held it out to the owner.

"We're no cheerity charities, Margery," she said. "I'll get Patience a balloon."

"You're an awful liar and a cruel beast, Lydia!" cried Margery. She snatched the string and tied it about the baby's wrist. "You know you can't buy her one and you know she'll cry herself sick for one, now she's seen mine, and I guess I love her as much as you do."

Lydia looked from the cherub in the perambulator, crowing ecstatically over the red bubble that tugged at her wrist, to the defiant Margery.

"I'll let her have it, Margery," she said reluctantly. "I'll make you a doll's high chair."

"All right," said Margery, nonchalantly. "Face tag! So long!"

Lydia ran the perambulator along the board walk. The street was macadamized and bordered with thrifty maple trees. Back of the maple trees were frame houses, of cheap and stupid construction. Before one of these Lydia paused. It was a dingy brown house, of the type known as "story and a half." There was a dormer window at the top and a bow window in the ground floor and a tiny entry porch at the front.

Lydia opened the gate in the picket fence and tugged the perambulator through and up to the porch.

"There, baby mine, shall Lydia take you in for your supper?"

"Supper," cooed little Patience, lifting her arms.

Lydia lifted her to the porch with surprising ease. The little two year old should have been no light weight for the little mother of twelve. She stood on the porch, watching Lydia arrange Florence Dombey in her place in the perambulator. Her resemblance to Lydia was marked. The same dusty gold hair though lighter, the square little shoulders, and fine set of the head. The red balloon tugging at her wrist, her soiled little white dress blowing in the summer breeze, she finally grew impatient of Lydia's attentions to Florence Dombey.

"Baby eat now," she cried with a stamp of her small foot.

Lydia laughed. She ran up the steps, took the baby's hand and led her through the entry into a square little room, evidently the parlor of the home. It was dusty and disorderly. The center-table of fine old mahogany was littered with pipes and newspapers. A patent rocker was doing duty as a clothes rack for hats and coats. A mahogany desk was almost indistinguishable under a clutter of doll's furniture. The sunset glow pouring through the window disclosed rolls of dust on the faded red Brussels carpet.

Lydia disgorged the contents of her blouse upon the desk, then followed little Patience into the next room. This was larger than the first and was evidently the dining room and sitting room. A huge old mahogany table and sideboard, ill kept and dusty, filled the bow window end of the room. Opposite the sideboard was a couch, draped with a red and green chenille spread. The floor was covered with oil cloth.

A short, stout old woman was setting the table. She had iron grey hair. Her face was a broad wreath of wrinkles, surrounding bespectacled black eyes and a thin mouth that never quite concealed a very white and handsome set of false teeth.

"See! Liz! See!" cried little Patience, pattering up to the old woman with the tugging balloon.

"Ain't that grand!" said Lizzie. "Where'd you git the money, Lydia? Baby's milk's in the tin cup on the kitchen table. Your father's home. You'd better fry the steak. He complains so about it when I do it."

Lydia left the baby clinging to Lizzie's skirts and went on into the kitchen. Her father was washing his hands at the sink.

"Hello, Dad!" she said. The child had a peculiar thread of richness in her voice when she spoke to little Patience and it was apparent again as she greeted the man at the sink. He turned toward her.

"Well, young woman, it's about time you got home," he said. "Baby all right?"

Lydia nodded and turned toward the litter of dishes and paper parcels on the kitchen table. Amos Dudley at this time was about forty years old, — a thin man of medium weight, his brown hair already grey at the temples. Lydia evidently got from him the blue of her eyes and the white of her teeth. He began to peel off a pair of brown overalls.

"What's for supper?" he asked.

"Round steak," said Lydia.

"For heaven's sake, don't let Liz touch it."

"I won't," said the child, piling up dishes deftly. "I'm going to give baby her cup of milk, and then I'll fix it in my patent way."

Amos nodded. "You're a natural cook, like your mother." He paused, one leg of his overalls off, disclosing his shiny black trousers. Lydia carried the cup of milk toward the dining room. From where he sat he could see her kneel before little Patience, and hold the cup, while the baby drank thirstily. Little motes of the sunset light danced on the two curly golden heads. He looked from the children toward the dusty kitchen table.

"What a hell of a mess Liz does keep going," he muttered. "Patience would break her heart, if she knew. Oh! Patience, Patience! —"

Lydia came back with the empty cup. "Now for the steak," she exclaimed. "Gosh, what a fire —"

She attacked the greasy stove with enthusiasm and in a short time a savory smell of steak filled the house. Amos went into the dining room and sat in a rocking chair with little Patience and the balloon in his lap. Old Lizzie hummed as she finished setting the table and Lydia whistled as she seasoned the potatoes Lizzie had set to frying.

"Where'd she get the balloon?" asked Amos as Lydia brought in the platter of meat.

"Margery gave it to her," answered the child. "Supper's ready."

"Got it at the circus, I suppose. I wish I could 'a' let you go, Lydia, but at a dollar and a half a day, I swan I —"

"I didn't want to go," returned Lydia, sitting the baby in her high chair. "I'm getting too big for circuses."

"Too big for a circus!" Her father looked at her with understanding eyes. "I guess heaven is paved with lies like yours, Lydia. John Levine will be over tonight. Get some of the mess dug out of the parlor, will you, Lizzie?"

"Sure," said Lizzie, good-naturedly. Lydia sat opposite her father and poured tea. The ancient maid of all work sat beside Patience and dispensed the currant sauce and the cake.

The baby was half asleep before the meal was ended. "She didn't finish her nap this afternoon," said Lydia. "I'll take her up to bed now and finish my cake afterward."

She tugged the baby out of the high chair that was becoming too close a fit and toiled with her up the narrow stairs that led from the entry.

The little sisters slept together in a slant-ceilinged bedroom. Here again was dust and disorder, the floor covered with clothing and toys, the bed unmade, the old fashioned mahogany bureau piled high with books, brushes, and soiled teacups that had held the baby's milk.

There was still light enough to see by. Lydia stood Patience on the bed and got her into her nightdress after gently persuading the baby to let her fasten the balloon to the foot of the bed. Then she carried her to the little rocker by the window and with a look that was the very essence of motherhood began to rock the two year old to sleep. Presently there floated down to Amos, smoking his pipe on the front step, Lydia's childish, throaty contralto:

"I've reached the land of corn and wine
  With all its riches surely mine,
  I've reached that beauteous shining shore,
  My heaven, my home, forevermore."

A little pause, during which crickets shrilled, then, in a softer voice:

"Blow him again to me
  While my little one, while my pretty one sleeps."

Another pause – and still more softly:

"Wreathe me no gaudy chaplet;
  Make it from simple flowers
  Plucked from the lowly valley
  After the summer showers."

The coolness of the August wind touched Amos' face, "Oh! Patience, Patience –" he murmured.

Lydia sat for a moment or two with the sleeping baby in her arms, looking down on her with a curious gentle intentness. Then she rose carefully, and as carefully deposited little Patience on the bed. This done, she untied the balloon and carried it out with her to the little landing. There was a window here into which the August moon was beginning to shine. Lydia sat down with the balloon and felt of it carefully.

"Aren't balloons the most wonderful things, almost as wonderful as bubbles," she murmured. "I love the smell of them. Think what they can do, how they can float, better than birds! How you want to squeeze them but you don't dast! I'd rather have gone to the circus than to heaven."

In a moment she heard steps and greetings and her father leading his friend into the house. Then she slipped down the stairs and into the night. A dozen times she ran up and down the yard, the balloon like a fettered bird tugging at her wrist.

"I love it as much as little Patience does," she murmured. "Oh, I wish it was mine."

Finally, she ran out of the gate and up the street to the one fine house of which the street boasted. She stole up to the door and fastened the string of the balloon to the door bell, gave the bell a jerk and fled.

As she ran down the street, a boy, leaning against the gatepost next her own, cried, "What's the rush, Lydia?"

"Oh, hello, Kent! Did you like the circus?"

"The best ever! You should have taken that ticket I wanted you to. Didn't cost me anything but carrying water to the elephants."

"I can't take anything I don't pay for. I promised mother. You know how it is, Kent."

"I guess your mother fixed it so you'd miss lots of good times, all right — Now, don't fly off the handle — look, I got a trick. I've rubbed my baseball with match heads, so's I can play catch at night. Try it?"

"Gosh, isn't that wonderful!" exclaimed Lydia. The boy, who was a little taller than Lydia, led the way to the open space between his home and Lydia's. Then he spun Lydia a brisk ball.

"It's like a shooting star," she cried, spinning back a quick overhand shot, "but it makes your hands smell like anything."

"Lydia," called her father from the bow window, "it's time to come in."

"All right!" Then aside to Kent, "I'll wait till he calls me twice more, Kent. Keep them coming."

"Lydia!"

"Yes, Dad. Not so hard, Kent. Don't throw curves, just because I can't."

"Lydia! I shan't call again."

"Coming, Dad! Good night, Kent. Face tag!"

"Face tag yourself, smarty. Maybe I'll be over, tomorrow, if I ain't got anything better to do."

Lydia sauntered slowly up to the kitchen steps. "Well, I haven't anything pleasant at all to look forward to now," she thought. "The circus parade is over and I've returned the balloon. Gee, yes, there is too! I didn't eat my cake yet!"

She turned up the lamp in the kitchen and foraged in the cake box, bringing out the cake Lizzie had saved for her. With this in her hand she entered the dining room. An extraordinarily long, thin man was stretched out in one armchair, Amos in the other.

"You ought to sit in the parlor, Dad," said Lydia, reproachfully.

"It's too stuffy," said Amos.

"Oh, hello, young Lydia!" said the tall man. "Come here and let me look at you."

Levine drew the child to his knee. She looked with a clear affectionate gaze on his thin smooth-shaven face, and into his tired black eyes.

"Why do you always say 'young' Lydia?" asked the child.

"That's what I want to know, too," agreed Amos.

"Because, by heck! she's so young to be such an old lady." He smoothed the short curly hair with a gesture that was indescribably gentle. "I tell you what, young Lydia, if you were ten years older and I were ten years younger —"

Lydia leaned against his knee and took a large bite of cake. "You'd take me traveling, wouldn't you, Mr. Levine?" she said, comfortably.

"You bet I would, and you should have your heart's desire, whatever that might be. If anyone deserves it you do, young Lydia."

Amos nodded and Lydia looked at them both with a sort of puzzled content as she munched her cake.

"I brought a newly illustrated copy of 'Tom Sawyer' for you to see, Lydia," said Levine. "Keep it as long as you want to. It's over on the couch there."

Lydia threw herself headlong on the book and the two men returned to the conversation she had interrupted.

"My loan from Marshall comes due in January," said Amos. "My lord, I've got to do something."

"What made you get so much?" asked Levine.

"A thousand dollars? I told you at the time, I sorta lumped all my outstanding debts with the doctor's bill and funeral expenses and borrowed enough to cover."

"He's a skin, Marshall is. Why does he live on this street except to save money?"

Lydia looked up from "Tom Sawyer." There were two little lines of worry between her eyes and the little sick sense in the pit of her stomach that always came when she heard money matters discussed. Her earliest recollection was of her mother frantically striving to devise some method of meeting their latest loan.

"I'd like to get enough ahead to buy a little farm. All my folks were farmers back in New Hampshire and I was a fool ever to have quit it. It looked like a mechanic could eat a farmer up, though, when I was a young fellow. Now a little farm looks good enough to me. But on a dollar and a half a day, I swan —" Amos sighed.

"Land's high around here," said Levine. "I understand Marshall sold Eagle Farm for a hundred dollars an acre. Takes a sharp farmer to make interest on a hundred an acre. Lord — when you think of the land on the reservation twenty miles from here, just yelling for men to farm it and nothing but a bunch of dirty Indians to take advantage of it."

"Look here, John," said Amos with sudden energy. "It's time that bunch of Indians moved on and gave white men a chance. I wouldn't say a word if they farmed the land, but such a lazy, lousy outfit!"

"There are more than you feel that way, Amos," replied Levine. "But it would take an Act of Congress to do anything."

"Well, why not an Act of Congress, then? What's that bunch we sent down to Washington doing?"

"Poor brutes of Indians," said John Levine, refilling his pipe. "I get ugly about the reservation, yet I realize they've got first right to the land."

"The man that can make best use of the land's got first right to it," insisted Amos. "That's what my ancestors believed two hundred and fifty years ago when they settled in New Hampshire and put loopholes under the eaves of their houses. Our farmhouse had loopholes like that. Snow used to sift in through 'em on my bed when I was a kid."

Lydia, lying on her stomach on the couch, turning the leaves of "Tom Sawyer," looked up with sudden interest.

"Daddy, let's go back there to live. I'd love to live in a house with loopholes."

The two men laughed. "You should have been a boy, Lydia," said Amos.

"A boy," sniffed Levine, "and who'd have mothered little Patience if she'd been a boy?"

"That's right — yet, look at that litter on the desk in the parlor."

Both the men smiled while Lydia blushed.

"What are you going to do with that doll furniture, Lydia?" asked John Levine.

"I'm going to make a doll house for little Patience, for Christmas." Lydia gave an uncomfortable wriggle. "Don't talk about me so much."

"You're working a long way ahead," commented Amos. "That was your mother's trait. I wish I'd had it. Though how I could look ahead on a dollar and a half a day — Lydia, it's bedtime."

Lydia rose reluctantly, her book under her arm.

"Don't read upstairs, child," Amos went on; "go to bed and to sleep, directly."

Lydia looked around for a safe place for the book and finally climbed up on a chair and laid it on the top shelf of the sideboard. Then she came back to her father's side and lifted her face for her good night kiss.

"Good night, my child," said Amos.

"How about me," asked Levine. "Haven't you one to spare for a lonely bachelor?"

He pulled Lydia to him and kissed her gently on the cheek. "If you were ten years older and I were ten years younger —"

"Then we'd travel," said the child, with a happy giggle as she ran out of the room.

There was silence for a moment, then John Levine said, "Too bad old Lizzie is such a slob."

"I know it," replied Amos, "but she gets no wages, just stayed on after nursing my wife. I can't afford to pay for decent help. And after all, she does the rough work, and she's honest and fond of the children."

"Still Lydia ought to have a better chance. I wish you'd let me —" he hesitated.

"Let you what?" asked Amos.

"Nothing. She'd better work out things her own way. She'll be getting to notice things around the house as she grows older."

"It is the devil's own mess here," admitted Amos. "I'm going to move next month. This place has got on my nerves."

"No, Daddy, no!" exclaimed Lydia.

Both men started as the little girl appeared in the kitchen door. "I came down to put Florence Dombey to bed," she explained. "Oh, Daddy, don't let's move again! Why, we've only been here two years."

"I've got to get into a place where I can have a garden," insisted Amos. "If we go further out of town we can get more land for less rent."

"Oh, I don't want to move," wailed Lydia. "Seems to me we've always been moving. Last time you said 'twas because you couldn't bear to stay in the house where mother died. I don't see what excuse you've got this time."

"Lydia, go to bed!" cried Amos.

Lydia retreated hastily into the kitchen and in a moment they heard her footsteps on the back stairs.

"It's a good idea to have a garden," said John Levine. "I tell you, take that cottage of mine out near the lake. I'll let you have it for what you pay for this. It'll be empty the first of September."

"I'll go you," said Amos. "It's as pretty a place as I know of."

Again silence fell. Then Amos said, "John, why don't you go to Congress? Not today, or tomorrow, but maybe four or five years from now."

Levine looked at Amos curiously. The two men were about the same age. Levine's brown face had a foreign look about it, the gift of a Canadian French grandfather. Amos was typically Yankee, with the slightly aquiline nose, the high forehead and the thin hair, usually associated with portraits of Daniel Webster.

"Nice question for one poor man to put to another," said Levine, with a short laugh.

"No reason you should always be poor," replied Amos. "There's rich land lying twenty miles north of here, owned by nothing but Indians."

Levine scratched his head.

"You could run for sheriff," said Amos, "as a starter. You're an Elk."

"By heck!" exploded John Levine. "I'll try for it. No reason why a real estate man shouldn't go into politics as well as some of the shyster lawyers you and I know, huh, Amos?"

Upstairs, Lydia stood in a path of moonlight pulling off her clothes slowly and stifling her sobs for the sake of the little figure in the bed. Having jerked herself into her nightdress, she knelt by the bedside.

"O God," she prayed in a whisper, "don't let there be anymore deaths in our family and help me to bring little Patience up right." This was her regular formula. Tonight she added a plea and a threat. "And O God, don't let us move again. Seems though I can't stand being jerked around so much. If you do, God, I don't know what I'll say to you — Amen."

Softly as a shadow she crept in beside her baby sister and the moonlight slowly edged across the room and rested for a long time on the two curly heads, motionless in childhood's slumber.

Chapter II

THE HEROIC DAY

"Where the roots strike deepest, the fruitage is best."
— *The Murmuring Pine*

*L*ittle Patience had forgotten the red balloon, overnight. Lydia had known that she would. Nevertheless, with the feeling that something was owing to the baby, she decided to turn this Saturday into an extra season of delight for her little charge.

"Do you care, Dad," asked Lydia, at breakfast, "if baby and I have lunch over at the lake shore?"

"Not if you're careful," answered Amos. "By the way," he added, "that cottage of John Levine's is right on the shore." He spoke with studied carelessness. Lydia had a passion for the water.

She stared at him now, with the curiously pellucid gaze that belongs to some blue eyed children and Amos had a vague sense of discomfort, as if somehow, he were not playing the game quite fairly. He dug into his coat pocket and brought up a handful of tobacco from which he disinterred two pennies.

"Here," he said, "one for each of you. Don't be late for supper, chickens."

He kissed the two children, picked up his dinner pail and was off. Lydia, her red cheeks redder than usual, smiled at Lizzie, as she dropped the pennies into the pocket of her blouse and stuffed a grey and frowsy little handkerchief on top of them.

"Isn't he the best old Daddy!" she exclaimed.

"Sure," said Lizzie absentmindedly, as she poured out her third cup of coffee. "Lydia, that dress of yours is real dirty. You get into something else and I'll wash it out today."

"I haven't got much of anything else to get into, have I, Lizzie? — except my Sunday dress."

"You are dreadful short of clothes, child, what with the way you grow and the way you climb trees. I'm trying to save enough out of the grocery money to get you a couple more of them galatea dresses for when school opens, but land — your poor mother was such a hand with the needle, you used to look a perfect picture. There," warned by the sudden droop of Lydia's mouth, "I tell you, you'll be in and out of the water all day, anyhow. Both of you get into the bathing suits your Aunt Emily sent you. They're wool and it's going to be a dreadful hot day."

"Jefful hot day," said little Patience, gulping the last of her oatmeal.

"All right," answered Lydia, soberly. "Wouldn't you think Aunt Emily would have had more sense than to send all those grown up clothes? Who did she think's going to make 'em over, now?"

"I don't know, child. The poor thing is dead now, anyhow. Folks is always thoughtless about charity. Why I wasn't taught to sew, I don't know. Anyhow, the bathing suits she got special for you two."

"You bet your life, I'm going to learn how to sew," said Lydia, rising to untie the baby's bib. "I'm practicing on Florence Dombey. Mother had taught me straight seams and had just begun me on over and over, when —"

"Over and over," repeated the baby, softly.

Lizzie put out a plump, toil-scarred hand and drew Lydia to her. "There, dearie! Think about other things. What shall poor old Liz fix you for lunch?"

The child rubbed her bright cheek against the old woman's faded one. "You are a solid comfort to me, Lizzie," she said with a sigh. Then after a moment she exclaimed, eagerly, "Oh! Lizzie, do you think we could have a deviled egg? Is it too expensive?"

"You shall have a deviled egg if I have to steal it. But maybe you might dust up the parlor a bit while I get things ready."

Lydia established little Patience on the dining room floor with a linen picture book, brought in a broom and dustpan from the kitchen and began furiously to sweep the parlor. When the dust cleared somewhat she emerged with the dustpan heaped with sweepings and the corners of the room still untouched. She hung the coats and hats in the entry and rubbed off the top of the table with her winter Tam o' Shanter, from which the moths flew as she worked. She gazed thoughtfully at the litter on the desk and decided against touching it. Then with a sense of duty well done, she lifted little Patience and carried her up into the little bedroom.

The bathing suits were pretty blue woolen things, and when the two presented themselves to Lizzie in the kitchen the old woman exclaimed, "Well, if ever I seen two fairies!"

"A thin one and a fat one," chuckled Lydia. "Push the baby carriage down over the steps for me, Lizzie, and I'll prepare for our long, hard voyage."

Patience was established in her perambulator with her linen picture book. Florence Dombey was settled at her feet, with "Men of Iron." The bits of cigar box and the knife packed in a pasteboard box were tied to one edge of the carriage. Patience's milk, packed in a tin pail of ice, was laid on top of "Men of Iron." The paper bag of lunch dangled from the handle-bar and Lydia announced the preparations complete.

The way to the lake shore led under the maple trees for several blocks. Then the board walk turned abruptly to cross a marsh, high-grown now with ripening cat-tails. Having safely crossed the marsh, the walk ended in a grass-grown path. Lydia trundled the heavy perambulator with some difficulty along the path. The August sun was hot.

"'A life on the ocean wave —'"

she panted. "You are getting fat, baby!

"'A home on the rolling deep.
  Where the scattered waters rave
  And the winds their revels keep.'

Darn it, I wish I had a bicycle!"

"Ahoy there! Hard aport with your helm, mate!" came a shout from behind her. A boy in a bright red bathing suit jumped off a bicycle.

"Hello, Kent!" said Lydia.

"Hello, yourself!" returned Kent. "Wait and I'll hitch to the front axle."

He untied a stout cord from his handle-bars and proceeded to fasten it from his saddle post to the perambulator. Lydia watched him with a glowing face. She was devoted to Kent, although they quarreled a great deal. He was a handsome boy, two years Lydia's senior; not tall for his years, but already broad and sturdy, with crinkly black hair and clear, black-lashed brown eyes. His face was round and ruddy under its summer tan. His lips were full and strong — an aggressive, jolly boy, with a quick temper and a generous heart. He and Lydia had been friends since kindergarten days.

"I'm going to stay in the Willows all day," said Lydia. "Don't go too fast, Kent."

"Dit-up! Dit-up, horsy!" screamed little Patience.

"Toot! Toot! Express for the Willows!" shouted Kent, mounting his wheel, and the procession was off, the perambulator bounding madly after the bicycle, while Patience shouted with delight and Lydia clung desperately to the handle-bars.

The path, after a few moments, shifted to the lake shore. The water there lapped quietly on a sandy beach, deep shaded by willows. Kent dismounted.

"Discharge your cargo!" he cried.

"Don't be so bossy," said Lydia. "This is my party."

"All right, then I won't play with you."

"Nobody asked you to, smarty. I was going to give you my deviled egg for lunch."

"Gosh," said Kent, "did you bring your lunch? Say, I guess I'll go home and get mother to give me some. But let's play pirates, first."

"All right! I choose to be chief first," agreed Lydia.

"And I'm the cannibal and baby's the stolen princess," said Kent.

The three children plunged into the game which is the common property of childhood. For a time, bloody captures, savage orgies, escape, pursuit, looting of great ships and burial of treasure, transformed the quiet shore to a theater of high crime. At last, as the August noon waxed high, and the hostage princess fell fast asleep in her perambulator cave, the cannibal, who had shifted to captured duke, bowed before the pirate.

"Sir," he said in a deep voice, "I have bethought myself of still further treasure which if you will allow me to go after in my trusty boat, I will get and bring to you — if you will allow me to say farewell at that time to my wife and babes."

"Ha!" returned the pirate. "How do I know you'll come back?"

The duke folded his arms. "You have my word of honor which never has, and never will, be broken."

"Go, duke — but return ere sundown." The pirate made a magnificent gesture toward the bicycle, "and, say Kent, bring plenty to fill yourself up, for I'm awful hungry and I'll need all we've got."

As Kent shot out of sight, Lydia turned to arrange the mosquito bar over little Patience, then she stood looking out over the lake. The morning wind had died and the water lay as motionless and perfect a blue as the sky above. Faint and far down the curving shore the white dome of the Capitol building rose above soft billows of green tree tops. Up the shore, woods crowned the gentle slopes of the hills. Across the lake lay a dim green shore-line of fields. Lydia gave a deep sigh. The beauty of the lake shore always stirred in her a wordless ecstasy. She waded slowly to her waist into the water, then turned gently on her back and floated with her eyes on the sky. Its depth of color was no deeper nor more crystal clear than the depths of her own blue gaze. The tender brooding wonder of the lake was a part and parcel of her own little face, so tiny in the wide expanse of water.

After some moments of drifting, she turned on her side and began to swim along the shore. She swam with a power and a precision of stroke that a man twice her size would have envied. But it must be noted that she did not get out of eye and ear shot of the perambulator beneath the willows; and she had not been swimming long before a curious agitation of the mosquito netting brought her ashore.

She wrung the water from her short skirt and was giving little Patience her bread and milk, when Kent returned with a paper bag.

"Ma was cross at me for pestering her, but I managed to get some sandwiches and doughnuts. Come on, let's begin. Gee, there's a squaw!"

Coming toward the three children seated in the sand by the perambulator was a thin bent old woman, leaning on a stick.

"Dirty old beggar," said Kent, beginning to devour his sandwiches.

"Isn't she awful!" exclaimed Lydia. Begging Indians were no novelty to Lake City children, but this one was so old and thin that Lydia was horrified. Toothless, her black hair streaked with grey, her calico dress unspeakably dirty, her hands like birds' claws clasping her stick, the squaw stopped in front of the children.

"Eat!" she said, pointing to her mouth, while her sunken black eyes were fixed on Kent's sandwiches.

Little Patience looked up and began to whimper with fear.

"Get out, you old rip!" said Kent.

"Eat! Eat!" insisted the squaw, a certain ferocity in her manner.

"Did you walk clear in from the reservation?" asked Lydia.

The squaw nodded, and held out her scrawny hand for the children's inspection. "No eats, all time no eats! You give eats – poor old woman."

"Oh, Kent, she's half starved! Let's give her some of our lunch," exclaimed Lydia.

"Not on your life," returned Kent. "Dirty, lazy lot! Why don't they work?"

"If we'd go halves, we'd have enough," insisted Lydia.

"You told me you'd only enough for yourself. Get out of here, you old she-devil."

The squaw did not so much as glance at Kent. Her eyes were fastened on Lydia, with the look of a hungry, expectant dog. Lydia ran her fingers through her damp curls, and sighed. Then she gave little Patience her share of the bread and butter and a cookie. She laid the precious deviled egg in its twist of paper on top of the remainder of the bread and cookies and handed them to the Indian.

"You can't have any of mine, if you give yours up!" warned Kent.

"I don't want any, pig!" returned Lydia.

The old squaw received the food with trembling fingers and broke into sobs, that tore at her old throat painfully. She said something to Lydia in Indian, and then to the children's surprise, she bundled the food up in her skirt and started as rapidly as possible back in the direction whence she had come.

"She's taking it back to someone," said Kent.

"Poor thing," said Lydia.

"Poor thing!" sniffed Kent. "It would be a good thing if they were all dead. My father says so."

"Well, I guess your father don't know everything," snapped Lydia.

"Evyfing," said Patience, who had finished her lunch and was digging in the sand.

Kent paused in the beginning of his attack on his last sandwich to look Lydia over. She was as thin as a half-grown chicken in her wet

bathing suit. Her damp curls, clinging to her head and her eyes a little
heavy with heat and weariness after her morning of play, made her look
scarcely older than Patience. Kent wouldn't confess, even to himself,
how fond he was of Lydia.

"Here," he said gruffly. "I can't eat this sandwich. Mother made me
too many. And here's a doughnut."

"Thanks, Kent," said Lydia meekly. "What do you want to play, after
lunch?"

"Robinson Crusoe," replied Kent promptly. "You'll have to be Friday."

As recipient of his bounty, Lydia recognized Kent's advantage and
conceded the point without protest.

She held Patience's abbreviated bathing suit skirt with one hand.
"Where are you heading for, baby?" she asked.

"Mardy! Mardy!" screamed Patience, tugging at her leash.

"Oh, rats, it's Margery Marshall. Look at the duds on her. She makes
me sick," groaned Kent.

"She's crazy about little Patience," answered Lydia, "so I put up with
a lot from her."

She loosed her hold on Patience. The baby trundled along the sand
to meet the little girl in an immaculate white sailor suit, who approached
pushing a doll buggy large enough to hold Patience. She ran to meet
the baby and kissed her, then allowed her to help push the doll carriage.

"Mardy tum! Mardy tum!" chanted Patience.

Margery's black hair was in a long braid, tied with a wide white
ribbon. Margery's hands were clean and so were her white stockings and
shoes. She brought the doll's carriage to pause before Lydia and Kent
and gazed at them appraisingly out of bright black eyes — beautiful eyes,
large and heavily lashed. Kent's face was dirty and sweat streaked. His
red bathing suit was grey with sand and green with grass stain. On his
head he wore his favorite headgear, a disreputable white cotton cap with
the words "Goldenrod Flour Mills" across the front.

"Well," he said belligerently, to Margery, "do you see anything green?"

Margery shrugged her shoulders. "Watcha playing?"

"Nothing! Want to play it?" replied Lydia.

"Thanks," answered Margery. "I'll watch you two while I sit with the
baby. Isn't she just ducky in that bathing suit?"

Lydia melted visibly and showed a flash of white teeth. "You bet!
How's Gwendolyn?" nodding toward the great bisque doll seated in the
wonderful doll carriage. "I wish I had a doll like that."

"She isn't in it with Florence Dombey," said Kent. "Florence is some
old sport, she is. Guess I'd better cut her down."

It was remarkable that while on most occasions Lydia was the tenderest of mothers to Florence Dombey, she was, when the fever of "play and pretend" was on her, capable of the most astonishing cruelties. During the game of pirates, Florence Dombey had been hung from a willow branch, in lieu of a yardarm, and had remained dangling there in the wind, forgotten by her mother.

Kent placed her in Patience's carriage. "I'll tell you what I'll do," he said. "I'll go up the shore and get Smith's flat boat. We'll anchor it out from the shore, and that'll be the wreck. We'll swim out to her and bring stuff in. And up under the bank there we'll build the cave and the barricade."

"Gee," exclaimed Lydia, "that's the best we've thought of yet. I'll be collecting stuff to put in the wreck."

All during the golden August afternoon the game waxed joyfully. For a long time, Margery sat aloof, playing with the baby. But when the excavating of the cave began, she succumbed, and began to grovel in the sand with the other two. She was allowed to come in as Friday's father, and baby Patience, panting at her work of scratching the sand with a crooked stick, was entered as the Parrot. Constant small avalanches of sand and soil from the bank powdered the children's hair and clothes with grey-black dust.

"Gosh, this is too much like work," groaned Kent, at last. "I'll tell you, let's play the finding of Friday's father."

"I don't want to be tied up in a boat," protested, Margery, at once.

"Mardy not in boat," chorused little Patience, toddling to the water's edge and throwing in a handful of sand.

"Isn't she a love!" sighed Margery.

"Huh, you girls make me sick," snorted Kent. "We won't tie you in the boat. We'll bring the boat in and get you, then we'll anchor it out where it is now, and — and — I'll go get Smith's rowboat, and Friday and I'll come out and rescue you."

Margery hesitated. "Aw, come on!" urged Kent. "Don't be such a 'fraid cat. That's why us kids don't like you, you're such a silly, dressed-up doll."

The banker's daughter flushed. Though she loved the pretty clothes and though the sense of superiority to other children, carefully cultivated by her mother, was the very breath of her nostrils, she had never been quite so happy as this afternoon when grubbing on an equality with these three inferior children.

"I'm not afraid at all and I'm just as dirty as Lydia is. Go ahead with your old boat."

They tethered Patience with Kent's cord to one of the willow trees and Margery was paddled out several boat lengths from the shore and the great stone that served for anchor was dropped over. Kent took a clean dive overboard, swam ashore and disappeared along the willow path. Little Patience set up a wail.

"Baby turn too. Baby turn, too," she wept.

"I'll go stay with her till Kent comes," said Lydia, diving into the water as casually as if she were rising from a chair.

"I won't stay in this awful boat alone!" shrieked Margery.

Lydia swam steadily to the shore, then turned. Margery was standing up in the boat.

"Sit down! Sit down!" cried Lydia.

Margery, beside herself with fear, tossed her arms, "I won't stay in this old —"

There was a great splash and a choking cry as Margery's black braid disappeared beneath the water.

"And she can't swim," gasped Lydia. "Kent!" she screamed, and made a flying leap into the water. Her slender, childish arms seemed suddenly steel. Her thin little legs took a racing stroke like tiny propellers. Margery came up on the far side of the boat and uttered another choking cry before she went down again. Lydia dived, caught the long black braid and brought the frenzied little face to the surface. Margery immediately threw an arm around Lydia's neck, and Lydia hit her in the face with a clenched small fist and all the strength she could muster.

"Let go, or I'll let you drown. Turn over on your back. There isn't a thing to be afraid of."

Margery, with a sob, obeyed and Lydia towed her the short distance to the boat. "There, catch hold," she said.

Both the children clung to the gunwale, Margery choking and sobbing.

"I can't lift you into the boat," panted Lydia. "But quit your crying. You're safe. There's Kent."

The whole episode had taken but a few minutes. Kent had heard the call and some note of need in it registered, after a moment, in his mind. He ran back and leaped into the water.

He clambered into the flat boat and reaching over pulled Margery bodily over the gunwale. The child, sick and hysterical, huddled into the bottom of the boat.

"Are you all right, Lyd?" he asked.

"Sure," replied Lydia, who was beginning to recover her breath.

It was the work of a minute to ground the boat. Then unheeding little Patience's lamentations, the two children looked at each other and at Margery.

"I'll run for her mother," said Kent.

"And scare her to death! She isn't hurt a bit," insisted Lydia. "Margery, stop crying. You're all right, I tell you."

"I'll tell you," said Kent, "let's put her in Patience's carriage, and carry her home. The water she swallowed makes her awful sick at her stomach, I guess."

The fright over, the old spirit of adventure, with an added sense of heroism, animated Kent and Lydia.

Margery was teased out of the boat and assisted into the perambulator, with her dripping white legs dangling helplessly over the end. Little Patience's tears were assuaged when she was placed in the doll buggy, with Margery's doll in her arms. Florence Dombey was tied papoose fashion to Lydia's back. The bicycle was hidden in the cave and with Kent wheeling Margery and Lydia, Patience, the procession started wildly for home.

By the time they had turned into the home street, Margery was beginning to recover, but she was still shivering and inclined to sob. Other children followed them and it was quite an imposing group that turned in at the Marshall gate, just as Mrs. Marshall came to the door to bid a guest good-bye.

The scene that followed was difficult for either Lydia or Kent to describe afterward. There was a hullabaloo that brought half the mothers of the neighborhood into the yard. The doctor was sent for. Margery was put to bed and Kent and Lydia were mentioned as murderers, low-down brats and coarse little brutes by Mrs. Marshall, who ended by threatening them with the police.

Old Lizzie appeared on the scene in time to take Lydia's part and Kent disappeared after Mrs. Marshall had told him that Margery's father would be around to see his father that evening.

"Is the child dead?" demanded old Lizzie, holding Patience on one arm while Lydia clung to the other.

"She was able to walk upstairs," said a neighbor. "It's just Mrs. Marshall's way, you know."

"I'll way her," snorted Lizzie. "Fine thanks to Lydia for saving the child. Come home with your old Liz, dearie, and get into the nice clean dress I've got for you."

Lydia told the story to Amos at suppertime. He was much disturbed.

"I've told you often and often, Lydia, never to endanger a child that can't swim. You and Kent should have had more sense."

The quick tears sprang to the child's eyes. She was still much shaken.

"Is this lesson enough for you, or must I forbid your playing in the water? I thought I could trust you absolutely."

"Stop your scolding her, Amos Dudley," exclaimed old Lizzie. "I won't have it. She's too nervous a child."

Amos was saved a reply by a ring at the doorbell. Lizzie let Margery's father in. He was a short, red-faced man with black hair and eyes. He was too much excited now to stand on ceremony, and he followed Lizzie into the dining room.

"This won't do, Dudley. These wild young ones of yours —"

"Wait a minute, Marshall," interrupted Amos, with a dignity that he had brought with him from New England. "Margery is all right, so we can go over this thing calmly. Sit down and listen to Lydia's story. Tell him, Lydia."

Lydia left her place and crowded up against her father's side. Old Lizzie was holding the baby.

"It was like this," Lydia began. "Baby and me were going to play by ourselves under the willows. Then Kent, he came and he played pirates with us."

"Why wasn't Kent out playing with the boys?" interrupted Marshall.

Lydia's eyes widened. "Why, I'm as good as a boy to play with, any day! Mostly he does play with other boys, but when they aren't round, he and I play pirates. And then, right after we'd had our lunch, Margery she came along and Kent and I were mad —"

The child paused uncomfortably and rubbed her curly yellow head with her thin little hand in an embarrassed way.

"Why were you mad, Lydia?" In spite of himself, Marshall's voice was softening, as Amos had known it would. Lydia made a deep appeal somehow to the tenderness of men.

"Tell Mr. Marshall all you told me, Lydia," said Amos.

"Well — well, you see, it's like this. Margery's always so *clean* and she has lovely clothes and — and she — she looks down on us other kids so we won't generally let her play with us — and she's an awful 'fraid cat and — and a tattle-tale. But when we got to playing Robinson Crusoe, and were digging the cave she helped and got terrible dirty, just like us, and then she wanted to be Friday's father, and then — well — now — I guess the rest of it was Kent's and my fault. We forgot she couldn't swim and we forgot what a cry-baby she was. 'Cause you see, water's almost like land to Kent and me and we'd been swimming 'most all day, and Margery's the only kid around here that can't swim."

"Why can't she swim?" demanded Marshall. "How'd all the rest of you learn? Don't you think you were mean not to let her learn?"

Again Lydia's pellucid eyes widened. "Why her mother won't let her play with common kids like us! And us kids never learned. We've just played in the water ever since we was as big as baby. She'll be swimming by the time she's five," added Lydia, looking at the sleeping Patience and speaking with the curious note of richness in her voice.

David Marshall scowled and stirred uncomfortably. He did not look at Amos, who sat with his arm about Lydia, his thin face a lesser replica of the old engraving of Daniel Webster hanging on the wall above.

"Well, go on! How'd she come to fall overboard?"

"She and I was sitting in the boat, and baby, she was tied to a tree by a long string and she began to cry to come too, and I jumped over to go quiet her. Kent he'd gone to get another boat. And Margery she jumped up and began to yell and wave her arms and fell overboard. Then I remembered she couldn't swim and I went back and got her and Kent came and pulled us in shore. It wasn't anything, but Margery's such a cry-baby. Lizzie, she's terrible uncomfortable."

Lydia's attention had returned to little Patience. "I'll take her up to bed," she said, "it won't take but a few minutes."

"I'll carry her," said Lizzie.

The baby opened her eyes. "No, no one cally but Lyd."

"Let Daddy carry you," begged Amos.

Patience's little voice rose to a wail. "No one cally but Lyd."

"You don't have to be so polite," sniffed Lydia, "I carry her all the time."

She lifted the sleepy baby easily and Patience dropped her soft cheek against Lydia's and closed her eyes again. Lydia turned to Marshall. Her face was very serious.

"I know I was awful bad, Mr. Marshall, and maybe you feel as if you ought to lick me."

"Put your little sister to bed," said Marshall gravely, "and then we'll see."

There was silence in the room for a moment after Lydia left it, then Amos said, "I'll be glad to do anything I can, Marshall."

"Neither of you'll lay a finger on Lydia," interrupted Lizzie. "If you want to lick anyone, go lick Elviry Marshall, the fool! Why, I knew her when she was my niece's hired girl and you, Dave Marshall, was selling cans of tomatoes over a counter. And she's bringing that young one up to be a silly little fool. Mark my words, she'll be the prey of the first fortune-hunter that comes along."

To Amos's surprise, Marshall only scowled at Lizzie, who now began to remove the supper dishes, talking in a whisper to herself. She paused once in front of Marshall with the teapot in one hand and the milk pitcher in the other.

"Coming and going with your nose in the air, Dave, I suppose you never notice Lydia, but you've had a good look at her tonight, and mind well what I mean when I say you know as well as I that children like Lydia are rare and that your young one ought to consider it a privilege to be pulled out of the water by her."

Old Lizzie pounded out of the room and there was a clatter of dishes that ably expressed her frame of mind. Above the clatter and down from the children's bedroom floated Lydia's little contralto lilt:

"Wreathe me no gaudy chaplet;
  Make it from simple flowers
  Plucked from the lowly valley
  After the summer showers."

Neither Amos nor his caller spoke. In a few minutes Lydia's step sounded on the stairs. The last of the sunset glow caught her hair, and the fine set of her head on her square little shoulders was never more pronounced than as she walked slowly toward Dave Marshall.

"I never had a licking," she said, "but I guess I deserve one and so you'd better do it and get it done, Mr. Marshall."

Chapter III

THE COTTAGE

"The young pine knows the secrets of the ground. The old pine knows the stars."

— *The Murmuring Pine*

*M*arshall cleared his throat and reaching out, took Lydia by the arm and pulled her toward him. He could feel her muscles stiffen under his touch. The bright red color left her cheeks.

"I wouldn't think much of your father, my child," he said, huskily, "if he let me whip you, even if I wanted to."

Lydia took a quick look up into his face. Then she gave a little gasping sigh, her lips quivered and she leaned against his knee.

"Look here, Lydia," said Dave Marshall, "this is to be your punishment. I want you and Kent to teach Margery how to swim and how to get dirty, see? Let her play with you 'common kids,' will you?"

"Will her mother let her?" asked Lydia.

"Yes," answered Dave, grimly.

"All right," said Lydia, with a little sigh.

"I know it'll be a hard job," Marshall interpreted the sigh quickly; "that's where the punishment comes in."

"Lydia'll do it. I'll see to it," said Amos.

"You keep out, Dudley. This is between Lydia and me. How about it, Lydia?"

"If you'll boss her mother, I'll boss Margery and Kent," said Lydia, with a sudden laugh.

"It's a bargain." Marshall rose. "Good night, Dudley."

"Good night, Marshall."

Amos followed his caller to the door. As he did so Lydia heard Kent's whistle in the back yard. She joined him and the two withdrew to a bench behind the woodshed.

"I saw him through the window," said Kent, in a low voice. "What's he going to do to us? Dad's licked me, so that much is done."

Lydia told of their punishment. "Darn it," groaned Kent, "I'd rather had another licking. I certainly do hate that girl."

"So do I," agreed Lydia.

The two sat staring into the summer twilight. "Anyhow," said Lydia, "I hit her an awful smack in the face today. Of course, I had to, but that's why her nose bled so."

"I wish you'd busted her old snoot," grumbled Kent. "She's always turning it up at everybody. We saved somebody's life today, by golly, and you'd think we'd committed a crime."

Lydia sighed. "Nothing to look forward to but worry now. O gee, Kent, I've got two pennies! One's Patience's. But let's go spend the other at Spence's!"

"Gum or all day sucker?" asked Kent, who, in spite of the fact that he owned a second-hand bicycle, was not above sharing a penny.

"Gum lasts longer," suggested Lydia.

"What kinda gum, spruce or white or tutti-frutti?"

"You can choose."

"Spruce then. It makes the most juice. Come on, Lyd, before you're called in."

And thus ended the heroic day.

No one ever knew what Dave Marshall said to Elviry, his wife, but a day or so after, little Margery, in a fine white flannel bathing suit, appeared on the sand, about a quarter of a mile below the Willows. Here any bright day from the last of June to the first week in September, a dozen children might be found at play in and out of the water. There was usually a mother or an older sister somewhere about, but it was to be noted that Mrs. Marshall never appeared. Margery came and went with Lydia.

Kent was a quitter! After the rescue he decided to eschew the society of girls forever and he struck a bargain with Lydia that she could have the use of his bicycle one day a week till snow came if she would undertake the disciplining of the banker's daughter alone. For such a bribe Lydia would have undertaken to teach Elviry Marshall, herself, to swim — and so the bargain was struck.

Margery, it was quickly discovered, sousing in the water with the other children was quite "a common kid" herself and though there seemed to be an inherent snobbishness in the little girl that returned to her as soon as she was dried and clothed, in her bathing suit she mucked about and screamed and quarreled as did the rest.

Lydia's method of teaching was one employed by most of the children of Lake City when a new child moved into the town. She forced Margery to float face downward in the water, again and again, while she counted ten. After one afternoon of this, the banker's daughter had forever lost her fear of the water and the rest was easy.

In spite of the relationship Dave Marshall had established between the two children, Margery and Lydia did not like each other. One Saturday afternoon, after banking hours, Marshall was seated on his front porch, with Elviry and Margery, when Lydia appeared. She stood on the steps in her bathing suit, her bare feet in a pair of ragged "sneakers." Her face and hands and ankles were dirty but her eyes and the pink of her cheeks were clear.

"Come on, Marg," said Lydia, "and, Mr. Marshall, please, won't you come too and see how well she does it?"

"Run and get into your bathing suit, daughter," said Marshall. "Elviry, want to come?"

"No," snapped Elviry. "Lydia, how do you manage to get so dirty, when to my positive knowledge, you're in the water an hour every day?"

Lydia blushed and tried to hide one ankle behind the other. "I think you're terrible impolite," she murmured.

Dave roared with laughter. "Right you are, Lydia! I guess I'll have to hitch up and drive us all over."

They drove to the Willows and Margery went through her paces, while her father watched and applauded from the shore. When they had finished and had run up and down to warm up and dry off and were driving home, Dave said,

"You'd better come in to supper with us, Lydia."

"No, thank you," answered the child. "Mr. Levine's coming to supper at our house and I have to cook it."

"Hum! What does John Levine do at your house, so much?"

"Oh, he's going into politics," answered Lydia, innocently, "and Dad advises him."

"Well, tell them you've done a fine job as a swimming teacher," Dave spoke carelessly. "I don't see why Levine wants to get into politics. He's doing well in real estate."

"Oh!" exclaimed Lydia, with a child's importance at having real news to impart, "he's going into politics so's to get some Indian land."

"Like hell he is!" exclaimed Marshall.

"Oh, Daddy!" Margery's voice was exactly like her mother's.

They were turning into the Marshall driveway and Marshall's face was a curious mixture of amusement and irritation. He kissed his little daughter when he lifted her from the buggy and bade her run to the house. Before he lifted Lydia down he paused and as he stood on the ground and she sat in the surrey, she looked levelly into his black eyes.

"I wish I had another little daughter like you, Lydia," he said. "I don't see why — but God, you can't get swans from barnyard fowl." He continued to study Lydia's face. "Some day, my child, you'll make some man's heart break, or lift him up to heaven."

Lydia squirmed.

"Well, Margery's taught now," she said hastily, "so I don't have to be punished anymore, do I?"

Marshall scowled slightly. "What do you mean? Don't you want Margery to play with you?"

"Oh, sure, she can play, if she wants to, but I mean I don't have to go get her and bring her into our games."

"No," said Dave slowly, "but I think it would be nice of you to sort of keep an eye on her and get her dirty once in a while. There! Run home, child, you're shivering."

With puzzled eyes, Lydia obeyed.

The most important result, as far as Lydia was interested, of the talk between her father and Levine that night was that Amos decided definitely to move the following week. Lydia cried a little over it, reproached God in her prayers and then with a child's resignation to the inevitability of grown up decision, she began to say good-bye to the neighborhood children and to help old Lizzie to pack.

Lydia did not see the new home until she rode out with the first dray-load of furniture. She sat in the high seat beside the driver, baby Patience in her lap, her thin, long little legs dangling, her cheeks scarlet with excitement and the warmth of a hot September morning. The cottage was a mile from the old home. They drove along the maple shaded street for the first half of the distance, then turned into a dirt road that led toward the lake shore. The dirt road emerged on the shore a half mile above the Willows and wound along a high embankment, crowned with oaks.

"Whoa!" shouted the driver.

"Oh, isn't it pretty!" exclaimed Lydia.

An old-fashioned white cottage, with green blinds and a tiny front porch, stood beside the road, its back to the lake. There were five acres or so of ground around the house, set off by a white picket fence. At the gate a pine tree stood. There were oaks and lilac bushes in the front yard. Through the leaves, Lydia saw the blue of the lake.

"Our yard runs right down to the water!" she cried, as the driver lifted the baby down and she followed after. "Gee! I'm glad we moved!"

"It is a nice little spot," said the driver, "but kinda lonely." He set the perambulator inside the fence, then balanced the dining room table on his head and started up the path to the door.

Lydia looked along the road, where an occasional house was to be seen.

"I hope kids live in those houses," she said, "but if they don't, baby and the lake are company enough for me, and Kent can come out on his wheel."

She strapped Patience into the perambulator, then ran up to the house. The front door gave directly into a living room of good proportions. Out of this folding doors led into a small dining room and beyond this a kitchen of generous size with a wonderful view of the glimmering lake from its rear windows. A comfortable-sized bedroom opened off each of these rooms. Lydia ran through the little house eagerly. It was full of windows and being all on one floor, gave a fine effect of spaciousness. It was an old house but in excellent repair as was all John Levine's property.

"I'm going to have the bedroom off the kitchen, 'cause you can see the lake from it," she told the driver.

"It'll be colder'n charity in the winter. Better take the middle one," he remarked, setting the kitchen stove down with a bang.

"No, old Lizzie'll want to have that. Well, I'll begin to get things settled."

Lizzie arrived on the third and final load. She brought with her a lunch that they shared with the driver. He good-naturedly set up the kitchen stove and the three beds for them and departed with the hope that they would not be too lonesome.

Lydia and old Lizzie put in an afternoon of gigantic effort. By six o'clock, the beds were made, dishes unpacked and in the china closet, the table was set for supper and an Irish stew of Lydia's make was simmering on the stove.

When Amos came up the path at a half after six, his dinner pail in his hand, he found Lydia flat on her back on the little front porch. Her curly head was wet with perspiration; face, hands and blouse were black. The baby sat beside her, trying to get Florence Dombey to sleep.

"Well," said Amos, looking down on his family, "how do you like it, Lydia?"

"It's great! My back's broken! Supper's ready."

"You shouldn't lift heavy things, child! How often have I told you? Wait until I get home."

"I want to get things done," replied Lydia, "so's I can do a little playing before school opens. Come on in and see all we've done, Daddy."

She forget her aching back and led the way into the house. Amos was as excited and pleased as the children and Lizzie, so tired that her old hands shook, was as elated as the others.

"It's much more roomy than the old house and all on one floor. 'Twill save me the stairs. And the garden'll be fine," she said, failing to call attention to the fact that the water was far from the house and that there was no kitchen sink.

"We've got to try to keep this place cleaner than we did the other," said Amos. "Lydia, better wash up for supper."

"Oh, Daddy," said Lydia, "I'm too tired! Don't make me!"

"All right," answered Amos, "but your mother was always clean and so am I. I don't see where you get it."

"Maybe one of my ancestors was a garbage man," suggested Lydia, sliding into her place at the table.

She allowed Lizzie to carry Patience into their bedroom after supper and Amos, smoking in the yard and planning the garden for next year, waited in vain to hear "Beulah Land" and "Wreathe me no gaudy chaplet" float to him from the open window.

"Where's Lydia, Lizzie?" he asked as the old lady came out to empty the dish water.

"She ain't come out yet. Maybe she's fell asleep too."

The two tiptoed to the window. On the bed under the covers was little Patience, fast asleep, and beside her, on top of the covers, fully dressed, lay Lydia, an arm across her little sister, in the sleep of utter exhaustion.

"I'll just take her shoes off and cover her and leave her till morning," said Lizzie.

But Amos, gazing at his two ill-kempt little daughters, at the chaotic room, did not answer except to murmur to himself, "Oh, Patience! Patience!"

The cottage was somewhat isolated. Amos was three quarters of a mile from his work. The schoolhouse was a mile away and the nearest trolley, which Lizzie must take to do the family shopping, was half a mile back along the dirt road.

Nevertheless, all the family felt that they had taken a distinct step upward in moving into lake shore property and nobody complained of distances. Amos began putting in his Sundays in cleaning up the bramble-grown acres he intended to turn into a garden in the spring. He could not afford to have it plowed so he spaded it all himself, during the wonderful bright fall Sabbaths. Nor was this a hardship for Amos. Only the farm bred can realize the reminiscent joy he took in wrestling with the sod, which gave up the smell that is more deeply familiar to man than any other in the range of human experience.

A dairy farmer named Norton, up the road, gave him manure in exchange for the promise of early vegetables for his table. After his spading was done in late September, Amos, with his wheelbarrow, followed by the two children, began his trips between the dairy farm and his garden patch and he kept these up until the garden was deep with fertilizer.

There never had been a more beautiful autumn than this. There was enough rain to wet down the soil for the winter, yet the Sundays were almost always clear. Fields and woods stretched away before the cottage, crimson and green as the frosts came on. Back of the cottage, forever gleaming through the scarlet of the autumn oaks, lay the lake, where duck and teal were beginning to lodge o' nights, in the rice-fringed nooks along the shore.

Lydia was happier than she had been since her mother's death. She took the long tramps to and from school, lunch box and school bag slung at her back, in a sort of ecstasy. She was inherently a child of the woods and fields. Their beauty thrilled her while it tranquilized her. Some of the weight of worry and responsibility that she had carried since her baby sister of two weeks had been turned over to her care left her.

Kent was enchanted with the new home. Football was very engrossing, yet he managed to get out for at least one visit a week. He and Lydia discovered a tiny spring in the bank above the lake and they began at once to dam it in and planned a great series of ditches and canals.

The doll's furniture was finished by October and Lydia began work on the doll's house.

One Saturday afternoon early in October she was established on the front steps with her carpentry when a surrey stopped at the gate. Little Patience, in a red coat, rolled to her feet. She had been collecting pebbles from the gravel walk.

"Mardy!" she screamed. "Baby's Mardy!" and started down the walk to meet Margery and her father.

"Darn it," said Lydia to herself. "Hello, Marg! How de do, Mr. Marshall."

"Well! Well!" Dave Marshall lifted the tails of his light overcoat and sat down on the steps. "Gone into house building, eh, Lydia? Did you do it all yourself? Gee! that's not such a bad job."

Lydia had the aptitude of a boy for tools. On one end of the cracker box was a V-shaped roof. There were two shelves within, making three floors, and Lydia was now hard at work with a chisel and jackknife hacking out two windows for each floor.

She stood, chisel in hand, her red coat sleeves rolled to her elbows, her curly hair wind-tossed, staring at Marshall half proudly, half defiantly.

Dave laughed delightedly. "Lydia, anytime your father wants to sell you, I'm in the market." He looked at the nails hammered in without a crack or bruise in the wood, then laughed again.

"Get your and the baby's hats, Lydia. We stopped to take you for a ride."

Lydia's eyes danced, then she shook her head. "I can't! The bread's in baking and I'm watching it."

"Where's Lizzie?"

"She went in town to do the marketing! Darn it! Don't I have awful luck?"

Lydia sighed and looked from baby Patience and Margery, walking up and down the path, to Mrs. Marshall, holding the reins.

"Well, anyhow," she said, with sudden cheerfulness, "Mrs. Marshall'll be glad I'm not coming, and some day, maybe you'll take me when she isn't with you."

Dave started to protest, then the polite lie faded on his lips. Lydia turned her pellucid gaze to his with such a look of mature understanding, that he ended by nodding as if she had indeed been grown up, and rising, said, "Perhaps you're right. Good-bye, my dear. Come, Margery."

Lydia stood with the baby clinging to her skirts. There were tears in her eyes. Sometimes she looked on the world that other children lived in, with the wonder and longing of a little beggar snub-nosed against the window of a French pastry shop.

John Levine came home with Amos that night to supper. Amos felt safe about an unexpected guest on Saturday nights for there was always a pot of baked beans, at the baking of which Lizzie was a master hand, and there were always biscuits. Lydia was expert at making these. She had taken of late to practicing with her mother's old cook book and Amos felt as if he were getting a new lease of gastronomic life.

"Well," said Levine, after supper was finished, the baby was asleep and Lydia was established with a copy of "The Water Babies" he had brought her, "I had an interesting trip, this week."

Amos tossed the bag of tobacco to Levine. "Where?"

"I put in most of the week on horseback up on the reservation. Amos, the pine land up in there is something to dream of. Why, there's nothing like it left in the Mississippi Valley, nor hasn't been for twenty years. Have you ever been up there?"

Amos shook his head. "I've just never had time. It's a God-awful trip. No railroad, twenty-mile drive —"

Levine nodded. "The Indians are in awful bad shape up there. Agent's in it for what he can get, I guess. Don't know as I blame him. The sooner the Indians are gone the better it'll be for us and all concerned."

"What's the matter with 'em?" asked Lydia.

"Consumption — some kind of eye disease — starvation —"

The child shivered and her eyes widened.

"You'd better go on with the 'Water Babies,'" said John. "Has Tom fallen into the river yet?"

"No, he's just seen himself in the mirror," answered Lydia, burying her nose in the delectable tale again.

"It's a wonderful story," said Levine, his black eyes reminiscent.

"'Clear and cool, clear and cool,
   By laughing shallow and dreaming pool;

*

Undefiled, for the undefiled;
Play by me, bathe in me, mother and child.'

It has some unforgettable verse in it. Well, as I was saying, Amos, that timber isn't going to stay up there and rot — *because, I'm going to get it out of there!*"

"How?" asked Amos.

"Act of Congress, maybe. Maybe a railroad will get a permit to go through, eh? There are several ways. We'll die rich, yet, Amos."

Amos pulled at his pipe and shook his head. "You will but I won't. It isn't in our blood."

"Shucks, Amos. Where's your nerve?"

Amos looked at Levine silently for a moment. Then he said huskily,

"My nerve is gone with Patience. And if she isn't in heaven, there isn't one, that's all."

Lydia looked up from her story with a quick flash of tragedy in her eyes.

"Well," said John, smiling at her gently, "if you don't want to be rich, Amos, Lydia does. I'll give her the cottage here, the first fifty thousand I make off of Indian pine lands."

"I swan," exclaimed Amos, "if you do that, I'll buy a cow and a pig and some chickens and I can pretty near make a living right here."

"You're foolish, Amos. This isn't New England. This is the West. All you've got to do is to keep your nerve, and anyone with sense can make a killing. Opportunity screams at you."

"I guess she's always on my deaf side," said Amos.

"When I grow up," said Lydia, suddenly, "I'm going to buy a ship and sail to Africa and explore the jungles."

"I'll go with you, Lydia,," exclaimed Levine, "hanged if I don't sell my Indian lands for real money, and go right along with you."

"Mr. Marshall says 'like Hell you'll get some Indian lands,'" mused the child.

Both men exclaimed together, "What!"

Lydia was confused but repeated her conversation with Marshall.

"So that's the way the wind blows," said Levine.

"You don't think for a minute there's a banker in town without one hand on the reservation," said Amos. "Lydia, you're old enough now not to repeat conversations you hear at home. Don't you ever tell anybody the things you hear me and Mr. Levine talk over. Understand?" sharply.

"Yes, Daddy," murmured Lydia, flushing painfully.

"You don't have to jaw the child that way, Amos." Levine's voice was impatient. "Just explain things to her. Why do you want to humiliate her?"

Amos gave a short laugh. "Takes a bachelor to bring up kids. Run along to bed, Lydia."

"Lydia's not a kid. She's a grown-up lady in disguise," said Levine, catching her hand as she passed and drawing her to him. "Good night, young Lydia! If you were ten years older and I were ten years younger —"

Lydia smiled through tear-dimmed eyes. "We'd travel!" she said.

Cold weather set in early this year. Before Thanksgiving the lake was ice-locked for the winter. The garden was flinty, and on Thanksgiving Day, three inches of snow fell. The family rose in the dark. Amos, with his dinner pail, left the house an hour before Lydia and the sun was just flushing the brown tree tops when she waved good-bye to little Patience, whose lovely little face against the window was the last thing she saw in the morning, the first thing she saw watching for her return in the dusk of the early winter evening.

Amos, always a little moody and a little restless, since the children's mother had gone to her last sleep, grew more so as the end of the year approached. It was perhaps a week before Christmas on a Sunday afternoon that he called Lydia to him. Patience was having her nap and Lizzie had gone to call on Mrs. Norton.

Lydia, who was re-reading "The Water Babies," put it down reluctantly and came to her father's side. Her heart thumped heavily. Her father's depressed voice meant just one thing — money trouble.

He was very gentle. He put his hand on the dusty yellow of her hair. He was very careful of the children's hair. Like many New England farm lads he was a jack of all trades. He clipped Lydia's hair every month himself.

"Your hair will be thick enough in another year, so's I won't have to cut it anymore, Lydia. It's coming along thick as felt. Wouldn't think it was once thin, now."

Lydia eyed her father's care-lined face uneasily. Amos still hesitated.

"Where'd you get that dress, my dear?" he asked.

"Lizzie and I made it of that one of mother's," answered the child. "It isn't made so awful good, but I like to wear it, because it was hers."

"Yes, yes," said Amos absently.

The dress was a green serge, clumsily put together as a sailor suit, and the color fought desperately with the transparent blue of the little girl's eyes.

"Lydia," said her father abruptly. "You're a big girl now. You asked for skates and a sled for Christmas. My child, I don't see how you children are going to have anything extra for Christmas, except perhaps a little candy and an orange. That note with Marshall comes due in January. By standing Levine off on the rent, I can rake and scrape the interest together. It's hopeless for me even to consider meeting the note. What Marshall will do, I don't know. If I could ever get on my feet — with the garden. But on a dollar and a half a day, I swan —"

"No Christmas at all?" quavered Lydia. "Won't we even hang up our stockings?"

"If you'll be contented just to put a little candy in them. Come, Lydia, you're too big to hang up your stocking, anyhow."

Lydia left her father and walked over to the window. She pressed her face against the pane and looked back to the lake. The sun was sinking in a grey rift of clouds. The lake was a desolate plain of silvery gold touched with great shadows of purple where snow drifts were high. As she looked, the weight on her chest lifted. The trembling in her hands that always came with the mention of money lessened. The child, even as early as this, had the greatest gift that life bestows, the power of deriving solace from sky and hill and sweep of water.

"Anyhow," she said to her father, "I've still got something to look forward to. I've got the doll house to give baby, and Mr. Levine always gives me a book for Christmas."

"That's a good girl!" Amos gave a relieved sigh, then went on with his brooding over his unlighted pipe.

And after all, this Christmas proved to be one of the high spots of Lydia's life. She had a joyous 24th. All the morning she spent in the woods on the Norton farm with her sled, cutting pine boughs. As she trudged back through the farmyard, Billy Norton called to her.

"Oh, Lydia!"

Lydia stopped her sled against a drift and waited for Billy to cross the farmyard. He was a large, awkward boy several years older than Lydia. He seemed a very homely sort of person to her, yet she liked his face. He was as fair as Kent was dark. Kent's features were regular and clean-cut. Billy's were rough hewn and irregular, and his hair and lashes were straight and blond.

What Lydia could not at this time appreciate was the fact that Billy's grey eyes were remarkable in the clarity and steadiness of their gaze, that his square jaw and mobile mouth were full of fine promise for his manhood and that even at sixteen the framework of his great body was magnificent.

He never had paid any attention to Lydia before and she was bashful toward the older boys.

"Say, Lydia, want a brace of duck? A lot of them settled at Warm Springs last night and I've got more than I can use."

He leaned his gun against the fence and began to separate two birds from the bunch hanging over his shoulder.

Lydia began to breathe quickly. The Dudleys could not afford a special Christmas dinner.

"I — I don't know how I could pay you, Bill —"

"Who wants pay?" asked Bill, indignantly.

"I dasn't take anything without paying for it," returned Lydia, her eyes still on the ducks. "But I'd — I'd rather have those than a ship."

Billy's clear gaze wandered from Lydia's thin little face to her patched mittens and back again.

"Won't your father let you?" he asked.

"I won't let myself," replied the little girl.

"Oh!" said Billy, his grey eyes deepening. "Well, let me have the evergreens and you go back for some more. It'll save me getting Ma hers."

With one thrust of her foot Lydia shoved the fragrant pile of boughs into the snow. She tied the brace of duck to the sled and started back toward the wood, then paused and looked back at Billy.

"Thank you a hundred times," she called.

"It was a business deal. No thanks needed," he replied.

Lydia nodded and trudged off. The boy stood for a moment looking at the little figure, then he started after her.

"Lydia, I'll get that load of pines for you."

She tossed a vivid smile over her shoulder. "You will not. It's a business deal."

And Billy turned back reluctantly toward the barn.

In an hour Lydia was panting up the steps into the kitchen. Lizzie's joy was even more extreme than Lydia's. She thawed the ducks out and dressed them, after dinner, with the two children standing so close as at times seriously to impede progress.

"I'm lucky," said Lydia. "There isn't anybody luckier than I am or has better things happen to 'em than I do. I'd rather be me than a water baby."

"Baby not a water baby. Baby a duck," commented Patience, her hands full of bright feathers.

"Baby is a duck," laughed Lydia. "Won't Daddy be glad!"

Amos was glad. Plodding sadly home, he was greeted by three glowing faces in the open door as soon as his foot sounded on the porch. The base burner in the living room was clear and glowing. The dining room was fragrant with pine. He was not allowed to take off his overcoat, but was towed to the kitchen where the two birds, trussed and stuffed for the baking, were set forth on the table.

"I got 'em!" shouted Lydia. "I got 'em off Billy Norton for a load of pine. Christmas present for you, Daddy, from yours truly, Lydia!" She seized the baby's hands and the two did a dance round Amos, shouting, "Christmas present! Christmas present!" at the top of their lungs.

"Well! Well!" exclaimed Amos. "Isn't that fine! If Levine comes out tomorrow we can ask him to dinner, after all. Can't we, Lizzie?"

"You bet we can!" said Lizzie. "And look at this. I was going to keep it for a surprise. I made it by your wife's recipe."

She held an open Mason jar under Amos' nose.

"Mince meat!" he exclaimed. "Why, Lizzie, where'd you get the makings?"

"Oh, a bit here and a bit there for the last two months. Ain't it grand?" offering a smell to each of the children, who sniffed ecstatically.

When the baby was safely asleep, Lydia appeared with two stockings which she hung on chair backs by the stove in the living room.

"I'm putting them up to hold the candy," she explained to her father, suggestively.

He rose obediently and produced half a dozen oranges and a bag of candy.

"Oh, that's gorgeous," cried Lydia, whose spirits tonight were not to be quenched. She brought in the doll house.

"See, Daddy," she said, with the pride of the master builder. "I colored it with walnut juice. And I found the wall paper in the attic."

Amos got down on his knees and examined the tiny rooms and the cigar box furniture. He chuckled delightedly. "I swan," he said, "if Patience doesn't want it you can give it to me!"

"I'm going to let Lizzie put the candy in the stockings," mused Lydia, "then I'll have that to look forward to. I'm going to bed right now, so morning will come sooner."

Alone with the stockings, into which Lizzie put the candy and oranges, Amos sat long staring at the base burner. Without, the moon sailed high. Wood snapping in the intense cold was the only sound on the wonder of the night. Something of the urgent joy and beauty of the Eve touched Amos, for he finally rose and said,

"Well, I've got two fine children, anyhow." Then he filled up the stoves for the night and went to bed.

Chapter IV

THE RAVISHED NEST

"The young pine bends to the storm. The old pine breaks."
— *The Murmuring Pine*

It would be difficult to say which enjoyed the doll house more, Lydia or Patience. It would be difficult to say which one was the more touched, Lizzie or Amos by the package each found on the breakfast table. Amos unwrapped his to find therein a pipe tray fashioned from cigar box wood and stained with Lydia's walnut dye. Lizzie's gift was a flat black pincushion, with "Lizzie, with love from Lydia," embroidered crazily on it in red. Florence Dombey showed no emotion over her gift, a string of red beads that had a curious resemblance to asparagus seed-pods, but she wore them gracefully and stared round-eyed at all the festivities. Lydia and Patience each wore pinned to her dress a cotton handkerchief, Lizzie's gift.

John Levine appeared at noon, laden like a pack horse. This was his great opportunity during the year to do things for the Dudley children and he took full advantage of the moment. Books for Lydia, little toys for the baby, a pipe for Amos, a woolen dress pattern for Lizzie, a blue sailor suit for Lydia, a fur hood for Patience.

John's thin, sallow face glowed, his black eyes gleamed as he watched the children unwrap the packages. In the midst of the excitement, Lydia shrieked.

"My ducks! My ducks!" and bolted for the kitchen.

"The pie!" cried Lizzie, panting after her.

"Don't tell me they're spoiled!" groaned Amos, as with John and the baby, he followed into the kitchen.

"Safe!" shouted Lydia, on her knees before the oven. "Just the pope's nose is scorched! The pie is perfect."

"Let's eat before anything else happens," said Amos, nervously.

"Lord!" said John Levine, "who'd miss spending Christmas where there are children? I'd a gotten out here today if I'd had to come barefooted."

The dinner was eaten and pronounced perfect. The gifts were re-examined and re-admired. John Levine, with Lydia and Florence Dombey on his lap, Amos with the drowsy little Patience in his arms, and Lizzie, her tired hands folded across her comfortable stomach, sat round the base burner while the wind rose outside and the boom of the ice-locked lake filled the room from time to time.

"Fearful cold when the ice cracks that way," said Amos.

"'The owl, for all his feathers was a-cold,'" murmured Lydia.

"Where'd you get that and what's the rest of it?" asked Levine.

"Selected Gems," replied Lydia. "It's a book at school.

"'St. Agnes Eve – Ah, bitter chill it was!
  The owl for all his feathers was a-cold;
  The hare limp'd trembling through the frozen grass
  And silent was the flock in woolly fold.'

I forget the rest."

The grown-ups glanced at each other over the children's heads.

"Say your pretty Christmas poem you spoke at school, Lydia," suggested old Lizzie.

Lydia rested her head back comfortably on John's shoulder and rambled on in her childish contralto.

"Sing low, indeed: and softly bleat,
  You lambing ewes about her feet,
  Lest you should wake the child from sleep!
  No other hour so still and sweet
  Shall fall for Mary's heart to keep
  Until her death hour on her creep,
  Sing soft, the Eve of Mary."

There was silence for a moment.

"Why did you choose that one, young Lydia?" asked Levine.

"I don't know. I seemed to like it," answered Lydia. "It's a girl's poem. Gosh, I've been happy today! Daddy, you thought we'd have an awful poor Christmas, didn't you? Poor old Daddy! Why, I've just felt all day as if my heart was on tiptoes."

It had indeed been a high day for the child. Perhaps she remembered it for years after as one of her perfect days, because of the heart breaking days that followed.

For little Patience for the first time in her tiny life was taken ill. For three or four days after Christmas she was feverish and cross with a hoarse cold. When Amos came home the fourth night, he thought she had the croup and sent Lydia pelting through the darkness for the dairy farmer's wife. Mrs. Norton, the mother of Billy, was not long in coming to a decision.

"'Tain't regular croup. You go after the doctor, Mr. Dudley."

Patience, frightened by her difficult breathing, would let no one but Lydia touch her. Under Mrs. Norton's supervision, she packed the baby in hot water bottles while Lizzie heated water and stoked the fires till the stove doors glowed red.

Amos came back with the doctor about nine o'clock. Patience was in a stupor. The doctor sent Lydia away while he made his examination. The child clenched her fists and walked up and down the living room, cheeks scarlet, eyes blazing. Suddenly she dropped on her knees by the window and lifted her clasped hands to the stars.

"God! God, up there!" she called. "If you let her die, I'll never pray to you again! Never! I warned You when You let mother die!"

She remained a moment on her knees, staring at the stars while fragments of Sunday School lore flashed through her mind. "Our Father who art in heaven," she said. "No, that won't do. Suffer little children to come unto me. Oh, no, no."

The door opened and Lizzie came out, tears-running down her cheeks. Lydia flew to her.

"They say I got to tell you. Diphtheritic croup — her lungs is full — no hope."

Lydia struck the kind old hand from her shoulder and dashed out of the house. She ran through the snow to a giant pine by the gate and beat her fists against it for how long she did not know. Pain in her bruised hands and the intense cold finally brought her to her senses. A self-control that was partly inherent and partly the result of too early knowledge of grief and of responsibility came to her rescue. With a long sigh, she walked steadily into the house and into the room where the baby sister lay in a stupor, breathing stertorously.

The doctor and Amos were there. Mrs. Norton was now soothing Lizzie in the kitchen, now obeying the doctor's orders. Amos did not stir from his chair by the bed, nor speak a word, all that night. The doctor was in his shirt sleeves, prepared to fight as best he could.

"Go out, Lydia," said Dr. Fulton, quietly.

"She'll want me," replied the child.

The doctor looked at Lydia keenly. He knew her well. He had ushered her as well as Patience into the world. He pulled her to him, with one hand, not relinquishing his hold on the baby's pulse with the other.

"She's in a stupor and won't miss you, Lydia. She is not suffering at all. Now, I want you to go to bed like a good girl."

"I won't," said Lydia, quietly.

"Lydia," the doctor went on, as if he were talking to a grown person, "all your life you will be grateful to me, if I make you obey me now. I know those wild nerves of yours, too much and too early controlled. *Lydia, go to bed!*"

Not because she feared him but because some knowledge beyond her years told her of his wisdom, Lydia turned, found Florence Dombey in the living room and with her and a blanket, crept under her father's bed, into the farthest corner where she lay wide-eyed until dawn. Someone closed the door into the room then, and shortly, she fell asleep.

In three days, the like of which are the longest, the shortest days of life, the house had returned to the remnant of its old routine. The place had been fumigated. Lydia had placed in her bedroom everything that had belonged to the baby, had locked the door and had moved herself into Lizzie's room. Amos departed before dawn as usual with his dinner pail, stumbling like an old man, over the road.

The quarantine sign was on the house and no one but the undertaker, the doctor, Mrs. Norton and John Levine had been allowed to come to see the stricken little family, excepting the minister. He, poor man, had babies of his own, and had been nervous during the few short minutes of the service.

Lydia and Lizzie put in the morning cleaning the cottage. Never since they had lived in it had the little house been so spic and span. At noon, they sat down to lunch in a splendor of cleanliness that made the place seem stranger than ever to them both. Neither talked much. At intervals, tears ran down old Lizzie's wrinkled cheeks and Lydia looked at her wonderingly. Lydia had not shed a tear. But all the time her cheeks were scarlet, her hands were cold and trembled and her stomach ached.

"You must eat, childie. You haven't eat enough to keep a bird alive since — since —"

There was a bang on the door, and Lizzie trundled over to open it.

"For the Lord's sake, Kent!"

Kent it was, big and rosy with his skates over his shoulders. He walked into the living room deliberately.

"Hello, Lydia," he said, "I came out to see your Christmas presents."

Lydia clasped her hands. "Oh, Kent, I'm so glad! But you can't stay! We're quarantined."

"What the seventeen thunder-bugs do I care," returned Kent, gruffly, looking away from Lydia's appealing eyes.

Lydia laughed, as she always did at Kent's astonishing oaths. At the sound of the laughter, old Lizzie gave a sigh as though some of her own tense nerves had relaxed.

"Now see here," growled Kent, "they've got no business to shut you up this way. You come out and skate for a while. The wind's blown the snow till there's lots of clear places. I got up here without much trouble. We won't meet anybody at this end of the lake."

"Just the thing, quarantine or not!" exclaimed, Lizzie, briskly. "And I'll cook a surprise for the two of you. Keep her out an hour, Kent."

Lydia silently got into overcoat and leggings and pulled on her Tam o' Shanter. She brought her skates from the kitchen and the two children made their way to the lake shore.

It was a brilliant afternoon. The vast white expanse of the lake was dotted with the flash of opals wherever the wind had exposed the ice to the winter sun. Far down the lake toward the college shore, the flitting sails of ice-boats gleamed, and faint and far up the wind came the clear "cling-pling" of their steel runners. The mercury was hovering around ten or twelve above zero as the fierce booming of the expanding ice attested.

With unwonted consideration, Kent helped Lydia strap on her skates. Then the two started, hand in hand, up the lake. They skated well, as did most of the children of the community. The wind in their faces was bitter cold, making conversation difficult. Whether or not Kent was grateful for this, one could not say. He watched Lydia out of the tail of his eye and as the wind whipped the old red into her cheeks, he began to whistle. They had been going perhaps fifteen minutes when the little girl stumbled several times.

"What's the matter, Lyd?" asked Kent.

"I don't know," she panted. "I — I guess I'm tired."

"Tired already! Gosh! And you've always worn me out. Come on up to the shore, and I'll make a fire, so's you can rest."

Lydia, who always had scorned the thought of rest, while at play, followed meekly and stood in silence while Kent without removing his skates hobbled up the bank and pulled some dead branches to the shore. Shortly he had a bright blaze at her feet. He kicked the snow off a small log.

"Sit down — here where you get the warmth," he ordered, his voice as gruff as he could make it.

Lydia sat down obediently, her mittened hands clasping her knees. Kent stood staring at his little chum. He took in the faded blue Tam, the outgrown coat, the red mittens, so badly mended, the leggings with patches on the knees. Then he eyed the heavy circles around her eyes and the droop to the mouth that was meant to be merry.

"I'm sorriest for Lydia," his mother had said that morning. "No mother could feel much worse than she does, and she's got no one to turn to for comfort. I know Amos. He'll shut up like a clam. Just as soon as they're out of quarantine, I'll go out there."

Kent was only a boy, but he was mature in spite of his heedless ways. Staring at the tragedy in Lydia's ravished little face, a sympathy for her pain as real as it was unwonted swept over him. Suddenly he dropped down beside her on the log and threw his boyish arms about her.

"I'm so doggone sorry for you, Lydia!" he whispered.

Lydia lifted startled eyes to his. Never before had Kent shown her the slightest affection. When she saw the sweetness and sympathy in his brown gaze,

"Oh, Kent," she whispered, "why did God let it happen! Why did He?" and she buried her face on his shoulder and began to sob. Softly at first, then with a racking agony of tears.

Even a child is wise in the matter of grief. Kent's lips trembled, but he made no attempt to comfort Lydia. He only held her tightly and watched the fire with bright, unseeing eyes. And after what seemed a long, long time, the sobs grew less. Finally, he slipped a pocket-handkerchief into Lydia's hand. It was grey with use but of a comforting size.

"Wipe your eyes, old lady," he said in a cheerful, matter of fact tone. "I've got to put the fire out, so's we can start home."

Lydia mopped her face and by the time Kent had the fire smothered with snow, she was standing, sad-eyed but calm except for dry sobs. Kent picked up one of the sticks he had brought for the fire.

"Catch hold," he said, "I'll pull you home."

Old Lizzie was watching for them and when they came stamping into the dining room, they found a pitcher of steaming cocoa and a plate of bread and butter with hot gingerbread awaiting them.

"See if you can get her to eat, Kent," said Lizzie.

"Sure, she'll eat," Kent answered her. "Gimme back my hanky, Lyd!"

Lizzie gave a keen look at Lydia's tear-stained face and turned abruptly into the kitchen. She came back in a moment to find Lydia silently eating what Kent had set before her.

Kent ate hugely and talked without cessation. About what, Lydia did not know, for the sleep that had been long denied her was claiming her. She did not know that she almost buried her head in her second cup of cocoa, nor that Kent helped carry her to the couch behind the living room base burner.

"Is she sick? Shall I get the doctor?" he whispered as old Lizzie tucked a shawl over her.

"Sick! No! No! She's just dead for sleep. She's neither cried nor eat nor had a decent hour of sleep since it happened. And now, thanks to you, she's done all three. You are a good boy, Kent Moulton."

Kent looked suddenly foolish and embarrassed. "Aw — that's nothing," he muttered. "Where's my coat? Maybe I'll come out again tomorrow, if I ain't got anything better to do."

All the rest of the winter afternoon, Lydia slept. The sun dipped low beyond the white hills, filling the living room with scarlet for one breathless moment, before a blanket of twilight hid all save the red eyes of the base burner. Amos came home at seven and he and Lizzie ate supper in silence except for the old lady's story of Kent's visit.

"Poor young one," muttered Amos, looking slowly toward the quiet blond head on the faded brown cushion. "I'm glad she's a child and 'll forget it soon."

Lizzie gave Amos a curious glance. "You don't know Lydia, Amos," she said.

He did not seem to hear her. He moved his chair toward the stove, put his feet on the fender, lighted his pipe and then sat without moving until a stamping of feet and a hearty rap on the door roused him. Lizzie let John Levine in.

"Where's Lydia?" was Levine's first Question.

Lizzie pointed to the couch, where, undisturbed, Lydia slept on.

"Good!" said John. He drew his chair up beside Amos' and the two fell into low-voiced conversation.

It must have been nine o'clock when Lydia opened her eyes to hear Amos say fretfully,

"I tell you, I went to him today as I'll go to no man again. I begged him to renew the note, but he insisted his duty to the bank wouldn't let him. I told him it would put you in a terrible fix, that you'd gone on the note when you couldn't afford it. He grinned a devil's grin then and said, 'Amos, I know you've got nothing to lose in this. If you had, for the sake of your children — I mean Lydia, I'd hold off. But Levine can fix it up!'"

"So I could, ordinarily," said Levine in a troubled voice. "But it just happens that everything I've got on earth is shoestringed out to hang onto that pine section of mine up in Bear county. I'm mortgaged up to my eyebrows. Marshall knows it and sees a chance to get hold of the pines, damn him!"

Lydia sat up and rubbed her eyes.

"Well! Well! young Lydia," cried Levine. "Had a fine sleep, didn't you!"

"I'm awful hungry," said the child.

"Bless your soul," exclaimed Lizzie. "I'll warm your supper up for you in a minute."

Lydia stood with hands outstretched to the base burner, her hair tumbled, her glance traveling from Amos to Levine.

"What makes Mr. Marshall act so?" she asked.

"Sho," said Levine, "little girls your age don't know anything about such things, do they, Amos? Come here. You shall eat your supper on my lap."

"I'm getting too old for laps," said Lydia, coming very willingly nevertheless within the compass of John's long arms. "But I love you next to Daddy now, in all the world."

John swept her to his knees and put his cheek against hers for a moment, while tears gleamed in his black eyes.

"Eat your supper and go to bed, Lydia," said Amos.

"Don't be so cross, Amos," protested Levine.

"God knows I'm not cross — to Lydia of all people in the world," sighed Amos, "but she worries over money matters just the way her mother did and I want to finish talking this over with you."

"There's nothing more to talk about," Levine's voice was short. "Let him call in the loan, the fat hog!"

Lydia slept the long night through. She awoke refreshed and renewed. After first adjusting herself to the awful sense of loss, which is the worst of waking in grief, the recollection of the conversation she had heard the night before returned with sickening vividness. After she had wiped the breakfast dishes for Lizzie she stood for a long time at the living room window with Florence Dombey in her arms staring at the lake. Finally, she tucked the doll up comfortably on the couch and announced to Lizzie that she was going skating.

An hour later, Dave Marshall heard his clerk protesting outside his door and a childish voice saying, "But please, just for a minute. He likes me. He truly does."

Then the door opened and Lydia, breathless and rosy and threadbare, came into his little private office. She closed the door and stood with her back against it, unsmiling.

"I'm in quarantine," she said, "so I won't come near you."

"Why, Lydia!" exclaimed Marshall, "where did you come from!"

"Home. Mr. Marshall, won't you fix Daddy's note if he gives you me?"

"Huh!" ejaculated Marshall.

"You said last fall," the child went on, her voice quavering but her eyes resolute, "that if Daddy ever wanted to sell me, you'd buy me. I think I ought to be worth a thousand dollars. I can do so much work around the house and help you train Margery! I can work hard. You ask John Levine."

Marshall's fat face was purple and then pale.

"Does your father know you're here, Lydia?" he asked.

She clasped her mittened hands in sudden agitation.

"Nobody knows but you," she exclaimed. "Oh! you mustn't tell the man out there my name. I'm in quarantine and I'd be arrested, if the health office knew!"

"I won't tell," said Dave, gently. "Come over here by me, Lydia. Margery is away on a visit so I'm not afraid for her."

Lydia crossed the room. Marshall took the skates from her shoulders and unfastened her coat.

"Sit down on that chair and let's talk this over. You know what a note is, do you, Lydia?"

"It's money you owe," she said, her blue eyes anxiously fixed on Marshall's face.

He nodded. "Yes. When your mother was sick, your father asked my bank here to lend him a thousand dollars for two years. Now, your father is very poor. He doesn't own anything that's worth a thousand dollars and I knew he could never pay it back. So I told him he must get someone to promise to pay that money for him if he couldn't, at the end of the two years. Understand?"

Lydia nodded.

"Well, he got John Levine. Now the two years are up and unless that thousand dollars is paid, the people whose money I take care of in the bank, will each lose some of that thousand. See?"

Lydia stared at him, struggling to take in the explanation. "I see," she said. "But if you'd pay a thousand dollars for me, that would fix it all up."

"Why Lydia, do you mean you would leave your father?"

"I wouldn't want to," she answered earnestly, "but Lizzie could take care of Daddy. He doesn't really need me. There isn't anybody really needs me — needs me — now —"

She swallowed a sob, then went on. "Mr. Levine just mustn't pay it. He's awful worried. His land's fixed so's he'd never get over it. And he's the best friend we have in all the world. He just mustn't pay it. It would kill mother, if she knew. Oh, she hated borrowing so."

Marshall chewed his cigar. "Levine," he growled, "is a long legged crook."

Lydia flew out of her chair and shook her fist in the banker's face. "Don't you dare say that!" she cried. "He's a dear lamb, that's what he is."

Dave's fat jaw dropped. "A dear lamb, eh? Ask him some time what a land shark is — a dear lamb?"

He went on chewing his cigar and Lydia returned to her chair. Whether it was the anxious round eyes, above the scarlet cheeks, whether it was the wistful droop of the childish lips, whether it was the look that belongs to ravished motherhood and seemed grossly wrong on a child's face, whether it was some thought of his own pampered little daughter, whether it was that curious appeal Lydia always made to men, or a combination of all, that moved Marshall, he could not have told. But suddenly he burst forth.

"Good God, I've done hard things in my life, but I can't do this! Lydia, you go home and tell your father I'll renew that note, but he's got to pay the interest and ten percent of the principal, every year till he's paid it up. Here, I'll write it down. And tell him that I'm not doing it for him or for that skunk of a Levine, but I'm doing it for you. Here, I'll write that down, *too.*"

He folded the bit of paper and put it in an envelope. "Come here," he said. He pinned the note into the pocket of her blouse. "Understand, Lydia," he said in a low voice, tilting her head up so that he looked down into her eyes, "I'm buying your friendship with this. You go on living with your father and taking care of him, but I'm buying your friendship for me and Margery — for good and all." He looked out of the window with a curious air of abstraction. Then, "Button your coat and run along."

"I haven't thanked you," exclaimed Lydia, "I can't thank you. Oh, but thank you, Mr. Marshall — I — I —" she began to tremble violently.

"Stop!" roared Marshall. "And you tell your father to look out for your nerves. Now skip." And Lydia's trembling stopped and she skipped.

She did not tell Lizzie of her errand and that faithful soul was too glad to see her eat her dinner to think to ask her why she had skated so long. Kent came out in the afternoon and the two fished through the ice until sunset, when they came in with a string of fish sufficiently long to divide and make a meal for the Dudleys and the Moultons. At dusk, Kent departed with his fish and "Men of Iron," loaned by Lydia as a special favor, under his arm.

Old Lizzie cleaned the fish and Lydia fried them, with the daintiness and skill that seemed to have been born in her. She laid an envelope at her father's plate and when he sat down, silent and abstracted, without heeding the fish, she shook her head at Lizzie who was about to protest.

"Where'd this come from?" he asked, absentmindedly opening the envelope. Then, "For God's sake! Lydia — where? how?"

"It was like this," said Lydia. "Set the fish back to warm, while I explain, Lizzie. It was like this —" and she gave a full history of her morning's visit, to her two speechless listeners. "And I ran all the way to the lake and I skated like the wind, and I never told Lizzie a word, though I nearly busted!"

Amos looked from Lydia to Lizzie, from Lizzie to Lydia.

"Lydia — my little daughter —" he faltered.

The tears flew to Lydia's eyes and she spoke hastily, "Lizzie, show him the fish we caught!"

Amos smiled while he shook his head. "I won't forget it, Lydia. In spite of little Patience's going, you've taken ten years off me this night. What do you suppose John Levine will say?"

"He'll say," replied Lydia, taking her serving of fish, "'If you were ten years older, Lydia, and I were ten years younger,' and I'll say — 'then we'd travel.'"

Chapter V

ADAM

"A thousand deaths have fed my roots — yet to what end?"
                                                    — *The Murmuring Pine*

*T*he days slipped by, as days will, even though they are grief laden. Slowly and inarticulately for the most part, Lydia struggled to adjust herself to her new loss. She went back to school, after the quarantine was lifted and the familiar routine there helped her. She was a good student and was doing well in the eighth grade. During school hours her books absorbed her, and she worried through the evenings reading or sewing, with Florence Dombey always in her lap.

Florence Dombey was a great comfort to the child. She slept at night with her black head beside Lydia's yellow one. Sometimes she slipped into the middle of the bed and fat Lizzie rolled on her and woke with a groan.

"I'd just as soon sleep with a cannon-ball at my back," the good soul told Lydia. But she never uttered a more violent protest.

Lydia never entered the locked bedroom off the kitchen. Amos, self-absorbed and overworked, asked no questions, but one night in April, John Levine saw Lydia at work on a night dress for Florence Dombey.

"Where does the young lady sleep?" he asked.

Lydia explained and Lizzie uttered her mild plaint, adding, "Lydia ought to be getting back to her own bed, now warm weather will be coming in."

Lydia caught her lower lip in her teeth but said nothing. Levine scrutinized the curly head bent over the sewing, then went on with his conversation with Amos. He was working quietly on his campaign, a year hence, for the office of sheriff and Amos, who was an influential Mason, was planning to use his influence for his friend. Lydia, absorbed in sad little memories over her sewing or happily drugged in some book, heeded these discussions only subconsciously.

Just before leaving, John asked for a drink of water and Amos went to the pump to bring in a fresh pail. He stopped while there to fuss over a barrel in which he had an old hen setting on some eggs he had got from Mrs. Norton. Lizzie had gone to bed early.

"Young Lydia," said John, as soon as they were alone, "come here."

When she was perched in her old place on his knee, "Don't you think it's time for you to get back to your own bedroom with its view of the lake?" he asked.

Lydia looked at him dumbly.

"You don't like to sleep in that stuffy bedroom with Lizzie, do you, dear?"

"No," replied the child. "She's fat and snores and won't have the window open — but —"

"But what?" Levine's voice was gentle.

"I'm afraid to sleep alone."

"Afraid? Lydia — not of any memory of dear little Patience!"

"No! No! but I have nightmares nearly every night — she — she's choking and I — I can't help her. Then I wake up and catch hold of Lizzie. Oh, don't make me sleep alone!"

"Why, my dear little girl —" John caught the child's thin hands in a firm, warm grip. She was trembling violently and her fingers twitched. "This won't do! That's what keeps the dark rings round your eyes, is it? Of course you shan't sleep alone! How does school go?"

"Fine," answered the child. "I hate grammar and diagramming, but the rest is easy."

"And what book are you reading now?"

"I'm starting *David Copperfield.*"

"Here comes your father. It's bedtime, isn't it? Good night, my dear."

Lydia picked up Florence Dombey and went slowly off to bed as her father came in with a glass of water.

"That fool hen isn't fully convinced she wants a family," he said.

The bedroom door closed after Lydia.

"Amos," said John, "that child's nerves are all shot to pieces." He related his conversation with Lydia.

"What can I do?" asked Amos, with a worried air. "Seems to me she's just got to wear it out. It's awful hard she's had to be up against these things — but, I swan! —"

Levine grunted and put on his hat. "I wish she was my daughter," he said. "If you'll ask Brown to come around to the Elks Club tomorrow, I'll talk to him."

Amos nodded and John mounted his bicycle and rode away. On the Friday afternoon following when Lydia got home from school, she found the house apparently deserted. But there issued from the neighborhood of the kitchen a yipping and ki-yi-ing that would have moved a heart of stone. Lydia ran into the kitchen. The puppy wails came from behind the door of the old bedroom.

"Who's in there!" she called.

The yipping changed to deep barks of joy. Lydia tried the door. It opened easily and a great, blundering puppy hurled himself at her. Lydia was a dog lover.

"You love! You lamb!" she cried. She squatted on the floor and the pup crowded his great hulk into her lap, licking her face and wagging his whole body.

There was a note tied to his collar. Lydia untied it: "Dearest Young Lydia: — Here is a friend who wants to share your bedroom with you. You must bring him up to be a polite, obedient dog, and a credit to your other friend, John Levine."

"Oh!" squealed Lydia. "Oh! but why did they tie you in here!" She looked about the room. The old bed had been moved out and the dining room couch moved in. The bureau had been shifted to another corner.

There was nothing to be seen of all little Patience's belongings. It did not look like the same room.

As she clung to the squirming puppy and stared, Lizzie came in.

"Ain't it nice?" she asked. "Mr. Levine came out with the dog this afternoon and suggested the change. He helped me. We stored all the other things up in the attic. See the old quilt in the corner? That's for the dog to sleep on. Ain't he as big as an elephant! I'm afraid he'll eat as much as a man."

"He can have half of my food," cried Lydia. "Oh, Lizzie, isn't he beautiful!"

"Well, no," replied Lizzie, truthfully. "He looks to me as if someone had stepped on his face. You'd better take him out for a run."

John Levine never did a wiser or a kinder thing than to give the brindle English bulldog to Lydia. He was a puppy of nine months, well bred and strong. Lydia took him into her empty little heart with a completeness that belongs to the natural dog lover and that was enhanced by her bereavement. And he, being of a breed that is as amiable and loyal as it is unlovely to look upon, attached himself unalterably and entirely to Lydia. She and Kent cast about some time before deciding on a name. At first they thought seriously of naming him John, after the donor, but decided that this might lead to confusion. Then they discovered that Levine's middle name was Adam, and Adam the brindle bull became, forthwith.

Lydia made no objection to returning to the old room. It had lost its familiar outlines. And Adam, refusing the quilt on the floor, established himself on the foot of the couch where all night long he snuffled and snored and Lydia, who had objected to Lizzie's audible slumbers, now, waking with nightmares, heard Adam's rumbling with a sigh of relief, pressed her feet for comfort against his warm, throbbing body, and went off to sleep immediately.

In May the garden was planted and in June, Lydia graduated from the eighth grade, and the long summer vacation had begun. Margery Marshall, although Lydia's age, was not a good student and was two grades below her. After the episode of the note, Lydia made a conscientious effort to play with Margery at recess and when vacation began, she called for the banker's daughter regularly every week to go swimming.

Occasionally Elviry would invite her into the house to wait for Margery. At such times Lydia would stare with wondering delight at the marvels of the quartered oak, plush upholstered furniture, the "Body-Brussels" rugs, and the velour portières that adorned the parlor.

Outwardly this summer was much like the previous one, except that there was a quiet contentment about Amos in spite of his real mourning for his baby daughter, that had been foreign to him for years. It was the garden that did this. Not only was it a wonderful garden to look on and to eat from, but with it Amos paid for milk and butter from the Nortons and for a part of his groceries. This made possible the year's interest and payment on the note.

Lydia sewed for Florence Dombey, climbed trees, swam and played pirates with Kent. But as a matter of fact, the old childish zest for these things had gone. For Lydia's real childhood had left her that December night she had spent under the far corner of her father's bed. She had not prayed since then. Her young faith in the kindness and sweetness of life, badly shaken by her mother's death, had been utterly destroyed when little Patience had been taken from her.

With Adam at her heels, she took to solitary tramping through the neighboring woods where at times she met Indians from the reservation – a buck asleep on a log – a couple of squaws laughing and chatting while they ate food they had begged – an Indian boy, dusty and tired, resting after a trip to Lake City. Lydia was a little afraid of these dark folk, though they always smiled at her. She would jerk at Adam's collar and cuff his ears for growling, then make off toward home.

It was a walk of just a mile from the cottage to the High School. Lydia was very nervous about her first day at High School. Kent was entering at the same time and she would have liked to have asked to go with him but she knew he would resent violently being associated with a girl on so important an occasion.

So it was that one of the teachers observed a child in a faded but clean galatea sailor suit, with curly blond hair barely long enough to tie in her neck, standing in one of the lower halls after the mob of seven or eight hundred boys and girls had been successfully herded into the great Assembly room.

"What is your name, my dear?" asked the teacher.

Lydia silently presented her promotion card. The teacher nodded.

"Come along, Miss Dudley, or you'll miss the principal's speech."

She seated Lydia near her in the Assembly room, then looked her over curiously. The child's face was remarkably intelligent, a highbred little face under a finely domed head. The back of her ears and the back of her neck were dirty, and her thin hands were rough as if with housework. The galatea sailor suit was cheap and coarse.

"A sick mother or no mother," was the teacher's mental note. "I must inquire about her. Almost too bashful to breathe. Precocious mentally, a child physically. I'll look out for her today."

Miss Towne had the reputation of an unfeeling disciplinarian among the pupils, but Lydia did not know this. She only knew that by some miracle of kindness she came to understand the classroom system of recitations, that she was introduced to different teachers, that she learned how to decipher the hours of her recitations from the complicated chart on the Assembly room blackboard, and that at noon she started for home with a list of textbooks to be purchased, and a perfectly clear idea of what to do when she returned on the morrow.

The streets were full of children of all ages flocking toward the book stores. Lydia walked along slowly, thinking deeply. She knew that her list of books came to something over five dollars. She knew that this sum of money would floor her father and she knew that she would rather beg on the streets than start Amos on one of his tirades on his poverty.

She pegged along homeward, half elated over the excitement of the day, half depressed over her book problem. When she turned into the dirt road. Billy Norton overtook her. He was wearing a very high starched collar and a new suit of clothes. Billy was a senior and felt his superiority. Nevertheless, he wanted to tell his troubles — even to a first year pupil.

"Gee, don't I have the luck!" he groaned. "I could get on the School football team, I know it, if I didn't have to come home right after school to deliver milk. Hang it!"

Lydia looked at him quickly. "How much milk do you have to deliver?"

"Aw, just a snag. Two quarts up the road to Essers' and two to Stones'. They both got babies and have to have it. Think of putting me off the school team for four quarts of baby milk!"

"Oh, Billy," gasped Lydia, "I'll do it for you — if — Billy, have you got your freshman textbooks still?"

"Sure," answered the boy. "They're awful banged up, but I guess all the pages are there."

Lydia was breathless with excitement. "Billy, if you'll let me have your books, I'll carry the milk for you, all winter."

The big boy looked at the little girl, curiously.

"They're a ratty lot of old books, Lydia. Half the fun of having schoolbooks is getting new ones."

"I know that," she answered, flushing.

"Hanged if I'll do it. Let your dad get you new ones."

"He'd like to as well as anyone, but he can't right now and I'm going to look out for my own. Oh, Billy, let me do it!"

"You can have 'em all and welcome," exclaimed Billy, with a sudden huskiness in his voice. "Gosh, you're awful little, Lydia."

Lydia stamped her foot. "I won't take anything for nothing. And I'm not little. I'm as strong as a horse."

"Well," conceded Billy, "just till after Thanksgiving is all I want. Come on along home now and we'll fix it up with Ma."

Ma Norton twisted Lydia around and retied her hair ribbon while she listened. They all knew Lydia's pride, so she quenched the impulse to give the child the books and said, "Till Thanksgiving is plenty of pay, Billy, and when the snow comes, the two mile extra walking will be too much. Get the books out of the parlor closet. You got a — a — ink on the back of your neck, Lydia. Wait till I get it off for you."

She wet a corner of a towel at the tea kettle and proceeded to scour the unsuspecting Lydia's neck and ears. "Children in the high school are apt to get ink in the *back* of their necks and *ears,*" she said. *"Always* scrub there, Lydia! Remember!"

"Yes, Ma'm! Oh, gosh, what a big pile! Thank you ever so much, Billy. I'll be here right after school tomorrow, Mrs. Norton."

Lydia spent a blissful evening mending and cleaning Billy's text-books, with Adam snoring under her feet and her father absorbed in his newspaper.

The delivering of the milk was no task at all, though had it not been for Adam trudging beside her with his rolling bulldog gait and his slavering ugly jaw, she would have been afraid in the early dusk of the autumn evenings.

The High School was a different world from that of the old ward school. The ward school, comprising children of only one neighborhood with the grades small, was a democratic, neighborly sort of place. The High School gathered together children from all over town, of all classes, from the children of lumber kings and college professors, to the offspring of the Norwegian day laborer and the German saloon keeper. There were even several colored children in the High School as well as an Indian lad named Charlie Jackson. In the High School, class feeling was strong. There were Greek letter societies in the fourth grade, reflecting the influence of the college on the lake shore. Among the well-to-do girls, and also among those who could less well afford it, there was much elaborate dressing. Dancing parties were weekly occurrences. They were attended by first year girls of fourteen and fifteen as well as by the older girls, each lass with an attendant lad, who called for her and took her home unchaperoned.

It took several months for Lydia to become aware of the complicated social life going on about her. She was so absorbed while in school in adjusting herself to the new type of school life, — a different teacher for each study, heavier lessons, the responsibility of collateral reading — that the Christmas holidays came before she realized that except in her class room work, she had nothing whatever in common with her classmates.

All fall she saw very little of Kent. He was on the freshman football squad and this was a perfectly satisfactory explanation of his dereliction — had he cared to make any — as far as Saturdays went. In the Assembly room because he had chosen the Classical course, his seat was far from Lydia's, who had chosen the English course.

Saturday was a busy day for Lydia at home. Old Lizzie, who was nearing sixty, was much troubled with rheumatism and even careless Lydia felt vaguely that the house needed a certain amount of cleaning once a week. So, of a Saturday morning, she slammed through the house like a small whirlwind, leaving corners undisturbed and dust in windrows, but satisfied with her efforts. Saturday afternoon, she worked in the garden when the day was fair, helping to gather the winter vegetables. Before little Patience's death she had gone to Sunday School, but since that time she had not entered a church. So Sunday became her feast day. She put in the entire morning preparing a Sunday dinner for her father and nearly always John Levine. After dinner, the three, with Adam, would tramp a mile up the road, stopping to lean over the bars and talk dairying with Pa Norton, winter wheat with Farmer Jansen, and hardy alfalfa with old Schmidt. Between farms, Amos and John always talked politics, local and national, arguing heatedly.

To all this, Lydia listened with half an ear. She loved these walks, partly because of the grown up talks, partly because Adam loved them, mostly because of the beauty of the wooded hills, the far stretch of the black fields, ready plowed for spring and the pale, tender blue of the sky that touched the near horizon. If she missed and needed playmates of her own age, she was scarcely conscious of the fact.

Christmas came and went, sadly and quietly. Lydia was glad when the holidays were over and she was back in school again. On her desk that first morning lay a tiny envelope, addressed to her. She opened it. In it was an invitation from Miss Towne to attend a reception she was tendering to the members of her Algebra and Geometry classes, freshmen and seniors.

For a moment Lydia was in heaven. It was her first formal invitation of any kind. Then she came rapidly to earth. She had nothing to wear! It was an evening party and she had no way to go or come. She put the precious card in her blouse pocket and soberly opened her Civil Government.

At recess, she sat alone as she was rather prone to do, in the window of the cloak room, when she heard a group of girls chattering.

"Who wants to go to grouchy old Towne's reception when you can go to a dance? I've got two bids to the Phi Pi's party," said a fourteen-year-old miss.

"Oh, we'll have to go or she'll flunk us in Algebra," said another girl. "I'll wear my pink silk organdy. What'll you wear?"

"My red silk. Maybe she'll let us dance. I suppose Charlie and Kent'll both want to take me."

"Terrible thing to be popular! Hasn't Kent the sweetest eyes! Do you know what he said to me the other night at the Evans' party?"

The girls drifted out of the cloak room. Lydia sat rigid. Pink organdy! Red silk! Kent's "sweetest eyes!" Then she looked down at the inevitable sailor suit, and at her patched and broken shoes. So far she had had few pangs about her clothes. But now for the first time she realized that for some reason, she was an alien, different from the other girls — and the realization made her heart ache.

The bell rang and she went to her recitation. It was in Civil Government. Lydia sat down dejectedly next to Charlie Jackson, the splendid, swarthy Indian boy of sixteen.

"Did you learn the preamble?" he whispered to Lydia.

She nodded.

"He didn't say we had to," Charlie went on, "but I like the sound of it, so I did."

The rest of the class filed in, thirty youngsters of fourteen or fifteen, the boys surreptitiously shoving and kicking each other, the girls giggling and rearranging their hair. Mr. James rapped on his desk, and called on young Hansen.

"Can you give the preamble to the Constitution?" he asked, cheerfully.

The boy's jaw dropped. "You never told us to learn it," he said.

"No, I merely suggested that as Americans, you ought to learn it. I talked to you during most of yesterday's period about it. I wondered if you were old enough to take suggestions and not be driven through your books. Miss Olson?"

Miss Olson, whose hair was done in the latest mode, tossed her head pertly.

"I was too busy to learn anything extra."

Mr. James' eyebrows went up. "A dance last night, I suppose." He continued with his query halfway round the class, then paused with a sigh. "Has anyone in the class learned it?"

A muscular brown hand shot up, boldly. A thin white one timidly followed.

"Ah!" Mr. James' face brightened. "Miss Dudley, try it."

Lydia clutched the back of the seat before her and began timidly. Then the dignity and somewhat of the significance of the words touched her and her voice became rich and full.

"'We, the people of the United States, in order to form a more perfect union, establish justice, insure domestic tranquility, provide for the common defense, promote the general welfare and secure the blessings of liberty to ourselves and our posterity, do ordain and establish this Constitution for the United States of America.'"

"Good. Try it, Mr. Jackson."

The young Indian rose and began. "We, the people of the United States —" He too was letter perfect.

After he was seated, the teacher, a grey-haired, stern-faced man, looked at the two attentively.

"Miss Dudley," he said finally, "does the preamble *mean* anything to you?"

Lydia's round childish eyes regarded him steadfastly. "Two of my ancestors were delegates to the first Convention," she said hesitatingly. "One of 'em lived in a log farmhouse with loopholes in it. They used to shoot Indians —" she paused and looked at Charlie Jackson, then went on. "I — I like the sound of the words."

The teacher nodded. "And you, Jackson?"

The boy scowled. "I know the words are lies as far as Indians are concerned. And I know they needn't have been if whites weren't natural hogs. Anyhow, I'm the only real American in the class."

Lydia looked up at the brown face eagerly, questioningly. Mr. James nodded. "Quite right, Jackson."

Young Hansen spoke up. "We're all Americans. What's he giving us?"

"Has your father been naturalized, Hansen?" asked the teacher.

The Norwegian boy shook his head, shamefacedly.

"And were you born in this country?"

"I was a baby when they came over."

"Well then, are you an American, or aren't you? You don't really know, do you? And you haven't enough interest in the country you've lived in fourteen years to find out — or to know what was the impulse that gave birth to our laws, the thing that makes an American different from a Norwegian, for instance. The two people in the class who needed the preamble least are the ones that have learned it. I'm disappointed. We'll go on to the lesson. Reisenweber, what is a demesne?"

Lydia sat looking from the teacher's face to Charlie Jackson, and from Charlie to the blond faces of the other pupils. Vague wonderments were stirring in her mind; the beginnings of thoughts she never had had before. Tramping home that night through the snowy road she had a new set of thoughts. What had made her stiffen and at the same time feel sorry and ashamed when Charlie Jackson had said the Preamble was a lie for Indians! And could she, could she possibly in the two weeks before Miss Towne's reception make herself a dress that would be presentable?

Adam, slavering and slobbering, was waiting for her as usual by the front gate. His deep brown eyes always showed phosphorescent glimmers of excitement when Lydia came. He lunged up against her now with howls of delight and she knelt in the snow, as she always did, and hugged him. Then he seized her book strap and lugged her Algebra and English Composition up to the house.

Lizzie was as excited as Lydia when she heard of the invitation.

"There's that grey serge of your mother's," she said. "It's awful faded. And there's a piece of a light blue serge waist she had, Lydia, let's get 'em dyed red. Smitzky's will do it in a couple of days for us. They did lots of work for me in bygone days and I'll pay for it out of the grocery money."

"Do you think we can fix it so it won't look made over?" asked Lydia, torn between hope and doubt.

"Of course we can. You choose your pattern tomorrow and I'll get in to town in the morning with the goods, rheumatiz or no rheumatiz."

Amos heard of the invitation with real pleasure. Nor did the clothes problem trouble him. "Pshaw, wear that green Sunday dress of yours. You always look nice, Lydia; whatever you wear. And I'll take you up there and call for you. If all the boys in school was running after you, I wouldn't let one of 'em beau you round before you was eighteen. So put that kind of a bee out of your bonnet for good and all."

Lydia lived the next two weeks in the clouds. The new-old dress was finished the day before the reception. There had been minutes of despair in creating this festive garment. The dyeing process had developed unsuspected moth holes. The blue and the grey serge did not dye exactly the same shade, nor were they of quite the same texture. However, by twisting and turning and adding a yoke of black silk, which had for years been Lizzie's Sunday neck scarf, a result was produced that completely satisfied the little dressmaker and old Lizzie.

Miss Towne was the only daughter of one of the old New England families of Lake City. Teaching was an avocation with her and not a bread and butter necessity. She lived in one of the fine old stone houses that crowned the lake shore near the college. At eight o'clock on a Saturday evening, Amos left Lydia at the front door of the house, and in a few minutes Lydia was taking off her hat and coat in the midst of a chattering group of girls. The pink organdy was there as well as the red silk, — so were blue organdies and white, as well as dainty slippers.

After a general "Hello," Lydia slipped downstairs to find her hostess. Miss Towne, the grouchy, the strict and the stern Miss Towne, moving among her guests, saw the thin little figure hesitating in the doorway, saw the cobbled red dress, with skirt that was too short and sleeves that were too long and neck that was too tight, saw the carefully blacked school shoes, saw the intelligent highbred head nobly set on straight shoulders and the wonderful dusty gold of the curly hair, and the puzzled, bashful blue eyes.

"Oh, Lydia!" cried the grouchy Miss Towne, "weren't you a dear to come clear into town for my party. Mother — -" this clearly for all the children to hear, "this is the pupil I've told you of, the one of whom we're all so proud. Come over here, Lydia."

Lydia moved carefully. Her most moth eaten breadth was at the back and it was difficult to cross the room without unduly exposing that back. But she reached the safe haven of Miss Towne's side before the bevy of multi-colored organdies entered the room.

Kent was there. He had brought the pink organdy. He waved a gay hand to Lydia, who waved back, gaily too. Her cheeks were beginning to burn scarlet, partly because a real party was a wonderful thing and partly because of the multi-colored organdies. Charlie Jackson was there. He lived with Dr. Fulton as office boy and general helper and the doctor was clothing and educating him. Charlie was half-back of the school football team, a famous player and a great favorite. The girls flirted with him. The boys were jealous of his favor. Even in the snob-ridden High School there was here a hangover of the pure democracy of childhood.

Miss Towne had provided games and refreshments bountifully. The elocution teacher recited some monologues and the music teacher sang. But it was a difficult matter to entertain these youngsters already accustomed to a grown up social life. Miss Towne had declared that there should be no dancing. But the games were neglected and the guests stood about in frankly bored groups. So when a bevy of organdies begged for permission to dance, Miss Towne, with obvious reluctance, gave in.

From that moment, the party was an assured success. Lydia, who had stuck like a little burr at Miss Towne's side all the evening, looked on with wonder and a growing lump in her throat.

"Don't you dance, my dear?" asked Mrs. Towne.

"Of course she doesn't, Mother," answered Miss Towne, "she's just a child. There's time enough for those things after High School. I don't know what's going to become of this generation."

This was small comfort to Lydia, watching the pretty groups twirl by.

Kent, hugging the pink organdy, stopped on the far side of the room from Lydia to get a drink of lemonade.

"Isn't Lydia's dress a scream," said Olga.

"Huh?" asked Kent in surprise. He followed his partner's glance across the room.

Chapter VI

THE COOKING CLASS

"We pines have been useful to man and so he has destroyed us."
— *The Murmuring Pine*

*L*ydia with parted lips and big, wistful eyes stood quietly beside Miss Towne.

"What you giving us," said Kent. "Red's my favorite color."

"Red's all right," Olga tossed her head, "but that dress! She ought to know better. A five cent cheese cloth would have been better'n that."

Kent was truly enamored of pretty Olga but he looked at her angrily.

"You girls make me sick," he grunted and started dodging among the dancers, across the room to Lydia's side. Olga stood pouting.

"What's the matter?" asked Charlie Jackson.

"Oh, I just said Lydia's dress was a fright and Kent went off mad." Charlie in turn stared at Lydia.

Kent in the meantime was grinning at Lydia amiably.

"Hello, Lyd! Want to dance?"

"I can't. Don't know how," replied Lydia, despondently.

"Easy as anything. Come on, I'll teach you."

Lydia seized Kent's lapel with fingers that would tremble slightly. "Kent, I dassn't stir. My back breadth don't match and my skirt hangs awful."

"Oh, shucks!" replied Kent, angrily, "you girls are all alike. Red's my favorite color."

"Mine too," said Charlie Jackson at his elbow. "What're you two arguing about?"

"Her dress," growled Kent, "I don't see anything the matter with it, do you?"

"Nope, and it's on the prettiest girl in the room too, eh, Kent?"

"You bet," returned Kent, believing, though, that he lied, for Olga was as pretty as a tea rose.

Lydia blushed and gasped.

"If you won't dance, come on over and have some lemonade," suggested Kent.

"If I sit in the window, will you bring me a glass?" asked Lydia, still mindful of the back breadth.

"You take her to the window and I'll get the lemo, Kent," said Charlie.

Kent led the way to the window-seat. "You're a good old sport, Lyd," he said. "Charlie'll look out for you. I gotta get back to Olga."

he returned to make peace with the pink organdy. She was very lovely and Kent was having his first flirtation. Yet before he went to sleep that night the last picture that floated before his eyes was of a thin little figure with worn mittens clasped over patched knees and a ravished child's face looking into his.

Charlie Jackson sat out two whole dances with Lydia. Their talk was of Adam and of fishing. Lydia longed to talk about Indians with him but didn't dare. Promptly at ten, Amos appeared at the front door.

Lydia's first party was over. Amos and old Lizzie were charmed with Lydia's description of it and were sure she had had a wonderful time. But Lydia felt that the dress had made of the party a hideous failure. She knew now that she was marked among her mates as a poverty stricken little dowd whom popular boys like Kent and Charlie pitied.

And yet because life is as kind to us as we have the intelligence to let it be, it was out of the party that grew slowly a new resolve of Lydia's — to have some day as pretty hands and as well shod feet as Olga and Hilda and Cissy, to learn how to make her dresses so that even the composing of an organdy might not be beyond her.

They saw less of John Levine during the late winter and early spring. He was running for sheriff on the Republican ticket. He was elected early in April by a comfortable majority and invited Amos and Lydia to a fine Sunday dinner in celebration at the best hotel in town. Kent's father in April was promoted from a minor position in the office of the plow factory to the secretaryship of the company. The family immediately moved to a better house over on the lake shore and it seemed to Lydia that Kent moved too, out of her life.

She missed him less than might have been expected. Her life was so different from that of any of the children that she knew, that growing into adolescence with the old bond of play disappearing, she fell back more and more on resources within herself. This did not prevent her going faithfully once a month to call on Margery Marshall. And these visits were rather pleasant than otherwise. Margery was going through the paper doll fever. Lydia always brought Florence Dombey with her and the two girls carried on an elaborate game of make-believe, the intricacies of which were entirely too much for Elviry Marshall, sitting within earshot.

Elviry Marshall had two consuming passions in life — Margery and gossip. The questions she asked always irritated Lydia vaguely.

"What wages is your Pa getting now, Lydia?"

"Just the same, Mrs. Marshall."

"Don't you pay Lizzie anything yet?"

"No, Ma'am."

"How much is your grocery bill this month?"

"I don't know."

"Does your Pa ever talk about getting married again?"

"No, Ma'am! Oh, no, Ma'am!"

Lizzie almost exploded with anger when Lydia retailed these questions, but Amos only laughed.

"Pshaw, you know Elviry!"

"Yes, I know Elviry! She's a snake in the grass. Always was and always will be."

"She's a dandy housekeeper," murmured Lydia. "I wonder where she learned. And she isn't teaching Margery a thing. I like Mr. Marshall."

"Dave's a miser. He always was and he always will be," snapped Lizzie. "I despise the whole kit and biling of them, money or no money. Dave never earned an honest cent in his life."

"Lots of rich men haven't," replied Amos.

Amos' garden was a thing of beauty. Its trim rows of vegetables were bordered with sunflowers, whose yellow heads vied in height with the rustling ears of corn. Amos had a general grudge toward life. He had a vague, unexpressed belief that because he was a descendant of the founders of the country, the world owed him an easy living. He had a general sense of superiority to his foreign born neighbors and to the workmen in the plow factory.

But in his garden, all his grudges disappeared. Every evening until dark and every Sunday he worked away, whistling softly to himself. He always felt nearer to his wife, in the garden. She too had been bred on a New England farm. He always felt as if the fine orderliness of the rows was for her.

Lydia greatly preferred weeding the garden to cleaning the house. Indeed the contrast between the fine garden, the well kept patch of lawn and the disorderly house was startling. Amos grumbled and complained but Lydia was in the hobble-de-hoy stage — she didn't care and she had no one teach her.

One afternoon in August, clad in her bathing suit, now much too small for her, she was working in the garden, when a voice behind her grunted,

"Eat!"

Lydia jumped and turned. The old squaw of two years before stood begging. She was as pitifully thin as ever. As she stared at the ugly old Indian, Lydia's throat tightened. She seemed to feel baby Patience's fingers clinging to hers in fear.

"Want some vegetables?" she asked, motioning toward the garden.

The squaw nodded eagerly and held up the dirty apron she was wearing. Lydia began slowly to fill it, talking as she worked.

"Where do you live?" she asked.

The Indian jerked her grey head toward the north. "Big Woods."

"But that's twenty miles. It must take you a long time to walk it. Poor thing!"

The squaw shrugged her shoulders. Lydia stared at the toothless, trembling old mouth, hideous with wrinkles, then at the gnarled and shaking old hands.

"Haven't you anyone to take care of you?"

"All sick — boy sick — man sick — girl sick. All time sick, all time nothing to eat."

"But won't some other Indian make you a garden, a little one?"

Again the squaw shrugged her shoulders. Her apron was full now. She produced a string from inside her waist and tying the apron up baglike, she slung it over her shoulder. Then she gave Lydia a keen glance.

"Friend," she said, briefly, and turning, she tottered painfully out of the gate.

Followed by Adam, Lydia walked thoughtfully out upon the little pier Amos had built. They had no boat, but Lydia fished and dived from the pier. It was hard to understand how the Indians with all their rich pine land could be so poor. She resolved to ask her father and Levine about it and turned a somersault into the water. She swam about until tired, then turned over on her back to rest. Lying so a shadow drifted across her face and she raised her head. A grey birch bark canoe floated silently beside her. In it, in a grey bathing suit, sat Charlie Jackson.

"Goodness!" exclaimed Lydia. "How in the world you do it so quietly, I don't see."

"I saw something that looked like a wet yellow pup in the water, and stole up on it," grinned Charlie.

"Come on in. It's as warm as suds."

Charlie shot his canoe to the pier and in a moment, was floating beside Lydia. She took a deep breath, let herself sink and a moment or two later came up several yards beyond him. He did not miss her for a moment, then he started for her with a shout. A game of tag followed ending in a wild race to the pier which they reached neck and neck. Adam wept and slobbered with joy over their return.

"You certainly are a little sunfish in the water," panted Charlie, as they sat with feet dangling off the pier.

"Ought to be, I'm in it enough," returned Lydia. "Charlie, there's a poor old squaw came here today. What's the matter with the Indians? Why don't they work?"

Charlie turned to look at the white child, uneasily. The two made a wonderful contrast. Charlie was big and bronze and deep chested, with regular features although they were a little heavy. Lydia, growing fast, was thinner than ever but cheeks and eyes were bright.

Charlie's mouth twisted in a sneer. "Why don't they work? Why don't the whites give 'em a chance? Dirty thieves, prowling round like timber wolves. Ask Dave Marshall. Ask that gumshoeing crook of a Levine. Don't ask me."

"Levine's not a crook," shouted Lydia. "He's my friend."

The sneer left Charlie's face and he laughed. "Your friend is he, little sunfish!"

"Yes," said Lydia, furiously. "He gave me Adam," hugging the dog's ugly, faithful head. He immediately tried to sit in her wet lap. "And he's done as much for me as my own father."

"If he's your friend," said the Indian gently, "I won't speak against him to you again."

Lydia instantly was mollified. Charlie was so old and so young! He was so different from Kent that staring into his deep black eyes, Lydia suddenly felt his alien race.

"I must go in and dress," she said. "It's time to get supper."

Charlie nodded and untied his canoe. After he was seated with paddle lifted, he glanced up at her mischievously.

"You're a very nice little girl," he said; "I shall come again. You may call me Uncle Charlie."

Lydia put out her tongue at him. "Good-bye, Uncle!" she called and raced up the bank to the house.

"Daddy," she said that night at supper, "why should Mr. Marshall and Charlie Jackson both say Mr. Levine is a crook?"

Amos ate a piece of bread meditatively before replying. "Any man that goes into politics in this country leaves his reputation behind him. You and I'll never have a better friend than John Levine."

Lydia nodded. She was only a child after all and still retained implicit faith in the opinion of those she loved. She went back to school that fall full of interest and importance. She was a sophomore now and very proud of the fact that she knew the ropes. Her arrangement with Billy held for his second year books. With much pinching of the grocery money, Lizzie had achieved two new galatea sailor suits and so while she felt infinitely inferior to the elaborately gowned young misses of her grade, Lydia was not unhappy.

There was a new course of study offered the pupils this year. It was called the Cookery Course and was elective, not required. Lydia turned her small nose up at it. She was a good cook, without study, she told herself. But Miss Towne thought differently. She called Lydia into her room one day, early in the term. "Lydia, why don't you take the Cooking Course?"

"I can cook, Miss Towne. I do all our cooking and Daddy says I'm fine at it."

"I know, my dear, but there are other things connected with the Course that you need."

"What things?" asked Lydia, a trine obstinately.

"That's what I want you to find out for yourself. Come, Lydia, take my word for it. It's only two hours a week and no outside study required. If after a term of it, you still think it's useless, why drop it."

So behold Lydia entered in the Cooking Course which was not popular. The mothers of the majority of the girls did not, they said, send their daughters to school to be taught kitchen service. But by the efforts of Miss Towne and one or two other teachers, a dozen children ranging in age from fourteen to eighteen, with Lydia as the infant of the class, were enticed into the bright model kitchen in the basement.

It was not long after this that Lydia said to her father, one evening, "Daddy, I've got to have twenty-five cents."

Amos looked up from his newspaper. "What for, Lydia? A quarter's a good deal of money. Takes me pretty near two hours to earn it."

"I know it," answered Lydia, wincing, "but I've got to buy a nail file. You ought to see my hands compared with the other girls. And you ought to see dirty finger nails under the microscope. The cooking school teacher showed us before we made bread, today."

Amos looked at Lydia thoughtfully for a moment, then he carefully abstracted a quarter from his pocket, laid it on the table and went back to his reading.

Lydia planned a real feast for Thanksgiving. She negotiated with Billy Norton for the exchange of two pounds of fudge for a brace of wild duck. The Saturday before Thanksgiving, she gave the house its usual "lick and promise" and then started out with her skates to enjoy the first ice of the season.

She had a glorious morning. There was no snow and the lake had frozen crystal clear. The air was breathless. As she skated she chanted, to improvised tunes, bits of verse.

"The stag at eve had drunk his fill
Where danced the moon on Monan's rill
And deep his midnight lair had laid
In lone Glenartney's hazel shade.

"I sprang to the stirrup, and Joris and he,
I galloped, Dirk galloped, we galloped all three.
'Good speed!' cried the watch as the gate bolts undrew,
'Speed' echoed the wall to us galloping through."

She hunted through Scottish mountains and moors, she whirled from Ghent to Aix and still high hearted and in the land of visions, took off her skates and entered the house. She banged the door, then stood for a moment staring. Elviry and Margery were seated before the living room stove, while old Lizzie sat on one edge of Amos' armchair eyeing the two belligerently.

Margery was wearing a new fur coat. Her beautiful black eyes looked out from under a saucy fur-trimmed hat with a scarlet quill on the side. Elviry wore black broadcloth with fox collar and muff. Lydia, in a remodeled coat of her mother's, and her old Tam and mended mittens, recovered from her surprise quickly.

"Hello!" she said. "When did you come? This is the first time you've ever been in our house, Mrs. Marshall, isn't it?"

"Yes," replied Elviry, "and," with a glance at Lizzie, "I wouldn't be here now if Mr. Marshall hadn't made me."

"Oh, Mamma," protested Margery, "I wanted to come."

"You hush up, Margery! What I came for is that Mr. Marshall would like to have the three of you come to our house for Thanksgiving dinner."

Lydia suddenly giggled. "Don't worry, Mrs. Marshall, we can't come. We're going to have company ourselves for Thanksgiving."

Elviry gave a huge sigh of relief. "Well, that's too bad," she said. "We're going to have a grand dinner, too."

"So are we," retorted Lydia.

"How's Florence Dombey?" asked Margery. "Mamma, can't I stay and play with Lydia a while?"

"We'll stay a few minutes," said Elviry, loosing her furs and settling back in her chair. "It's a real small place, Lizzie, but you can do so little work now, I s'pose it's just as well."

Lydia had produced a pasteboard shoe box of paper dolls which she gave to Margery. She cuddled Florence Dombey in her arms and gave one ear to Margery's question as to the names and personalities of the paper dolls, the other to Elviry's comments.

"It ain't so small," sniffed Lizzie. "It's bigger'n anything you ever lived in, Elviry, till Dave sold enough lumber he stole from the Government to start a bank."

Elviry was not to be drawn into a quarrel. "You always was a jealous body, Lizzie. That old mahogany belonged to both Amos and his wife's folks, I've heard. Why don't you get rid of it and buy more of this here new Mission stuff that's coming in? Though I suppose you'd better wait till Lydia's old enough to take more interest in keeping the house clean. Butter's awful high this winter. How much does your grocery bill average, Lizzie?"

"None of your business," replied Lizzie.

"I don't think Imogen is as good looking as Marion. I'd rather have Marion marry Prince Rupert, then these can be their children," Margery murmured on.

"Land, Lizzie, don't be so cross," said Elviry. "I suppose you've heard the talk about John Levine? He's getting in with that half breed crowd up on the reservation that the Indian agent's such friends with. They say Levine's land hungry enough to marry a squaw. He's so dark, I wouldn't be surprised if he had Indian blood himself. Land knows nothing would surprise me about him. They say he's just naturally crooked."

Lydia and Florence Dombey suddenly stood in front of Elviry.

"Don't you say such things about Mr. Levine," said Lydia slowly, cheeks bright, eyes as blue as Florence Dombey's.

"Well!" exclaimed Elviry, beginning to pull her furs up, "I don't seem to be able to please you two with my conversation, so I'll be going. Margery, get up off that dirty floor. I never cared much about Amos' wife, she was too proud, but at least she was clean. She'd turn over in her grave if she knew what this house looked like. Come, Margery, the horse will be cold, standing so long."

Lizzie opened her mouth to speak but Lydia shook her head, and the two stood in silence, watching the departure of the visitors. When the door had closed Lizzie burst forth in an angry tirade, but Lydia only half listened. She looked slowly around the living room, then walked into the dining room and thence into the kitchen. She opened the pantry door and stared at the dust and disorder, the remnants of food, the half washed dishes. Suddenly she thought of the shining and orderly kitchen in the High School basement. Supposing the cooking teacher should come out to supper, sometime! Lydia had asked her to come.

She came slowly back into the living room. Old Lizzie was replenishing the stove, still muttering to herself. Lydia observed for the first time that her apron was dirty. Thinking it over, she could not recall ever having seen Lizzie with a clean apron. A deep sense of shame suddenly enveloped Lydia.

"Oh, I wish someone had taught me," she groaned. "I wish mother had lived. Everybody has to go and die on me! I suppose Lizzie and Dad'll be next. Adam helps to keep the house dirty. There's dog hair everywhere."

"Don't you get worked up over Elviry Marshall, child," said Lizzie.

"I hate her," exclaimed Lydia, "but what she said about the house is true. Anyhow, I've learned how to clean pantry shelves, so here goes."

She tied one of Lizzie's aprons round her neck, pushed a chair into the pantry and began her unsavory task. It was dusk when she finished and led Lizzie out to observe the shiny, sweet smelling orderliness of the place.

"Land, it does make a difference! If the rheumatiz didn't take all the ambition out of me, I'd keep it that way for you," said the old lady.

"I'll do it, every Saturday. Gosh, I'm tired!" groaned Lydia, throwing herself on the living room couch. "Lizzie, give me some of your mutton tallow to rub on my hands. The cooking teacher says it's fine for hands."

Lydia lay in the twilight, watching the coals glow in the base burner, while the aroma of the baked beans and brown bread Lizzie was tending in the kitchen floated in to her. Adam lay on the floor by the stove, where he could keep one drowsy eye on her every motion. She was thinking of her mother and of little Patience. She could think of them now without beginning to tremble. She tried to picture every detail of her mother's face. They had no picture of her nor of the baby, and Lydia was afraid she would forget. She wondered if they were together, if they knew how hard she was trying to obey her mother's injunction to "make something" of herself. "Be a lady!" "Never be coarse." There was nobody to show her things, she thought. How could she ever learn to be a lady? "If I believed in praying anymore, I'd pray about lots of things," she thought, sadly. "But either there isn't any God, or else He don't believe in prayer, Himself. Gee, supper smells good. I'm awful hungry. I wonder why Mrs. Marshall hates me so. I suppose because I'm such a common kid and she still thinks I almost drowned Margery. And I don't believe a word she says about Mr. Levine, either. Hateful old beast! If I believed in prayer, you bet I'd tell God a few things about her."

The highly satisfactory Thanksgiving feast was eaten and praised. The dishes were washed and set away in the immaculate pantry, and Amos and John Levine were smoking by the fire.

"Seems to me this room looks all slicked up," said Levine.

Amos nodded. "Lydia's coming along. Says the cooking school teacher told her to sprinkle wet tea leaves over the carpet before sweeping to keep down the dust. Place was like a cyclone this morning for an hour, but the result pays. She's growing like her mother."

"She's only a child, and small for her age, at that," said John. "It's a shame for her to work so hard."

"I know it," answered Amos, "but what can I do? On a dollar and a half a day — I swan —"

There was a rap on the door. Lizzie admitted Dave Marshall and Margery.

"Out for a tramp as a digester," explained Dave. "Came to call on my friend Lydia. I ain't seen her for ages."

He and Levine nodded to each other. Amos shook hands and Dave kissed Lydia, catching a dark scowl on Levine's face as he did so.

"Let's play paper dolls," said Margery, as soon as she had pulled off her coat.

"You play 'em," replied Lydia, "I'm awful tired."

"Why should a baby like you be tired?" inquired Marshall, pulling her to his side as he seated himself in Amos' armchair.

"If you'd tasted our dinner," said Amos, "you'd know why she and Lizzie should be half dead."

"I wish I could 'a' tasted it," replied Marshall. "Have a smoke, friends?"

Amos took a cigar but Levine refused.

"Come, John, come," said the stout banker, banteringly. "This is a legal holiday and you and I at least agree on Lydia. Let's stop war for the day, eh?"

Levine's sallow face hardened, then he caught Lydia's blue gaze on him as she stood beside Marshall. It was such a transparent, trusting gaze, so full of affection, so obviously appealing to him to "be nice," that in spite of himself he grinned and took a cigar.

Amos settled back with a sigh of satisfaction. He enjoyed company and had had no one but John since his wife's death.

"Looks as if the country'd go Republican next fall," he said by way of starting a conversation.

"I don't see why," returned Marshall, who was a Democrat.

"Folks are sick of Democratic graft," said Levine.

"And Republicans think it's their turn, eh?" inquired Marshall. "Well, maybe it is, maybe it is!"

Amos laughed genially. "Satisfied with your share, Dave?"

"Got my eye on just one more little mite. Just one little mite, then I'm through," chuckled Marshall.

"Then you good Republicans can get your feet into the trough."

"Co-ee! Lydia!" came a call from the lake shore.

Lydia ran to the kitchen door. Charlie Jackson and Kent were skating up to the bank.

"Come out for a while," cried Kent.

"I can't. I've got company. Come on up and get warm," returned Lydia.

The two boys slipped off their skates and came up to the cottage. Kent needed no introduction, and Lydia made short work of Charlie by saying to the assemblage at large, "This is Charlie Jackson. Come on up by the stove, boys."

The boys established themselves on the couch back of the baseburner.

"Hello, Marg," said Kent. "What you doing?"

"Paper dolls," returned Margery from her corner, without looking up. Charlie Jackson stared at the beautiful little black head bent over the bright colored bits of paper with interest.

Amos took up the interrupted conversation. "If we could get a Republican Congress, that block o' pine and black loam twenty miles north would be given to its rightful owners."

"Meaning the full bloods, I suppose," said Levine with a short laugh.

"Yes — full blooded whites," returned Amos.

Charlie Jackson suddenly threw back his head and rose.

"I'm a full blood Indian," he said, quietly. The three men looked at him as if they saw him for the first time.

"Well, what of it?" asked Marshall, shortly.

"This of it," said Charlie, tensely, "that you whites with your Constitution and your Declaration of Independence are a lot of liars and thieves."

Marshall turned purple, but John Levine spoke quickly. "Easy there, my boy! You're talking of things you don't understand."

"Oh, but he does," interrupted Lydia eagerly. "'Governments derive their just powers from the consent of the governed.' We had it in school. It must mean Indians too."

John Levine laughed. "There you have it. And Charlie is right, we are liars and thieves, but we have to be. Might is right in this world."

"Speak for yourself, Levine," cried Marshall.

"Levine!" exploded Charlie. "Are you Levine? You're the man then that my sister —" his voice rose to a shout. "I'll beat the face off of you right now."

And he made a sudden spring for the astonished Levine.

Chapter VII

THE REPUBLICAN CANDIDATE

"Nature counts no day as wasted."

— The Murmuring Pine

*A*mos and Kent caught Charlie by either arm as his hands clutched for Levine's throat. Marshall did not stir out of his chair. During the remainder of the episode his face wore a complacent expression that, though Lydia did not consciously observe it at the time, returned to her in after years with peculiar significance.

"Here! Here! This won't do, my young Indian!" cried Amos.

"Let me get at him!" panted Charlie.

Lydia moved away from Lizzie and Margery. The three had automatically jumped to grab Adam's collar for Adam always assisted in a fight, human or otherwise. She ran over to the Indian.

"Charlie," she pleaded, looking up into his face, "you mustn't hurt Mr. Levine. He's my best friend. And it is not polite to come to call at my house and make a row, this way."

"That's right," commented Marshall. "Do your fighting outdoors."

John had not stirred from his chair. He looked up at the Indian and said slowly and insolently, "Get out of here! You know what I can do to you, don't you? Well, get out before I do it!"

Charlie returned John's look of contempt with one of concentrated hatred. Then he turned to Kent.

"Come on, Kent," he growled and followed by his friend, he marched out of the kitchen door.

"Whew!" said Amos, "talk about civilizing Indians!"

Lydia was trembling violently. "What made him act so — *Did* you hurt his sister, Mr. Levine?"

"Didn't even know he had a sister," returned John, coolly relighting his cigar.

Marshall rose and stretched his fat body. "Well, you serve up too much excitement for me, Amos. I'll be getting along. Come, Margery."

"Wait and we'll all have some coffee," said Lizzie. "Land, I'm all shook up."

"Pshaw! 'twan't anything. Kent should have had more sense than to bring him in here," said Levine.

"Why, he's usually perfectly lovely," protested Lydia. "Goes to parties with the girls and everything."

"I wouldn't go to a party with a dirty Indian," said Margery, her nose up in the air.

"What do you know about parties, chicken?" asked Marshall, buttoning her coat for her.

"Mama says I can go next year when I enter High School," replied Margery.

"First boy, white or Indian, that comes to call on you before you're eighteen, I'll turn the hose on," said Dave, winking at the men.

Amos and John laughed and Dave made his exit in high good humor.

When the door had closed Amos said, "Any real trouble with the boy, John?"

"Shucks, no!" returned Levine. "Forget it!"

And forget it they did while the November dusk drew to a close and the red eyes of the stove blinked a warmer and warmer glow. About eight o'clock, after a light supper, Levine started back for town. He had not been gone five minutes when a shot cracked through the breathless night air.

Amos started for the door but Lizzie grasped his arm. "You stay right here, Amos, and take care of the house."

"What do you s'pose it was?" whispered Lydia. "I wish Mr. Levine was here. He's sheriff."

"That's what I'm afraid of — that something's happened, to him — between his being sheriff and his other interests. I'll get my lantern."

"Wait! I'll have to fill it for you," said Lydia.

So it was that while Amos fumed and Lydia sought vainly for a new wick, footsteps sounded on the porch, the door opened and Billy Norton and his father supported John Levine into the living room. Levine's overcoat showed a patch of red on the right breast.

"For God's sake! Here, put him on the couch," gasped Amos.

"Billy, take Levine's bicycle and get the doctor here," said Pa Norton.

"Hot water and clean cloth, Lydia," said Amos. "Let's get his clothes off, Norton."

"Don't touch me except to cut open my clothes and pack the wound with ice in a pad of rags," said John weakly. Then he closed his eyes and did not speak again till the doctor came.

Lydia trembling violently could scarcely carry the crushed ice from Lizzie to her father. No one spoke until the gentle oozing of the blood yielded to the freezing process. Then Amos said in a low voice to Pa Norton,

"What happened?"

"Can't say. Billy and I were coming home from town when we heard the shot ahead of us. It took us a minute or two to come up to Levine. He was standing dazed like, said the shot had come from the lake shore way and that's all he knew about it."

The beat of horses' hoofs on the frozen ground broke the silence that followed. In a moment Dr. Fulton ran into the room. Lydia seized Florence Dombey and hurried to the kitchen, nor did she leave her station in the furthest corner until the door closed softly after the doctor. Amos came out into the kitchen and got a drink at the water pail.

"Doc got the bullet," said Amos. "Grazed the top of the lungs and came to the surface near the backbone. Lord, that was a narrow escape!"

"Will he — will he die?" whispered Lydia.

"Of course not," answered Amos, with a quick glance at the blanched little face. "He's got to have good nursing and he can't be moved. Lizzie's as good a nurse as anyone could want. Doctor'll be back at midnight and stay the rest of the night."

"Who did it, Daddy?"

Amos shook his head. "It might have been Charlie Jackson or it might have been a dozen others. A sheriff's liable to have plenty of enemies. Billy started a bunch hunting."

Lydia shivered.

"Go to bed, child," said Amos. "We're going to be busy in this house for a while."

"I want to see him first, please, Daddy."

"Just a peek then, don't make a noise."

Already the living room had a sick room aspect. The light was lowered and the table was littered with bandages and bottles. Lydia crept up to the couch and stood looking down at the gaunt, quiet figure.

John opened his eyes and smiled faintly. "Making you lots of trouble, young Lydia."

"Oh, no!" exclaimed Lydia. "Just get well, we don't mind the trouble."

"I've got to get well, so's you and I can travel," whispered Levine. "Good night, dear."

Lydia swallowed a sob. "Good night," she said.

At first, Amos planned to have Lydia stay out of school to help, but Levine grew so feverishly anxious when he heard of this that the idea was quickly given up and Ma Norton and a neighbor farther up the road arranged to spend the days turn about, helping Lizzie.

As soon as the shooting was known, there was a deluge of offers of help. All the organizations to which Levine belonged as well as his numerous acquaintances were prodigal in their offers of every kind of assistance.

But John fretfully refused. He would have no nurse but Lizzie, share no roof but Amos'. "You're the only folks I got," he told Amos again and again.

The shooting was a seven days' wonder, but no clue was found as to the identity of the would-be assassin. Charlie Jackson had spent the evening with Kent. As the monotony of Levine's convalescence came on, gossip and conjecture lost interest in him. John himself would not speak of the shooting.

It was after Christmas before John was able to sit up in Amos' armchair and once more take a serious interest in the world about him. Lydia, coming home from school, would find Adam howling with joy at the gate and John, pale and weak but fully dressed, watching for her from his armchair by the window. The two had many long talks, in the early winter dusk before Lydia started her preparations for supper. One of these particularly, the child never forgot.

"Everybody acted queer about Charlie Jackson, at first," said Lydia, "but now you're getting well, they're all just as crazy about him as ever."

"He'll kill someone in a football scrimmage yet," was John's comment.

"No, the boys say he never loses his temper. The rest of them do. I wish girls played football. I bet I'd make a good quarterback."

John laughed weakly but delightedly. "You must weigh fully a hundred pounds! Why, honey, they'd trample a hundred pounds to death!"

"They would not!" Lydia's voice was indignant. "And just feel my muscles. I get 'em from swimming."

John ran his hand over the proffered shoulders and arm. "My goodness," he said in astonishment. "Those muscles are like tiny steel springs. Well, what else would you like to be besides quarterback, Lydia?"

"When I was a little girl I was crazy to be an African explorer. And I'd still like to be, only I know that's not sensible. Adam, for Pete's sake get off my feet."

Adam gave a slobbery sigh and withdrew a fraction of an inch. Levine watched Lydia in the soft glow of the lamp light. Her hair was still the dusty yellow of babyhood but it was long enough now to hang in soft curls in her neck after she had tied it back with a ribbon. She was still wearing the sailor suits, and her face was still thin and childish for all she was a sophomore.

"I don't suppose you could explore," said Levine, meditatively.

"Oh, I could, if I had the money to outfit with, but I'll tell you what I really would like best of all." Lydia hitched her chair closer to Levine and glanced toward the kitchen where Lizzie was knitting and warming her feet in the oven. "I'd like to own an orphan asylum. And I'd get the money to run it with from a gold mine. I would find a mine in New Mexico. I know I could if I could just get out there."

"Seems to me all your plans need money," suggested John.

"Yes, that's the trouble with them," admitted Lydia, with a sigh. "And I'll always be poor — I'm that kind."

"What are you really going to do with yourself, Lydia, pipe dreams aside?"

"Well, first I'm going to get an education, clear up through the University. 'Get an education if you have to scrub the streets to do it,' was what Mother always said. 'You can be a lady and be poor,' she said, 'but you can't be a lady and use poor English.' And then I'm going to be as good a housekeeper as Mrs. Marshall and I'm going to dress as well as Olga Reinhardt, and have as pretty hands as Miss Towne. And I'm never going to move out of the home I make. Maybe I'll get married.

I suppose I'll have to 'cause I want at least six children, and someone's got to support them. And I'll want to travel a good deal."

"Travel takes money," John reminded her.

"Not always. There was The Man Without a Country, but I wouldn't want to have what he had. Seems to me it was a little thing he said after all. Mr. Levine, why did he feel so terrible about the poem?"

"What poem?" asked Levine.

Lydia cleared her throat.

"'Breathes there a man with soul so dead
  Who never to himself hath said
  This is my own, my native land?'

— and you know the rest."

John Levine looked at Lydia strangely. There was a moment's pause, then she said, "But I don't understand just what it all means."

"Lots of us don't," commented John, briefly. "But if I had a son I'd beat understanding of it into him with a hickory club."

Lydia's jaw dropped. "But — but wouldn't you beat it into your daughter?"

"What's the use of trying to teach patriotism to anything female?" There was a contemptuous note in Levine's voice that touched Lydia's temper.

"Well, there's plenty of use, I'd have you know!" she cried. "Why, I was more interested in Civil Government last year than any of the boys except Charlie Jackson."

Levine laughed, then said soberly, "All right, Lydia, I'd be glad to see what you can do for your country. When you get that orphan asylum, put over the door, 'Ducit Amor Patriae.'"

Lydia looked at him clearly. "You just wait and see."

She went soberly toward the kitchen for her apron, and Levine looked after her with an expression at once wistful and gentle. Lydia looked up "Ducit Amor Patriae" in a phrase book the next day. She liked the sound of it.

By the middle of January, Levine was sufficiently recovered to leave. The Saturday before he left occurred another conversation between him and Lydia that cemented still further the quaint friendship of the two.

It snowed heavily all day. Lydia had put in the morning as usual cleaning the house. This was a very methodical and thorough process now, and when it was finished the cottage shone with cleanliness. In the afternoon, she dug a path to the gate, played a game of tag in the snow with Adam, then, rosy and tired, established herself in Amos' armchair with a book. Lizzie was taking a long nap. The dear old soul had been exhausted by the nursing. Levine lay on the couch and finally asked Lydia to read aloud to him. She was deep in "The Old Curiosity Shop" and was glad to share it with her friend.

During the remainder of the afternoon John watched the snowflakes or Lydia's sensitive little red face and listened to the immortal story.

Suddenly he was astonished to hear Lydia's voice tremble. She was reading of little Nell's last sickness. "She was dead. Dear, patient, noble Nell was dead. No sleep so beautiful and calm. She seemed a creature fresh from the hand of God. Not one who had lived and suffered death."

Lydia suddenly broke off, bowed her yellow head on the book and broke into deep, long drawn sobs that were more like a woman's than a child's.

John rose as quickly as he could. "My dearest!" he exclaimed. "What's the matter?" He pulled her from the armchair, seated himself, then drew her to his knees.

"I can't bear it!" sobbed Lydia. "I can't. Seems sometimes if I couldn't have little Patience again I'd die! That's the way she looked in her coffin, you remember? 'F-fresh from the hand of God — not one who h-had lived and s-suffered death.' O my little, little sister!"

John took "The Old Curiosity Shop" from the trembling fingers and flung it upon the couch. Then he gathered Lydia in his arms and hushed her against his heart.

"Sweetheart! Sweetheart! Why, I didn't realize you still felt so! Think how happy Patience must be up there with God and her mother! You wouldn't wish her back!"

"If I believed that I could stand it — but there isn't any God!"

Levine gasped. "Lydia! Hush now! Stop crying and tell me about it."

He rocked slowly back and forth, patting her back and crooning to her until the sobs stopped.

"There!" he said. "And what makes you think there's no God, dear?"

"If there was a God, He'd answer prayers. Or He'd give some sign." Lydia lifted a tear-stained face from John's shoulder. "He's never paid any attention to me," she said tensely. "I've tried every way to make Him hear. Sometimes in the dusk, I've taken Adam and we've gone deep into the woods and I've sat and thought about Him till — till there was nothing else in the world but my thought of Him. And I never got a sign. And I've floated on my back in the lake looking up into the sky trying to make myself believe He was there — and I couldn't. All I knew was that Mother and Patience were dead and in coffins in the ground."

Levine's sallow face was set with pain. "Why, child, this isn't right. You're too young for such thoughts! Lydia, do you read the Bible?"

She nodded. "I've tried that too — but Jesus might have believed everything He said was true, yet there mightn't have been a word of truth in it. Do you believe in God?"

John's hold on the thin hands tightened. He stared long and thoughtfully at the snowflakes sifting endlessly past the window.

"Lydia," he said, at last. "I'll admit that my faith in the hereafter and in an All-seeing God has been considerably shaken as I've grown older. But I'll admit too, that I've refused to give the matter much thought. I tell you what I'll do. Let's you and I start on our first travel trip, right now! Let's start looking for God, together. He's there all right, my child. But you and I don't seem to be able to use the ordinary paths to get to Him. So we'll hack out our own trail, eh? And you'll tell me what your progress is — and where you get lost — and I'll tell you. It may take us years, but we'll get there, by heck! Eh, young Lydia?"

Lydia looked into the deep black eyes long and earnestly. And as she looked there stole into her heart a sense of companionship, of protection, of complete understanding, that spread like a warm glow over her tense nerves. It was a sense that every child should grow up with, yet that Lydia had not known since her mother's death.

"Oh!" she cried, "I feel happier already. Of course we'll find Him. I'll begin my hunt tomorrow."

John smoothed her tumbled hair gently. "We're great friends, aren't we, Lydia! I've an idea you'll always believe in me no matter what folks say, eh?"

"You bet!" replied Lydia solemnly.

John Levine went back to his duties as sheriff and Lydia and Amos and Lizzie missed him for a long time. But gradually life fell back into the old routine and spring, then summer, were on them almost before they realized winter was gone.

Lydia did well at school, though she still was an isolated little figure among her schoolmates. The cooking teacher added sewing to the course, after Christmas, and Lydia took up "over and over stitch" at the point where her gentle mother had left off five years before. She progressed so famously that by the time school closed she had learned how to use a shirtwaist pattern and how to fit a simple skirt. With her plans for a summer of dress-making she looked with considerable equanimity on the pretty spring wardrobes of her schoolmates.

They saw less than ever of Levine when summer came, for he was beginning his campaign for Congressman. He came out occasionally on Sunday and then he and Lydia would manage a little stroll in the woods or along the lake shore when they would talk over their progress in the Spiritual Traveling they had undertaken in January. Lydia had decided to give the churches a chance and was deliberately attending one Sunday School after another, studying each one with a child's simple sincerity.

One source of relief to Lydia during the summer was that Mrs. Marshall and Margery spent two months in the East. Lydia had faithfully kept in touch with Margery ever since her promise had been given to Dave Marshall. But she did not like the banker's daughter — nor her mother. So again as far as playmates were concerned Lydia spent a solitary summer.

Yet she was not lonely. Never before had the lake seemed so beautiful to her. Sitting on the little pier with Adam while her father worked in his garden, she watched the sunset across the water, night after night. There was nothing that seemed to bring her nearer to a sense of God than this. Night after night the miracle, always the same, always different. The sun slipped down behind the distant hills, the clouds turned purple in the Western hill tops, fading toward the zenith to an orange that turned to azure as she watched. The lake beneath painted the picture again, with an added shimmer, a more mysterious glow. Little fish flashed like flecks of gold from the water, dropping back in a shower of amethyst. Belated dragon flies darted home. And the young girl watching, listening, waiting, felt her spirit expand to a demand greater than she could answer.

Amos was keenly interested in Levine's campaign. His attitude toward politics was curiously detached, when one considered that he was saturated with information — both as to state and national politics. He was vicious in his criticism of the Democrats, ardent in his support of the Republicans, yet it never seemed to occur to him that it was his political duty to do anything more than talk. He seemed to feel that his ancestors in helping to launch the government had forever relieved him from any duty more onerous than that of casting a vote.

He did, however, take Lydia one September evening just before school opened to hear John make a speech in the Square. Lydia up to this time had given little heed to the campaign, but she was delighted with the unwonted adventure of being away from home in the evening.

It was a soft, moonlit night. The old Square, filled with giant elms, was dotted with arc lights that threw an undulating light on the grey mass of the Capitol building. When Amos and Lydia arrived the Square was full of a laughing, chattering crowd. Well dressed men and women from the University and the lake shore, workingmen, smoking black pipes, pushing baby carriages, while their wives in Sunday best hung on their arms. Young boys and girls of Lydia's age chewed gum and giggled. Older boys and girls kept to the shadows of the elms and whispered.

On the wooden platform extended from the granite steps of the Capitol, a band dispensed dance music and patriotic airs, breaking into "America" as Levine made his way to the front of the platform.

Almost instantly the crowd became quiet. A curious sort of tenseness became apparent as Levine began to speak.

Lydia stared up at him. He looked very elegant to her in his frock coat and grey trousers. She was filled with pride at the thought of how close and dear he was to her. She wished that the folk about her realized that she and her shabby father were intimate with the hero of the evening.

The first part of the address interested Lydia very little. It concerned the possibility of a new Post Office for Lake City and made numerous excursions into the matter of free trade. It did not seem to Lydia that in spite of their attitude of tenseness, the people around her were much more interested than she.

Then of a sudden Levine launched his bolt.

"But after all," he said, "my friends, what is free trade or a new Post Office to you or me? Actually nothing, as far as our selfish and personal interests go. And who is not selfish, who is not personal in his attitude toward his community and his country? I frankly admit that I am. I suspect that you are.

"Ladies and gentlemen, twenty miles north of this old and highly civilized city, lies a tract fifty miles square of primitive forest, inhabited by savages. That tract of land is as beautiful as a dream of heaven. Virgin pines tower to the heavens. Little lakes lie hid like jewels on its bosoms. Its soil is black. Fur bearing animals frequent it now as they did a century ago.

"Friends, in this city of white men there is want and suffering for the necessities of life. Twenty miles to the north lies plenty for every needy inhabitant of the town, lies a bit of loam and heaven-kissing pines for each and all.

"But, you say, they belong to the Indians! Friends, they belong to a filthy, degenerate, lazy race of savages, who refuse to till the fields or cut the pines, who spend on whiskey the money allowed them by a benevolent government and live for the rest, like beasts of the field.

"Why, I ask you, should Indians be pampered and protected, while whites live only in the bitter air of competition?

"I am not mincing words tonight. I do not talk of taking the lands from the Indians by crooked methods. You all know the law. An Indian may not sell the lands allotted to him. I want you to send me to Congress to change that law. I want the Indian to be able to sell his acreage."

Levine stopped and bowed. Pandemonium broke loose in the Square. Clapping, hisses, cheers and cat-calls. Lydia clung to her father's arm while he began to struggle through the crowd.

"Well," he said, as they reached the outer edge of the Square and headed for the trolley, "the battle is on."

"But what will the Indians do, Daddy, if they sell their land?" asked Lydia.

"Do! Why just what John intimated. Get out and hustle for a living like the rest of us do. Why not?"

Why not indeed! "What did some of the people hiss for?" asked Lydia.

"Oh, there's a cheap bunch of sentimentalists in the town, — all of 'em, you'll notice, with good incomes, — who claim the Indians are like children, so we should take care of 'em like children. Then there's another bunch who make a fat living looting the Indians. They don't want the reservation broken up. I'm going to sit on the back seat of the car and smoke."

Lydia clambered into the seat beside her father. "Well — but — well, I suppose if Mr. Levine feels that way and you too, it's right. But they are kind of like children. Charlie Jackson's awful smart, but he's like a child too."

"I don't care what they're like," said Amos. "We've babied 'em long enough. Let 'em get out and hustle."

"Do you think Mr. Levine'll get elected?"

Amos shrugged his shoulders. "Never can tell. This is a Democratic town, but Levine is standing for something both Democrats and Republicans want. It'll be a pretty fight. May split the Democratic party."

This was the beginning of Lydia's reading of the newspapers. To her father's secret amusement, she found the main details of Levine's battle as interesting as a novel. Every evening when he got home to supper he found her poring over the two local papers and primed with questions for him. Up to this moment she had lived in a quiet world bounded by her school, the home, the bit of lake shore and wood with which she was intimate, and peopled by her father and her few friends.

With John Levine's speech, her horizon suddenly expanded to take in the city and the vague picture of the reservation to the north. She realized that the eyes of the whole community were focused on her dearest friend. Up on the quiet, shaded college campus — the newspapers told her — they spoke of him contemptuously. He was a cheap politician, full of unsound economic principles, with a history of dishonest land deals behind him. It would be a shame to the community to be represented by such a man. They said that his Democratic opponent, a lawyer who had been in Congress some five terms, was at least a gentleman whose career had been a clean and open book.

When these slurs reached Levine, he answered in a vitriolic speech in which he named the names of several members of the faculty who had profited through the Indian agent in quiet little sales of worthless goods to Indians.

The saloon element, Lydia learned, was against Levine. It wanted the reservation to stand. That the saloon element should be in harmony with them was galling to the college crowd, though the fact that their motives for agreement were utterly different was some solace.

The "fast crowd" were for John. Clubmen, politicians, real estate men were high in his praise. The farmers all were going to vote for him.

Lake City was always interested in the national election but this year, where the presidential candidates were mentioned once, Levine and his opponent were mentioned a hundred times. Ministers preached sermons on the campaign. The Ladies' Aid Society of the Methodist Church, the Needlework Guild of the Episcopalian, the Woman's Auxiliary of the Unitarian, hereditary enemies, combined forces to work for Levine, and the freeing of the poor Indian from bondage.

Chapter VIII

THE NOTE

"Each year I strew the ground with cones, yet no young pines grow up. This has been true only since the Indians went."
— *The Murmuring Pine*

*M*argery Marshall had entered High School this fall. She had returned from New York with a trousseau that a bride might have envied. She was growing tall, and her beauty already was remarkable. Her little head carried its great black braid proudly. The pallor of her skin was perfectly healthy — and even the Senior lads were seen to observe her with interest and appreciation.

The results of Lydia's summer dressmaking had not been bad. She had made herself several creditable shirtwaists and a neat little blue serge skirt. Her shoes were still shabby. Poor Lydia seemed somehow never to have decent shoes. But her hands and the back of her neck were clean; and her pile of Junior schoolbooks already had been paid for — by picking small fruit for Ma Norton during the summer and helping her to can it. She came back to school with zeal and less than her usual sense of shabbiness.

It was a day toward the first of October at the noon hour that Lydia met Kent and Charlie Jackson. She had finished her lunch, which she ate in the cloakroom, and bareheaded and coatless was walking up and down the sidewalk before the schoolhouse.

"Hello, Lyd! How's everything?" asked Kent. "I haven't seen you to talk to since last spring."

"Did you have a fine summer?" said Lydia.

"Aw, only part of it. Dad made me work till the middle of August, then Charlie and I camped up on the reservation."

"Shame he had to work, isn't it?" grinned Charlie. "Poor little Kent!"

The three laughed, for Kent now towered above Lydia a half head and was as brawny as Charlie.

"There comes Margery," said Lydia. "She hardly speaks to me now, she's been to New York."

"She *is* a peach," exclaimed Charlie, eying Margery in her natty little blue suit appraisingly.

"Some swell dame, huh?" commented Kent, his hands in his trousers' pockets, cap on the back of his head. "Hello, Marg! Whither and why?"

"Oh, how de do, Kent!" Margery approached languidly, including Lydia and Charlie in her nod.

"Got any paper dolls in your pocket, Miss Marshall?" inquired Charlie.

Margery tossed her head. "Oh, I gave up that sort of thing long ago!"

"Land sakes!" The young Indian chuckled.

"How do you like High School, Margery?" asked Lydia.

"Oh, it's well enough for a year or so! Of course Mama, I mean — Mother's going to send me to New York to finish."

"'Mother!' suffering cats!" moaned Kent. "Marg, you're getting so refined, I almost regret having pulled you out of the lake that time."

"*You!* Why Kent Marshall, I pulled her out myself!" exclaimed Lydia.

"And I saved both of you — and got licked for it," said Kent.

"I hope you all had a pleasant summer," observed Margery, twisting up the curls in front of her small ears. "Mother and I were in New York."

Kent, Lydia and Charlie exchanged glances.

"I had a pretty good summer," said Lydia. "I sewed and cooked and scrubbed and swam and once Adam, Dad, Mr. Levine and I walked clear round the lake, eighteen miles. Adam nearly died, he's so fat and bow-legged. He scolded all the way."

"I don't see how your father can let that Mr. Levine come to your house!" exclaimed Margery with sudden energy. "My father says he's a dangerous man."

"He's a crook!" said Charlie, stolidly and finally.

Lydia stamped her foot. "He's not and he's my friend!" she cried.

"You'd better not admit it!" Margery's voice was scornful. "Daddy says he's going to speak to your father about him."

"Your father'd better not go up against Levine too hard," said Kent, with a superior masculine air. "Just tell him I said so."

"You don't stick up for Levine, do you, Kent?" asked Charlie, indignantly.

"Why, no, but Dave Marshall's got no business to put his nose in the air over John Levine. I don't care if he is Margery's father. Everybody in town knows that he's as cruel as a wolf about mortgages and some of his money deals won't bear daylight."

"Don't you dare to say such things about my father," shrieked Margery.

"He was awful good to Dad and me about a money matter," protested Lydia.

"Aw, all of us men are good to you, Lyd," said Kent impatiently. "You're that kind. Being good to you don't make a man a saint. Look at Levine. He's got a lot of followers, but I'll bet you're the only person he's fond of."

"He's a crook," repeated Charlie, slowly. "If what he's trying to do goes through, my tribe'll be wanderers on the face of the earth. If I thought it would do any good, I'd kill him. But some other brute of a white would take his place. It's hopeless."

The three young whites looked at the Indian wonderingly. Their little spatting was as nothing, they realized, to the mature and tragic bitterness that Charlie expressed. A vague sense of a catastrophe, epic in character, that the Indian evidently saw clearly, but was beyond their comprehension, silenced them. The awkward pause was broken by the school bell.

Lydia had plenty to think of on her long walk home. Charlie's voice and words haunted her. What did it all mean? Why was he so resentful and so hopeless? She made up her mind that when she had the opportunity to ask him, she would. She sighed a little, as she thought of the comments of her mates on John Levine. Little by little she was realizing that she was the only person in the world that saw the gentle, tender side of the Republican candidate for Congress. The realization thrilled her, while it worried her. She had an idea that she ought to make him show the world the heart he showed to her. As she turned in at the gate and received Adam's greetings, she resolved to talk this matter over with Levine.

The opportunity to talk with Charlie came about simply enough. At recess one day a week or so later he asked her if she was going to the first Senior Hop of the year. Lydia gave him a clear look.

"Why do you ask me that? Just to embarrass me?" she said.

Charlie looked startled. "Lord knows I didn't mean anything," he exclaimed. "What're you so touchy about?"

Lydia's cheeks burned redder than usual. "I went to a party at Miss Towne's when I was a Freshman and I promised myself I'd never go to another."

"Why not!" Charlie's astonishment was genuine.

"Clothes," replied Lydia, briefly.

The Indian boy leaned against a desk and looked Lydia over through half-closed eyes. "You're an awful pretty girl, Lydia. Honest you are, and you've got more brain in a minute than any other girl in school'll have all her life."

Lydia blushed furiously. Then moved by Charlie's simplicity and obviously sincere liking, she came closer to him and said, "Then, Charlie, why hasn't any boy ever asked me to a party? Is it just clothes?"

Looking up at him with girlish wistfulness in the blue depths of her eyes, with the something tragic in the lines of her face that little Patience's death had written there irradicably, with poverty speaking from every fold of the blouse and skirt, yet with all the indescribable charm of girlish beauty at fifteen, Lydia was more appealing than Charlie could stand.

"Lydia, I'll take you to a party a week, if you'll go!" he cried.

"No! No! I couldn't go," she protested. "Answer my question — is it clothes?"

"No, only half clothes," answered Charlie, meeting her honestly. "The other half is you know too much. You know the fellows like a girl that giggles a lot and don't know as much as he does and that's a peachy dancer and that'll let him hold her hand and kiss her. And that's the honest to God truth, Lydia."

"Oh," she said. "Oh —" Then, "Well, I could giggle, all right. I can't dance very well because I've just picked up the steps from watching the girls teach each other in the cloakroom. Oh, well, I don't care! I've got Adam and I've got Mr. Levine."

"He's a nice one to have," sneered Charlie.

"Why do you hate him so, Charlie?" asked Lydia.

"Lots of reasons. And I'll hate him more if he gets his bill through Congress."

"I don't see why you feel so," said Lydia. "You get along all right without the reservation, why shouldn't the other Indians. I don't understand."

"No, you don't understand," replied Charlie, "you're like most of the other whites round here. You see a chance to get land and you'd crucify each other if you needed to, to get it. What chance do Indians stand? But I tell you this," his voice sank to a hoarse whisper and his eyes looked far beyond her, "if there is a God of the Indians as well as the whites, you'll pay some day! You'll pay as we are paying."

Lydia shivered. "Don't talk so, Charlie. I wish I knew all about it, the truth about it. If I was a man, you bet before I voted, I'd find out. I'd go up there on that reservation and I'd see for myself whether it would be better for the Indians to get off. That poor old squaw I gave my lunch to, I wonder what would become of her —"

"Look here, Lydia," exclaimed Charlie, "why don't you come up on the reservation for a camping trip, next summer, for a week or so?"

"Costs too much," said Lydia.

"Wouldn't either. I can get tents and it wouldn't cost you anything but your share of the food. Kent'll go and maybe one of the teachers would chaperone."

Lydia's eyes kindled. "Gee, Charlie, perhaps it could be fixed! I got nine months to earn the money in. It's something to look forward to."

Charlie nodded and moved away. "You'll learn things up there you never dreamed of," he said.

The conversation with John Levine did not take place until the Sunday before the election. The fight in the Congressional district had increased in bitterness as it went on. Nothing but greed could have precipitated so malevolent a war. The town was utterly disrupted. Neighbors of years' standing quarreled on sight. Students in the University refused to enter the classrooms of teachers who disagreed with them on the Levine fight. Family feuds developed. Ancient family skeletons regarding pine grafts and Indian looting saw the light of day.

On the Saturday a week before election, Lydia went to pay her duty call on Margery. Elviry admitted her. It was the first time Lydia had seen her since the New York trip.

"Margery'll be right down," said Elviry. "She's just finished her nap."

"Her what?" inquired Lydia, politely.

"Her nap. A New York beauty doctor told me to have her take one every day. Of course, going to school, she can't do it only Saturdays and Sundays. She went to the Hop last night. She looked lovely in a cream chiffon. One of the college professors asked who was that little beauty. Come in, Margery."

Margery strolled into the room in a bright red kimono. "How de do, Lydia," she said.

"Hello, Margery. Want to play paper dolls?"

"Paper dolls!" shrieked Elviry. "Why, Margery, you are fifteen!"

"I don't care," replied Lydia obstinately. "I still play 'em once in a while."

"I haven't touched one since last spring," said Margery. "Want to see my New York clothes?"

"No, thank you," answered Lydia. "I'd just as soon not. I've got to get home right away."

"What's in that big bundle?" asked Elviry, pointing to the huge paper parcel in Lydia's lap.

"Nothing," she said shortly, looking at the rope portières in the doorway.

"I got new ones in the East," said Elviry, following her glance. "Shells strung together. But I put 'em up only when we have parties. We don't use anything but doilies on the dining table now, no tablecloths. It's the latest thing in New York. Who made your shirtwaist, Lydia?"

"I did," answered Lydia, not without pride.

"I thought so," commented Elviry. "How much was the goods a yard — six cents? I thought so. Hum — Margery's every day shirtwaists were none of them less than thirty-nine cents a yard, in New York. But of course that's beyond you. I don't suppose your father's had a raise, yet. He ain't that kind. Does he pay Levine any rent for that cottage?"

"Of course, every month!" exclaimed Lydia, indignantly.

"Oh! I just asked! Your father's been talking strong for him at the plow factory, they say, and we just wondered. He's old enough to be your father, but you're getting to be a young lady now, Lydia, and it's very bad for your reputation to be seen with him. You haven't any mother and I must speak."

"I don't see how John Levine's reputation about Indians or pine lands can hurt me any," protested Lydia, angrily, "and I just think you're the impolitest person I know."

Elviry snorted and started to speak but Margery interrupted.

"You are impolite, Mama! It's none of our business about Lydia — if she wants to be common."

Lydia rose, holding the paper parcel carefully in her arms. "I *am* common, just common folks! I always was and I always will be and I'm glad of it — and I'm going home."

The front door slammed as she spoke and Dave Marshall came in.

"Hello! Well, Lydia, this is a sight for sore eyes. Thought you'd forgotten us. What's in your bundle?"

Lydia spoke furiously, tearing the paper off the bundle as she did so.

"Well, since you're all so curious, I'll show you!" And Florence Dombey, with the hectic gaze unchanged, emerged. "There!" said Lydia. "I never shall be too old for Florence Dombey and I thought Margery wouldn't be either — but I was wrong. I wrapped Florence Dombey up because I do look too big for dolls and I don't want folks to laugh at her."

"Of course you're not too big for dolls," said Dave. "You and Margery go on and have your play."

"Daddy!" cried Margery. "Why, I wouldn't touch a doll now."

"There, you see!" said Lydia, laying Florence Dombey on a chair while she pulled on her coat — made this year from one that Lizzie had grown too stout to wear — "It's no use for me to try to be friends anymore with Margery. She's rich and I'm common and poor. She has parties and beaux and clothes and I don't. I'll be friends with you but I can't be friends with her."

Dave looked from his two women folks to Lydia. "What've you two been saying now?" he asked gruffly.

Elviry tossed her head. "Nothing at all. I just showed a decent interest in Lydia, as I would in any motherless girl and she got mad."

"Yes, I know your decent interest," grunted Dave. "You make me sick, Elviry. Why I was ever such a fool as to let you spend a summer in New York, I don't know."

"Now, Dave," said Elviry in a conciliating tone, "you said that Lydia and Amos ought to be warned about Levine."

"Yes, I did," exclaimed Dave, with a sudden change of voice. "You tell your father to come round and see me this evening, Lydia. I don't like his attitude on the reservation question. Tell him if I can't change his views any other way, I may have to bring pressure with that note."

Lydia blanched. She looked at Marshall with parted lips. She never had heard before the peculiar, metallic quality in his voice that she heard now. She buttoned her coat with trembling fingers.

"Yes, sir, I'll tell him," she said. "I guess it's no use to try to be friends with you either. We'll pay that note up, somehow. Even it can't be allowed to keep us from believing what we believe." Her voice strengthened suddenly. "What's the use of being an American if you can't believe what you want to? We'll pay that note! If I have to quit school and go out as a hired girl, we will."

Dave Marshall looked from Lydia to Margery and back again. Margery was patting her curls. Lydia, holding the doll, returned his look indignantly.

"I'm not going to tell my father to come to see you. I'll answer right now. We'll think and say what we please and you can do whatever you want to about that nasty old note."

Dave suddenly laughed. "There, Elviry, that's what I mean about Lydia's being the real thing. You can't help my being your friend, Lydia, no matter what happens. But," grimly, "I'll call in that note unless your father shuts up."

"Good-bye!" exclaimed Lydia abruptly and she marched into the hall, head held high, and closed the outside door firmly behind her.

It had been a long time since she had known the heavy sinking of the heart that she felt now. In spite of their desperate poverty, since her interview in the bank with Marshall four years before, she had not worried about money matters. She had an utter horror of repeating Marshall's message to her father. Money worry made Amos frantic. She plodded along the October road, unheeding the frosty sunshine or the scudding brown leaves that had charmed her on her earlier trip.

In the midst of one of her longest sighs, Billy Norton overtook her.

"Well, Lydia," he said, "isn't it chilly for your lady friend?"

"Hello, Billy," said Lydia, looking up at the young man soberly. Billy was a sophomore in college.

"I'll carry her, if your hands are cold, though I'd hate to be caught at it," he said.

Lydia ignored his offer. "Billy, is there any way a girl like me could earn $600?" she asked him.

"Golly, not that I know of! Why?"

"Oh, I just asked. I wish I was a man."

Billy looked at the scarlet cheeks and the blowing yellow curls. "I don't," he said. "What's worrying you, Lyd?"

"Nothing," she insisted. Then, anxious to change the subject, she asked, "What're you studying to be, Billy?"

"A farmer. Next year I shift into the long agric. course."

"Goodness!" exclaimed Lydia, "I don't see what you want to study to be a farmer for. I should think you'd want to be something classy like a lawyer or — or something."

"Lots of folks think the same way, but I believe a farmer's the most independent man in the world. And that's what I want to be, independent — call no man boss."

"That's me too, Billy," cried Lydia, pausing at her gate. "That's what I want to be, independent. That's what real Americans are."

"You're a funny little girl," said Billy. "What made you think of that?"

"I often think about it," returned Lydia, running up the path to the door.

Billy stood for a minute looking after her thoughtfully. Then he smiled to himself and went on homeward.

Lydia did not tell her father that night of Marshall's threat. He was in such a tranquil mood that she could not bear to upset him. But the next day she gathered her courage together and told him. Amos was speechless for a moment. Then to her surprise instead of walking the floor and swearing, he gave a long whistle.

"So it's that serious, is it? I wonder just what he's up to! The old crook! Huh! This will be nuts for John though. If he doesn't come out this afternoon, I'll go look him up this evening."

Lydia's jaw dropped. "But, Daddy, you don't seem to realize we'll have to pay $600 the first of January," she urged, her voice still trembling. She had scarcely slept the night before in dread of this moment.

For the first time, Amos looked at her carefully. "Why, my dear child, there's nothing to worry about!" he exclaimed.

"You mean you're going to stop talking for Mr. Levine? Oh, Daddy, don't do that! We can borrow the money somewhere and I'll help pay it back. I'm almost grown up now."

"'Stop talking'!" roared Amos. "I've fallen pretty far below what my ancestors stood for, but I ain't that low yet. Now," his voice softened, "you stop worrying. Levine and I'll take care of this."

Lydia looked at her father doubtfully and suddenly he laughed unsteadily and kissed her. "You get more and more like your mother. I've seen that look on her face a hundred times when I told her I'd fix up a money matter. I don't know what I'd do without you, Lydia, I swan."

This was rare demonstrativeness for Amos. The reaction from anxiety was almost too much for Lydia. She laughed a little wildly, and seizing Adam by his fore paws put him through a two step that was agony for the heavy fellow. Then she put on her coat, and bareheaded started for a walk. Amos stood in the window staring after the bright hair in the October sun until it disappeared into the woods. Then he sighed softly. "Oh, Patience, Patience, I wonder if you can see her now!"

Levine stole away from his various councils and reached the cottage about supper time.

"If I didn't get out here once in a while," he said as he sat down to the waffles and coffee that made the Sunday night treat Lydia had lately developed, "I'd get to believe everyone was playing politics."

Lizzie, pouring the coffee, looked Levine over. "A bullet'd have hard work to hit you now," she remarked, "you're so thin. If you'd listen to me, you'd be taking Cod Liver Oil."

Levine smiled at the wrinkled old face opposite. "If I didn't listen to you, I don't know who I would. Aren't you and Lydia all the women folks I got? If you'll fix me up some dope, I'll take a dose every time I come out here."

Lizzie sniffed and loaded his plate with another waffle. Amos was giving no heed to these small amenities. He was eating his waffles absentmindedly and suddenly burst forth,

"Lydia, tell John about Dave Marshall."

Lydia, flushing uncomfortably, did so. Levine did not cease his onslaught on the waffles during the recital. When she had finished, he passed his coffee cup.

"Another cup, young Lydia. Your coffee is something to dream of."

Lydia was too surprised to take the cup. "But — but *six hundred dollars.* Mr. Levine!" she gasped.

"Good news, eh, Amos?" said Levine. "Getting anxious, isn't he!" Then catching Lydia's look of consternation, "Why, bless your soul, Lydia, what are you upset about? Let him call in the loan. I can pay it."

Amos nodded. "Just what I said."

"But I think that's awful," protested Lydia. "We owe Mr. Levine so much now."

The effect of her words on John was astonishing. He half rose from his chair and said in a tone not to be forgotten, "Lydia, never let me hear you speak again of owing me anything! Between you and me there can never be any sense of obligation. Do you understand me?"

There was a moment's silence at the table, Amos and Lizzie glanced at each other, but Lydia's clear gaze was on the deep eyes of Levine. What she saw there she was too young to understand, but she answered gravely,

"All right, Mr. Levine."

John sank back in his chair and passed his plate for a waffle.

"I'll make my interest and payments to you then, thank the Lord!" said Amos.

"We'll make them on time just as usual," remarked Lydia, in a voice that had both reproof and warning in it. "Ain't debts perfectly awful," she sighed.

"So Marshall's worried," repeated John, complacently, when they were gathered round the stove. "Well, it behooves him to be. I don't know what he'll do when the Indians are gone."

"Mr. Levine," asked Lydia, "where'll the Indians go?"

John shrugged his shoulders. "Go to the devil, most of them."

"Oh, but that seems terrible!" cried Lydia.

"No more terrible than the way they live and die on the reservation. My dear child, don't develop any sentiment for the Indian. He's as doomed as the buffalo. It's fate or life or evolution working out — whatever your fancy names it. No sickly gush will stop it. As long as the Indian has a pine or a pelt, we'll exploit him. When he has none, we'll kick him out, like the dead dog he is."

Lydia, her eyes round, her lips parted, did not reply. For a moment she saw the Levine that the world saw, cold, logical, merciless. John interpreted her expression instantly and smiled. "Don't look at me so, young Lydia. I'm just being honest. The rest talk about 'freeing the Indian.' I say damn the Indian, enrich the whites."

"It — it makes me feel sort of sick at my stomach," replied Lydia, slowly. "I suppose you're right, but I can't help feeling sorry for Charlie Jackson and my old squaw."

Levine nodded understandingly and turned to Amos. "What's the talk in the factory?" he asked.

During the half hour that followed, Lydia did not speak again nor did she hear any of the conversation. New voices were beginning to whisper to her. Try as she would to hush them with her faith in her father and John, they continued to query: How about the Indians? Whose is the land? What do you yourself believe?

When Levine rose at nine to leave, she followed him to the door. "Adam and I'll walk a way with you," she said, "while Dad puts his chickens to bed."

"Fine!" exclaimed John. "My wheel is out of commission so I have to walk to the trolley."

He glanced at Lydia a trifle curiously however. This was a new venture on her part. It was a clear, cold, starlit night. Lydia trudged along for a few moments in silence. Then Levine pulled her hand through his arm.

"Out with it, young Lydia," he said.

"Do you suppose," she asked, "that God is something like ether — or like electricity — in the air, everywhere, something that sort of holds us together, you know?"

"Well," replied John, slowly, "I wouldn't want to believe that. I want to find a God we can know and understand. A God that's tender and — and human, by Jove."

Lydia looked up at him quickly in the starlight. "After what you said about Indians tonight, you can't believe God could be tender and — and let that happen!"

Levine returned her look and smiled. "You score there, honey. Lydia, you're growing up. Your head's above my shoulder now."

The young girl nodded carelessly. "But I wanted to talk to you about taking the reservation, not about me."

"I guess we'd better do that another time. I don't dare to have you walk further with me. This is a lonesome road back for you. And besides, I don't want you to scold me."

"Scold you!" Lydia paused in her astonishment. "Why, I love you as much as I do anybody in the world. How could I scold you?"

Levine looked down into the shadowy, childish eyes. "Couldn't you? Well, you're a dear, anyhow. Now scoot and I'll watch till you reach the gate."

Lydia hesitated. She felt a change in John's manner and wondered if she had hurt his feelings. "Kiss me good night, then," she said. "You don't do it as regularly as you used to. If I don't watch you, you'll be finding someone else to travel with you."

John turned the little face up and kissed her gently on the forehead, but Lydia with rare demonstrativeness threw her arms about his neck and kissed his lips with a full childish smack.

"There!" she said complacently. "Come on, Adam! Don't wait, Mr. Levine. I'm safe with Adam."

But John Levine did wait, standing with his hand against his lips, his head bowed, till he heard the gate click. Then he lifted his face to the stars. "God," he whispered, "why do You make me forty-five instead of twenty-five?"

Chapter IX
THE ELECTION

"Perhaps, after all, I have fulfilled my destiny in being a lute for
the wind. But then why the cones and the broken boughs?"
                                              — *The Murmuring Pine*

*I*t rained on Election Day, a cold November drizzle that elated the
Democrats. "A rainy day always brings a Democratic victory," said
Amos, gloomily, voicing the general superstition.

The day was a legal holiday and even the saloons were closed. Yet Lake
City was full of drunken men by noon. Every hack, surrey and hotel
bus in town was busy in the pay of one faction or the other hauling
voters to the booths. The Capitol square was deserted but groups of
men, some of them very drunk and some of them very sober, were to
be found throughout the business section of the city, bitterly debating
the reservation question.

There were a great number of Indians in town that day, big dark
fellows in muddy moccasins and faded mackinaws who stood about
watching the machinations of the whites without audible comments.

Toward night the rain stopped and Lydia begged her father to take
her into town to see the parade that would be indulged in by the
victorious party. Amos was not at all averse to taking in the parade,
himself. So nine o'clock found the two at the Square with a great waiting
crowd. There were very few women in the crowd. Those that Lydia saw
were painted and loud-voiced. Amos told her vaguely that they were
"hussies" and that she was not to let go of his arm for an instant.

Lydia didn't know what a hussy was, but she didn't want to stir an
inch from her father's side because of her fear of drunken men. She was
in a quiver of excitement; torn with pity and doubt when she thought
of Charlie Jackson; speechless with apprehension when she thought of
the possibility of Levine's being defeated.

It was close on ten o'clock when the sound of a drum was heard from
the direction of the Methodist Church. The crowd started toward the
sound, then paused as Binny Bates, the barber, in a stove-pipe hat,
mounted on a much excited horse, rode up the street. Binny was a Levine
man and the crowd broke into cheers and cat-calls.

After Binny came the band, playing for dear life "Hail the Conquer-
ing Hero" and after the band, two and two a great line of citizens with
kerosene torches. After the torches came the transparencies: "Levine
Wins!" "The Reservation is Ours." "Back to the land, boys!" "We've
dropped the white men's burden."

And following the transparencies came a surprise for crowd and paraders alike. Close on the heels of the last white man strode Charlie Jackson, with a sign, "The land is ours! You have robbed us!" and after Charlie, perhaps a hundred Indians, tramping silently two by two, to the faint strain of the band ahead,

"Columbia, the gem of the ocean
 The home of the brave and the free —"

For a moment, the crowd was surprised into silence. Then a handful of mud caught Charlie's sign and a group of college students, with a shout of "Break up the line! Break up the line," broke into the ranks of the Indians and in a moment a free for all fight was on.

Amos rushed Lydia down a side street and upon a street car. "Well! Well! Well!" he kept chuckling. "John ate 'em alive! Well! Well!" Then in the light of the car he looked at Lydia. "For heaven's sake! What are you crying for, child?"

"I don't know," faltered Lydia. "I'm — glad for Mr. Levine — but poor Charlie Jackson! You don't suppose they'll hurt him?"

"Oh, pshaw," replied Amos. "Nothing but an election night fight! The young Indian went into the parade just to start one."

"How soon will the Indians have to get off the reservation?" asked Lydia.

"Oh, in a year or so! John's got to get a bill through Congress, you know."

"Oh." Lydia gave a great sigh of relief; a year or so was a very long time. She decided to forget the Indians' trouble and rejoice in Levine's triumph.

It was a triumph that John himself took very quietly. He realized that he had ahead of him in Congress a long and heavy campaign. The forces against him were not going to lie down, defeated by his election. But after the fashion of American elections, there were no protests or quarrels afterward. The town settled immediately to its old routine and Levine was dropped from the front pages of the newspapers.

Charlie Jackson was taciturn for a week or so, then he played brilliantly in the Thanksgiving football game and at the banquet which followed he was his old genial self.

After Christmas Lydia began seriously to consider how she could earn the twenty-five dollars that her share in the camping trip would cost. Lizzie was aghast at the size of the sum and didn't approve of the idea of camping anyhow. Amos gave his consent to her going, feeling that it was quite safe; that Lydia never could earn the money.

Lydia was dampened but not daunted. One (in January) Saturday afternoon, she went to call on Ma Norton. Ma was sitting in her bright kitchen sewing carpet rags. Ma's hair was beginning to turn grey but her plump cheeks were red and her grey eyes behind her spectacles were as clear as a girl's.

"Who's going to chaperone you children?" she asked Lydia.

"Miss Towne. The rest kicked, but I like her."

"You use a good deal of unnecessary slang, my dear," said Ma. "Who of the boys and girls are going?"

"Charlie and Kent and Olga and I. Margery's crazy to go, only her mother hasn't given in yet. If she does go, we'll ask Gustus Bach too."

Ma Norton looked at Lydia searchingly. "I didn't know you had anything to do with Olga or with Margery either, now."

"Goodness!" exclaimed Lydia, "this is Charlie's, party! None of 'em would go on my invitation. I — I don't quite see why, but I don't have chums like the rest."

"I wouldn't let it worry me," said Ma. "You've never had time to lollygag. That's the secret of it."

Lydia turned this over in her mind thoughtfully for a moment and the older woman, looking up from her sewing caught on the young face the look of sadness that should not have been there.

"It would be nice for you to have the camping trip, dear," said Ma. "You've had so little to do with children your own age. I suppose you're worrying over the money end?"

Lydia nodded. "That's what I wanted to talk to you about. Every spring you get someone in to help you clean house. If you'll do it in Easter vacation, this year, and let me help, why, that would be a couple of dollars, wouldn't it?"

Ma Norton looked at the slender little figure and thought of the heavy carpet beating, the shoving of furniture, the cleaning of mattresses that the stout old colored man hustled through for her every spring. And she thought of the winter's butter and egg money (nearly forty dollars it amounted to already) that she was saving for new parlor curtains. Then she recalled the little figure that had nightly trudged two miles delivering milk rather than take Billy's schoolbooks as a gift. And Ma Norton smiled a little ruefully as she said,

"All right, you can help me instead of old Job and I'll pay you five dollars."

"Five dollars for what?" asked Billy. He had come in the side door, unheeded.

His mother explained the situation. Billy listened attentively, warming his hands at the stove.

"If I didn't have so much to do at home," said Lydia, "I could work here Saturdays and Sundays and earn a little, that way."

"Well, you wouldn't, you know," growled Billy. Lydia and Ma Norton looked up, startled at his tone.

"For the land's sake, Billy, why not?" exclaimed Ma.

"Because, Lydia's getting too big now to do these hired girl stunts. It was bad enough when she was little. But folks'll never forget 'em and always think of her as a hired girl if she keeps on."

Lydia gasped and turned scarlet. Ma Norton stared at her son as if she never had seen him before. Strong and blonde and six feet tall, he seemed suddenly to his mother no longer a boy but a mature man, and a very handsome one at that. As a matter of fact, although Billy's gaunt frame was filling out and his irregular features were maturing into lines of rugged strength, he never would be handsome. He was looking at Lydia now with the curious expression of understanding that she always brought to his grey eyes.

"I'm not ashamed to be a hired girl for your mother, Billy Norton," snapped Lydia.

"Well, I'm ashamed for you," answered the young man. "You earn your money some other way."

Lydia looked meaningly at Billy's big hands, rough and red with milking and farm work.

"You do hired man's work for your father. How'll you live that down?"

It was Billy's turn to blush. "I'm a man," he replied.

Lydia's voice suddenly quivered. "Then how can I earn money?"

"Dead easy! You make the best fudge in the world. Put some for sale in the University book store. I'm clerking there an hour every day."

"The very thing!" cried Ma Norton.

"Billy, you are a duck!" shrieked Lydia.

"Gimme something to eat, Ma, before I go out to milk," said Billy, with a grin that struggled to be modest.

Billy's suggestion proved indeed to be a happy one. He was a willing pack horse and middleman for Lydia and though the demand for fudge was never overwhelming, Lydia by the end of May had cleared something over thirty-five dollars.

Her joy over this method of earning money was not confined to its relation to her camping trip. She saw herself helping to pay up their indebtedness to Levine, Marshall having made good his threat to call in the note. She saw herself gradually developing an enormous trade that finally should demand a whole store for itself. The store would develop into a candy factory. The candy factory would grow into a business that would send Lydia, admired and famous, traveling about the world in a private yacht.

In the meantime, she expended the whole of four dollars on a pair of buckskin outing boots and eight dollars on a little corduroy hunting coat and skirt. When the clothes arrived from the Chicago mail order house, Amos, Lizzie and Lydia had an exciting hour. Amos had brought the package home from town with him, and supper had been held back while Lydia tried on the clothes. Amos and Lizzie smiled when the young girl pranced out before them. The suit was cheap but well cut, with belt and pockets and welted seams. The soft buckskin shoes fitted the slender calves like velvet. With her bright cheeks and her yellow hair above the fawn-colored corduroy, Lydia looked half boy, half woman.

"My soul, Lydia, they're just grand!" cried Lizzie.

"What boys are going in that crowd?" demanded Amos.

"Charlie and Kent and — Margery's mother's given in — 'Gustus Bach. I told you. Daddy, don't you like the suit?"

"Like it!" exclaimed Amos. "Lydia, I'm stunned by it! It makes me realize my little girl's growing up to be a pretty woman. I wish I could have bought you your first suit myself, Lydia. But on a dollar and a half a day, I swan —"

The brightness suddenly left Lydia's face. "Oh, Daddy," she exclaimed, "I'm a pig to spend all this money on myself! You take the rest of the money, for the note."

Amos gave a laugh that was half gay, half grim. "Lydia, you spend every cent of that money on yourself. You've earned it in more ways than one. I wish John Levine could see you in it. I guess he will though. Congress will rest most of the summer. Let's have supper now."

Lydia spun through her Junior examination blissfully. For once marks and final averages were of little importance to her. For the week after school closed, she was going camping!

Charlie and Kent were making all the camp preparations. Miss Towne and the three girls were to be at Lydia's gate with their suitcases at nine o'clock of a Monday morning. Other than this, they had received no orders.

Amos had been very sober when he said good-bye to Lydia, at half past six. "It's your first trip, Lydia. Don't do anything you wouldn't want your mother to see."

Lydia looked at him wonderingly, then threw her arms about his neck. "Oh, Daddy, I don't want to go off and leave you two whole weeks!"

"It's too late to back out now. Go on and have a good time," said Amos, picking up his dinner pail. Lydia watched him down the road. Suddenly she realized how lonely her father must be without her mother.

"I oughtn't to go, Lizzie," she said.

"Shucks! Think of all you'll have to tell us when you get home. Don't be a cry baby, child."

Promptly at nine Charlie and Kent whirled up to the gate in a carryall. The driver was the same man who had moved the Dudley family five years before. He greeted Lydia with a grin.

"You've grow'd some, eh, Lydia? Where's the rest of the women folks?"

"Here come Miss Towne and Olga!" cried Kent. "Margery'll be late, of course."

At nine-fifteen Margery was driven up in state by Elviry, and at nine-twenty the carryall was off to the north in a cloud of dust, leaving Adam howling dismally at the gate.

For fifteen miles the way led up and down hill over a dusty country road that wound for the most part past great wheat farms and grazing lands, vividly green under the June sky. Here and there were woods of young oak and birch, self sowed, replacing the pine long since cleared off. For the last five miles there were few farms. The rolling hills disappeared and low lying lakes, surrounded by marshes took their places. The young rice bordering the lakes was tenderly green and the marshes were like fields of corn with their thick growth of cat-tail. Beyond the marshes the hills rose again, with the road winding like a black ribbon over their curving bosoms into the vivid sky beyond.

"Where the hills begin again, that's the reservation," said Charlie.

"Where are the pines?" asked Lydia. "I thought it was all pines."

"You'll see plenty, before the trip's over. Just beyond that group of buildings is the reservation line."

The buildings Charlie pointed to were the first that had appeared in several miles. A two-story, unpainted frame house with several barns and sheds comprised the group. There was a sign on the front of the house.

"Last Chance," read Margery, as they clattered by. "For goodness' sake!" she giggled, "is it a hotel?"

"Look at all the women! One in every window!" cried Olga. "Why, they must have a lot of maids! Do people come up here in the summer, Kent?"

Kent gave Miss Towne an appealing glance.

"It's a miserable, disreputable place, girls," said the teacher. "Why look at that when you have these beautiful hills before you? How far into the reservation do we go, Charlie?"

"About four miles. It's where I camp every year. Margery, did you bring some paper dolls?"

Margery dimpled and tossed her head. "I wonder how old I'll have to be before you realize I'm grown up, Charlie!"

Charlie looked at her critically. "Well, when you're eighteen, maybe."

"Lydia'll be twenty-five before she gets through looking like a baby, but Olga's a young lady now," said Kent. He was eying the girls with the air of a connoisseur. "Three peaches, aren't they, Miss Towne?"

"I don't see why you say three," objected Gustus. "Ask me and say four."

The young people laughed and looked at Miss Towne, half startled by Gustus' audacity. Miss Towne herself was blushing and Olga exclaimed, "Why, Miss Towne, you *are* good looking when you blush! And I don't believe you're so frightfully old!"

It was true. Miss Towne in her outing blouse, a soft felt hat crushed down on her brown hair, which was now wind-tossed and loosened, her smooth skin flushed, her grey eyes full of laughter, did not look her frightful age of thirty-five. In fact, she looked charmingly young. Her youthful charges looked her over with frank amazement. It was a tradition in the school to fear and dislike Miss Towne. Charlie had asked a number of teachers to act as chaperone before he had approached Miss Towne. She too had at first refused, then had said, "Well, it's Lydia's first outing. I'll do it for her sake. But don't tell her I said so." Charlie had kept his own counsel and Miss Towne had delayed her summer trip to Europe, for the camping trip on the reservation.

"Thank you, children, you brighten my old age very much. Look at the neat farms we are passing."

"Indian farms," said Charlie. "This one belongs to Chief Cloud."

"Are there many Indian farms?" asked Lydia.

"No, there's not much use for Indians to farm. The Agent is their middleman, and he eats up all the profits."

"For the Lord's sake, Charlie," protested Kent, "don't begin any funeral oration! We're no investigating committee. We're out for some fun."

"Second the motion," said Gustus. "Can I smoke, Miss Towne?"

Miss Towne gave Gustus a clear look. He was a tall, thin boy of seventeen, with the dark eyes of the Rhine German and with thin hawklike features that went with his hollow chest. His father was a rich brewer and Gustus, always elegantly dressed, was very popular with the girls. Margery had insisted on his being invited.

"If I were a boy with a chest like yours, I wouldn't smoke," said Miss Towne, "but do as you please."

With a nonchalant "Thanks," Gustus lighted a cigarette.

"Going to stay in training all summer, Charlie?" asked Kent.

"Yes," grunted Charlie, "but next summer I'll be through with foot-ball, and I'll smoke my head off."

"Oh! the pines!" shrieked Lydia.

A sudden silence fell. The road, curving around a hill, had without warning entered the pine woods.

In every direction as far as the eye could pierce stretched brown, columnar aisles, carpeted with the brown of needles and the green of June undergrowth: aisle on aisle, green arch on green arch, flecked with sunshine, mighty trunks supporting great swaying boughs, drooping with their weight of needles.

Except for a muffled thud of horses' hoofs, the carryall moved soundlessly for the road was thick carpeted with needles.

The others fell to chatting again, but Lydia was too moved for words. The incense of the pines, their curious murmuring stillness, roused in her memories that were perhaps half racial. She never had been in a pine wood before, yet the hushed sense of solemnity it wakened in her was perfectly familiar. Its incense breathed to her secrets she never had known, never would understand, yet it seemed to her startled fancy that she had known and understood them, always.

She was still in a half dream when the blue of a lake glimmered beyond the far aisles and the carryall drew up with a flourish before three tents set in the pines on the water's edge.

Charlie and Kent had made their preparations well and they dis-played them proudly. They had rented the three old A tents from the agent, as well as the seven canvas cots, the dishes and the cooking utensils. The middle tent had been arranged with a rough slab-table and benches for a dining- and living room. The boys' tent with three cots and the girls' with four, were crowded but comfortable.

"The Indian school is closed for the summer," explained Charlie, "and the Agent was glad to make a little money extra. He'll pocket it, you bet. Everything's clean," he added hastily in answer to Miss Towne's lifting eyebrows. "Blankets, cots and all, even the hammocks yonder, I had scrubbed with soap and water. I don't live with a doctor for nothing."

"It's very nice, indeed, boys," said Miss Towne. "Come girls, get out your aprons. I suppose you're all starved."

"Wait! Wait!" cried Kent. "That's not the way this camp's going to be run. Charlie, Gustus and me do the cooking. You ladies are company and don't have to do anything except wash the dishes and make your own beds."

"Gee!" exclaimed Lydia. "I'd rather cook than wash dishes, any day."

"I never wash dishes," protested Margery.

"I can't do it either," said Olga.

"Can you boys really cook?" asked Miss Towne, in her sharp way.

"Yes, *Ma'am!*" replied Kent. "Charlie learned in the Indian school, even baking, you know, and he's taught me a lot. Gustus can peel potatoes, clean fish and such stunts."

Gustus groaned but made no protest.

"I think it's a very nice arrangement," decided Miss Towne. "Come girls, let's unpack and arrange the tent."

Kent's statement proved no idle boast. The boys could cook. And though the fare was simple during the entire holiday consisting of fish, caught in the lake, potatoes, baking powder biscuits and occasional additions of canned stuff, it was well prepared and there was plenty of it.

The little camp quickly settled into an orderly routine. The girls wrangled among themselves about the dish-washing and Gustus was inclined to complain over the number of potatoes he was obliged to peel, but beyond this the camp work caused little friction.

Miss Towne was well supplied with French books and made, the young folks thought, an ideal chaperone. She was tired after her year's work and spent almost all her time in a hammock. She saw to it that the girls were in bed by ten o'clock and that all were accounted for at meal time. Apparently, beyond this, she left her charges to their own devices. She had taught in the High School too long not to know that spying and nagging are more demoralizing than no chaperoning at all.

There was a very early pairing off in the camp. Kent devoted himself to Olga, Gustus to Margery and Charlie to Lydia. Kent and Olga kept the camp supplied with fish. Excepting at meal time and the bathing hour, they spent the day in a birch-bark canoe on the lake. Gustus and Margery were the least strenuous of the party and caused Miss Towne, as a consequence, more uneasiness than the rest. They spent long hours sitting side by side in a hammock, talking, heaven knows of what! In the evening when the campfire was lighted they were always being routed out of the shadows by the others and teased into joining the story telling and singing.

Charlie undertook to show to Lydia the reservation as the Indians knew it. If Lydia was a little puzzled by his eagerness to make her understand conditions on the reservation, she gave little thought to the riddle. This adventure was affecting her deeply. There was the sudden freedom and relaxation from home responsibilities. There was the daily and intimate companionship with young people, than whom none were better dressed than she! — and there were the pines.

She knew and loved the woods at home. But they were second growth hardwood and birch, and had little in common with the splendor of the pines. Waking early in the morning, she would creep from the tent and steal beyond sound and sight of the camp. There in the cathedral beauty of the pines she would stand drawing deep breaths and staring as if her eyes must pierce through the outward solemn loneliness of the forest, to its deeper meaning. She often wondered if in his search for God, John Levine had ever stood so.

Tramping through the woods with Charlie, she did not talk much, nor did he. They visited one or two neat Indian farms, but for the most part Charlie led her from one wick-i-up to the other, deep set in recesses of the wood, where the only whites to intrude on the Indians were the occasional government wood cruisers. These wick-i-ups were hovels, usually in the last stages of poverty and desolation. A squaw, braiding reed mats, a buck returning with a string of fish, a baby burrowing in the moss — all of them thin, ragged and dirty, and about them the hallowed beauty and silence of the primeval pines; this was the picture Lydia carried of most of the dwellers in these huts. Sometimes the wick-i-up was occupied by a solitary Indian, nearly always sick and always old.

Once they came upon a white haired squaw crawling feebly from her doorway toward a fish that lay at the foot of a tree. Charlie picked up the fish and he and Lydia helped the old woman back to her hut. In the hut was an iron pot and a pile of reed mats. That was all.

"She says," explained Charlie, "that she's been sick all winter and she'd have starved to death only one of her neighbors drops a fish for her there, every day or so."

"Let's get some food for her at the camp," said Lydia eagerly.

Charlie shook his head. "What's the use! It would just prolong her agony. She's nearly dead now. The old can go. It's the young ones' starving that hurts me."

He led Lydia out and again they tramped through the long green aisles. It was later in the day that they came upon a wick-i-up where there were three children, besides the father and mother. Two of the children were half blind with eye trouble. The whole family was sitting in the sun, about a pot of fish. The grown-ups chatted eagerly with Charlie, and he translated for Lydia.

"They say it's been a fearful winter. They only had ten dollars this year out of their Government allowance and they couldn't get work. They lived on fish and potatoes. The Catholic priest gave them some wild rice. The baby froze to death or starved, or both. We'll bring some food over to these folks, Lydia, because there are kids — eh?"

"But, Charlie, what's the Government allowance?"

"Oh, didn't you know? — and you're one of the white lords of creation too! The Government set aside this land for the Indians in solemn treaty with them, forever and ever. Then it deliberately sold off a big block of it and deposited the money at Washington. The income from this was to be given to the Indians. There's over two million dollars there. But by the time it's filtered from Washington to the Indians, this is the result." He nodded at the half-starved group about the fish pot. "Damn the dirty, thieving whites," he said, quietly.

Lydia had had four days of this. As they made their way back to the camp for supper, she said to him, in an unsteady voice, "Charlie, I can't stand it! Think of that baby that froze to death. And all these beautiful woods are full of half-starved Indians! Charlie, I can't stand it!" And Lydia bowed her head on her arm and leaned against a tree trunk.

"Good Lord, Lydia!" exclaimed Charlie, "I didn't want you to feel that bad! I just wanted you to see, because you're Levine's friend and because I like you so much. Please, don't cry!"

"I'm not crying," Lydia lifted reddened eyes to his, "I was just thinking. What can I do about it, Charlie?"

"You can't do anything. It's too late. But I wanted you to see. I don't care what girl understands as long as you do. I think an awful lot of you, Lydia."

He took Lydia's hand and patted it. Lydia looked up at him, thrilled by his bronze beauty and the note in his voice.

"If I were a white man," said Charlie, "I'd make you love me and marry me. But I'm an Indian and sooner or later I'll go back to my people. I'm just making believe I can play the white man's game for a while." He eyed Lydia wistfully. "But we'll be friends, eh, Lydia? — Always? Even if I go back to the wick-i-up, you'll be my friend?"

"Oh, yes, Charlie, always," replied Lydia, earnestly, even while there flashed through her head the half whimsical thought, "Queer kinds of men want to be friends with me, Mr. Levine, Mr. Marshall, and Charlie. And they all hate each other!"

After this episode, Charlie was less strenuous about showing Lydia Indian conditions. That night he resumed a mild flirtation with Olga that he had dropped when school closed and Olga met him more than halfway.

"Wouldn't that come and get you!" growled Kent to Lydia as Charlie and Olga paddled away in the canoe, the next morning. "Have you and Charlie had a fight?"

"Nope," replied Lydia. "But I got sick of investigating the reservation. Are you and Olga mad at each other?"

"Not so very! Say, Lyd, let's kill time," Kent interrupted himself with a yawn, "with a tramp up to the settlement for some gum."

Lydia stifled an elaborate yawn, at which Kent grinned. "All right, I can stand it if you can," she said. "Will you come along, Miss Towne?"

Miss Towne, who had been highly edified by the morning's maneuvering shook her head and settled herself in her hammock. "No eight mile walk for me. I'm taking a rest cure. Better wear a hat, Lydia. You're getting dreadfully burned."

"That's right. Your nose is peeling something fierce," said Kent as they started off.

"Huh, yours looks like a pickled beet," returned Lydia. "Come on, pretend I'm Olga and be happy."

Chapter X

THE CAMP

"The humans I have known lack root hold. Perhaps that is why they die and leave no trace."

— *The Murmuring Pine*

*T*here was no clear-cut trail between the camp and the settlement. The settlement lay four miles northeast and there were little-used, needle-covered roads to be found that led here, there and everywhere, over which the initiated could find the way to the store.

But Lydia and Kent did not want to use the roads. It was with the old familiar sense of make believe adventure that they started on what they called a Bee-line southwest. And it was mid-afternoon before, hungry and leg weary, they reached the store that backed up against the Indian school!

They bought sardines, crackers and cheese and ate them perched on a dry goods box near the hitching rack.

"There! I feel happier," said Kent as he threw away the empty sardine cans. "How are you, old lady?"

Lydia swung her feet contentedly. "Fine! Let's start back. We'll be there by supper time, I'm sure we know the way now."

Kent nodded, offered Lydia a stick of gum, took one himself, put a huge supply in his pocket and they were off.

But alas for the vanity of amateur woods-craftsmen! The late June dusk found them still threading the endless aisles of pine, their sense of direction completely obscured by the sinking of the sun.

"Scared, Lyd?" inquired Kent as they paused for a moment's rest on a log.

"No, but I'm awful hungry and I've chewed gum till I'll scream if I see another piece. We ought to come on another wick-i-up soon."

"We've come on a dozen of them," grumbled Kent. "If we could make the Indians understand where the camp is, it would be all right. And I don't know what Charlie's Indian name is, so that doesn't help."

Lydia drew a trifle closer on the log to Kent. "Supposing we have to stay out here all night!" She shivered a little.

"Well, I'd light a fire," said Kent in a matter of fact manner that Lydia suspected was assumed, "and fix you up on a bed of pine needles. Then I'd stand guard all night, like a little tin hero."

"No, we'd guard in turns," corrected Lydia. "Kent, what's the use of starting on until the moon comes up?"

"None at all," returned the boy. "It's due about nine, isn't it! I hope the folks won't worry about us. In the meantime, you and I can have a good old talk, like the old days. Remember?"

It was entirely dark now in the woods. Fireflies darted about. Crickets shrilled and an occasional owl hooted. Lydia moved still closer to Kent, until his shoulder touched hers.

"I remember! Kent, are you afraid?"

"I should say not! I like the woods at night. Don't the fern and the needles smell fine? Lyd, what're you going to do after you finish High School?"

"Go on to the University. Aren't you?"

"Dad wants me to, but I guess I'll go to work. Why waste four years learning a lot of stuff that'll never earn me a cent?"

"But you could take engineering, or law."

"All lawyers are crooks and I've no head for figures. I'm going into the real estate business. There's real money in that, particularly if Levine gets his bill through. What do you want to go to the University for?"

"Kent, I promised Mother I'd go. And I want to anyhow. We're so poor, that I'll never be anything but a scrub woman if I don't get educated. And all our folks back East were college people, even if they were farmers — all but Dad. He thought he was too smart to go to college."

Kent stirred uncomfortably. "I don't think I'm too smart, but I want to make money, quick."

"I don't see what the hurry is. Is it Olga?"

"Of course it isn't Olga! She's all right to flirt with and a peachy looker, but you don't suppose a fellow wants to marry every girl he gets crazy about!"

"I didn't know," said Lydia, meekly. "Nobody was ever crazy about me."

"You aren't that kind, thank heaven. If I ever catch you running round flirting, I'll slap your face."

There was nothing humorous in Kent's tone, nevertheless Lydia giggled. "Lots you'd know about it when you don't see me for months at a time."

"I'd know, never fear. You're growing up the way a girl ought to. I know all about it."

Lydia sat, staring into the darkness, thinking this over. She was getting an amount of comfort out of the conversation that made her realize how sore a spot there had been within her.

"But why do you flirt?" she asked finally.

"Aw, boys are that way. You don't understand. A fellow can't help flirting with girls like Margery and Olga — or any other old girl, as far as that goes."

"Kent," asked Lydia, suddenly, "what's a hussy?"

"Huh!" exclaimed Kent. "What makes you ask that?"

"What you said about flirting. Election night there were lots of women, flashily dressed, around, and father said they were hussies. And I saw Gustus flirting with one of them, and some of the Senior boys, too. And I saw some of the best dressed of the Indians with them."

"You'd better ask your father," said Kent.

"I did and he said I'd know when I got older."

There was silence again. The wind sighed through the pines, the crickets chirped, the all-hallowing scent of the pine enveloped them as if blown from some heavenly incense burner. Kent was only seventeen. He sat staring with puzzled eyes into the darkness. He tried to picture Olga putting a question like this to him, and failed. A sudden realization of the loneliness of Lydia's unmothered girlhood, of her innocent faith

in him, touched the best that was in him. His voice was a little husky
but he answered coolly.

"A hussy, Lyd, is a flirt who's gone to the bad. Those around Lake
City chase after the students and the Indians who've got Government
allowances, and get their money away from them."

"Oh," said Lydia. "Oh!" Then thoughtfully, "Aren't men silly!"

"Yes, they are," agreed Kent. "And, Lyd, whenever you want to know
about such things, you ask me. It's a man's place to tell a girl the things
she ought to know."

"All right," replied Lydia, "and of course, you're just like a brother
to me."

"Oh, I don't feel so brotherly as — Gee, there's a fire, Lydia!"

Faintly through the trees gleamed a distant blaze. The two jumped
to their feet and, weariness forgotten, started hastily toward it.

"It's the camp crowd, I guess," said Lydia.

"No, it isn't, it's a bunch of men," corrected Kent. "Hold on a minute,
Lydia. Let's see what we're getting into."

He pulled her into the shelter of a giant pine trunk and the two
peered at the group around the fire.

"Some kind of an Indian powwow, half breeds, mostly," whispered
Kent.

Lydia shivered. "Don't they look fierce in the firelight," she murmured. "Let's get out of here, Kent."

"Shucks! Be a sport, Lyd! We'll watch them a minute, then I'll brace
up and speak to 'em."

There were six half breeds in "store" clothes and moccasins squatting
around the blaze. None of them was speaking.

"They act as if they were waiting for someone," whispered Lydia, with
some of the old thrill of pirate plays returning to her. "Kent, they've all
got guns!"

"Hush! There comes someone else. For the love of cats!"

John Levine emerged from the darkness of the forest into the fire
glow.

"How!" he grunted, slipping into an empty space, opposite the two
eavesdroppers.

"How," returned the Indians.

Silence in the woods, except for the crackling fire.

"Kent, let's go! I don't want to listen, I don't want to know." The
cold sweat was standing on Lydia's forehead.

Kent seized her arm. "You've got to stay. It's your business to know,"
he whispered sharply.

"Where's Eagle's Feather?" asked Levine.

"Sick," replied an Indian.

John nodded. "I got back from Washington today. Big fight there. Marshall and his crowd, they'll make a big fight. I may have to compromise. I may make my bill read, only mixed bloods can sell their lands, not full bloods."

"Good!" said an Indian. "Full blood don't want to sell, anyhow."

"Better for you mixed bloods," agreed Levine, "because you'll get higher prices for your land, but worse for us whites, for there'll be less land, unless — you mixed bloods should happen to swear the full bloods are mixed too."

No one spoke for a minute, then a fat, yellow-faced half-breed laughed. "I'll swear old Chief Dawn had a white great-grandmother. I'll get even with him, for throwing me out of the council."

"Exactly," said Levine. "It'll be a good way for all of you to pay up old debts. Any of Marshall's men been up here lately?"

After a pause, one of the younger Indians said, "Some young fellows been going through the woods measuring out a road and they acted like they was just out for a vacation when anyone was around. A year ago I see one of the fellows riding out with Marshall."

Levine grunted. Lydia's heart was pounding so hard that it really pained her. She stared at John unbelievably. Yet it was the same familiar, sallow face, with the gaunt look about the cheeks. Only the eyes were strange. Lydia had never seen them so hard, so searching before. Kent was breathing deep and he did not loose his hold on her arm.

"Well," said Levine, "is that all you folks have got to report, after six months? What do you think I'm paying you for?"

An old mixed blood, almost as dark as a full blood, removed his pipe from his mouth. "All the shoes we buy this year made out of paper, cost four dollars, melt when they get wet. Woman at Last Chance tell me Injun Agent tell her he gets those shoes from Marshall."

"The hog!" grunted Levine. "Anything more?"

What more might have come Lydia did not know for an old squaw came tottering into the fire glow. She was grey headed and emaciated.

"Oh, that's our old squaw, Kent, remember?" whispered Lydia.

"Shut up!" murmured Kent.

The squaw made her way up to John. There was something sinister in the look of her and he rose.

"What you do now, white man," she snarled. "Steal! Steal more, eh?"

Levine looked down on her and his voice was pitying. "Why, you poor old devil, you look half starved." He dug into his pocket and brought out a silver dollar. "Go get some grub," he said.

The old woman stared from the dollar to Levine's face and her voice rose to a shriek.

"Steal! Steal! Make our young men drunk! Make our young girls have babies that grow like these snakes," she pointed a trembling, scrawny finger at the scowling mixed bloods. "White man — dirty fool — dirty thief," and she spat at Levine, at the same time striking the dollar from his hand. It rolled out onto the needles and lay shining in the firelight.

John stiffened and the mixed bloods watched him curiously. But the squaw suddenly burst into the feeble yet deep drawn sobs of the old, and tottering over to the silver she picked it up. "Hungry!" she sobbed. "All the time much hungry." And she started slowly away from the fire in the direction of Kent and Lydia's hiding place.

"Quick!" whispered Kent, and noiselessly the two ran back into the darkness of the woods, through which, however, a silver light was beginning to filter. "There's the moon," he said in a low voice. "Now I can find the lake."

He took Lydia's hand and they hastened in silence toward the rising moon. In less than half a mile they found the lake and far around its curving shore, the gleam of their own campfire.

"Holy Mike! What do you think of that!" demanded Kent as they headed for the fire. "Isn't Levine a wonder!"

"Oh, Kent!" gasped Lydia. "What shall we do!"

"Do!" cried Kent. "Why keep our mouths shut and see what happens. Lord, what an adventure! Lyd, I wouldn't have missed this day for a hundred dollars!"

Lydia scarcely heard him. "John Levine!" she murmured. "My best friend! Oh, I can't believe it."

"Shucks! Why, that's life! Gee, what rich pickings! Me for the real estate business!"

"Kent, it's stealing, just as my squaw said. And it's just the meanest, dirtiest kind of stealing!"

"It's nothing of the kind. The whites have got to have that land and if a lot of sentimental grannies won't let us get it openly, we've got to get it quietly."

They were nearing the camp now and Kent stopped and in the moonlight took Lydia by the shoulders. "Look here, Lyd, don't you tell a soul about what we saw. Promise me!"

"I'll do nothing of the kind," snapped Lydia.

The two stood staring at each other. The lad, tall and broad, his dark face tense; the girl, slender, her fair hair shimmering, her eyes clear in the moonlight.

"Promise!" repeated Kent.

"I will not!" returned Lydia.

Kent's hold on her shoulders tightened. He wanted to box her ears and yet, as he gazed at the wistful, sensitive lips, he felt a sudden desire to kiss her.

"Well, promise me, you'll say nothing while we're in camp, anyhow."

Lydia hesitated. After all, she thought, to whom could she tell the story and what could anyone do! "All right, I'll promise that," she agreed, slowly.

Kent took his hands from her shoulders. "Come on then, old lady. Gee, this beats hanging poor old Florence Dombey under the willows. Give me your hand and I'll tow you along."

It was scarcely nine o'clock, after all, when they trudged into the camp. Charlie and Gustus came in a moment later, having heard Miss Towne's call.

"Oh, Lydia! Lydia! I've worried myself sick." And the cruel Miss Towne, the grouchy Miss Towne, threw her arms about Lydia, with a little murmur that was curiously like a sob.

"We were just going to the settlement for help," said Charlie, "though we were pretty sure nothing serious could have happened."

"Of course nothing serious!" protested Kent. "We were too smart to follow the roads and got lost going and coming. We waited for the moon to come up and we haven't had anything to eat but chewing gum."

"We saved your supper," said Margery. "Come on, Gustus, we'll heat it for 'em."

"Margery'd be a real human being, if she'd stay away from her mother," observed Kent. "For the love of Mike, let me sit down!"

"Here, get in the hammock and let me fix the cushions for you!" cried Olga, who had been eying Lydia closely.

"Thanks, I prefer the dining room bench, right now," returned Kent. "Come on, Lyd. Food!"

Lydia was tired the next day and elected to stay in camp with Miss Towne while the others, including even Margery and Gustus, went on an all day strawberry hunt.

Lydia lay in a hammock with a book all the morning, but the greater part of the time, Miss Towne observed, her eyes were fastened broodingly on the lake and not on the printed page. The two went bathing alone, at noon, and afterward lay on the grassy shore, drying their hair.

"Lydia, wasn't Kent nice to you, yesterday?" asked the chaperone, abruptly.

Lydia turned a startled, sunburned face toward the questioner. "Nice! Why, of course! Kent's like my brother."

"No man but a brother can be like a brother, my dear. Always remember that. What happened yesterday to worry you?"

"Nothing that had anything to do with Kent. Gosh! I should say not!"

"Lydia!" cried Miss Towne. "Please don't use such dreadful language! If you knew how coarse it sounds! Oh, my dear, I'm not trying to hurt your feelings," as she watched the scarlet face and quivering lips. "It's just that you are so fine, I can't bear to have you do anything that isn't fine. I've been planning to talk to you for a long time about your slang. Leave that sort of thing to Olga and the rest. Use only the purest Anglo-Saxon. Be a credit to your fine Puritan stock in speech. You already are, in character."

Lydia said nothing. She sat struggling to keep back the tears when a horse's hoof beats sounded under the trees and Levine rode into the camp.

Lydia had been wondering how, when she saw him in town, she was going to meet him, what she was going to say to him. But now, her only thought was that here was the devoted friend who had understood her since babyhood.

As he dismounted, she jumped to her feet. "Oh, my dear Mr. Levine! My dear! My dear!" she cried and hair flying, she ran to him and threw her arms about his neck, burying her face against his rough corduroy coat.

John threw a long arm about her, and held her to him closely, while with his free hand he smoothed back the glory of her hair. And Miss Towne, watching, saw his long saturnine face transformed.

"Why, Lydia, my little sweetheart! I didn't realize you'd missed me so." He held her silently for a moment, then, catching Miss Towne's gaze, he smiled.

"Lydia has few loves, but they're strong," he said. "I'm her foster father. My name's John Levine."

Lydia disengaged herself. "And this is Miss Towne," she said, "my dearest teacher."

"I've heard your praises sung for a long time," said Levine.

"And I've heard Lydia sing yours," returned Miss Towne.

"And no one else, I'll bet," laughed John.

"Sit down," said the chaperone, with what dignity she could muster with her hair down her back, "while Lydia and I finish dressing."

"You'll have lunch with us?" called Lydia as she retreated toward the tent.

"Yes, but I can't stay longer. Must be back in Lake City for supper," replied Levine, tying up his horse.

The luncheon was a success. Lydia was delighted to put her hand to cooking again, and while Miss Towne set the table, John chatted with both of them of his Washington experiences. He rode away immediately after he had finished eating. Miss Towne wiped the dishes thoughtfully.

"It's hard to realize that he's the scandalous John Levine," she said. "He's simply charming!"

Lydia flared, flushed and subsided. Never again, she realized, could she contradict aspersions cast on Levine's character. And yet, how like a bad dream the episode of last night seemed. If only it had been a dream!

"You're not resentful still about my criticism of your slang using, are you, Lydia?" asked Miss Towne, anxiously.

"No," muttered Lydia, "I deserved it."

Miss Towne's face cleared. "Well, then, tell me all about your friend. He interests me."

Nothing could have soothed Lydia more in her half guilty feeling of having spied unfairly on John than to spend the rest of the afternoon in a history of his relationship to her family.

Side by side in the hammock the two lay during the rest of the sunny summer afternoon, gazing up into the pines and talking of the curious personality that was making history for Lake City. In after years, whenever she thought of Levine, Miss Towne's memory brought her two pictures — one of the tall, sardonic faced man clasping the golden haired girl in his arms. The other was of pine boughs, murmuring sadly and persistently above the gentle flow of Lydia's young voice.

That night the young people sat alone around the campfire. The chaperone complained of a headache and went to bed soon after supper. When she had disappeared, and the tent flap had dropped behind her, Gustus chanted softly,

"School's closed!
 Teacher's dead!
  Hooray!"

and deliberately put his arm about Margery and kissed her. Margery gave a little shriek but blushed and looked pleased and Gustus settled down with his head in her lap. Margery sat looking into the fire, and smoothing Gustus' hair.

Olga, who was sitting with Charlie on the opposite side of the blaze, her back against a log, arranged her skirts. "Come on, Charlie," she said, with a glance at Kent. And Charlie ensconced himself comfortably with his head on Olga's knee.

Lydia, who was sitting with Kent, eyed this grouping with interest, and mingled with a little sense of shock and disapproval was just the least little feeling of regret that the boys didn't feel "crazy" about her. She was sitting bolt upright, with her cheeks flaming a little when she felt Kent's arm stealing round her. She did not resist when he pulled her softly against him. She was utterly surprised at the pleasurable sensation she experienced at having Kent's arm about her. The others were singing but for once Lydia's throaty contralto did not join in.

So this was spooning! Of course, she wouldn't let anybody but Kent do this. And what did it amount to, anyhow! If this was all there was to spooning, why did people think it was wrong?

Under cover of the singing, Kent giving her a little squeeze said, "Didn't think you were such a flirt, Lydia! Let me put my head in your lap, will you?"

"All right," said Lydia nonchalantly. And presently she was smoothing Kent's hair, and he was holding her unoccupied hand. It was the same crisp black hair Lydia had pulled in many a childish quarrel and Kent had held her hands many a time to keep her from slapping his face. And yet there was a thrill about this!

Kent evidently called this flirting. Flirting! Lydia began going back over the conversation with Kent that the eavesdropping episode had crowded from her thoughts. Kent didn't respect girls that flirted and he told her he'd slap her if she flirted and yet, here he was! Lydia went on smoothing the crisp hair, with the thin hand that had the calluses of hard work across the palm.

The others were singing one of Lydia's favorite airs and she joined in.

"The thirst that from the soul doth rise
  Doth ask a drink divine."

She sang the words unthinkingly — and stopped. John Levine was helping her in her search for God, and robbing and betraying the Indians as he did so! And here was Kent, warning her against doing that which he was persuading her to do. What was the matter with men! Was there no trusting them? And yet, she liked to "spoon" with Kent!

"Oh," she thought, "I wish I knew more about men. I wish I could ask Mother."

And memory, like a gentle alarm clock rang its warning. "Lydia," her father had said, "don't do anything you'd be ashamed to have your mother know."

Lydia yawned and gave Kent's hair a little tweak. "Get up, Kent, my foot's asleep," she said.

Kent sat up. The others sang on and Lydia said, "I thought you didn't want me to flirt."

"I don't, but with me it's different!" replied Kent.

Lydia jumped to her feet. "You make me sick, Kent Moulton!" she snapped. "All men make me sick. I'm going to bed." And she stalked off in her hunting boots, without a good night to anyone.

Kent looked after her with an expression half sheepish, half admiring.

"What's the matter with Lyd?" asked Olga.

"Doesn't care about the spooning bee," replied Kent.

"Proper is Lydia's middle name," commented Gustus.

"Lydia is absolutely O. K.," said Charlie.

"Bet your life," agreed Kent. "Get your big head over, Gustus, and give me a piece of Margery's knee."

"Darn it," said Charlie, "Lydia's left the tent flap up. We might as well go to bed."

Which, after another song or two, they did.

Chapter XI

LYDIA GIGGLES

"Nature is neither cruel nor sad. She is only purposeful, tending to an end we cannot see."

— *The Murmuring Pine*

*T*he days flew lightly by, lightly for Lydia, too, in spite of the heavy secret she carried of Levine's plotting. Lightly, in spite of the fact that Lydia was undergoing some soul-changing experiences in this short holiday, experiences that were to direct her life's course.

The day before they broke camp, Lydia's old squaw appeared and asked for Charlie Jackson.

Charlie and Kent were cooking dinner.

"Dear me," said Miss Towne, "tell him to take the poor thing away, Lydia."

"He must feed her, first," exclaimed Lydia, leading the old Indian over to the cooking shelter.

Kent and Lydia exchanged glances as Charlie led the squaw — Susie, he called her — into the woods, after Lydia had heaped her old arms with food. Kent and Gustus had put the dinner on the table and they all were seated at the meal when Charlie returned.

"What did she want, Charlie?" asked Olga.

"You wouldn't care if I told you," replied Charlie, grimly. "But," he burst forth suddenly, "some day you whites will pay. Some day the Japs or the Jews will do to you Americans what you've done to us."

"Who cares!" cried Olga, pertly. "Have a pickle, Charlie, and cheer up." She pushed the pickle dish toward him.

"Or some catsup," suggested Gustus, depositing the bottle by Charlie's plate.

"Or a sardine," added Margery.

Charlie's lips twitched and he smiled and Miss Towne sighed in a relieved way. The meal progressed without a further crisis.

After the dishes were done, Kent followed Lydia, who was strolling off for a last walk in the woods.

"Do you suppose she told Charlie about Levine?" he asked, as he overtook her.

"Look out, Charlie's coming," said Lydia and in a moment the Indian had joined them.

"Look here, Lydia," he began, "Levine is up to some new cussedness. Old Susie came on him in council the other night with six of the worst half breeds in the reservation. She lost her head and began to jaw him so she didn't find out what it was about. And he's getting the last of my timber now. Lydia, you've *got* to help me. When you get home, talk to Levine."

"Getting the last of your timber!" exclaimed Kent.

"Yes, the law lets 'em get the 'dead and down' stuff and who's going to swear it's fresh stuff that he cut this summer and will get out next winter?"

"Do you mean he's up cutting your pines now?" cried Lydia, aghast.

"No! No!" impatiently. "His half breeds do that."

"But how does he come to be taking your wood? Why don't you go to see him yourself?" asked Kent.

"I can't answer either of those questions," replied Charlie, sullenly.

The two young whites thought of the attack on Levine, and looked at each other apprehensively.

"Won't the Indian Agent stop him?" asked Lydia.

"He! Why, he's deep in the mire himself with Dave Marshall. My God, Margery Marshall went to New York on a blind Indian boy's pines! Lydia, save my pines for me! They belong to my tribe. My father kept them and so did his father for his people. As long as they had those miles of pines, they had a place for the tribe to live. Father was going to Washington three years ago to tell the president about the graft when they shot him from ambush. If I put up a fight, they'll shoot me. My father wanted me to learn white ways so I could protect the tribe. And the more I learn of white ways the more I realize I'm helpless. Lydia, won't you help us?"

Neither Kent nor Lydia ever had seen Charlie thus before. He was neither arrogant nor sullen. He was pleading with a tragic hopelessness that moved his two hearers profoundly.

"Oh, Charlie! I *will* try," cried Lydia. "I truly will."

"I knew you would," said Charlie, huskily, and he turned back abruptly to the camp.

"Gee!" exclaimed Kent. "Chapter number two!"

Lydia stamped her foot. "How can you speak so, Kent! It's a frightful thing!"

"Sure it's frightful, but it can't be helped. The whites have got to have this land. Might's right."

"What makes the whites so crazy for it?" asked Lydia.

"Money," returned Kent.

Lydia stared about her. Supposing, she thought, that she owned a hundred acres of this pine land. She forgot Kent and concentrated every force of her mind on sensing what land ownership would mean. And suddenly there woke in her, her racial hunger for land. Suddenly there stirred within her a desire for acreage, for trees, soil, stream and shrub, a wide demesne that should be hers and her children's forever. She was still too young to trace the hunger back to its primal source, the desire for permanency, the yearning to possess that which is the first and the last of existence, which neither moth nor dust can corrupt nor thieves break through and steal. But somewhere back in her still childish mind a lust for a wide domain of pine land bestirred itself to begin battle with the sense of right and justice that her heart of hearts told her Levine was outraging.

"Are you really going to talk to Levine?" Kent roused her from her reverie.

"Yes! Didn't I promise to?"

"Lots of good it'll do," grunted Kent. "And if you tell him we overheard him in the woods, I'll be sore."

"I don't see why."

"Because, after I finish High School, I'm going to tell him I know, to make him let me in on the deal. Look here, Lyd, don't tell him I was with you, anyhow."

"Oh, all right," replied Lydia, crossly. "For goodness' sake, don't let's talk about it anymore. I don't see why men always have to be plotting! I'm going back to camp and help pack."

The driver arrived with the carryall at nine o'clock the next morning, and at mid-afternoon, Lydia was dropped at the gate, where Adam took possession of her. It was earlier than she had been expected, and Lizzie had not returned from her Saturday marketing. Lydia lugged her suitcase up the path, glad to be at home, yet murmuring to herself a little disconsolately.

"Nothing to look forward to now, but school in the fall."

The house seemed small and dingy to her, after the open splendor of the pine woods. Old Lizzie had "let things go" and the rooms were dusty and disorderly. Lydia dropped her suitcase in the kitchen.

"I've just got to train old Lizzie," she said, "so that she won't leave her old carpet slippers and her apron in the middle of the kitchen every time she goes out. And Dad just must quit leaving his pipe on the dining room table. I do wish we had Mission furniture instead of this everlasting old mahogany. I just guess there's got to be some reforming in this house, this summer. If I've got to leave off slang, Dad and Lizzie can leave off a few of their bad habits."

She carried the suitcase on into her bedroom and Lizzie, coming in, hot and bundle-laden an hour later, found the living room in immaculate order and Lydia, in an old dress, blacking the kitchen stove.

"For the land's sake, child," said Lizzie as Lydia kissed her and took her bundles from her, "how tanned you are! And you shouldn't have begun work the minute you got home."

"I had to. I couldn't stand the dirt," answered Lydia, briskly. "Is Daddy all right? You'll find your slippers where they belong, Lizzie."

The old lady, in her rusty black alpaca which she always wore to town, gave Lydia a look that was at once reproachful and timid. Lydia had shown signs lately of having reached the "bringing up the family" stage of her development and Lizzie dreaded its progress.

Amos came in the gate shortly after six. Lydia was waiting for him at the front door. He looked suddenly shabby and old to Lydia and she kissed him very tenderly. It required all the supper hour and all the remainder of the evening to tell the story of the camp and to answer Lizzie's and Amos' questions. There were several episodes Lydia did not describe; that of the half breed council in the wood, for example, nor the "spooning" with Kent.

It was ten o'clock when Amos rose with a sigh. "Well, you had a good time, little girl, and I'm glad. But I swan, I don't want you ever to go off again without me and Liz and Adam. Adam howled himself to sleep every night and I'd 'a' liked to. I'm going out to see if the chickens are all right."

"I got everything that belongs to you mended up, Lydia," said Lizzie, following into the kitchen bedroom.

Lydia looked from the gnarled old hands to the neat rolls of stockings on the bureau. She had been wishing that Lizzie was a neat maid with a white apron! A sense of shame overwhelmed her and she threw her arms about her kind old friend.

"Lizzie, you're a lot too good to me," she whispered.

Lydia was sitting on the front steps, the next afternoon, with a book in her lap and Adam at her feet, when Billy Norton called. He stopped for a chat in the garden with her father, before coming up to greet Lydia.

"He is awful homely. A regular old farmer," she thought, comparing him with the elegant Gustus and with Kent's careless grace.

Billy was in his shirtsleeves. His blond hair was cropped unbecomingly close. Lydia did not see that the head this disclosed was more finely shaped than either of her friends. He was grinning as he came toward Lydia, showing his white teeth.

"Hello, Lyd! Awful glad you're back!"

He sat down on the step below her and Lydia wrinkled her nose. He carried with him the odor of hay and horses.

"How's your mother?" asked Lydia. "I'm coming over, tomorrow."

"Mother's not so very well. She works too hard at the blamed canning. I told her I'd rather never eat it than have her get so done up."

"I'll be over to help her," said Lydia. "We had a perfectly heavenly time in camp, Billy."

"Did you?" asked her caller, indifferently. "Hay is fine this year. Never knew such a stand of clover."

"Miss Towne was grand to us. And Kent and Charlie are the best cooks, ever."

"Great accomplishment for men," muttered Billy. "Are you going to try to sell fudge, this winter, Lyd?"

"I don't know," Lydia's tone was mournful, "Daddy hates to have me. Now I'm growing up he seems to be getting sensitive about my earning money."

"He's right too," said Billy, with a note in his voice that irritated Lydia.

"Much you know about it! You just try to make your clothes and buy your schoolbooks on nothing. Dad's just afraid people'll know how little he earns, that's all. Men are selfish pigs."

Astonished by this outburst, Billy turned round to look up at Lydia. She was wearing her Sunday dress of the year before, a cheap cotton that she had outgrown. The young man at her feet did not see this. All he observed were the dusty gold of her curly head, the clear blue of her eyes and the fine set of her head on her thin little shoulders.

"You always look just right to me, Lyd," he said. "Listen, Lydia. I'm not going to be a farmer, I'm —"

"Not be a farmer!" cried Lydia. "After all you've said about it!"

"No! I'm going in for two years' law, then I'm going into politics. I tell you, Lydia, what this country needs today more than anything is young, clean politicians."

"You mean you're going to do like Mr. Levine?"

"God forbid!" exclaimed the young man. "I'm going to fight men like Levine. And by heck," he paused and looked at Lydia dreamily, "I'll be governor and maybe more, yet."

"But what's changed you?" persisted Lydia.

"The fight about the reservation, mostly. There's something wrong, you know, in a system of government that allows conditions like that. It's against American principles."

His tone was oratorical, and Lydia was impressed. She forgot that Billy smelled of the barnyard.

"Well," she said, "we'd all be proud of you if you were president, I can tell you."

"Would you be!" Billy's voice was pleased. "Then, Lydia, will you wait for me?"

"Wait for you?"

"Yes, till I make a name to bring to you."

Lydia flushed angrily. "Look here, Billy Norton, you don't have to be silly, after all the years we've known each other. I'm only fifteen, just remember that, and I don't propose to wait for any man. I'd as soon think of waiting for — for Adam, as for you, anyhow."

Billy rose with dignity, and without a word strode down the path to the gate and thence up the road. Lydia stared after him indignantly. "That old *farmer!*" she said to Adam, who wriggled and slobbered, sympathetically.

She was still indignant when John Levine arrived and found her toasting herself and the waffles for supper, indiscriminately. Perhaps it was this sense of indignation that made her less patient than usual with what she was growing to consider the foibles of the male sex. At any rate, she precipitated her carefully planned conversation with Levine, when the four of them were seated on the back steps, after supper, fighting mosquitoes, and watching the exquisite orange of the afterglow change to lavender.

The others were listening to Lydia's account of her investigating tour with Charlie.

"I shouldn't say it was the best idea in the world for you to be wandering through the woods with that young Indian," was Levine's comment when Lydia had finished.

"I don't see how you can speak so," cried Lydia, passionately, "when this minute you're taking his pine wood."

"Lydia!" said Amos, sharply.

"Let her alone, Amos," Levine spoke quietly. "What are you talking about, Lydia?"

For a moment, Lydia sat looking at her friend, uncertain how much or how little to say. She had idealized him so long, had clung so long to her faith in his perfection, that a deep feeling of indignation toward him for not living up to her belief in him drove her to saying what she never had dreamed she could have said to John Levine.

"The Indians are people, just like us," she cried, "and you're treating them as if they were beasts. You're robbing them and letting them starve! Oh, I saw them! Charlie showed the poor things to me — all sore eyes, and coughing and eating dirt. And you're making money out of them! Maybe the very money you paid our note with was made out of a starved squaw. Oh, I can't stand it to think it of you!"

Lydia paused with a half sob and for a moment only the gentle ripple of the waves on the shore and the crickets were to be heard Levine, elbow on knee, chin in hand, looked through the dusk at the shadowy sweetness of Lydia's face, his own face calm and thoughtful.

"You're so good and kind to me," Lydia began again, "how can you be so hard on the Indians? Are you stealing Charlie's logs? *Are* you, Mr. Levine?"

"I bought his pine," replied Levine, quietly.

"He doesn't believe it. He thinks you're stealing. And he's so afraid of you. He says if he makes a fuss, you'll shoot him. Why does he feel that way, Mr. Levine?"

Lydia's thin hands were shaking, but she stood before the Congressman like a small accusing conscience, unafraid, not easily to be stilled.

"Lydia! What're you saying!" exclaimed Amos.

"Keep out, Amos," said Levine. "We've got to clear this up. I've been expecting it, for some time. Lydia, years ago before the Government began to support the Indians, they were a fine, upstanding race. The whites could have learned a lot from them. They were brave, and honorable, and moral, and in a primitive way, thrifty. Well, then the sentimentalists among the whites devised the reservation system and the allowance system. And the Indians have gone to the devil, just as whites would under like circumstances. Any human being has to earn what he eats or he degenerates. You can put that down as generally true, can't you, Amos?"

"You certainly can," agreed Amos.

"Now, the only way to save those Indians up there is to kick them out. The strong ones will live and be assimilated into our civilization. The weak ones will die, just like weak whites do."

"But how about Charlie's pines?" insisted Lydia.

Something like a note of amusement at the young girl's persistence was in John's voice, but he answered gravely enough.

"Yes, I've bought his pines and I'll get them out, next winter. There's no denying we want the Indians' land. But there's no denying that throwing the Indian off the reservation is the best thing for the Indian."

"But what makes Charlie think you're stealing them? And he says that when the pines go, the tribe will die."

"I paid for the pine," insisted Levine. "An Indian has no idea of buying and selling. It's a cruel incident, this breaking up of the reservation, but it's like cutting off a leg to save the patient's life. Sentiment is wasted."

"That's the great trouble with America, these days," said Amos, his pipe bowl glowing in the summer darkness. "All these foreigners coming in here filled the country with gush. What's become of the New Englanders in this town? Well, they founded the University, named the streets, planted the elms and built the Capitol. Since then they've been snowed under by the Germans and the Norwegians, a lot of beer drinkers and fish eaters. Nobody calls a spade a spade, these days. They rant and spout socialism. The old blood's gone. The old, stern, puritanical crowd can't be found in America today."

Lydia was giving little heed to her father. Amos was given to fireside oratory. She was turning over in her mind the scene in the woods between John and the half breeds. That then was a part of the process of removing the patient's leg! The end justified the means.

She heaved a great sigh of relief. "Well, then, I don't have to worry about that anymore," she said. "Only, I don't dare to think about those starving old squaws, or the baby that froze to death."

"That's right," agreed Levine, comfortably. "Don't think about them."

Old Lizzie snored gently, gave a sudden sigh and a jerk. "Land! I must have dozed off for a minute."

Lydia laughed. "It was nip and tuck between you and Adam, Lizzie. Let's get in away from the mosquitoes — I'm so glad I had this talk with you, Mr. Levine."

"Lydia should have been a boy," said Amos; "she likes politics."

"I'd rather be a girl than anything in the world," protested Lydia, and the two men laughed. If there was still a doubt in the back of Lydia's mind regarding the reservation, for a time, at least, she succeeded in quieting it. She dreaded meeting Charlie and was relieved to hear that Dr. Fulton had taken him East with him for a couple of weeks to attend a health convention.

One of the not unimportant results of the camping trip was that Lydia rediscovered the pine by the gate. It was the same pine against which she had beaten her little fists, the night of Patience's death. She had often climbed into its lower branches, getting well gummed with fragrant pitch in the process. But after her return from the reservation, the tall tree had a new significance to her.

She liked to sit on the steps and stare at it, dreaming and wondering. Who had left it, when all the rest of the pines about it had been cleared off? How did it feel, left alone among the alien oaks and with white people living their curious lives about it? Did it mourn, in its endless murmuring, for the Indians — the Indians of other days and not the poor decadents who shambled up and down the road? For the Indians and the pines were now unalterably associated in Lydia's mind. The life of one depended on that of the other. Strange thoughts and perhaps not altogether cheerful and wholesome thoughts for a girl of Lydia's age.

So it was probably well that Margery about this time began to show Lydia a certain Margery-esque type of attention. In her heart, in spite of her mother's teachings, Margery had always shared her father's admiration for Lydia. In her childhood it had been a grudging, jealous admiration that seemed like actual dislike. But as Margery developed as a social favorite and Lydia remained about the same quiet little dowd, the jealousy of the banker's daughter gave way to liking.

Therefore several times a week, Margery appeared on her bicycle, her embroidery bag dangling from the handle bars. The two girls would then establish themselves on cushions by the water, and sew and chatter. Lizzie, from the kitchen or from the bedroom where she was resting, could catch the unceasing sound of voices, broken at regular intervals by giggles.

"Lydia's reached the giggling age," she would say to herself. "Well, thank the Lord she's got someone to giggle with, even if Margery is a silly coot. There they go again! What are they laughing at?"

Hysterical shrieks from the lawn, with the two girls rolling helplessly about on the cushions! Overhearing the conversation would not have enlightened old Lizzie, for the girls' talk was mostly reminiscent of the camp experiences or of their recollections of Kent's little boyhood, of Charlie's prowess at school, or of Gustus' "sportiness" and his fascinating deviltry. Lydia was enjoying the inalienable right of every girl of fifteen to giggle, and talk about the boys, the two seemingly having no causative relation, yet always existing together.

Lizzie had not realized how quiet and mature Lydia had been since little Patience's death until now. She would mix some lemonade and invite the girls into the house to drink it, just for the mere pleasure of joining in the laughter. She never got the remotest inkling of why the two would double up with joy when one or the other got the hiccoughs in the midst of a sentence. But she would lean against the sideboard and laugh with them, the tears running down her old cheeks.

It was no uncommon occurrence during this summer for Amos to come on the two, giggling helplessly on a log by the roadside. Lydia would have been walking a little way with Margery to come back with her father, when their mirth overcame them. Amos had no patience with this new phase of Lydia's development.

"For heaven's sake," he said to John Levine, one Sunday afternoon, when hysterical shrieks drifted up from the pier, "do you suppose I'd better speak to Doc Fulton or shut her up on bread and water?"

"Pshaw, let her alone. It's the giggles! She's just being normal," said John, laughing softly in sympathy as the shrieks grew weak and maudlin.

The two did have lucid intervals during the summer, however. During one of these, Lydia said, "I wish we had hard wood floors like yours."

"What kind are yours?" inquired Margery.

"Just pine, and kind of mean, splintery pine, too."

"Upstairs at Olga's all the floors were that way," said Margery, "and they had a man come and sandpaper 'em and put kind of putty stuff in the cracks and oil and wax 'em and they look fine."

"Gee!" said Lydia, thoughtfully. "That is, I don't mean 'Gee,' I mean whatever polite word Miss Towne would use for 'Gee.'"

The girls giggled, then Lydia said, "I'll do it! And I'll cut our old living room carpet up into two or three rugs. Lizzie'll have to squeeze enough out of the grocery money for fringe. I'd rather have fringe than a fall coat."

Amos, coming home a night or so later found the living room floor bare and Lydia hard at work with a bit of glass and sand paper, scraping at the slivers.

"Ain't it awful?" asked Lizzie from the dining room. "She would do it."

Lydia's knees and back had given out and she was lying on her stomach and one elbow, scraping away without looking up.

"Lizzie's complained all day," she said. "She doesn't realize how our house looks like 'poverty and destruction' compared with other folks. I'm going to get some style into it, if I have to tear it down. Oh, Daddy, don't you get sick of being poor?"

"Yes," said Amos, shortly, "and I think you're a silly girl to wear yourself out on this kind of thing."

Lydia sat up and looked at him. She was growing fast and was thinner than ever, this summer. "If mother was alive," she said, "she'd know exactly how I feel."

Suddenly there came to Amos' memory a weak and tender voice, with contralto notes in it like Lydia's, "Lydia's like me, Amos. You'll never have trouble understanding her, if you'll remember that."

"Lydia," he said, abruptly, "make the house over if you want to, my dear," and he marched out to the kitchen to wash and take off his overalls.

It took Lydia several days to complete her task. When it was done the cracks were still prominent and the oily finish was spotted. But in Lydia's eyes it was a work of art and she cut the old carpet into three parts with enthusiasm. She sewed the fringe on the rugs, on the front porch. Sitting so, she could see Margery when she appeared far down the road, could view the beauty of the Nortons' wide fields, and could hear the quiet sighing of the pine by the gate. On the afternoon on which she finished the last of the rugs, Charlie Jackson and not Margery appeared. Lydia's heart sank a little as he turned in the gate, though in his greeting he seemed his usual genial self.

He admired the rugs and the gleam of the shining floor through the doorway. Then without preamble, he asked, "Did you talk to Levine, Lydia?"

"Yes," she said. "He — he just doesn't see it any way but his, Charlie!"

The young Indian's face fell. "I certainly thought you could influence him, Lydia. Did you really try?"

"Of course I tried," she exclaimed, indignantly. "He insists that the only way to save you Indians is to make you work for a living."

"He's doing it all for our good, huh?" sneered Charlie.

"He doesn't pretend. He says he wants the land. He's paying for it though."

"Paying for it!" cried the Indian. "How's he paying, do you know?"

"No, and I don't want to know! I'm tired of hearing things against Mr. Levine."

"I don't care if you are," said Charlie, grimly. "If you're going to keep on being his friend, you've got to be it with your eyes open. And you might as well decide right now whether you're going to take him or me for your friend. You can't have us both."

"I wouldn't give up Mr. Levine for anyone on earth." Lydia's voice shook with her earnestness. "And I don't see why I have to be dragged into this business. I've nothing to do with it."

"You have too! You're white and it's every white's business to judge in this. You'll be taking some of the profits of the reservation if it's thrown open, yourself."

"I will not!" cried Lydia. "I wouldn't want an inch of that land." Then she caught her breath. Something within her said, "Wouldn't, eh — not the vast acres of cathedral pines, you thought of as yours, at camp?" She flushed and repeated vehemently, "Not an inch!"

Charlie smiled cynically. "Listen, Lydia, I'll tell you how Levine pays for his Indian lands."

Chapter XII

THE HIGH SCHOOL SENIOR

"Where the pine forest is destroyed, pines never come again."
— *The Murmuring Pine*

*L*ydia sighed helplessly and began to stitch again on the fringe, thrusting her needle in and out viciously.

"Years ago," began Charlie, grimly, "my father foresaw what the whites were trying to do. None of the other full bloods believed him. He had nothing to do with half-breeds."

"I don't see why you always speak so of the mixed bloods," interrupted Lydia. "Their white blood ought to improve them."

"It ought, yes, — but it doesn't. And the reason is that only the rottenest kind of a white man'll make a squaw a mother. And only the low harpies in places like Last Chance will let an Indian father a child."

Lydia flushed but compressed her lips and let Charlie speak on. She knew that it was useless to try to stem the tide of protest that was rising to his lips.

"Father was the chief of the tribe and he called council after council until at last they all decided he'd better go to Washington and see if he could get help from the Indian Commissioner. Even then John Levine had a following of half-breeds. He told the yellow curs to kidnap my father and he'd see if he could make him more reasonable. So the half-breeds laid in ambush the day father started for Washington. Father put up an awful fight and they killed him!"

"Oh, Charlie!" cried Lydia, dropping her sewing. "Oh, Charlie!"

"Yes," said the Indian, tensely, "and though Levine wasn't there he was just as much my father's murderer as if he'd fired the shot. Of course, nothing was ever done by the authorities. It was hushed up as an Indian brawl. But my sister, she was twenty then, she found out about Levine and she came in and set fire to his house one night, thinking she'd burn him to death. Instead of that, she just scared his old hired man who was drunk. Levine was away from home. But he's a devil. He found out it was my sister and he told her the only way she could keep from being jailed was to sell him all our pines — for a hundred dollars. So she did, but she shot at him that Thanksgiving night when he'd been at your house."

"Oh, *Charlie!*" whispered Lydia, horror in her blue eyes and her parted lips. She looked at him in utter dismay. No longer was he the debonair favorite of the High School. In his somber eyes, his thin cold lips, his tense shoulders, the young girl saw the savage. She looked from Charlie to the familiar garden, to Adam, scratching fleas, and beyond to the quiet herds in the Norton meadows. Surely Charlie's tale of killings had no place in this orderly life. Then her glance fell upon the pine beside the gate. It murmured softly. Again Lydia saw the cloistered depths of the reservation pines and again there stirred within her that vague lust for ownership. And she knew that Charlie's tale was true.

She moistened her dry lips. "But what can I do, Charlie! I'm only a girl."

"I'll tell you what you can do. You can throw down your murderer friend and side with me. You can get everyone you know to side with me. And, Lydia, never tell Levine, or anyone else, what you know about him. It wouldn't be safe!"

He leaned toward her as he spoke and Lydia shivered. "I won't," she whispered. Then she said aloud in sudden resentment, "But I'm not going to throw Mr. Levine down without his having a chance to explain. Who are you to think you've got a right to ask me?"

Charlie caught her slender wrist in a firm grasp. "I'm a human being fighting for justice — no — fighting for existence. That's who I am."

"Oh, I don't want to know about it!" cried Lydia. "I don't want to think about it! I'm just a girl. I want to be happy just a little while before I grow up. I've had too much unhappiness."

"Yes, you have had," agreed Charlie, grimly, "and that's why you will think about it in spite of yourself. You understand how I feel because you've suffered. When are you going to throw Levine down?"

Lydia's face whitened. "Never!" she said.

"What! When you know he's a murderer?"

"He never intended to kill your father. Anyhow, I can't help what he's done. He's like my own father and brother and mother all in one to me."

The two young people sat looking into each other's eyes. Suddenly Charlie threw Lydia's hand from him, and like Billy Norton, he strode down the path and out of the gate without a word. Lydia was trembling violently but she picked up her sewing and forced herself to finish the rugs and spread them on the living room floor. They looked very well, she thought. Later on, they showed a vicious tendency to turn up, to wrinkle and scuffle easily, threatening the life and limb of the heavy treading Lizzie and of Amos a dozen times a day. But the evening after Charlie's visit she was too distrait to notice the complaints of her elders.

Levine did not appear at the cottage for several days. During that time Lydia tried to put Charlie's story out of her mind. With housework and swimming and giggling with Margery, she managed to do this during the day, but at night she dreamed of it and woke, and spoke to Adam.

When John did come out she avoided talking to him and he caught her several times looking at him with a sad and puzzled expression. When they started on their usual Sunday walk, Amos went back to the house for his cane and Levine said, abruptly, "Out with it, young Lydia!"

"I promised I wouldn't," she said.

"Been hearing more stories about my wickedness?" asked John.

Lydia nodded, miserably.

"My dear," Levine said quietly, "this is a man's game. I'm playing a rough-and-tumble, catch-as-catch-can fight. In it, the weak must fail and maybe die. But out of it a great good will come to this community. As long as the Indians are here to exploit, this community will be demoralized. I'm using every means fair or foul to carry my purpose. Can't you let it go at that?"

Lydia set her teeth. "Yes, I can and I will," she said, as her father came up with his cane.

And though this was more easily said than done and the thought of murdered chiefs and starved babies troubled her occasionally, she did not really worry over it all as much as she might have were she not entering her senior year in the High School.

If life holds any position more important, any business more soul satisfying than that of being a High School senior, few people are so fortunate as to have discerned it. Being a college senior is a highly edifying and imposing business, but the far greater advantages lie with the High School senior. He is four years younger. He has lost no illusions. He has developed no sense of values. He is not conscious of the world outside his vision. But in spite of a smug conviction of superiority, the college senior has heard life knocking at the door of his young illusions. He has moments of wistful uncertainty. No, it is the High School senior who is life's darling.

Lydia was not altogether an easy person to live with this year although both Lizzie and Amos realized that never had she been so altogether sweet and lovable as now. She objected to Lizzie's table manners. She was hurt because Amos would eat in his shirt-sleeves, and would sit in his stocking feet at night, ignoring the slippers she crocheted him. She stored in the attic the several fine engravings in gilt frames that her father and mother had brought with them from New England. In their place she hung passepartouted Gibson pictures clipped from magazines. And she gave up reading tales of travel and adventure, gave up Dickens and Thackeray and Mark Twain and took to E. P. Roe and other writers of a sticky and lovelorn nature.

In spite of the camping trip, Lydia saw little of her campmates. Charlie did not reenter school in the fall. Olga and Gustus were devoted to each other and, to Lydia's surprise, Kent took Margery to several parties.

"I thought you liked Gustus best," she said to Margery one Saturday afternoon late in the fall. Lydia was calling on Margery and the two were making fudge.

"Oh, that was last year! Gustus is too sickly for me. I'm crazy about Kent. He's so big and strong and bossy!"

A little pang shot through Lydia's heart. But she was saved a reply by Elviry, who as usual was within earshot.

"Kent Moulton doesn't amount to anything. His father's got nothing but a salary. Gustus'll have the brewery."

"Well, who wants to marry a brewery," sniffed Margery. "If you think I'm going to have any old bossy, beery German like Gustus'll be, you're mistaken. Kent comes of fine Puritan stock."

"Your ancestors don't pay the bills," said Elviry, sharply. "If your father has that extra money he's expecting at Christmas time, you'll just go East to boarding-school, Margery."

"I don't want to go," protested Margery. "I love High School."

"Makes no difference. You have common tastes, just like your father. I want you should have refined tastes in your friends particularly."

And Dave must have received his extra money, for after the Christmas holidays, Margery tearfully departed for the Eastern finishing school. The night after her departure, Kent made his first call on Lydia in many months. The two withdrew to the kitchen to make candy and there Lydia's surprise and pleasure gave way to suspicion. Kent seemed to want to talk for the most part about Margery!

"Hasn't she grown to be a beauty," he said, beating the fudge briskly.

"She always was beautiful," replied Lydia, who was cracking walnuts. "Didn't we use to hate her though! Well, she was the whiniest little snip!"

"Oh, that was her mother's fault! The only good thing about this boarding-school deal is that it gets her away from Elviry Marshall. Put more nuts in here, Lyd. You like her now, don't you?"

"Yes, I do," replied Lydia, honestly, "though she's an awful silly. She never reads anything, and she flunked all her Thanksgiving examinations."

"Anybody as pretty as Margery doesn't need to be brilliant," said Kent.

"And she spoons, and you don't think much of girls that spoon." Lydia's cheeks were a deeper pink than usual.

"Shucks, don't be catty, Lydia!" growled Kent.

Lydia suddenly chuckled, though tears were very near the surface. "Well, when I'm an old maid here in the cottage, you and Margery can come out and call in your automobile."

"Who's talking about marrying or you being an old maid?" asked Kent, disgustedly. "Gee, you girls make me sick!"

Lydia's jaw dropped. Then she gave a laugh that ended abruptly. "Heavens, how clothes do count in life," she sighed. "Come on in and give Dad and Lizzie some fudge, Kent."

Kent called several times during the winter, but he never asked Lydia to go to a party nor did any of the other boy friends she saw daily in school — boys with whom she chummed over lessons, who told her their secrets, who treated her as a mental equal, yet never asked to call, or slipped boxes of candy into her desk or asked her into a drugstore for a sundae or a hot chocolate.

Nobody resented this state of affairs more than old Lizzie. After Kent's third or fourth call, she said to Lydia, closing the door behind him, "Yes, Kent'll come out here and see you, but I notice he don't take you anywhere. If you had fine party clothes and lived on Lake Shore Avenue, he'd be bowing and scraping fast enough."

Lydia tossed her head. "I don't care about going to parties."

"You do, too," insisted the old lady. "You're eating your heart out. I know. I was young once."

Amos looked up from his paper. "Lydia's too young to go if they did ask her. But why don't they ask?"

"It's because I'm too poor and I live so far out and I don't spoon," answered Lydia. "I don't care, I tell you." And just to prove that she didn't care, Lydia bowed her face in her hands and began to cry.

A look of real pain crossed Amos' face. He got up hastily and went to Lydia's side.

"Why, my little girl, I thought you were perfectly happy this year. And your clothes look nice to me." He smoothed Lydia's bright hair with his work-scarred hand. "I tell you, I'll borrow some money, by heck, and get you some clothes!"

Lydia raised a startled face. "No! No! I'd rather go in rags than borrow money. We're almost out of debt now and we'll stay out. Don't borrow, Daddy," her voice rising hysterically. "Don't borrow!" Adam began to howl.

"All right, dearie, all right!" said Amos.

"I'm an old fool to have said anything," groaned Lizzie. "What does it matter when she's the best scholar in her class and everybody, teachers and boys and girls alike, loves her."

Lydia wiped her eyes and hugged her father, then Adam and then Lizzie.

"I've got John Levine, anyhow," she said.

"You certainly have, hand and foot," said Amos.

The matter was not mentioned again directly. But the little scene rankled with Amos. A week or so later he said at supper, "Lydia, I'm thinking seriously of moving."

"Moving! Where? Why?" exclaimed Lydia.

"Well, I can borrow enough money, I find, to add to the rent we're paying, to rent the old stone house next to Miss Towne's. My idea is to move there just till you finish college! Then we'll go out on a farm. But it'll give you your chance, Lydia."

"Land!" murmured Lizzie.

Lydia hesitated. To move into the house next the Townes would be to arrive, to enter the inner circle, to cease to be a dowd. But — she looked about the familiar rooms.

"Daddy," she said, "would you really want to leave this cottage?"

"I'd just as soon," replied Amos. "Most places are alike to me since your mother's death. I could stand doing without the garden, if I had the farm to look forward to."

"How'd we pay the money back?" asked Lydia.

"After the Levine bill passes," said Amos, "I'll have a section of pines."

Instantly Lydia's sleeping land hunger woke and with it the memory of Charlie's tales. She sat in deep thought.

"Daddy," she said, finally, "we're not going to borrow, and we're not going to move again. I don't see why people want to keep moving all the time. I love this place, if it is only a cottage, and I'm going to stay here. I wish we could buy it and hand it down in the family so's it would be known forever as the Dudley place. Then nobody'd ever forget our name. What's the use of trying to make a splurge with borrowed money? We thought it was awful when the Barkers mortgaged their house to buy an automobile."

"All right," said Amos, reluctantly. "But remember, you've had your chance and don't feel abused about our poverty."

"I won't," replied Lydia, obediently.

And to her own surprise, she did feel less bitter about her meager, home-made clothing. She had had a chance to improve it and had resisted the temptation.

She told Ma Norton of Amos' plan, and her refusal. Ma heard her through in silence. They were sitting as usual in the kitchen of the Norton farmhouse. Lydia ran over nearly every Saturday afternoon but she seldom saw Billy. Amos had refused to allow Lydia to continue fudge selling and Ma supposed that that was why her son never spoke of Lydia or was about when she called.

"You did exactly right, Lydia," was Ma's verdict. "And you mustn't lay it all to clothes, though I've always maintained that party-going boys were just as silly about clothes as party-going girls. You're old for your age, Lydia. It takes older men to understand you. I suppose your class has begun to talk about graduation. It's March now."

"Yes," said Lydia. "We've chosen the class motto and the class color. I was chairman of the motto committee and we chose Ducit Amor Patriae — and purple and white's our color."

"For the land's sake," murmured Ma. "Why do you children always choose Latin or Greek mottoes? Hardly anybody in the audience knows what they mean. I never did get Billy's through my head."

Lydia laughed. "We just do it to be smart! But I chose this one. It's one John Levine gave me years ago. I thought it was a good one for young Americans — Love of Country leads them."

"Indeed it is. Especially with all the foreign children in the class. I'll have to tell Billy that. He's doing fine in his law but his father's broken-hearted over his giving up farming."

"I'll bet he goes back to it. He's a born farmer," said Lydia.

Late in March the valedictorian and salutatorian of the class were chosen. The custom was for the teachers to select the ten names that had stood highest for scholarship during the entire four years and to submit these to the pupils of the class, who by popular vote elected from these the valedictorian and the salutatorian.

To her joy and surprise Lydia's was one of the ten names. So were Olga's and Kent's.

"Olga and Kent will get it," Lydia told Amos and Lizzie. "I'm going to vote for them myself. All the boys are crazy about Olga and all the girls are crazy about Kent."

The day on which the election took place was cold and rainy. Amos plodding home for supper was astonished to see Lydia flying toward him through the mud a full quarter of a mile from home.

"Daddy, they elected me valedictorian! They did! They did!"

Amos dropped his dinner pail. "You don't mean it! How did it happen! I never thought of such a thing." He was as excited as Lydia.

She picked up his pail and clung to his arm as they started home.

"I don't know how it happened. They just all seemed to take it for granted. No one was surprised but me. Olga got four votes and Mamie Aldrich ten and I got sixty-six! Daddy! And Mamie wasn't cross but Olga was. Oh, isn't it wonderful!"

"Valedictorian! My little Lydia! Scholarship and popular vote! I wish your mother was here. What does Lizzie say?"

Lydia giggled. "I left Lizzie carrying on an imaginary conversation with Elviry Marshall, after she'd cried over me for half an hour. And, Daddy, nobody was surprised but me! Not the teachers or anybody!"

"Thank God, there's some democracy left in the world," said Amos. "Evidently those youngsters voted without prejudice. They can give us elders a few points. Lord, Lydia! and folks have been looking down on us because we were poor and I'm little better than a day laborer. I'll write to Levine tonight. He'll have to be here for the exercises."

"And Kent is salutatorian. He won by just two votes. I've got to begin to plan about my dress."

"Now, I'm going to buy that dress, Lydia, if I have to borrow money. You aren't going to begin any talk about earning it."

"Oh, all right," said Lydia, hastily. "You won't have to borrow. White goods is always cheap and I'll get it right away so I can put lots of hard work on it."

"What's your speech going to be about?" asked Amos, as they turned in the gate.

"I haven't had time to think about that. I'll plan it all out while I'm sewing. I must make a V neck so I can wear the dress without the collar to the Senior Ball."

Lizzie was waiting supper for them and poured the tea into the sugar bowl as she described to Amos the agonies of mind Elviry Marshall would endure on hearing the news. Ma Norton came over during the evening to exchange a setting of eggs but wouldn't sit down after Amos had forestalled Lizzie in telling of Lydia's honor. She said she couldn't wait to get home to tell Pa and Billy.

Billy did not congratulate Lydia. He passed her just as he had during all the months, with a curt little "Hello." To tell the truth Lydia was heartily ashamed of herself for her shabby reception of Billy's plea. Not that she had softened toward him! But she knew she had been unkind and she missed the desultory companionship she had had with Billy.

The preparation of the dress went on amazingly well. The speech making was less simple. As was customary, Lydia chose the class motto for her subject and sweated inordinately to find something to say. She complained bitterly to Miss Towne and Amos because during the four years at High School nothing at all was taught about love of country, or patriotism, or anything that would make the motto suggestive.

"How about your one term of Civil Government?" asked Miss Towne.

"Oh, I was a freshman then and I've forgotten it all, — except the preamble to the Constitution and the Declaration of Independence."

Lydia stopped thoughtfully.

Amos answered her plaint indignantly. "Well, for heaven's sake! And you a descendant of the Puritans! Lord, what's become of the old stock! No, I won't help you at all. Think it out for yourself."

And think it out Lydia did, sitting on the front steps with her sewing and listening to the sighing of the pine by the gate.

Spring flew by like the wind, and June came. There was but one flaw in Lydia's happiness. Nobody asked her to attend the Senior Ball that was to take place on Graduation night. To be sure, it was not an invitation affair. The class was supposed to attend in a body but there was, nevertheless, the usual two-ing and only a very few of the girls who had no invitation from boys would go. Lydia, herself, would have cut off her hand rather than appear at her own Senior Ball without a young man.

She had pinned some faith to Kent, until she had heard that Margery was to be home in time for the graduating exercises. As June came on and the tenth drew near, a little forlorn sense of the unfairness of things began to obscure Lydia's pride and joy in her honor. On the ninth, the last rehearsal of the speech had been made; the dress was finished and hung resplendent in the closet; Amos himself had taken Lydia into town and bought her white slippers and stockings, taking care to inform the street-car conductor and the shoe clerk carelessly the wherefore and why of his mission.

And Lydia knew that none of her classmates was going to ask her to the ball. "They think they've done enough in giving me the valedictory," she thought. "As if I wouldn't exchange that in a minute for a sure enough invitation."

Mortified and unhappy, she avoided her mates during the last week of school, fearing the inevitable question, "Who's going to take you, Lyd?"

The tenth dawned, a lovely June day. Amos had half a day off and was up at daylight, whistling in the garden. The exercises began at ten and by half past eight, Lydia was buttoned into her pretty little organdy, Lizzie was puffing in her black alpaca and Amos was standing about in his black Sunday suit which dated back to his early married days. By nine-thirty they had reached the Methodist church and Amos and Lizzie were established in the middle of the front row of the balcony while Lydia was shivering with fright in the choir-room where the class was gathered.

Somebody began to play the organ and somebody else who looked like Miss Towne shoved Lydia toward the door and she led the long line of her mates into the front pews. The same minister who had buried little Patience, prayed and a quartette sang. A college professor spoke at length, then Kent appeared on the platform.

Good old Kent, even if he wouldn't take Lydia to parties! Kent, with his black eyes and hair, his ruddy skin and broad shoulders, was good to look on and was giving his speech easily and well. Lydia had heard it a dozen times in rehearsal but now not a word Kent said was intelligible to her. She was seeing him in a red bathing suit as he hung Florence Dombey from a yard arm of the willow. She was hearing him as he knelt in the snow with an arm about her shoulders, "I'm so doggone sorry for you, Lydia." What a dear he had been! Now it all was different. They were grown up. This day marked their growing up and Kent didn't want to take her to parties.

Kent bowed and took his seat. The quartette sang and somebody prodded Lydia smartly in the back. She made her way up to the platform and began to speak automatically.

It was a very young and girlish speech. It was delivered with tremendous sincerity. Yet it did not matter much what she said, for what counted was that Lydia's contralto voice was very young and rich, that her golden hair was like a nimbus about her head, that her lips were red and sweet, that her cheeks were vivid and that her eyes were very blue, very innocent and clear.

Amos with tight clenched fists and Lizzie with her lips a thin seam of nervous compression, were swelled with vanity and torn with fear lest she forget her lines.

But John Levine, who had dashed in late and stood unnoticed in the crowd under the gallery listened intently, while he yearned over Lydia's immature beauty like a mother.

"And so," she ended, "when we say good-bye, you all must remember that we go out into the world resolved to live up to our motto. That we believe with our forefathers that governments derive their just powers from the consent of the governed. That all men are endowed by their Creator with certain inalienable rights, among which are life, liberty and the pursuit of happiness. And that because the New England people in the Middle West are far from the cradle of liberty where these ideas were born, living among foreigners it behooves the members of our class to carry our motto into their daily life. Love of country leads us and so farewell!"

It was a foolish, sentimental little speech with one or two real thoughts in it and John Levine smiled even while the tears filled his eyes. He told himself that no one, least of all probably Lydia herself, realized the cynical application of the class motto to Lake City conditions.

The diplomas were distributed. The great morning was over. After the congratulations and the handshaking, Lydia found herself with her father, Lizzie, Levine and Ma Norton on the way to the trolley. Lydia walked between her father and John.

"You'll come out to dinner, Mr. Levine," asked Lydia.

"No, ma'am," replied the Congressman. "I return to Washington on the 12:30 train, which gives me just time to see you to the trolley."

"Why, what's the matter?" asked Amos.

"We vote on the Levine bill, the morning I get back to Washington. I just ran out to see young Lydia graduate."

Amos groaned, "John, you're a fool!"

Levine laughed. "Lydia, am I a fool?" He looked down at the flushed face above the dainty organdy.

"No," she answered, giving him a swift look. "You're a goose and a lamb."

"So! You see you don't understand me, Amos," said John, triumphantly as he helped Lydia aboard the street-car. "Good-bye, young Lydia. I'll be home in a week or so."

And so the great event ended. After dinner Amos rushed back to the factory, Lydia hung the graduation gown away in her closet and she and Adam spent the afternoon on the lake shore, where the delicate splendor and perfume of June endeavored in vain to prove to Lydia that the Senior Ball was of no consequence.

She was silent at supper, while Amos and Lizzie went over the details of the morning again. After the dishes were washed she sat on the steps in the dusk with Adam's head in her lap when a carriage rolled up to the gate. A man came swiftly up the path. As he entered the stream of lamplight from the door Lydia with a gasp recognized Billy Norton. Billy, wearing a dress suit and carrying a bouquet of flowers!

"Good evening, Lydia," he said calmly. "Will you go to the Senior Ball with me?"

Lydia was too much overcome for speech. She never before had seen a man in a dress suit! It made of Billy a man of the world. Where was the country boy she had snubbed?

"Here are some flowers I hope you'll wear," Billy went on, formally. "Would you mind hurrying? It's pretty late."

"Oh, Billy!" breathed Lydia, at last. "Aren't you an angel!"

She jumped to her feet and rushed through the house into her room, leaving Billy to explain to her father and Lizzie. In half an hour the two were seated in the carriage, an actual, party-going, city hack, and bumping gaily on the way to the Ball.

In her gratitude and delight, Lydia would have apologized to Billy for her last summer's rudeness, but Billy gave her no opportunity. He mentioned casually that he had been up on the reservation, for a week, returning only that afternoon so that he had missed her graduation exercises. They chatted quite formally until they reached Odd Fellows' Hall, where the dancing had already begun.

Lydia's first dancing party! Lydia's first man escort and he wearing a dress suit and there were only two others in the Hall! Who would attempt to describe the joy of that evening? Who would have recognized Billy, the farmer, in the cool blond person who calmly appropriated Lydia's card, taking half the dances for himself and parceling out the rest grudgingly and discriminatingly. Kent was allowed two dances. He was the least bit apologetic but Lydia in a daze of bliss was nonchalant and more or less uninterested in Kent's surprise at seeing her at a dance.

For three hours, Lydia spun through a golden haze of melody and rhythm. Into three hours she crammed all the joy, all the thrill, that she had dreamed of through her lonely girlhood. At half after eleven she was waltzing with Billy.

"We must leave now, Lydia," he said. "I promised your father I'd have you home by midnight."

"Oh, Billy! Just one more two step and one more waltz," pleaded Lydia.

"Nope," he said, smiling down into her wistful eyes. "I want to get a stand-in with your Dad because I want to take you to more parties."

"Oh, Billy! Do you!" breathed Lydia. "Well, I don't think there's anyone in the world has nicer things happen to them than I do! Oh, Billy, just this waltz!"

It would have taken a harder heart than Billy's to resist this. He slipped his arm about her and they swung out on the floor to the strains of The Blue Danube, than which no lovelier waltz has ever been written.

They did not speak. Billy, holding the slender, unformed figure gently against his breast, looked down at the golden head with an expression of utter tenderness in his eyes, of deep resolve on his lips.

At the end, Lydia looked up with a wondering smile. "I didn't know anyone could be so perfectly happy, Billy. I shall always remember that of you — you gave me my happiest moment."

On the way home in the bumping hack, Billy seemed to relax. "Well, did I give you a good time, Miss, or didn't I? Could Kent or Gustus have done better?"

"Oh, they!" cried Lydia indignantly. "But, Billy, I didn't know you could dance."

"I couldn't, but I've been taking lessons all winter. I'm not going to give a girl a chance twice to call me down the way you did last summer. Of course, this is just a second-hand dress suit, but I think it looks all right, don't you?"

"Billy," said Lydia, "last summer I was just a silly little girl. Now, I'm grown up. You were the *swellest* person at the ball tonight. You just wait till I tell your mother about it."

Billy went up the path with Lydia to the steps and held her hand a moment in silence after he said, "It's a wonderful night!"

A wonderful night, indeed! The moon hung low over the lake and the fragrance of late lilac and of linden blooms enveloped them. Youth and June-moonlight and silence! A wonderful night indeed!

"You are very sweet, Lydia," whispered the young man. He laid his cheek for a moment against her hand, then turned quickly away.

Lydia watched the carriage drive off, stood for a moment trying to impress forever on her mind the look and odor of the night, then with a tremulous sigh, she went indoors.

Chapter XIII

THE INDIAN CELEBRATION

"The oak, the maple, the birch, I love them all, but nothing is so dear to the pine as the pine."
— *The Murmuring Pine*

*L*ydia was tired the day after the party, tired and moody. After she had told Lizzie and Ma Norton all about the evening, she spent the rest of the day lying on the lake shore, with a book but not reading. Late in the afternoon she went into the house and took Florence Dombey from her accustomed seat in a corner of the living room.

For a long time she sat with Florence Dombey in her arms, looking from the hectic china face to the scintillating turquoise of the lake and listening to the hushed whispering of the pine. Finally with Adam lumbering jealously after her, she climbed the narrow stairs into the attic.

Back under the eaves stood a packing box into which Lydia never had looked. It contained all of little Patience's belongings. Holding Florence Dombey in one arm, she lifted the lid of the box, catching her breath a little as she glimpsed the cigar box furniture and a folded little white dress. Very carefully she laid Florence Dombey beside the furniture, leaned over and kissed her china lips and closed down the lid of the box. Then of a sudden she dropped to the floor with her head against the box and sobbed disconsolately. Adam gave a howl and crowded into her lap and Lydia hugged him but wept on.

The late afternoon sun sifted through the dusty attic window on her yellow head. Somewhere near the window a robin began to trill his vesper song. Over and over he sang it until at last Lydia heard and raised her head. Suddenly she smiled.

"There, Adam," she said, "now I'm really grown up and I feel better. Let's go meet Dad."

It was three or four days later that news came that the Levine bill had passed. It was a compromise bill as John had intimated it would be to the half breeds in the woods. Only the mixed bloods could sell their lands. Nevertheless there was great rejoicing in Lake City. Plans were begun immediately for a Fourth of July celebration upon the reservation. Kent to his lasting regret missed the celebration. Immediately after school closed he had gone into Levine's office and had been sent to inspect Levine's holdings in the northern part of the State.

Levine returned the last week in June and took charge of the preparations. Amos, who never had been on the reservation, planned to go and Levine rented an automobile and invited Lydia, Amos, Billy Norton and Lizzie to accompany him.

It rained on the third of July, but the fourth dawned clear and hot. Lydia really saw the dawn for she and Lizzie had undertaken to provide the picnic lunch and supper for the party of five and they both were busy in the kitchen at sunrise. At eight o'clock the automobile was at the door.

John drove the car himself and ordered Lydia in beside him. The rest packed into the tonneau with the baskets. It seemed as if all Lake City were headed for the reservation, for Levine's automobile was one of a huge line of vehicles of every type moving north as rapidly as the muddy road and the character of the motive power would permit. As they neared the reservation, about eleven, they began to overtake parties of young men who had walked the twenty miles.

They passed the Last Chance, which was gaily hung with flags. Its yard was packed with vehicles. Its bar was running wide open. They swung on up the black road into the reservation, around a long hill, through a short bit of wood to the edge of a great meadow where John halted the car.

On all sides but one were pine woods. The one side was bordered by a little lake, motionless under the July sun. On the edge of the pines were set dozens of tents and birch-bark wick-i-ups. In the center of the meadow was a huge flagpole from which drooped the Stars and Stripes. Near by was a grandstand and a merry-go-round and everywhere were hawkers' booths.

Already the meadow was liberally dotted with sight-seers of whom there seemed to be as many Indians as whites. The mechanical piano in connection with the merry-go-round shrilled above the calls of vendors. Overhead in the brazen blue of the sky, buzzards sailed lazily watching.

"Isn't it great!" cried Lydia. "What do we do first?"

"Well," said Levine, "I'm free until three o'clock, when the speeches begin. There'll be all sorts of Indian games going until then."

"You folks go on," said Lizzie. "I'm going to sit right here. I never was so comfortable in my life. This may be my only chance to see the world from an automobile and I don't calculate to lose a minute. I can see all I want from right here."

The others laughed. "I don't blame you, Liz," said Amos. "I feel a good deal that way, myself. What's the crowd round the flagpole, John?"

"Let's go see," answered Levine.

"How did you get the Indians to come, Mr. Levine?" asked Billy.

"By offering 'em all the food they could eat. The majority of them haven't any idea what it's all about. But they're just like white folks. They like a party. Don't get crowded too close to any of them, Lydia. They're a dirty lot, poor devils."

The crowd about the flagpole proved to be watching an Indian gambling game. In another spot, a pipe of peace ceremony was taking place. The shooting galleries were crowded. Along the lake shore a yelling audience watched birch canoe races. The merry-go-round held as many squaws and papooses and stolid bucks as it did whites.

The four returned to the automobile for lunch hot and muddy but well saturated with the subtle sense of expectation and excitement that was in the air.

"This is just a celebration and nothing else, John, isn't it?" asked Amos as he bit into a sandwich.

"That's all," replied Levine. "We thought it was a good way to jolly the Indians. At the same time it gave folks a reason for coming up here and seeing what we were fighting for and, last and not least, it was the Indian Agent's chance to come gracefully over on our side."

"Did he?" asked Lydia.

"He did. He's done more of the actual work of getting the celebration going than I have."

"I wonder why?" asked Billy, suddenly.

"All there is left for him to do," said Levine. "Lydia, before the speeches begin, go up in the pines and choose your tract. I'll buy it for you."

Lydia glanced at Billy. He was thinner this summer than she had ever seen him. He was looking at her with his deep set grey eyes a little more somber, she thought, than the occasion warranted. Nevertheless she stirred uneasily.

"I don't want any Indian lands," she said. "I'd always see Charlie Jackson in them."

"The whole thing's wrong," muttered Billy.

Levine gave him a quick look, then smiled a little cynically. "You'd better go along with Lydia and take a look at the pines," he suggested. "Amos, I've already got your tract picked out. It's ten miles from here so you can't see it today. Come over to the speakers' stand and help me get things arranged."

"I'd like to look at the pines again, anyhow," said Lydia. "Come along, Billy."

Lydia was wearing the corduroy outing suit of the year before and was looking extremely well. Billy, in an ordinary business suit, was not the man of the world of Graduation night, yet there was a new maturity in his eyes and the set of his jaw that Lydia liked without really observing it. Old Lizzie watched the two as they climbed the slope to the woods. Billy strode along with the slack, irregular gait of the farmer. Lydia sprang over the ground with quick, easy step.

"Billy's a man grown," Lizzie said to herself, "and he's a nice fellow, but he don't tug at my old heart strings like Kent does — drat Kent, anyhow!" She settled herself as conspicuously as possible in the automobile. "If Elviry Marshall would pass now, I'd be perfectly happy," she murmured.

Billy and Lydia entered the woods in silence and followed a sun-flecked aisle until the sound of the celebration was muffled save for the shrill notes of the mechanical piano, which had but two tunes, "Under the Bamboo Tree" and the "Miserere."

"I hate to think of it all divided into farms and the pines cut down," said Lydia.

Billy leaned against one of the great tree trunks and stared thoughtfully about him.

"I'm all mixed up, Lydia," he said. "It's all wrong. I know the things Levine and the rest are doing to get this land are wrong, and yet I don't see how they can be stopped."

"Well," Lydia fanned herself with her hat, thoughtfully, "for years people have been telling me awful things Mr. Levine's done to Indians and I worried and worried over it. And finally, I decided to take Mr. Levine for the dear side he shows me and to stop thinking about the Indians."

"You can stop thinking, perhaps," said the young man, "but you can't stop this situation up here from having an influence on your life. Everybody in Lake City must be directly or indirectly affected by the reservation. Everybody, from the legislators to the grocery keepers, has been grafting on the Indians. Your own father says the thing that's kept him going for years was the hope of Indian lands. Margery Marshall's clothed with Indian money."

"And how about the influence on you, Billy?" asked Lydia with a keen look into the young fellow's rugged face.

"I'm in the process of hating myself," replied Billy, honestly. "I came up here last month to see how bad off the Indians were. And I saw the poor starving, diseased brutes and I cursed my white breed. And yet, Lyd, I saw a tract of pine up in the middle of the reservation that I'd sell my soul to own! It's on a rise of ground, with a lake on one edge, and the soil is marvelous, and it belongs to a full-blood."

There was understanding in Lydia's eyes. "Oh, the pines are wonderful," she exclaimed. "If one could only keep them, forever! And I suppose that's the way the Indians feel about them too!"

"It's all wrong," muttered Billy. "It's all wrong, and yet," more firmly, "the reservation is doomed and if we don't take some of it, Lydia, we'll not be helping the Indians — but just being foolish."

Lydia nodded. A hot breeze drifted through the woods and the pines sighed deeply.

"To have it and hold it for your children's children," exclaimed Lydia, passionately. "You and yours to live on it forever. And yet, I'd see a dead Indian baby and starving squaws behind every tree, I know I would."

"I tell you what I'm going to do," said Billy, doggedly. "I'm going to get hold of that tract. I'm not going to deceive myself that it's all anything but a rotten, thieving game we whites are playing, but I'm going to do it, anyhow."

"I'd like to myself," Lydia still had the look of understanding, "but I'm afraid to! I'd be haunted by Charlie Jackson's eyes."

"I'm going to get that tract. I'll pay for it, somehow, and I'll go on doing what I can to see that the Indians get what's left of a decent deal."

Again the two listened to the wind in the pines, then Lydia said, "We must get back for the speeches."

Billy started back, obediently.

"We're grown up, aren't we, Billy?" sighed Lydia. "We've got to decide what we're going to do and be, and I hate to think about it. I hate important decisions. Seems as though I'd been dogged by 'em all my life."

"If I had my way," cried Billy, unexpectedly, "you never should quite grow up. You'd always be the dear little yellow-haired girl that tramped her legs off to earn my miserable old schoolbooks. And that's what you always will be to me — the oldest and youngest little girl! And whether you like me or not, I'll tell you you're not going to have any worries that I can help you ward off."

They were emerging into the meadow and Lydia laughed up at him mischievously, "I've always thought I overpaid for those schoolbooks. They were fearfully used up. Oh, the speeches have begun," and Billy was hard put to it to keep close to her as she rushed toward the speakers' stand.

Levine had just finished his speech when Billy and Lydia got within hearing, and he introduced State Senator James Farwell as the chief speaker of the day. Farwell had considerable history to cover in his speech. He began with the Magna Charta and worked by elaborate stages through the French Revolution, the conquest of India, the death of Warren Hastings, the French and Indian War, the American Revolution and the Civil War to Lincoln's Gettysburg speech.

His audience, standing in the burning sun, was restless. The Indians, understanding little that was said, were motionless, but the whites drifted about, talked in undertones and applauded only when as a fitting peak to all the efforts of the ages toward freedom, Farwell placed the present freeing of the Indians from the reservation.

"The great fool!" said Billy to Lydia, as Farwell finally began to bow himself off the platform.

Levine rose and began, "Ladies and gentlemen, this ends our program. We thank —"

He was interrupted here by applause from the Indians. Looking round he saw Charlie Jackson leading forward old Chief Wolf.

"Chief Wolf wants to say a few words," cried Charlie.

"The program is closed," called Levine loudly.

There was a threat in Charlie's voice. "He is going to speak!" And there was a threat in the Indian voices that answered from the audience, "Let speak! Let speak."

Levine conferred hastily with Farwell and the Indian Agent, then the three with manifest reluctance — stood back and Charlie led the old Indian to the foot of the platform.

Old Wolf was half blind with trachoma. He was emaciated with sickness and slow starvation. Nevertheless, clad in the beaded buckskin and eagle feathers of his youth, with his hawk face held high, he was a heroic figure of a man.

He held up his right hand and began to speak in a trembling old bass, Charlie's young tenor translating sentence by sentence. With the first word, the audience became motionless and silent.

"I come from the wick-i-ups of my fathers to say one last word to the whites. I am an old, old man. The last winter was bitter hard and I may never see another July sun. I have lived too long. I have seen my race change from young men strong and daring as eagles, as thrifty and fat as brown bears, to feeble yellow wolves fit only to lap the carrion thrown them by the whites, and to lie in the sun and die.

"And I say to you whites, you have done this. You have moved us on and on, promising always that each resting place shall be ours forever. You swore by your God, in solemn council, that we could keep this reservation forever. With room for all the peoples of the world here, you could not find room for the Indian. You are a race of liars. You are a race of thieves. You have debauched our young men with your women. You have ruined our daughters with your men. You have taken our money. And now you are entering our last home with the hand of desolation. When the enemy enters the abiding place, the dweller is doomed. But I place the curse of the Indian Spirit on you and the land you are stealing. Some day it will be done to you as you have done to us. Some day —"

Levine stepped forward. "Jackson, take that Indian away," he commanded.

An angry murmur came from the Indians in the audience. A murmur that as Levine laid hold of old Wolf's arm, grew to strange calls. There was a surging movement toward the platform. Billy jumped on a box that he had found for a seat for Lydia.

"Charlie!" he roared, "Charlie! Remember there are women and children in this crowd."

"What do I care for your women and children?" shouted Charlie.

Then his glance fell on Lydia's golden head. She waved her hand to him beseechingly. Charlie hesitated for a moment, then spoke loudly in Indian to the crowd, and led old Wolf from the platform. The movement forward of the Indians ceased. The whites moved out of the crowd and for a moment there was a complete segregation of Indians and whites.

Then the mechanical piano which had stopped during the speech-making suddenly started up with a loud twang of "Under the Bamboo Tree." Two Indian boys laughed and started on a run for the merry-go-round and the crowd followed after.

Billy got down from his box with a sigh of relief. "That might have been an ugly moment," he said, "if Charlie hadn't seen you."

"The poor things! Oh, Billy, the poor, poor things!" exclaimed Lydia. Billy nodded. "It's all wrong."

The noise of hawkers began again, but something had gone out of the celebration. The Indians stood about in groups, talking, Charlie and Chief Wolf the center always of the largest group.

Amos and John joined Billy and Lydia at the machine. "The war dancing begins at sundown," said Levine. "I told the Indian Agent 'twas a risk to let them go on, after this episode. But he laughs at me. I don't like the look of things, though."

"They aren't armed?" asked Amos.

"No, but've got those pesky bows and arrows we were having them show off with. I don't know but what I'd better get you folks home."

"Shucks," said Amos, "I wouldn't let the Indians think they could scare us. What could they do, poor sickly devils, anyhow?"

"That's right," said Billy. "There's nothing can happen. I don't think Charlie Jackson would stand for any violence."

"I don't know about that," Levine spoke thoughtfully. "He's left Doc Fulton and is living on the reservation again. They always revert."

"Listen! Listen!" cried Lydia,

There was a red glow behind the clouds low in the west. From the foot of the flagpole came a peculiar beat of drum. A white can beat a drum to carry one through a Gettysburg. An Indian can beat a drum to carry one's soul back to the sacrifice of blood upon a stony altar. This drum beat "magicked" Lydia and Billy. It was more than a tocsin, more than a dance rhythm, more than the spring call. They hurried to the roped-off circle round the flagpole, followed by John and Amos.

An Indian in beaded buckskin squatted by the pole, beating a drum. Above him the flag stirred lazily. The west was crimson. The scent of sweet grass was heavy. There was a breathless interval while the drum seemed to urge Lydia's soul from her body.

Then there came the cry again followed by a wordless chant. Into the ring, in all the multicolored glory of beads and paint, swung a dozen moccasined braves. They moved in a step impossible to describe, — a step grave, rhythmic, lilting, now slow, three beats to a step, now swift, three steps to a beat. Old chiefs, half blind with trachoma, scarred with scrofula and decrepit with starvation; young bucks, fresh and still strong, danced side by side, turned by the alchemy of the drum into like things, young and vivid as dawn.

At intervals, at the bidding of the braves, squaws arose and moved sedately into the circle. In their dark dresses they moved about the outer edge of the circle with a side step that scarcely ruffled their skirts. The west lost its glow. Fires flashed here and there in the meadow. In the flickering, changing lights the dance went on and on. The flag fitfully revealed itself above the melting, gliding, opalescent group about the pole, that by degrees was growing larger as was the constant rim of somber squaws, with their dumb faces Sphinxlike in the half light.

Lydia shivered with excitement. Billy pulled her arm through his.

"I don't like this," he muttered.

"What's the matter?" exclaimed Lydia. "Do you think there's going to be trouble?"

"I don't know. It's just something in the air. I think we'd better find the folks and get you and Lizzie out of this."

"I don't believe they mean any harm," said Lydia. "Lots of the whites started home before sunset, anyhow."

"I wish you had," replied Billy. "Gee, here it comes."

The chant suddenly changed to a yell. The drum beat quickened, and the great circle of dancing Indians broke and charged the crowd of whites. A number of them drew revolvers and began firing them into the air. Others drew taut the great bows they carried. The whites plunged backward precipitately.

Billy thrust Lydia behind him. "Don't move, Lyd," he cried, pushing aside a threatening buck as he did so.

"Kill 'em whites!" shrieked the squaws.

"Run 'em whites off our reservation!" shouted half a dozen young bucks.

Lydia was trembling but cool. "Good for them! Oh, Billy, good for them!" she exclaimed.

He did not reply. His great body circled about her, with shoulder and elbow buffeting off the surging crowd. Thus far the whites had taken the proceedings as a joke. Then a white woman screamed, —

"Run! It's a massacre!"

"Massacre" is a horrifying word to use to whites in an Indian country. Men and women both took up the cry, —

"It's a massacre! Run!"

And the great crowd bolted.

Like pursuing wolves, the Indians followed, beating the laggards with their bows, shouting exultantly. Billy caught Lydia round the waist and held her in front of him as well as he could, and for a few moments the rush of the mob carried them on.

Then Lydia heard Billy's voice in her ear. "If this isn't stopped, it *will* be a massacre. We've got to find Charles Jackson."

"We may be killed trying to find him!" Lydia cried.

"We've got to make a try for it, anyhow," replied Billy. "Brace your shoulders back against my chest. I'll try to stop."

They succeeded in holding themselves steadily for a moment against the mob and in that moment, Billy caught a screaming squaw by the arm.

"Susie, where's Charlie Jackson?"

She jerked her thumb back toward the flag pole and twisted away.

"All right! Now we'll make for the pole, Lydia, get behind me and put your arms round my waist. Hang on, for heaven's sake."

Lydia did hang on for a few moments. But the flight was now developing into a free for all fight. And before she knew just how it happened, Lydia had fallen and feet surged over her.

She buried her face in her arms. It seemed an age to her before Billy had snatched her to her feet. In reality she was not down for more than two minutes. Billy swung her against his chest with one arm and swung out with his other, shouting at Indians and whites alike.

"You damned beasts! You dirty damned beasts."

Lydia, bruised and shaken, clung to him breathlessly, then cried, "Go ahead, Billy!"

He glanced down at her and saw a streak of blood on her forehead. His face worked and he began to sob and curse like a madman.

"They've hurt you, the hellhounds! I'll kill somebody for this."

Kicking, striking with his free arm, oaths rolling from his lips, he burst through the crowd and rushed Lydia to the free space about the flagpole where Charlie Jackson stood coolly watching the proceedings.

Billy shook his fist under the Indian's nose.

"Get down there and call the pack off or I'll brain you."

Jackson shrugged his shoulders, calmly. "Let 'em have their fun. It's their last blowout. I hope they do kill Levine and Marshall."

Lydia pulled herself free of Billy. Her voice was trembling, but she had not lost her head.

"Call them off, Charlie. It'll just mean trouble in the end for all of you if you don't."

Charlie looked at Lydia closely and his voice changed as he said, "You got hurt, Lydia? I'm sorry."

"Sorry! You damned brute!" raved Billy. "I tell you, call off this row!"

The two young men glared at each other. Afterglow and firelight revealed a ferocity in Billy's face and a cool hatred in Charlie's that made Lydia gasp. The shouting of the mob, the beating of the drum was receding toward the road. The flag snapped in the night wind.

Billy put his face closer to Charlie's. The muscles of his jaw knotted and his hands clenched and unclenched.

"Call it off!" he growled.

Charlie returned Billy's stare for a long moment. Then sullenly, slowly, he turned and threw out across the night a long, shrill cry. He gave it again and again. At each repetition the noise of the mob grew less, and shortly panting, feverish-eyed bucks began to struggle into the light around the pole.

Then, without a word, Billy led Lydia away. The Indians passing them shook their bows at them but they were unmolested.

"Can you walk, Lydia? Do you think you're badly hurt?" asked Billy.

"I'm not hurt except for this cut on my head. And I guess I'm scared and bruised from being stepped on. That's all."

"All! To think of me not scratched and you hurt! Your father ought to horsewhip me!"

"You saved me from being trampled to death!" cried Lydia, indignantly. "Oh there's the auto."

There it was, indeed, with old Lizzie standing in the tonneau, wringing her hands, and Amos and Levine, dust covered and disheveled, guarding the car with clubs.

They all shouted with relief when they saw the two. Lydia by now had wiped the blood from her face.

"Billy," cried Levine, "could you run the car and the two women down the road while Amos and I help the Agent get order here? The worst seems to be over, for some reason."

"Billy got Charlie Jackson to call the Indians in," said Lydia.

"Good work!" exclaimed Amos. "Are you both all right?"

"Yes," answered Lydia. "Go on! Billy'll take care of us."

"I'll wait for you at the willows, a mile below Last Chance," said Billy.

"Land," said Lizzie, as the car swung through the hurrying whites, to the road. "About one picnic a lifetime like this, would do me!"

Billy was an indifferent chauffeur but he reached the willows without mishap.

"Now," he said, "come out in front of the lamps, Lydia, till I see what happened to you."

"For heaven's sake, did Lydia get hurt?" screamed Lizzie.

"Don't fuss about me," said Lydia crossly, not offering to follow the other two out of the car.

Billy turned, lifted her down bodily and led her around to the lamps, while he told Lizzie what had happened.

The cut on the scalp was slight. Billy washed it out with water from the brook back of the willows and Lizzie produced a clean pocket-handkerchief with which to bind it. Then they went back to the car and ate their belated supper. After a time, Lizzie, who had the back seat to herself, began to snore comfortably.

Little by little, the stars were blotted out by a thin film of clouds. Sitting under the willows with the murmur of the brook and the fragrance of marsh grass enveloping them, the two young people did not talk much.

"Billy, were you scared?" asked Lydia.

"I don't know. I only know I went crazy when I saw you were hurt. God, Lydia — I couldn't stand that!"

"Billy," whispered Lydia, "you're so good to me and I was so horrid to you once."

Billy felt her fingers on his knee and instantly the thin little hand was enveloped in his warm fist. "Do you take it all back, Lydia?"

"Well, the horrid part of it, I do," she hedged.

"That's all right," returned the young man. "I'm willing to fight for the rest of it. Don't try to pull your hand away, because I intend to hold it till the folks come. You can't help yourself, so you have no responsibility in the matter."

So for an hour longer they sat, watching the summer night and waiting. And sometimes it seemed to Lydia that they were a pioneer man and woman sitting in their prairie schooner watching for the Indians. And sometimes it seemed to her that they were the last white man and woman, that civilization had died and the hordes were coming down upon them.

Finally two dim figures approached. "All right, Lydia?" asked Amos.

"Oh, yes! Yes!" she cried. "Are either of you hurt?"

"No," replied Levine, "but we stayed till I'd got my half-breeds distributed about to watch that none of the full bloods got out of the meadow."

"Was anyone hurt?" asked Billy.

"Oh, two or three broken heads among both Indians and whites. We got hold of Charlie Jackson about eleven and locked him up, then we felt secure."

"You aren't going to hurt Charlie!" cried Lydia.

"No, but we'll shut him up for a week or so," said Amos. "Move over, Lizzie."

"Goodness," exclaimed Lizzie, "I must have dozed off for a minute!"

In the laughter that followed, Levine started the car homeward.

During the trip, the story was told of Lydia's mishap, Billy and Lydia interpolating each other in the telling. Amos shook hands with Billy silently when they had finished and Levine turned round from the wheel to say,

"I'll not forget this night's work, Bill."

They reached home at daylight. The Celebration made table talk and newspaper space for several days. No real attempt was made to punish the Indians. For once, the whites, moved by a sense of tardy and inadequate justice, withheld their hands.

Kent never ceased to mourn that he had missed the affair. He confided the fact to Lydia one Sunday that he had told Levine of their eavesdropping on him in the woods.

"What did he say?" asked Lydia, flushing.

"Gave me this nice fat job," replied Kent.

Lydia stared, then she sighed. "Well, I don't understand men at all!" And Kent laughed.

Lydia saw a good deal of Billy during the summer. He never spoke of the accident to her at the Celebration, except to inquire about her bruises which troubled her for a week or so. Lydia wondered if he was ashamed of his wild flame of anger and his tears. She herself never thought of the episode without a thrill, as if she had been close for once to the primal impulses of life.

Margery Marshall and Elviry went to Atlantic City and Newport this summer. John Levine was sure to take supper at the cottage once or twice a week, but he was very busy with his political work and with the enormous sales of mixed-breed lands to the whites.

It was just before college opened that Amos announced that he was going to buy the one hundred and twenty acres John had set aside for him.

"How are you going to pay for it?" Lydia asked.

"Don't you worry, I'll tend to that," replied Amos.

Levine was taking supper with them. "Better tell her all about it, Amos," he said. "You know Lydia is our partner."

"Well, she'll just worry," warned Amos. "John's going to hold it for me, till I can get the pine cut off. That'll pay for the land."

"How much did you pay for it, Mr. Levine?" asked Lydia.

Levine grinned. "I forget!"

Lydia's gaze was still the round, pellucid gaze of her childhood. She sat now with her chin cupped in her palm, her blue eyes on Levine. To the surprise of both the men, however, she said nothing.

After the supper dishes were washed, and Amos was attending to the chickens, Lydia came slowly out to the front steps where Levine was sitting. He reached up and catching her hand pulled her down beside him on the topmost step. She leaned her head against his arm and they sat in silence, Lydia with her eyes on the dim outline of the pine by the gate.

"Lydia," said John, finally, "how does the Great Search go on? We haven't reported for a long time."

"I don't think I make much headway," replied Lydia. "The older I grow, the less I understand men and I've always felt as if, if there was a God, He was a man."

"You mean male, rather than female," agreed John.

"Lydia, dear, I wish you did have faith."

"But do you believe, yourself?" urged Lydia.

"Yes, I know that the soul can't die," said the man, quietly. "And the thing that makes me surest is the feeling I have for you, I know that I'll have another chance."

"What do you mean?" asked Lydia wonderingly.

"*That,* you'll never know," he replied.

"Well, I know that you're a dear," said the young girl, unexpectedly, "no matter how you get your Indian lands. And I love you to death."

She patted his cheek caressingly, and John Levine smiled sadly to himself in the darkness.

Chapter XIV

THE HARVARD INSTRUCTOR

"The saddest things that I have seen are the burned pine woods and the diseased Indians."

— *The Murmuring Pine*

*T*he University campus was a huge square of green, elm dotted, that was bordered on one edge for a quarter of a mile by the lake. The other three sides were enclosed by the college buildings, great Gothic piles of grey stone, ivy grown, with swallow haunted eaves. One entered the campus through wide archways, that framed from the street ravishing views of lake and elm, with leisurely figures of seniors in cap and gown in the foreground.

College life was not much unlike High School life for Lydia. She of course missed the dormitory living which is what makes University existence unique. The cottage was nearly three miles from the campus. Lydia took a street-car every morning, leaving the house with her father. She was very timid at first: suffered agony when called on to recite: reached all her classes as early as possible and sat in a far corner to escape notice. But gradually, among the six thousand students she began to lose her self-consciousness and to feel that, after all, she was only attending a larger High School.

It was curious, it seemed to her, in how short a time the real High School dropped out of her life. Miss Towne and the cooking teacher who had had so much to do with her adolescent development, became more or less dreamlike. And though Lydia did try to call on Miss Towne at the High School, her days were very full and little by little she slipped away entirely from the old environment.

Except for flying visits home, John Levine spent the year at Washington. He was returned to Congress practically automatically, at the end of his term. Kent throve mightily as a real estate man. He dashed about in a little "one lung" car with all the importance of nineteen in business for the first time. He continued to call on Lydia at irregular intervals in order to boast, she thought, of his real estate acumen and of his correspondence with Margery and Olga, both of whom were now at boarding-school.

Lydia was taking a general course in college. In a vague way, she was planning to become a teacher and partly because she had no aptitude for foreign languages, and partly because of the deep impression Miss Towne's little lecture on slang had made on her, she decided to teach English. She therefore took not only the required course in Freshman Composition, but an elective in Shakespeare, and was herded with fifty others into the classroom of a young instructor fresh from Harvard. He was a frail looking young man, smooth shaven and thin, with large, light brown eyes behind gold rimmed eyeglasses.

Lydia was deeply impressed from the very first by the young man's culture. He could quote Latin and Greek quite as freely as he could French and German and his ease in quoting the latter seemed as great as in quoting Palgrave's Lyrics, which Lydia was sure he could quote from cover to cover.

If his manner was a trifle impatient and condescending, this only served to enhance his impressiveness. And he knew his Shakespeare. Lydia entered under his guidance that ever new and ever old world of beauty that only the born Shakespeare lover discovers.

The Christmas recess had come and gone before Lydia became vaguely conscious that young Professor Willis called on her always to recite, whether he did on any other girl in the class or not. She did not know that from the first day she had entered his class the young professor had been conscious of the yellow head in the furthest corner of the classroom. It was a nobly shaped head bound round with curly yellow braids above a slender face, red cheeked yet delicate. He was conscious too of the home-made suit and the cheap shirtwaists, with the pathetic attempt at variety through different colored neckties. Little by little he recognized that the bashful young person had a mental background not shared by her mates, and he wondered about her.

It was early in January that he made an attempt to satisfy his curiosity. The snowfall had been light so far and heavy winds had blown the lake clear of drifts. Lydia often brought her skates to class with her and if the wind were favorable skated home after her last recitation.

She had just fastened on her skates one day when a rather breathless voice behind her said,

"Going for a skate, Miss Dudley?" and Professor Willis, skates over his shoulder, bore down on her.

Lydia blushed vividly — "I — I often skate home. I live three miles down the shore."

"Rather thought I'd have a try myself, if you don't mind."

"Heavens!" thought Lydia. "I hope he won't come clear home with me? The house looks awful!"

Willis fastened on his skates and stood up. "Which way?" he asked.

Lydia nodded homeward and started off silently, the Harvard man close beside her.

"You enjoy your Shakespeare work, Miss Dudley?" he asked.

"Oh, yes!" cried Lydia. "That most of anything. Don't you love to teach it?"

"Er — in some ways! I will admit that the co-educational end of it is very trying to an Eastern college man."

This was such a surprising view to Lydia that she forgot to be bashful. "Don't you like girls, Professor Willis?" she asked.

"Not in a boys' classroom — that is — at first the situation brought cold sweat to my face. But now, I carry on the work to a great extent for you. You are the only person with a background, don't you know."

Lydia didn't know. The Harvard man's voice, however, was entirely impersonal, so she ventured to explore.

"What do you mean by background?"

"If you wouldn't skate so outrageously fast," he panted, "I could tell you with more — more aplomb."

"But," explained Lydia, "I have to skate fast. There's always so much to be done and old Lizzie isn't well."

She looked at the Shakespeare professor innocently. He looked at his watch.

"Dear me!" he said, "I must be back in the classroom in half an hour. Supposing we continue this conversation tomorrow, in your own home, Miss Dudley? May I call tomorrow night?"

"Why yes," replied Lydia, in utter embarrassment again, "if you really want to! It's a dreadful trip, — to the end of the car line and half a mile along the road to a white cottage after that."

"That's nothing," said the Harvard man, gravely. "Till tomorrow night then," and lifting his cap, he skated back, leaving Lydia in a state of mind difficult to define.

She told Lizzie and her father that evening. Amos looked over his paper with a slight scowl. "You're too young to have a college professor calling."

"Well," cried Lydia, "you don't seem to realize how wonderful it is that he wants to take this awful trip out here, just to see *me*. And don't let it worry you, Daddy! He'll never want to come but once." She looked around the living room disgustedly.

Amos started to speak, looked at Lizzie, who shook her head, and subsided. The older Lydia grew, the more helpless he felt in guiding her. It seemed to him though that Patience would be pleased to have a professor calling on her daughter, and he let the matter go at that.

The next day was Saturday, and Lydia started an attack on the living room immediately after breakfast. She re-oiled the floors. She took down the curtains, washed and ironed them and put them up again. She blacked the base burner and gave the howling Adam a bath. The old mahogany worried her, even after she had polished it and re-arranged it until the worst of the scratches were obscured.

Her father's old wooden armchair, a solid mahogany that had belonged to his great-grandfather, she decided to varnish. She gave it two heavy coats and set it close to the kitchen stove to dry. By this time she was tired out. She lay in the dusk on the old couch watching the red eyes of the base burner, when Billy came in.

"Just stopped on my way home to see if you'd go skating tonight," he said. "Tired out? What've you been doing?"

Lydia enumerated the day's activities ending with, "Professor Willis is coming to call this evening."

Billy gave a low whistle. "Of course, I knew they'd begin to take notice sooner or later. But I don't see why you wanted to wear yourself out for a sissy like him."

"He's not a sissy. He's a gentleman," said Lydia, calmly. She was still curled up on the couch and Billy could just distinguish her bright hair in the red glow from the stove.

Billy was silent for a moment, then he said, "It's a shame you have to work so hard. I think of you so often when I see other girls in their pretty clothes, gadding about! Doggone it! and you're worth any ten of them. If I had my way —"

He paused and for a moment only the familiar booming of the ice disturbed the silence.

"I don't mind the work so much as I do going without the pretty clothes," said Lydia. "I suppose you'll think I'm awful silly," she suddenly sat up in her earnestness, "but when I get to thinking about how I'm growing up and that dresses never can mean to me when I'm old what they do now — oh, I can't explain to a man! It's like Omar Khayyam —

"'Yet ah, that Spring should vanish with the rose
    That youth's sweet scented manuscript should close —'

and my youth's going to close without the sweet scent of the rose."

Billy made one great stride over to the couch and sitting down beside Lydia he took her thin, work hardened little hands in his. "Lydia, no! You don't see yourself right! All the dresses in the world couldn't make you sweeter or more fragrant to a fellow's heart than you are now. The only importance to the clothes is that you love them so. Don't you see?"

Lydia laughed uncertainly. "I see that you're a dear old blarney, Billy. And I know one thing I have got that not one girl in a thousand has and that is the friendship of some of the best men in the world. In lots of ways, I'm very lucky. Honestly, I am! Trot on home, Billy. I've got to get supper. And I don't have to work so hard, remember that. Half my work is in trying to fix up the house."

Billy rose reluctantly. "I'm leaving you some marshmallows," he said. "I hope if you offer Willis one, it'll choke him, or," as he opened the door, "maybe he'll break his leg or his neck on the way out," and he shut the door firmly behind him.

Amos submitted with some grumbling to being relegated to the dining room with Lizzie for the evening. He complained somewhat bitterly, however, over the condition of his armchair which had refused to dry and was in a state of stickiness that defied description.

Old Lizzie, who was almost as flushed and bright-eyed over the expected caller as Lydia, finally squelched Amos with the remark, "For the land's sake, Amos, you talk like an old man instead of a man still forty who ought to remember his own courting days!"

Willis arrived, shortly after eight. If the trip had been somewhat strenuous, he did not mention the fact. He shook hands with Amos, who, always eager to meet new people, would have lingered. But Lizzie called to him and he reluctantly withdrew. Lydia established her guest with his back to the dining room door and the evening began.

The Harvard man was frankly curious. This was his first experience west of New York and he was trying to classify his impressions. The beauty of Lake City had intrigued him at first, he told Lydia, into believing that he was merely in a transplanted New England town. "And you know there are plenty of New Englanders on the faculty and many of the people of Lake Shore Avenue are second and third generation New Englanders. But the townspeople as a whole!" He stopped with a groan.

"What's the matter with them?" Lydia asked, a trifle belligerently. She was sitting on the couch, chin cupped in her hand, watching her caller so intently that she was forgetting to be bashful.

"Oh, you know they're so exactly like my classes in Shakespeare — raw-minded, no background, and plenty of them are of New England descent! I don't understand it. It's New England without its ancient soul, your Middle West."

"I don't know what you mean by background," said Lydia.

"But, Miss Dudley, you have it! Something, your reading or your environment has given you a mental referendum, as it were. You get more out of your Shakespeare than most of your mates because you understand so many of his references. You must have been a wide reader or your father and mother taught you well."

"I — you've got the wrong impression about me," Lydia protested. "I've read always and mostly good things, thanks to Mr. Levine, but so have many other people in Lake City."

Professor Willis looked at Lydia thoughtfully. "Levine? I thought he was a cheap scamp."

Lydia flushed. "He's my best friend and a finely read man. He's kept me supplied with books."

"Finely read, on the one hand," exclaimed Willis, "and on the other robbing Indians. How do you account for it?"

Lydia did not stir. She continued with her crystal gaze on this wise man from the East, struggling to get his viewpoint. There flashed into her mind the thought that perhaps, when she knew him better, he could help her on the Indian question.

"I can't account for it," she said. "I wish I could. Except for a French Canadian great-grandfather, Mr. Levine's a New Englander too."

"New Englander! Pshaw! Outside of Lake Shore Avenue and the college there are no New Englanders here. They are hollow mockeries, unless," he stared at Lydia through his gold-rimmed glass, "unless you are a reversion to type, yourself."

Lizzie spoke from the dining room. "The chocolate's all ready, Lydia."

"Oh, I forgot," exclaimed Lydia, flying out of the room and returning with a tray of chocolate and cake. "The cold walk must have made you hungry."

Willis drew up to the table, and over his cup of chocolate remarked, "Ah — pardon me if I comment on the wonderful pieces of mahogany you have."

Lydia set down her cup. "Why, I hate it!" she cried.

"Hate it! It's priceless! Family pieces? I thought so! What delicious cake! How kind of your mother! I'd like to meet her, if I may."

"I made the cake, Professor Willis. My — my mother is not living."

The Harvard man's stilted manner left him. He set down his cup hastily. "Oh, my dear!" he exclaimed. "I was tactless! Forgive me!" Again he looked about the room and back at Lydia's face above the meager dress fashioned the year before from a cheap remnant. Could a mother's death, he wondered, have put the look into her eyes and lips he had often surprised there. "I suppose," he said finally, "that one might explain you, eventually, if one had the privilege of knowing you long enough, I —"

Adam chose this moment to yelp at the dining room door which was barely ajar.

"Adam, be quiet!" roared Amos. "Liz, did you see my carpet slippers anywhere?" he added in a lower voice.

"I brought you a book," said Willis. "Browning's Dramatic Lyrics."

"I'd like to read them," Lydia spoke eagerly, with one ear on the dining room.

Amos yawned loudly. "Did you wind the clock, Lizzie? No? Well, I will!" Another loud yawn and Amos was heard to begin on the mechanism of the huge old wall clock which wound with a sound like an old-fashioned chain pump. Lydia set her teeth in misery.

"Yes, you must add Browning to your background," said the Harvard man, appearing undisturbed by the sounds in the next room. "Browning is difficult at times but —" He was interrupted by a great clattering in the dining room.

"Lizzie!" roared Amos. "Come here and pull this chair off of me. The next time Lydia varnishes anything —"

There was the sound of Lizzie pounding across the floor. The dining room door was banged and after that the murmur of Lizzie's voice and subdued roars from Amos. Lydia looked at Willis in an agony of embarrassment.

"Well," he said, rising, "it's quite a walk back to the trolley. Perhaps I'd better be going."

Lydia rose with alacrity. "I'm — I'm glad you like the mahogany," she said awkwardly.

"Er — yes. So am I," returned Willis, making for the door as Amos groaned again. "Good night, Miss Dudley."

"Good night," said Lydia, and closing the door with a gasp of relief she dashed for the dining room.

"Just when I'm trying to be refined and ladylike!" she wailed. Then she stopped.

"Lydia," roared Amos, "if you ever touch my chair again! Look at my shirt and pants!"

Lydia looked and from these to the chair, denuded of the two coats of varnish. "But you knew it wasn't dry," she protested.

"How could I remember?" cried Amos. "I just sat down a minute to put on my slippers you'd hid."

"I don't see why you couldn't have been quiet about it," Lydia half sobbed. "We were having such a nice time and all of a sudden it sounded like an Irish wake out here. It embarrassed Professor Willis so he went right home and I know he'll never come back."

"I should hope he wouldn't," retorted Amos. "Of course, what a college professor thinks is more important than my comfort. Why, that varnish went through my shirt to my skin. Liz, what are you laughing at?"

Lizzie had suppressed her laughter till she was weak. "At you, Amos! Till my dying day, I'll never forget how you looked prancing round the room with that chair glued to your back!"

"Oh, Daddy! It must have been funny!" cried Lydia, beginning to giggle.

Amos looked uncertainly at his two women folk, and then his lips twisted and he laughed till the tears ran down his cheeks.

"Lydia! Lydia!" he cried, "don't try to be elegant with anymore of your callers! It's too hard on your poor old father!"

"I won't," replied Lydia. "He likes the mahogany, anyway. But he'll never come again," she added, with sudden gloom. "Not that I care, stiff old Harvard thing," and she patted Adam and went soberly to bed.

But Professor Willis did come again. Not so frequently, of course, as to compromise his dignity. An instructor who called on freshman girls was always laughed at. But several times during the winter and spring he appeared at the cottage, and talked with Lydia earnestly and intellectually. Nor did he always confine his calls to the evening.

One Sunday afternoon in March Amos was in town with John Levine, who was on one of his hurried visits home, when Billy Norton came over to the cottage.

Lydia, who was poring over "The Ring and the Book," saw at once that something was wrong.

"What's worrying you, Billy?" she asked.

"Lydia," he said, dropping into Amos' chair and folding his big arms, "you know my tract of land — the one I was going to buy from an Indian? I paid young Lone Wolf a ten dollar option on it while I looked round to see how I could raise enough to pay him a fair price. He's only a kid of seventeen and stone blind from trachoma. Well, yesterday I found that Marshall had bought it in. Of course, I didn't really think Lone Wolf knew what an option was, but Marshall and the Indian Agent and Levine and all the rest knew what I was trying to do, so I thought they'd keep their hands off."

"What a shame!" exclaimed Lydia.

"Yes," said Billy grimly, a certain tensity in his tones that made Lydia look at him more closely, "Yes, a shame. The way Marshall did it was this. He looked young Lone Wolf up and gave him a bag of candy. The Indians are crazy for candy. Then he told him to make his cross on a piece of paper. That that was a receipt that he was to keep and if he'd show it at the store whenever he wanted candy, he'd have all he wanted, for nothing. And he had two half-breeds witness it. What Marshall had done was to get Lone Wolf to sign a warranty deed, giving Marshall his pine land. The poor devil of an Indian didn't know it till yesterday when he showed me his 'receipt' in great glee. Of course, they'll swear he's a mixed blood."

Lydia was speechless with disgust for a moment, then she burst out, "Oh, I wish that reservation had never been heard of! It demoralizes everyone who comes in contact with it."

"Lydia," said Billy, slowly, "I'm going to expose Marshall."

"What do you mean?" Lydia looked a little frightened.

"I mean that I'm going to show up his crooked deals with the Indians. I'm going to rip this reservation graft wide open. I'm not going to touch an acre of the land myself so I can go in with clean hands and I'm not going to forget that I came pretty close to being a skunk, myself."

"Oh, but, Billy!" cried Lydia. "There's John Levine and all our friends — oh, you can't do it!"

"Look here, Lydia," Billy's voice was stern, "are you for or against Indian graft?"

Lydia drew a long breath but was spared an immediate answer for there was a knock on the door and Kent came in, followed shortly by Professor Willis.

"Well," said Kent, after Lydia had settled them all comfortably, "I just left Charlie Jackson — poor old prune!"

"Oh, how is he?" asked Lydia eagerly, "and what is he doing?"

"He's pretty seedy," answered Kent. "He's been trying to keep the whites off the reservation by organizing the full bloods to stand against the half-breeds. But after a year of trying he's given up hope. The full bloods are fatalists, you know, and Charlie has gone back to it himself."

"Charlie Jackson is an old schoolmate of ours." Lydia turned to Willis and gave him a rapid sketch of Charlie's life. The Harvard man was deeply interested.

"Can't you get him back to his work with the doctor?" he asked Kent.

Kent shook his head. "The only way to keep an Indian from reverting is to put him where he never can see his people or the reservation. Charlie's given up. He's drinking a little."

"And still you folks will keep on, stealing the reservation!" exclaimed Billy.

Kent gave Billy a grin, half irritated, half whimsical. "I know it's Sunday, old man, but don't let's have a sermon. You're a farmer, Bill, anyhow, no matter what else you try to be."

"Thank God for that," laughed Billy.

"My word!" ejaculated Willis. "What a country! You spout the classics on week days and on holidays you steal from the aborigines!"

"Oh, here, draw it mild, Professor!" growled Kent.

"Well, but it's true," exclaimed Lydia. "Where's our old New England sense of fairness?"

"That's good too," said Kent. "Who was brisker than our forefathers at killing redskins?"

"Altogether a different case," returned the Harvard man. "Our forefathers killed in self-defense. You folks are killing out of wanton greed."

"That's the point, exactly," said Billy.

Kent gave his cheerful grin. "Call it what you please," he laughed. "As long as the whites *will* have the land, I'm going to get my share."

Nobody spoke for a moment. Lydia looked from Billy to Kent, and back again. Kent was by far the handsomer of the two. He had kept the brilliant color and the charming glow in his eyes that had belonged to his boyhood. He dressed well, and sat now, knees crossed, hands clasped behind his head, with easy grace. Billy was a six-footer, larger than Kent and inclined to be raw-boned. His mouth was humorous and sensitive, his grey eyes were searching.

"Let's not talk about it," Lydia said. "Let's go out in the kitchen and pop corn and make candy." This with a little questioning glance at the professor of Shakespeare. He, however, rose with alacrity, and the rest of the afternoon passed without friction. Willis developed a positive passion for making popcorn balls and he left with Kent at dusk proudly bearing off a bag of the results of his labors.

Billy stayed after the rest and helped Lydia to clean up the dishes. Kent would never have thought of this, Lydia said to herself with a vague pang. When they had finished Billy gravely took Lydia's coat from the hook and said, "Come, woman, and walk in the gloaming with your humble servant."

Lydia giggled and obeyed. There was still snow, in the hollows but the road was clear and frozen hard. They walked briskly till a rise in the road gave them a view of the lake and a scarlet rift in the sky where the sun had sunk in a bank of clouds.

"Now, Lydia," said Billy, "answer my question. Are you for or against Indian graft?"

"I just won't take sides," announced Lydia, obstinately.

Billy stepped round in front of the young girl and put both hands gently on her shoulders. "Look at me, Lydia," he said. "You have to take sides! You can't escape it. You mean too much to too many of us men. You've got to take a perfectly clear stand on questions like this. It means too much to America for you not to. Your influence counts, in that way if in no other, don't you see."

Lydia's throat tightened. "I won't take sides against Mr. Levine," she repeated.

"Do you mean that you don't want me to expose Marshall?" asked Billy.

"You've no right to ask me that." Lydia's voice was cross.

"But I have. Lydia, though you don't want it, my life is yours. No matter whether we can ever be anything else, we are friends, aren't we, friends in the deepest sense of the word, — aren't we, Lydia?"

Lydia stared at Billy in silence. Perhaps it was the glow from the west that helped to deepen and soften his grey eyes, for there was nothing searching in them now. There was a depth and loyalty in them and a something besides that reminded her vaguely of the way John Levine looked at her. A crow cawed faintly from the woods and the wind fluttered Billy's hair.

Friendship! Something very warm and high and fine entered Lydia's heart.

"Yes, we are friends. Billy," she said slowly. "But oh, Billy, don't make me decide that!"

"Lydia, you must! You can't have a friend and not share his problems and you can't live in a community and not share its problems, if you're going to be worth anything to the world."

"But if the problems really meant anything to you," protested Lydia, "you wouldn't depend on some girl to shove you into them."

"But men do. They are built that way. Not *some* girl but *the girl.* Every great cause was fought for some woman! Oh, Lydia, Lydia!"

"Billy," Lydia looked away from him to the lake, "you'll have to let me think about it. You see, it's deciding my attitude toward all my friends, even toward Dad. And I hadn't intended ever to decide."

"And will you tell me, tomorrow, or next day, Lydia?"

"I'll tell you as soon as I decide," she answered.

Amos brought John Levine home with him for supper. It seemed to Lydia that Levine never had been dearer to her than he was that evening. After supper, they drew up around the base burner in the old way, while the two men smoked. Lizzie sat rocking and rubbing her rheumatism-racked old hands and Adam, who snored worse as he grew old, wheezed with his head baking under the stove. Levine did not talk of the Indians, to Lydia's relief, but of Washington politics. As the evening drew to a close, and Amos went out to his chickens as usual after Lizzie had gone to bed, John turned to Lydia.

"What are you reading, these days, young Lydia?"

"Browning – 'The Ring and the Book,'" replied Lydia.

John shook his head. "Really grown up, aren't you, Lydia? Do you enjoy being a young lady?"

"Yes, I do, only I miss the old days when I saw so much of you."

"Do you, my dear?" asked Levine, eagerly. "In what ways do you miss me?"

"Oh, every way! No one will ever understand me as you do."

"Oh, I don't know. There are Billy and Kent."

Lydia shook her head, though Billy's face in the moonlight after the graduation party, returned unexpectedly to her memory as she did so.

"There'll never be anyone like you." Then moved by a sudden impulse she leaned toward him and said, "No matter what happens, you will always know that I love you, won't you, Mr. Levine?"

John looked at the wistful face, keenly. "Why, what could happen, young Lydia?"

"Oh, lots of things! I'm grown up now and – and I have to make decisions about the rightness and the wrongness of things. But no matter what I decide, *nothing* can change my love for you."

"Lydia, come here," said Levine, abruptly.

In the old way, Lydia came to his side and he pulled her down to the arm of his chair. For a moment they sat in silence, his arm about her, her cheek against his hair, staring into the glowing stove.

"When you were just a little tot," said Levine at last, "you were full of gumption and did your own thinking. And I've been glad to see you keep the habit. Always make your own decisions, dear. Don't let me or anyone else decide matters of conscience for you. 'To thine own self be true and it must follow as the night the day, thou canst not then be false to any man.' Eh, little girl?"

He rose as he heard Amos coming in the back door, and with his hand under Lydia's chin, he looked long and earnestly into her eyes. Then as Billy had done earlier in the evening, he sighed, "Oh, Lydia! Lydia!" and turned away.

Chapter XV

THE INVESTIGATION BEGINS

"Nothing is so proud or so brave as the young pine when it first tops the rest of the forest."

— *The Murmuring Pine*

For several days Lydia was unhappy and absent-minded. At first, in her thoughts she was inclined to blame Billy for forcing this turmoil of mind on her. But, a little later, she admitted to herself that for years, something within her had been demanding that she take a stand on the Indian question something to which Charlie Jackson and Billy had appealed, something which Kent and John Levine had ignored. Yet neither Charlie nor Billy had really forced her to a decision.

Lydia was grown up. All her young life she had carried the responsibilities and had faced the home tragedies that come usually only to grown folk. Now, in her young womanhood it was natural and inevitable that she should turn to the larger responsibilities of the living world about her in order to satisfy the larger needs of her maturity.

Yet, still old affection fought with new clarity of vision. Old loyalty quarreled with new understanding. Bit by bit she went over her thinking life, beginning with her first recollection of Charlie Jackson in the class in Civil Government, and all that was feminine and blind devotion in her fought desperately with all that education and her civic-minded forefathers had given her.

Coming home from her last recitation, one mild afternoon, she stopped at the gate and looked up into the pine tree. Its scent carried her back to the cloistered wood on the reservation and once more the desire for the soil was on her. She leaned against the giant tree trunk and looked out over the lake, steel blue and cold in the March sunshine. And there with the lowing of the Norton herds and the hoarse call of the crows mingling with the soft voice of the pine and the lapping of the lake, she made her decision. For clearly as though the pine had put it into words, something said to Lydia that it was not her business to decide whether or not the Indians deserved to live. It was her business to recognize that in their method of killing the Indians, the whites had been utterly dishonorable. That her refusing to take a stand could not exonerate them. History would not fail to record the black fact against her race that, a free people, the boasted vanguard of human liberty, Americans had first made a race dependent, then by fraud and faithlessness, by cruelty and debauchery, were utterly destroying it. And finally, that by closing her eyes to the facts, because of her love for Levine, she was herself sharing the general taint.

It was Lydia's first acknowledgment of her responsibility to America, and it left her a little breathless and trembling. She turned back to the road and made her way swiftly to the Norton place. She did not go into the house, but down the lane where she could see Billy putting up the bars after the cattle. He waited for her, leaning against the rails.

"Billy," she said, panting, her cheeks bright and her yellow hair blowing, "I'm against the Indian grafting."

Billy put out his hand, solemnly, and the two shook hands. For all Billy was four years older than Lydia, they both were very, very young. So young that they believed that they could fight single-handed the whole world of intrigue and greed in which their little community was set. So young that they trembled and were filled with awe at the vast importance of their own dreams. And yet, futile as they may seem, it is on young decisions such as these that the race creeps upward!

"What are you going to do, Billy?" asked Lydia.

"I'm going to get a government investigation started, somehow," he replied. "It'll take time, but I'll get it."

Lydia looked at him admiringly, then she shivered a little. "I hate to think of it, but I'll stand by you, Billy, whatever you do."

"I'm going into ex-Senator Alvord's law office this June. I'll bet he'll help. He's so sore at Levine. It'll be lovely muckraking, Lyd!"

"I hate to think of it," she said unsteadily. "Lizzie is miserable, today. Will you tell your mother, Billy, and ask her to come over to see her this evening? I mustn't stop any longer now."

Poor old Lizzie was miserable, indeed. For years, she had struggled against rheumatism, but now it had bound her, hand and foot. Ma Norton came over in the evening. Lizzie was in bed shivering and flushed and moaning with pain.

"Now, don't bother about me," she insisted. "Lydia's threatening to stay home tomorrow, and I tell you I won't have it," and the poor old soul began to cry weakly.

Ma pulled the covers over the shaking shoulders. "If I were you, Lizzie, I'd think about getting well and let Lydia do what she thinks best. A day or so out of school isn't going to count in the long run with a young thing like her."

She waited till Lizzie slept, then she told Lydia and Amos that Dr. Fulton had better be called, and Amos with a worried air, started for town at once.

Dr. Fulton shook his head and sighed.

"She's in for a run of rheumatic fever. Get some extra hot water bottles and make up your mind for a long siege, Lydia."

And it was a long siege. Six weeks of agony for Lizzie, of nursing and housework and worrying for Lydia. Ma Norton and the neighbors gave what time they could, but the brunt, of course, fell on Lydia. She fretted most about her college work. Sitting by Lizzie's bed, when the old lady dozed in her brief respites from pain, she tried to carry on her lessons alone, but with indifferent success. She was too tired to concentrate her mind. Trigonometry rapidly became a hopeless tangle to her; Ancient History a stupid jumble of unrelated dates. And most of all, as the days went by, she felt the indifference of University folk. Nobody cared that she had dropped out, it seemed to her.

Billy called every evening on his way home to supper. He filled water buckets, chopped wood and fed the chickens, that Amos might be free to take Lydia's place. John Levine sat up two or three nights a week. Kent came out once a week, with a cheery word and a basket of fruit. And at frequent intervals, the Marshall surrey stopped at the gate and

Elviry or Dave appeared with some of Elviry's delicious cookery for Lydia and Amos.

One afternoon in April when Lizzie had at last taken a turn for the better, Lydia elected to clean the kitchen floor. She was down on her hands and knees scrubbing when there came a soft tap on the open door. She looked up. Professor Willis was standing on the steps.

"Goodness!" exclaimed Lydia, rising with burning cheeks.

"I — I couldn't make anyone hear at the front door. I came to see why you didn't come to class."

Lydia was wearing a faded and outgrown blue gingham. Her face was flushed but there were black rings round her eyes, and she was too tired to be polite.

"I think it's just awful for you to come on me, scrubbing floors! You should have knocked at the front door, till I heard," she said, crossly.

The Harvard man looked at her seriously. "I really never saw a girl playing golf look as pretty as you do, scrubbing floors. May I come in?"

He did not wait for an invitation but stepped over the pail and brush to the chair beside the table. An open book lay on the chair. He picked it up. "'Ancient Rome,'" he read.

"I'm trying to keep up." Lydia was drying her red hands on the roller towel. Her shoulders drooped despondently. "What's the use of trying to be a lady," she said, suddenly, "when you have to fight poverty like this! You oughtn't to have come on me this way!"

The Harvard man looked from the immaculate kitchen to the slender girl, with her fine head, and then at the book in his hand.

"Of course, I've never known a girl like you. But I should imagine that eventually you'll achieve something finer out of your poverty than the other girls at the University will out of their golf and tennis. I don't fancy that our New England mothers were ashamed of scrubbing floors."

He looked at her with a smile on his pale face. Suddenly Lydia smiled in return. "Sit down while I make us some tea," she said. "I'll never try to play lady with you again."

Willis stayed with her an hour, sitting in the kitchen where the open door showed the turquoise lake through a grey-green net of swelling tree buds. He did not leave till Lizzie wakened. He cleared up the tangle in Lydia's trigonometry for her and went over the lost lessons in Shakespeare, all the while with a vague lump in his throat over the wistful eagerness in the blue eyes opposite his, over the thin, red, water-soaked hands that turned the leaves of the books.

When Billy called that evening he found Lydia more cheerful than she had been in weeks. When she told him of her caller he looked at her thoughtfully and growled, "I hope he chokes," and not another word did he say while he finished Amos' chores.

Professor Willis came out regularly after this and when Lydia returned to class work in May, she was able to work creditably through the reviews then taking place and in June to pass the examinations.

During all this time she said nothing to Billy about his muckraking campaign. In spite of her high resolves she half hoped he had given it up. But she did not know Billy as well as she thought she did. He finished his law course in June and entered ex-Senator Alvord's office as he had planned. There was another election in the fall and John Levine was returned to Congress, this time almost without a struggle. So many of the voters of the community were profiting by the alienating of the mixed-blood pines that it would have been blatant hypocrisy on the part of Republicans as well as Democrats to have opposed him. In fact, thanks to Levine, the town had entered on a period of unprecedented prosperity. The college itself had purchased for a song a section of land to be used as an agricultural experiment station.

Like a bomb, then, late in December fell the news that the Indian Commissioner had been called before a senate committee to answer questions regarding the relations of Lake City to the reservation. While following close on the heels of this announcement came word that a congressional commission of three had been appointed to sit at Lake City to investigate Indian matters.

"Billy, how did you do it?" asked Lydia, in consternation. He had overtaken her one bitter cold January afternoon, on her way home from college.

"I didn't do much," said Billy. "I just got affidavits, dozens of them, showing frauds, and gave them to Senator Alvord. He has a lot of influence among the Democratic senators and is a personal friend of the President. It was a wonderful chance, he saw, to hurt the Republicans, even though there were Democrats implicated. The Indian Commissioner and Levine are both Republicans, you know. Then, when he finally got the hearing before the Senate Committee, he smuggled Charlie Jackson and Susie and old Chief Wolf down there. Nobody here knows that."

Lydia's lips were set tightly as she plodded along the snowy road.

"Billy," she said, finally, "are you doing this to get even with Dave Marshall?"

"Lydia!" cried Billy, catching her arm and forcing her to stop and face him. "Don't you know me better than that? Don't you?"

"Then why are you doing it?" demanded Lydia.

"I'm doing it because I'm ashamed of what New Englanders have done with their heritage. And I'm doing it for you. To make a name for you. Look at me. No, not at the lake, into my eyes. You are going to marry me, some day, Lydia."

"I'm not," said Lydia flatly.

Billy laughed. "You can't help yourself, honey. It's fate for both of us. Come along home! You're shivering."

"When you talk that way, I hate you!" exclaimed Lydia, but Billy only laughed again.

Amos at first was furious when he heard of the investigation. He, with everyone else in town, was eager to know who had started the trouble.

"Some sorehead," said Amos, "who couldn't get all the land he wanted, I'll bet. And a sweet time the commission will have. Why, they'll have to dig into the private history of everyone in Lake City. It'll ruin Levine! Oh, pshaw! No, it won't either! He can get everything white-washed. That's the way American investigations always end!"

But Levine could not get everything whitewashed. The group of three commissioners sat for months and in that time they exposed to the burning sun of publicity the muck of thievery and dishonor on which Lake City's placid beauty was built.

By some strange turn of fortune, Congress had chosen three honest men for this unsavory task, three men grimly and unswervingly determined to see the matter through. They sat in rooms in the post office building. In and out of the building day after day passed the Indians to face the sullen and unwilling whites summoned to hear and answer what these Indians had to say of them. Charlie Jackson acted as interpreter. Lydia saw him once or twice on the street when he nodded coolly. He had dropped his white associates completely.

The local papers refused to report the commission's session. But papers outside the State were voracious for the news and little by little tales were published to the world that made Lake City citizens when out of the city, hesitate to confess the name of their home town.

The leading trustee of the Methodist Church was found to have married a squaw in order to get her pine and her pitiful Government allowance. His white wife and children left him when this was proved to them, and it was proved only when the starving squaw and her starving children were finally acknowledged by the trustee before the commission.

The Methodists were held up to scorn for a few months until a prominent Presbyterian who was the leading grocer in town was found to have supplied the Indian Agent for years with tainted groceries for the Indians.

The most popular dentist in town filled teeth for the Indians whenever they received their allowances. His method of filling was simple. He drove empty copper cartridge caps over the teeth. These when burnished made a handsome showing until gangrene set in. The afflicted Indians were then turned over to a popular young doctor of Lake City who took the next year's allowance from the bewildered patients.

Marriage after marriage of squaws with Lake City citizens was unearthed, most of these same citizens also having a white family. Hundreds of tracts of lands that had been obtained by stealing or by fraud from full bloods were listed. Bags of candy, bits of jewelry, bolts of cotton had been exchanged for pine worth thousands of dollars.

It was a nerve-racking period for Lake City. Whether purposely or not, the net did not begin to close round John Levine till toward the end of the hearing. Nor did Levine come home until late in the summer, when the commission had been sitting for some months.

In spite of a sense of apprehension that would not lift, the year was a happy one for Lydia. In the first place, she went to three college dancing parties during the year. The adaptability of the graduation gown was wonderful and although Lydia knew that she was only a little frump compared with the other girls, Billy, who took her each time, always wore the *dress suit!* So she shone happily in reflected elegance.

In the second place, three men called on her regularly — Billy, Kent and Professor Willis.

In the third place, Kent asked her to go with him to the last party and, to Lydia's mind, a notable conversation took place at that time.

"Thanks, Kent," said Lydia, carelessly, "but I'm going with Billy."

"Billy! Always Billy!" snorted Kent. "Why, you and I were friends before we ever heard of Billy!"

"Yes," returned Lydia calmly, "and in all these years this is the first time you've asked me to go to a party. I've often wondered why."

Kent moved uncomfortably. "Pshaw, Lyd, you know I always went with some girl I was having a crush on — that was why."

"And don't you ever ask a girl to go to a party unless you have a crush on her?" asked Lydia, mischievously.

Kent gave her a clear look. "No!" he replied.

Lydia flushed, then she said, slowly, "That's only half true, Kent. You've always liked me as I have you. But you've always been ashamed of my clothes. I don't blame you a bit, but you can imagine how I feel about Billy, who's taken me, clothes or no clothes."

It was Kent's turn to flush and he did so to such an extent that Lydia was sorry for him while she waited for him to answer.

"Hang it, Lyd, I've been an infernal cad, that's all!"

"And," Lydia went on, mercilessly, "I've got nothing to wear now but the same old graduating dress. I suppose you were hoping for better things?"

"Stop it!" Kent shouted. "I deserve it, but I'm not going to take it. I'm asking you for just one reason and that is, I've waked up to the fact that you're the finest girl in the world. No one can hold a candle to you."

There was a sudden lilt in Lydia's voice that did not escape Kent as she answered laughingly, "Well, if you feel the same after seeing Margery this summer, I'll be glad to go to one of the hops next fall with you, and thank you, deeply, Mr. Moulton."

"All right," said Kent, soberly. "The first hop next fall is mine and as many more as I can get."

It was late in the spring and after the conversation with Kent, that it began to be rumored about town that ex-Senator Alvord's office was at the bottom of the Indian investigation. Billy had been called in to testify and had shown an uncanny amount of knowledge of fraudulent land deals and Alvord had corroborated many of his statements.

Kent accused Billy of this openly, one Sunday afternoon at Lydia's. They were sitting on the lake shore, for the day was parching hot. Both the young men were in flannels and hatless, and lolled on the grass at Lydia's feet, as she sat with her back against a tree. She noticed how Kent was all grace, and ease, while Billy, whose face had lately become thinner, was all gaunt angles.

"I'm willing to take the blame, if necessary," said Billy.

Kent sat up with sudden energy. "Look here, if it once got round town that you're the father of this, you'll be run out of Lake City."

Billy laughed. "Oh, no I won't! All you respectable citizens have got too many troubles of your own."

"Nice thing to do to your friends and neighbors, Bill," Kent went on, excitement growing in his voice as he realized the import of Billy's acknowledgment. "What the deuce did you do it for?"

Billy shrugged his shoulders and said nothing. Kent appealed to Lydia. "Would you have gone to parties with him if you'd known what he was doing to his town, Lyd?"

Billy was still lying on both elbows, industriously herding a pair of ants. He did not look up at Lydia as she stared at his massive blond head.

"Kent, I knew it," said Lydia, after a pause.

"You knew it! You let a lot of sickly sentimentality ruin Lake City in the eyes of the world? Not only that. Think what's coming to John Levine! Think what's coming to me, though I've done little enough!"

"Then I'm glad it came to stop you; while you'd still done little!" cried Lydia.

"Nonsense!" snapped Kent. "Of course, you don't expect anything but gush from a girl about the Indians. But I don't see what you get out of it, Bill. Who's paying you? Are you going to run for president on the purity ticket?"

"There's no use in my trying to tell you why I did it," grunted Billy.

"No, there isn't," agreed Kent. "But I'll tell you this much. Bill, you and I break right here and now. I've no use for a sneak."

Again Billy shrugged his shoulders. Lydia looked at the two in despair, then she smiled and cried, "Oh, there's Margery! Isn't she lovely!"

It was Margery, just home from boarding-school, where she gaily announced as she shook hands she had been "finally finished."

"Though," she added. "Daddy wants to pack me right off again because of this silly investigation. As if I wanted to miss the fun of viewing all our best family skeletons!"

"Margery," cried Lydia, quickly, "you're so beautiful that you're simply above envy. What a duck of a dress!"

"Isn't it!" agreed Margery. "Kent, do get me a chair. I'll spoil all my ruffles on the grass. Well! Here I am! And what were you all discussing so solemnly when I interrupted?"

"Indian graft!" said Billy, laconically.

"Isn't it awful! And isn't it funny! You know, I was actually proud that I lived in Lake City. The girls used to point me out in school to visitors."

Margery, exquisite in her dainty gown, her wonderful black eyes gleaming with fun, as a sample of Lake City dishonesty appealed to the sense of humor of her audience and they all laughed, though Lydia felt her throat tighten strangely as she did so, — Margery, made exquisite on the money of blind squaws and papooses that froze to death!

"Daddy is all worked up, though I told him they certainly hadn't done anything much to him, so far, and I'd feel real neglected if they didn't find he had an Indian wife up his sleeve," Margery went on. "Oh, Billy, by the way. Daddy says he thinks Senator Alvord started the whole thing. Did he?"

"Yes, and I helped," replied Billy shortly.

"Well, I think you ought to be ashamed of yourself," cried Margery, airily. "Don't you, Lydia?"

"No, I don't, I'm proud of him, though I'm scared to death," said Lydia. "Things are so much worse than I thought they'd be."

"Well, I just tell you, Billy Norton," there was a sudden shrill note in Margery's voice, "if anything really horrid is unearthed about Daddy, I'll never speak to you again. Would you, Kent?"

"I don't intend to anyhow," replied Kent, coolly. "How'd you come out, Marg?"

"I walked from the trolley. I'd no idea it was so hot."

"Let me take you home in my toot-toot."

"But I just got here," protested Margery.

"It's now or never," said Kent, rising, "I've got to run along."

"Oh, if it's that serious!" Margery took Kent's arm. "By-by, Lydia! Come over and see my new dresses."

After they were gone, Billy sat up and looked at Lydia. Neither spoke for a few moments. The sun was sinking and all the world was enveloped in a crimson dust. There had been a drought now for six weeks. Even Amos' garden was languishing.

"Lydia," said Billy, "I'm going to quit. You know I've worked with Charlie Jackson right along."

"Quit? But Billy, why I — I didn't think you minded Kent and Margery that much!"

"I don't mind them at all. But, Lydia, I found yesterday my father got one hundred and twenty acres from a ten-year-old full-blood boy for five dollars and a bicycle. Last week Charlie unearthed a full-blood squaw from whom your father had gotten two hundred and forty acres for an old sewing machine and twenty-five dollars. I've done so much for the Indians and Charlie is so fond of you that he'll shut these Indians up, but I can't go on, after that, of course."

Lydia was motionless. Over the house top, the great branches of the pine were turned to flames. The long drawn notes of a locust sounded above the steady drone of the crickets. Lydia had a curiously old feeling.

"I can't go on, Lydia," Billy repeated. "My fine old father and dear old Amos! I can't."

"Yes, you'll go on, Billy," Lydia's voice was very low. "After I faced what would come to John Levine through this, I can face anything."

Billy gave a little groan and bowed his head on Lydia's knee. Suddenly she felt years older than Billy. She smoothed his tumbled blond hair.

"Go on, Billy. Our ancestors left England for conscience' sake. And our grandfathers both laid down their lives for the Union."

Lydia ended with a little gulp of embarrassment. Billy caught her hand and sat up, looking eagerly through the gloaming at her face.

"I told you all the battles of the world were fought for a woman," he said. "Dear, I'll go on, though it'll break mother's heart."

"It won't break her heart," said Lydia. "Women's hearts don't break over that sort of thing."

"Lydia!" called Amos from the doorway, "aren't you going to give me any supper tonight?"

"Lord, it's two hours past milking time!" groaned Billy, and he started on a dog-trot for home.

Chapter XVI

DUCIT AMOR PATRIAE

"The same soil that nourishes the Indian and the white, nourishes me. Yet they do not know that thus we are blood brothers."
— *The Murmuring Pine*

*I*t was the last week in August when John Levine was summoned before the commission. Lydia and Amos were summoned with him.

Lydia was frightened, Amos was irritable and sullen by turns after the summons finally came. They were due at the hearing at nine o'clock and arrived a little late. Amos had refused to be hurried.

The room in which the hearing was held was big and cool, with a heavily carpeted floor and walls lined with black walnut bookcases. There were two long tables at one end of the room behind one of which sat the three commissioners. At the other table were the official stenographers and Charlie Jackson. Before the tables were chairs and here were John Levine and Kent, Pa Norton, and Billy, old Susie and a younger squaw, with several bucks.

Lydia and her father dropped into empty seats and Lydia gave a little sigh of relief when Levine caught her eye across the room and smiled at her. She looked at the commissioners curiously. They were talking in undertones to one another and she thought that they all looked tired and harassed. She knew them fairly well from the many newspaper pictures she had seen of them. The fat gentleman, with penetrating blue eyes and a clean-shaven face, was Senator Smith of Texas. The roly-poly man, with black eyes and a grizzled beard, was Senator Elway of Maine, and the tall, smooth-shaven man with red hair was Senator James of New York.

"Mr. Levine," said Senator Smith, suddenly, "we are sorry to have to put you to this inconvenience. Believe us, we find our task no more savory than you do."

Levine gave his slow, sardonic grin. "Don't apologize, gentlemen. Only make the ordeal as short as you can."

"We have done that," said Elway. "We found that you had carried on so many — er — transactions that we finally decided to choose three or four sample cases and let our case stand on those. First, we have found that full bloods have been repeatedly sworn as mixed bloods, in order that their lands might be alienated. A curious idea, Mr. Levine, to attempt to legalize an illegality by false swearing. Jackson, call Crippled Bear."

Charlie, who had been sitting with arms folded, his somber eyes on Lydia, spoke quickly to one of the bucks, who rose and took the empty chair by Charlie.

He began to talk at once, Charlie interpreting slowly and carefully.

"I am a mixed blood. I speak English pretty well when I am with only one white. With so many, my English goes. Many moons ago the man Levine found me drunk in the snow. He picked me up and kept me in his house over night. When I was sober, he fed me. Then he made this plan. I was to gather half a dozen half-breeds together, he could trust. In the spring he would come up to the reservation and talk to us. I did this and he came. We were very hungry when he met us in the woods and he gave us food and money. Then he told us he was going to get the big fathers at Washington to let us sell our pines so we could always have money and food. Never be hungry anymore — never."

Charlie's voice was husky as he said this and he looked at Levine with his teeth bared, like a wolf, Lydia thought.

"Then he said while he was getting that done, he would pay us a little every month to go through the woods and chop down the best trees. The Big Father will let whites get 'dead and down' timber out of Indian woods, he said. But not let whites cut any. So we say yes, and though full bloods are very mad when we cut down big trees, we do it. For many moons we do it and in winter, white men haul it to sawmills.

"Every little while, Levine comes up there and we have a council and tell him everything that happens. All about things Marshall and other whites do. And he pays us always. Then he tells us that the Big Father will let mixed bloods sell their pine lands but not full bloods. So then we agree when he wants any full blood land to swear that any full blood is mixed. And we have done this now, perhaps twenty times."

The mixed blood and Charlie paused, and Levine leaned forward. "Crippled Bear," he said, "why did you tell all this?"

Crippled Bear Jerked a swarthy thumb at Billy Norton. "That white," he answered in English, "tell me if I tell truth, maybe I get back all lands and pine. I like that, you un'stand — for then I sell 'em again, un'stand."

A little ripple of laughter went through the room, though John himself did not smile. He looked at young Norton with his black eyes half closed.

Mr. Smith took up a paper. "I have here, Mr. Levine, a statement of your dealings with the Lake City Lumber Company. You have had sawed by them during the past six or eight years millions of feet of pine lumber. I find that you are holding Indian lands in the name of Lydia Dudley and her father, Amos Dudley, these lands legally belonging to full bloods. Amos Dudley is also the purchaser of land from full bloods, as is William Norton, Senior, through you."

Levine rose quickly. "Gentlemen," he exclaimed, "surely you can find enough counts against me without including Miss Dudley, who has never heard of the matters you mention."

Commissioner James spoke for the first time. "Suppose we go on with the witnesses before we open any discussion with Mr. Levine. Jackson, what have these squaws to tell? Or first, what about the other bucks?"

When Charlie had called the last of these Levine spoke, "I'd like to call the Government Roll-maker, Mr. Hardy."

A small man, who had slipped into the room unnoticed during the proceedings, came forward.

"What is your business, Mr. Hardy?" asked Levine.

"I am sent here by the Indian office to make a Roll of the Indians on this reservation, in the attempt to discover which are full and which mixed bloods."

"Do you find your task difficult, Mr. Hardy?" Levine's voice was whimsical.

"Very! The Government allows a man to claim his Indian rights when he has as little as one sixty-fourth of Indian blood in his veins. On the other hand, the older Indians are deadly ashamed of white blood in their veins and hate to admit it."

"Mr. Hardy, you have your Rolls with you? Yes? Well, tell me the blood status of each of these witnesses."

The room was breathless while the little Roll-maker ran through his list. According to this not one of the witnesses against Levine was a full blood nor one of the Indians from whom he had taken land. Even old Susie and Charlie's sister, he stated, had white blood in their veins.

"It's a lie!" shouted Charlie. "This man Hardy is paid by Levine!"

"Gently, Jackson!" said Senator James. "Mr. Levine, do you wish to call more witnesses?"

"Not for the present," replied John. "Let Jackson go on."

Charlie called old Susie. And old Susie, waving aside any attempts on Charlie's part to help, told of the death of her daughter from starvation and cold, this same daughter having sold her pines to Levine for a five-dollar bill and a dollar watch. She held out the watch toward Levine in one trembling old hand.

"I find this in dress, when she dead. She strong. It take her many days to die. I old. I pray Great Spirit take me. No! I starve! I freeze! I no can die. She young. She have little baby. She die."

Suddenly, she flung the watch at Levine's feet and sank trembling into her chair.

There was silence for a moment. In at the open window came the rumble of a street-car. Levine cleared his throat.

"All this is dramatic, of course, but doesn't make me the murderer of the squaw."

"No! but you killed my father!" shouted Charlie Jackson. And rising, he hurled forth the story he had told Lydia, years before. Lydia sat with her hands clasped tightly in her lap, her eyes fastened in horror on Charlie's face. A great actor had been lost in creating Charlie an Indian. He pictured his father's death, his sister's two attempts at revenge with a vividness and power that held even Levine spellbound. It seemed to Lydia that the noose was fastened closer round John's neck with every word that was uttered.

Suddenly she sprang to her feet. "Stop, Charlie! Stop!" she screamed. "You shan't say anymore!"

Senator Elway rapped on the table. "You're out of order, Miss Dudley," he exclaimed, sharply.

Lydia had forgotten to be embarrassed. "I can't help it if I am," she insisted, "I won't have Charlie Jackson picturing Mr. Levine as a fiend, while I have a tongue to speak with. I know how bad the Indian matters are. Nobody's worried about it more than I have. But Mr. Levine's not a murderer. He couldn't be."

The three commissioners had looked up at Lydia with a scowl when she had interrupted Charlie. Now the scowl, as they watched her flushed face, gave way to arched eyebrows and a little smile, that was reflected on every face in the room except Charlie Jackson's.

"Lydia, you keep out of this," he shouted. "You don't know what you're talking about."

"I do too!" stormed Lydia. "I —"

"Order! Let Jackson finish, Miss Dudley," said Senator Smith.

"I can't let him finish," cried Lydia, "until I tell you about Mr. Levine. He's been as much to me as my own father ever since my mother died when I was a little girl. He's understood me as only my own mother could, hasn't he, Daddy!"

Amos nodded, with a little apologetic glance at the commissioners. Levine's eyes were fastened on Lydia's face with an expression that was as sweet as it was fathomless. Charlie Jackson stood biting his nails and waiting, his affection for Lydia holding in abeyance his frenzied loyalty to his father.

"You think he could murder when he could hold a little girl on his knees and comfort her for the death of her little sister, when he taught her how to find God, when — oh, I know he's robbed the Indians — so has my own father, it seems, and so has Pa Norton, and so has Kent, and all of them are dear people. They've all been wrong. But think of the temptation, Mr. Commissioner! Supposing you were poor and the wonderful pines lay up there, *so easy to take.*"

Senator Elway would have interrupted, but Senator James laid a hand on his arm. "It's all informal, let her have her say," he whispered. "It's the first bright spot in all the weeks of the hearing."

"Did you ever feel land hunger yourself," Lydia went on eagerly, "to look at the rows and rows of pine and think what it would mean to own them, forever! It's the queerest, strongest hunger in the world. I know, because I've had it. Honestly, I have, as strongly as anyone here — only — I knew Charlie Jackson and this awful tragedy of his and I knew his eyes would haunt me if I took Indian lands."

"You're covering a good deal of ground and getting away from the specific case, Miss Dudley," said, Smith. "Of course, what you say doesn't exonerate Mr. Levine. On the other hand, Jackson has no means of proving him accessory to the murder of his father. We've threshed that out with Jackson before. What you say of Mr. Levine's character is interesting but there remains the fact that he has been proceeding fraudulently for years in his relations to the Indian lands. You yourself don't pretend to justify your acts, do you, Mr. Levine?"

Lydia sat down and Levine slowly rose and looked thoughtfully out of the window. "The legality or illegality of the matter has nothing to do with the broader ethics of the case, though I think you will find, gentlemen, that my acts are protected by law," he said. "The virgin land lies there, inhabited by a degenerate race, whose one hope of salvation lay in amalgamation with the white race. An ignorant government, when land was plenty and the tribe was larger, placed certain restrictions on the reservation. When land became scarce, and the tribe dwindled to a handful, those restrictions became wrong. It was inevitable that the whites should override them. Knowing that the ethics of my acts and those of other people would be questioned, I went to Congress to get these restrictions removed. If another two years could have elapsed, before these investigations had been begun, the fair name of Lake City never would have been smirched." Levine's hand on the back of his chair tightened as he looked directly at Billy Norton.

Once more Lydia came to her feet. "Oh, Mr. Levine," she exclaimed, "don't put all the blame on Billy! Really, it's my fault. He wouldn't have done it if I hadn't agreed that it was right. And he would have stopped when he found that Dad and his father had taken full blood lands only — why — why, I said that if I could stand his showing that you had been — crooked — up there, I could stand anything and I made him go on."

She stopped with a little break in her voice that was not unlike a sob. And for the first time there spread over John Levine's face a blush, so dark, so agonizing, that the men about him turned their eyes away. With a little groan, he sat down. Lydia clasped her hands.

"Oh, it is all my fault," she repeated brokenly, "all the trouble that's come to Lake City."

Billy Norton jumped up. "That's blamed nonsense!" he began, when Smith interrupted him, impatiently.

"Be seated, Norton." Then, gently, to Lydia, "My dear, you mean that, knowing what an investigation would mean to the people you love, you backed young Norton in instigating one. That you knew he would not go on without your backing?"

"Yes, sir," faltered Lydia.

"Can you tell us why?" asked Elway, still more gently.

Lydia, whose cheeks were burning and whose eyes were deep with unshed tears, twisted her hands uncomfortably and looked at Billy.

"Go ahead, Lyd," he said, reassuringly.

"Because it was right," she said, finally. "Because — Ducit Amor Patriae — -you know, because no matter whether the Indians were good or bad, we had made promises to them and they depended on us." She paused, struggling for words.

"I did it because I felt responsible to the country like my ancestors did, in the Civil War and in the Revolution, to — to take care of America, to keep it clean, no matter how it hurt. I — I couldn't be led by love of country and see my people doing something contemptible, something that the world would remember against us forever, and not try to stop it, no matter how it hurt."

Trembling so that the ribbon at her throat quivered, she looked at the three commissioners, and sat down.

James cleared his throat. "Mr. Dudley, did you know your daughter's attitude when you undertook to get some pine lands?"

Amos pulled himself to his feet. His first anger at Lydia had given way to a mixture of feelings. Now, he swallowed once or twice and answered, "Of course, I knew she was sympathetic with the Indians, but I don't know anything about the rest of it."

The commissioners waited as though expecting Amos to go on. He fumbled with his watch chain for a moment, staring out the window. With his thin face, his high forehead and sparse hair, he never looked more like the picture of Daniel Webster than now.

"Gentlemen," he said, "I'm a New Englander and I'm frank to admit that I've wandered a long way from the old ideals, like most of the New Englanders in America. But that isn't saying, gentlemen, that I'm not — not darned proud of Lydia!"

There was a little murmur through the room and Senator Elway smiled, a trifle sadly. "Mr. Dudley," he said, "we're all proud of Lydia. She's made our unsavory task seem better worth while."

"I suggest that we adjourn for lunch," said Smith. "Miss Dudley, you need not return."

While her father paused to speak to Kent and Levine, Lydia made her escape. She wanted more than anything in the world to be alone, but when she reached home, Ma Norton and Lizzie were waiting at the cottage, both of them half sick with anxiety. They were not reassured by Lydia's story of the morning session, although Ma said,

"Of course, it's the disgrace of the thing that worries us. Pa and Billy say all this commission can do is to present their evidence to Congress. I'm not saying, of course, that you weren't right plucky to take the stand you did, Lydia. And I'm proud of Billy though he is bringing trouble on his poor father!"

Lydia spent the afternoon with Adam in the woods. She expected John Levine to come home with her father to supper, and for the first time in her life, she did not want to meet her best loved friend. But she might have spared herself this anxiety, for Amos came home alone. Levine was busy, he said.

Amos was in a curiously subdued mood. Whatever Lydia had expected of him, she had not expected the almost conciliatory attitude he took toward her. It embarrassed her far more than recriminations would have.

"I do think, Lydia," he said mildly, after they had discussed the morning session, "you should have told me what was going on. But there, I suppose, I'd have raised Cain, if you had."

"Is Mr. Levine very angry with me?" asked Lydia.

"He didn't say. I don't see how he can be. After all, the stuff was bound to come out, sooner or later. He's got something up his sleeve. This experience's done one thing. It's brought all the different factions together. Disgrace loves company as well as misery."

"I'm so worried about it all!" sighed Lydia.

"Kind of late in the day for you to worry," sniffed Amos. "I suppose Billy's worrying too! But there, I guess you two have put some saving grace into Lake City, in the commission's eyes. Of course, I'm going to give up any claim on those lands."

Amos pulled at his pipe thoughtfully and looked at Lydia's tired, wistful face complacently. He did not tell her that the three commissioners had individually and collectively congratulated him on Lydia and their praise had been such that he felt that any disgrace he had suffered in connection with the Indian lands had been more than counteracted by Lydia's performance.

To Lydia's pain and disappointment, Levine did not come to the cottage before he returned to Washington, which he did the week following the hearing. And then, all thought of her status with him was swallowed up in astonishment over the revelations that came out early in September when Dave Marshall and the Indian Agent were called before the commission.

Dave Marshall was the owner of the Last Chance! The Last Chance where "hussies" lay in wait like vultures for the Indian youths, took their government allowances, took their ancient Indian decency, and cast them forth to pollute their tribe with drink and disease. The Last Chance! The headquarters for the illegal selling of whisky to Indians. Where Indians were taught to evade the law, to carry whisky into the reservation and where in turn the bounty for their arrest was pledged to Marshall. The Last Chance, the main source of Dave Marshall's wealth!

Even Lake City was horrified by these revelations. People began to remove their money from his bank and for a time a run was threatened, then Dave resigned as president and the run was stayed. The drugstore owned by Dave was boycotted. The women of the town began to cut

Margery and Elviry. The minister of the Methodist Church asked Dave for his resignation as Trustee.

To say that old Lizzie was pleased by the revelations would be perhaps to do the old lady an injustice. Yet the fact remains that she did go about with a knowing, "I told you so" air, that smacked of complacency.

"He always was just *skulch*," she insisted to Lydia. "When he was a child, he was the kind of a brat mothers didn't want their children to play with. I always prayed he'd get his come-uppers, and Elviry too. But I am sorry for Margery. Poor young one! Her future's ruined."

Lydia, sitting on the front steps in the lovely September afternoons, rubbed Adam's ears, watched the pine and the Norton herds and thought some long, long thoughts. Finally, one hazy Saturday afternoon, she gathered a great bunch of many colored asters and started off, without telling Lizzie of her destination.

It was nearly five o'clock when she stopped at the Marshalls' gate. The front of the house was closed, but nothing daunted, she made her way round to the kitchen door, which was open. Elviry answered her rap.

"Oh, it's Lydia," she said, brusquely. "What do you want?"

"I brought Marg some flowers," answered Lydia, awkwardly.

Elviry hesitated. "Margery's been having a headache and I don't know as she'd want to see you."

Lydia was not entirely daunted. "Well, if you're getting supper you might let me come and sit in the kitchen a few minutes. It's quite a walk in from the cottage."

Elviry opened the screen door and Lydia marched in and paused. Dave Marshall was sitting by the kitchen table, his hat on the back of his head, a pile of newspapers on the floor beside him. He did not speak to Lydia when she came in, but Lydia nodded brightly at him and said, "You like to sit in the kitchen, the way Dad does, don't you?"

She sat down in the rocker by the dining room door and Elviry began to stir a kettle of catsup that was simmering on the back of the stove.

This was worse than Lydia had thought it would be. She had not calculated on Dave's being at home. However, her fighting blood was up.

"You haven't asked me about my clothes, Mrs. Marshall," she said. "Don't you think I did pretty well with this skirt?"

Elviry glanced at the blue serge skirt. "It'll do," she answered listlessly.

Lydia looked at Dave desperately. At that moment there was a light step in the dining room, and Margery came into the kitchen. When she saw Lydia she gasped.

"Hadn't you heard? Oh, Lydia! You came anyhow!" and suddenly Margery threw herself down and sobbed with her face in Lydia's lap.

Elviry threw her apron over her head and Dave, with a groan, dropped his head on his chest. For a moment, there was only the crackling of the fire in the stove and Margery's sobs to be heard.

Then Dave said, "What did you come for, Lydia? You only hurt yourself and you can't help us. I don't know what to do! God! I don't know what to do!"

"I don't see why everybody acts so," cried Elviry, "as if what you'd done was any worse than everyone else's doings."

Margery raised her head. "Of course it's worse! A thousand times worse! I could have stood Dad's even having an Indian wife, better than this."

Dave looked at Margery helplessly and his chin quivered. Lydia noticed then how old he was looking.

"I want Margery and her mother to pack up and go away — for good," said Dave to Lydia. "I'll close up here and follow when I can. None of these cases will ever come to anything in our state court. It's the disgrace — and the way the women folks take it."

"I — I've been thinking," said Lydia, timidly, "that what you ought to do —"

Margery was sitting back on the floor now and she interrupted bitterly. "I don't see why you should try to help us, Lyd. Mother's always treated you dirt mean."

"It's not because of your mother," said Lydia, honestly. "I couldn't even try to forgive her — but — your father did a great favor to me and once I promised him then to be his friend. And you, Margery, you were fond of — of little Patience, and she did love you so! If she'd lived, I know she'd have wanted me to stand by you."

"She was a dear little kiddie," said Margery. "I always meant to tell you how I cried when she died, and then somehow, you were so silent, I couldn't."

The old lines round Lydia's mouth deepened for a minute, then she swallowed and said,

"I don't think it would do a bit of good for you all to go away. The story would follow you. Mr. Marshall ought to sell out everything and buy a farm. Let Mrs. Marshall go off for a visit, if she wants to, and let Margery come and stay with me a while and go to college."

Dave raised his head. "That's what I'd rather do, Lydia, for myself. Just stay here and try to live it down. I'd like to farm it. Always intended to."

Margery wrung her hands. "Oh, I don't see how I can! If it had been anything, anything but the Last Chance. Everybody will cut me and talk about me."

"Oh, well, Margery," said Lydia, a little impatiently, "it's the first trouble you've had in all your life and it won't kill you. Anybody that's as pretty as you are can live down anything. I know our house is awful scrimpy, but we'd have some good times, anyhow. Kent and Billy will stand by us and we'll pull through. See if we don't."

"I don't see why she needs to go to your house," said Elviry. "Let her stay right here, and go up to college with you if she will. And I don't want to go live on a farm, either."

"Mother, you don't understand, yet!" exclaimed Margery.

"Elviry," said Dave grimly, "our day is over. All we can hope to save out of the wreck is a future for Margery. Just get that through your head once and for all. I think Lydia's idea is horse sense. But it's for Margery to decide."

Margery got up from her place on the floor. "I thought we'd sell out and go to Europe for the rest of our lives," she said, "but as Lydia says, the story would follow us there. Dad," sharply, "you aren't going to *sell* the Last Chance and use that money?"

"I closed it up, last week," said Dave shortly. "I'm going to have the place torn down."

Margery rubbed her hand over her forehead. "Well," she said, "I don't see that I'd gain anything but a reputation for being a quitter, if I went to Lydia's. I'll stay with you folks, but I'll go to college, if Lydia'll stand by me."

Lydia rose. "Then that's settled. On Monday we'll register. I'll meet you on the eight o'clock car."

"I can't thank you, Lyd, —" began Margery.

"I don't want any thanks," said Lydia, making for the door, where Dave intercepted her with outstretched hand.

Lydia looked up into his dark face and her own turned crimson. "I can't shake hands," she said, "honestly, I can't. The Last Chance and the — the starving squaws make me sick. I'll stand by Margery and help you — but I can't do that."

Dave Marshall dropped his hand and turned away without a word and Lydia sped from the house into the sunset.

Amos heard Lydia's story of her call with a none too pleased face. "I don't think I want you mixing up with them, in any way," he said.

"But let me help Margery," pleaded Lydia, "Little Patience did love her so!"

"Well — Margery — you can help her," he agreed, reluctantly, "but you can't go near their house again. Margery will have to do all the visiting."

Chapter XVII

THE MILITARY HOP

"Who shall say that I do not understand what the wind sings in my branches or that I am less than the white or more than the Indian?"

— The Murmuring Pine

*I*n spite of the fact that Levine had avoided her, after the hearing, and in spite of all the many half tragic ramifications of the reservation trouble, Lydia was not unhappy. In fact, when Registration day dawned she awoke with a sense of something good impending, sang as she dressed, and piloted Margery gaily through the complications of entering the University as a "special" student.

Margery, for the first month or so, was silent and kept as close as possible to Lydia's apron strings. But Lydia had prophesied truly. No girl as beautiful as Margery could be kept in Coventry long and though she refused for a time to go to parties, it was not long before Margery was taking tramps with the college boys and joining happily enough in the simple pleasures at the cottage.

Lydia did not hear from Kent until a week before the first college hop, late in October. Then she received a formal note from him, reminding her of his invitation.

"Oh, Lyd!" exclaimed Margery, "aren't you lucky! I haven't seen Kent or heard from him since our trouble!"

"Neither have I," said Lydia. "And I suspect he's so cross with me that he hates to keep this engagement. But I don't care. I wish I had a new dress. But I've made the sleeves small in my organdy and made a new girdle. It looks as well as could be expected!" she finished, comically.

"Lydia," cried Margery, suddenly, "I've a whole closet full of party dresses I won't wear this year and you and I are just of a size, won't you wear one — take one and keep it — please, Lydia!"

Lydia flushed and shook her head.

"Is it because they were bought with Dad's money?" asked Margery.

Lydia's flush grew deeper. "I couldn't take it anyway, Margery," she protested. But Margery tossed her head and was silent for the rest of the afternoon.

The hop was a success, a decided success, in spite of the organdy. Kent was inclined to be stiff, at first, and to wear a slightly injured air, and yet, mingled with this was a frank and youthful bravado. And there could be no doubt that among the college boys, Kent was more or less of a hero. It was something to boast of, evidently, to have one's name coupled with Levine's in the great scandal.

Kent had supposed that he would have some trouble in filling Lydia's card for her, but to his surprise, he found that in her timid way, Lydia was something of a personage among the older college boys and the younger professors.

"Oh, you have Miss Dudley. Let me have three dances, will you," said the instructor in Psychology. "How pretty she is tonight!"

"Lydia is a peach," Kent stated briefly. "One two-step is the best I can do for you."

"Come now, Moulton, a two-step and a waltz," said Professor Willis. "I haven't seen Miss Dudley since college opened. Isn't her hair wonderful tonight!"

Gustus was there with Olga. "Gimme a waltz with Lydia, Kent," he demanded. "Who'd ever thought she'd grow up so pretty! If she could dress well —"

"Her card's full," grunted Kent. "And she dresses better'n any girl I know. What's the matter with that dress?"

The two young men stood watching Lydia, who was chatting with Professor Willis. The dress was out of style. Even their masculine eyes recognized that fact, yet where in the room was there a mass of dusty gold hair like Lydia's, where such scarlet cheeks, where such a look of untried youth?

"Oh, well, it was just something Olga said," began Gustus.

"Olga makes me sick," said Kent, and he stalked over to claim a waltz with Lydia.

It was altogether an intoxicating evening and at its end Lydia pulled on her last winter's overcoat and clambered into Kent's little automobile, utterly satisfied with life.

"Well, did I give you a good time, Miss?" asked Kent, as they chug-chugged down the Avenue.

"Oh, Kent, it was wonderful!"

"And you don't feel as if I were a villain anymore? You've forgiven me?"

"Forgiven you? For what?"

"For not agreeing with you on the Indian question. Gee, I was sore at you, Lyd, that morning at the hearing, and yet I was like your Dad. I was proud of you, too."

"Oh, don't let's talk about it, tonight, Kent," Lydia protested.

"All right, old girl, only just remember that I can't change. I back Mr. Levine to the limit. And maybe he hasn't a surprise party coming for all of you!"

"I don't care," insisted Lydia. "I'm going to be happy tonight, and I won't talk Indians. Oh, Kent, isn't Gustus getting good-looking?"

"Too fat," replied Kent. "He drinks too much beer. And let me call your attention to something funny. As you know, he's always had trouble getting in with the college set, because of the brewery. But his father is the only well-to-do man in town who's had nothing to do with the reservation, so now, by contrast, brewing becomes a highly honorable business! And Gustus goes with 'our very best families.'"

Lydia chuckled, then said, "Margery is feeling much better. She's at our house every Sunday. You must come round and see her!"

"Why shouldn't I come to see you, Lydia?" asked Kent, with a new note in his voice.

"Why, of course, you'd see me, but Margery's always been the main attraction with you."

"Has she? Seems to me I recall a time when I couldn't endure the sight of her. And when you were the best pal I had. That's what you are, Lydia, a real pal. A fellow can flirt round with the rest of 'em, but you're the one to look forward to spending a lifetime with!"

Lydia drew a quick breath, then laughed a little uncertainly. "You were the dearest boy! Do you remember how you hated to wash your hands and that funny cotton cap you liked to wear with Goldenrod Flour printed across it?"

"Of course, I remember. And I remember how the fellows used to tease me about you. I licked Gustus twice for it, when we were in the ward schools. Lydia, let's go over those old trails together again. Tomorrow's Sunday. Let's take a walk down to the Willows in the afternoon."

"All right, Kent," said Lydia, quietly, and silence fell on both of them till they drew up at the cottage gate.

Kent lifted Lydia to the ground, held both of her hands, started to speak, then with a half inarticulate, "Thank you, Lydia, and good-bye till tomorrow," he jumped into the little car and was gone.

For some reason, when she woke the next morning, Lydia half hoped that the soft patter against her window was of rain drops. But it was the wind-tossed maple leaves, whose scarlet and gold were drifting deep on the lawn and garden. There never was a more brilliant October day than this, and at three o'clock, Lydia and Kent set off down the road to the Willows.

Lizzie watched them from the living room window. "They're a handsome pair, Amos," she said. "Now aren't they?"

Amos looked up from his Sunday paper with a start. "Those young ones aren't getting sentimental, are they, Liz?" he asked, sharply.

"Well," returned Lizzie, "they might be, very naturally, seeing they're both young and good-looking. For the land sake! Don't you expect Lydia to find her young man and settle down?"

"No, I don't!" snapped Amos. "There isn't a man on earth good enough for Lydia. I don't want her to marry. I'll take care of her."

"Humph! Nothing selfish about a man, is there?" muttered Lizzie.

Kent and Lydia strolled along the leafy road, with the tang of the autumn in their nostrils, and the blue gleam of the lake in their eyes. It was only a half mile to the Willows and as they turned in, Kent took Lydia's hand and drew it through his arm.

"Look," he said, "I believe there is even a little left of our cave, after all this time. What a rough little devil I was in those days. And yet, even then, Lyd, I believe I had an idea of trying to take care of you."

"You were not a rough little devil!" exclaimed Lydia, indignantly. "You were a dear! I can never forget what you did for me, when little Patience died."

"I was a selfish brute in lots of ways afterward, though," said Kent, moodily. "I didn't have sense enough to appreciate you, to realize — yet, I did in a way. Remember our talks up at camp? Then, of course, we never shall agree on the Indian question. But what does that amount to?"

Kent dropped Lydia's hand and faced her. "Lydia, do you care for me — care for me enough to marry me?"

Lydia turned pale. Something in her heart began to sing. Something in her brain began to stir, uncomfortably.

"Oh, Kent," she began, breathlessly, then paused and the two looked deep into each other's eyes.

"Lydia! Lydia!! I need you so!" cried Kent. "You are such a dear, such a pal, so pretty, so sweet — and I need you so! Won't you marry me, Lydia?"

He seized both her hands and held them against his cheeks.

"I've always loved you dearly, Kent, and yet," faltered Lydia, "and yet, somehow, I don't think we'd ever make each other happy."

"Not make each other happy! I'd like to know why not! Just try me, Lydia! Try me!"

Kent's charming face was glowing. Into Lydia's contralto voice crept the note that had belonged to little Patience's day.

"I'd like to try you, dear if — Wait, Kent, wait! Let me have my playtime, Kent. I've never had a real one, you know, till now. Let me finish college, then ask me again, will you, Kent?"

Kent jerked his head discontentedly. "I think it would be better for us to tie to each other right now. Please, Lydia dear!"

Lydia shook her head slowly. "Let me have my playtime, Kent. I don't know that side of myself at all."

Kent looked at the lake and at the little cave of long ago and back into the clear tender blue of Lydia's eyes. Then he said softly, "All right, dear! You know best. But will you give me just one kiss, — for remembrance?"

"Yes," replied Lydia, lifting her face, and Kent pulled off his cap and kissed the warm, girlish lips, tenderly, lingeringly, then, without a word, gently turned Lydia homeward.

Kent's announcement that he had broken with Billy Norton did not amount to a great deal. As winter came on, he and Billy met constantly at the cottage and outwardly at least, were friendly. The commission finished its sitting and turned its findings over to Congress. Congress instructed the District Attorney to carry the matter to the state courts. When this had been done all the incriminated heaved a vast sigh of relief, and prepared to mark time.

To tell the truth, Lydia was not giving a great deal of thought to weighty problems, this winter. No girl who finds herself with two young men in love with her, can give much thought to the world outside her own. Nor did the fact that Professor Willis made a point of appearing at the cottage at least once a month detract any from her general joy in life.

She was doing well in her studies, though outside of the occasional hop she attended with Billy or Kent, she had no part in the college social life. She was not altogether contented with the thought of preparing herself to teach. The idea gave her no mental satisfaction. She could not bring herself to believe that her real talents lay in that direction.

Yet, though this dissatisfaction grew as the days went on, it did not prevent her from taking a keen pleasure in the books she read and studied.

She suddenly grew ashamed of her old E. P. Roe period and developed a great avidity for Kipling and Thomas Hardy, for Wordsworth and Stephen Phillips. To her surprise she found that Billy was more familiar with these writers than she. Kent read newspapers and nothing else.

During all Lydia's Junior year, but one fly appeared in her ointment. And this, of course, was with, reference to clothes! that perennial haunting problem of Lydia's, which only a woman who has been motherless and poverty-stricken and pretty can fully appreciate. The latter part of February, the great college social event of the year was to come, the Junior Prom. Lydia felt sure that either Kent or Billy would ask her to go and for this the organdy would not do. And for this she must have a party coat.

Lydia knew if she took the matter up with Amos he would go out and borrow money for her. She shuddered at the thought of this. He had been so bitter about her fudge selling that she dared not broach the matter of money earning to him again. Then she heard of the College Money Making Bureau. She discovered that there were girls who were earning their way through college and that the Bureau was one of the quiet ways used by the University to help them.

There was the Mending Department for example. Here were brought every week by the well-to-do students piles of mending of every variety from heelless socks and stockings, to threadbare underwear and frayed cuffs and collars. These were made into packages and farmed out to the money needing girls. The Department was located in a room in the rear of the Chemical laboratory, and was in charge of the old janitor, whose casual manner was a balm to the pride of the most sensitive.

Early in January, Lydia sneaked into the little room, and out again with a neat but heavy bundle. She got home with it and smuggled it into her room without old Lizzie's seeing it. Socks, wristbands and torn lace — there was fifty cents' worth of mending in the package! Lydia calculated that if she did a package a night for thirty nights, she would have enough money to buy the making of the party dress and cloak.

The necessity for secrecy was what made the task arduous. Lydia finished her studying as hurriedly as possible each night and went on to her room. It was bitter cold in the room when the door was closed, but she hung a dust cloth over the keyhole, a shawl over the window shade, wrapped herself in a quilt and unwrapped the bundle. By two o'clock she had finished and shivering and with aching eyes, crept into bed.

Within a week she was going about her daily work with hollow eyes and without the usual glow in her cheeks. Within two weeks, the casual glimpse of Lizzie darning one of Amos' socks gave her a sense of nausea, but she hung on with determination worthy of a better cause.

The third week she took cold, an almost unheard-of proceeding for Lydia, and in spite of all old Lizzie's decoctions, she could not throw it off. Amos insisted that Lizzie see her to bed each night with hot lemonade and hot water bottle. Lydia protested miserably until she found that it was really more comfortable to mend in bed than it was to sit quilt-wrapped in a chair. At the end of the fourth week she carried back her last bundle, and with fifteen dollars in her pocketbook, she boarded the street-car for home. She was trembling with fatigue and fever.

When she reached the cottage, she stretched out on the couch behind the old base burner with her sense of satisfaction dulled by her hard cough and the feverish taste in her mouth. She was half asleep, half in a stupor when Billy came in.

"How's the cold, Lyd?" he asked.

"I got it," she murmured hoarsely. "It'll be white mull and pink eider-down."

"What did you say?" asked Billy, coming over to the couch and peering down at her, through the dusk.

"Socks," whispered Lydia, "bushels of socks, aren't there, Billy?"

Billy picked up her hand and felt her pulse, pulled the shawl up over her chest, put his cheek down against her forehead for a moment as he murmured, "Oh, Lydia, don't be sick! I couldn't bear it!" then he hurried to the kitchen where Lizzie was getting supper.

The next thing that Lydia knew she was in her own bed and "Doc" Fulton was taking the clinical thermometer from her mouth. She was very much confused.

"Where's my fifteen dollars?" she asked.

"What fifteen dollars, little daughter?" Amos was sitting on the edge of the bed, holding her hand.

"For my party dress — white mull — with socks — please, Daddy."

Amos looked at Lizzie. "It's what she wanted for the Junior Prom, I guess," said the old lady, "poor child."

"You shall have fifteen dollars, just as soon as you get well, honey," said Amos.

"All right," said Lydia, hoarsely, "tell Kent so's he —" She trailed off again into stupor.

It was a hard pull, a sharp, hard struggle with badly congested lungs, for two weeks. It was the first real illness Lydia had had in all her sturdy young life. Ma Norton took charge and "Doc" Fulton was there night after night. Margery came every day, with a basket, for Elviry practically fed Amos during the two weeks. Billy did chores. Kent was errand boy with the little car. And Adam sat on the doorstep for hours and howled!

And all this time Lydia wandered in a world of her own, a world that those about her were utterly unable to picture through the erratic fragments of talk she uttered from time to time. She talked to them of little Patience, of John Levine, of old Susie, She seemed to be blaming herself for the starving of an Indian baby who was confused in her mind with little Patience. She sought her fifteen dollars through wild vicissitudes, until Amos found the little purse under the couch pillow and, wondering over its contents, put it in Lydia's feverish hands. Thereafter she talked of it no more.

But Lydia was splendidly strong. One night, after ten days of stupor and delirium, she opened her eyes on Amos' haggard face. She spoke weakly but naturally. "Hello, Dad! Ask Margery to get me the pattern we were talking about. In a day or so I'll be up and around."

Amos began to cry for sheer joy.

Once she began to mend, Lydia's recovery was unbelievably rapid. On a Sunday, a week before the Junior Prom., she was able to dress and to lie on the living room couch. During the afternoon, Kent came in. He had had one or two glimpses of the invalid before, but this was the first opportunity he'd had for a chat.

"Hello, Lyd!" he cried. "Are you going to go to the Junior Prom. with me, after all?"

"Kent, I can't go. I might be strong enough for one or two dances by that time, but I can't get my clothes done."

"Pshaw, isn't that hard luck!" Kent's voice was soft with sympathy. "Never mind, old lady! I'm so darned glad to have you getting well so fast, that the Prom. doesn't matter. Say, Lyd, Margery's come out fine, since you've been sick!"

"I know it," said Lydia. "Just think of Margery carrying Dad's meals in a basket, and helping Lizzie with the dishes. And I know she hates it worse than poison. She's out in the kitchen now, making fudge."

Kent brightened, perceptibly. "Is she? Er — Lydia, don't you think she'd go to the Prom. with me? Seems to me she's cut out society as long as she needs to."

Lydia buried her nose in a bunch of violets that Professor Willis had sent her. "I think she ought to go if she wants to," she said.

"Guess I'll ask her now," cried Kent, disappearing kitchenward.

Lydia lay watching snowflakes sift softly past the window. It was not long before Margery and Kent appeared.

"She's going!" cried Kent.

Margery's beautiful eyes were glowing. "Yes, I'm going, Lyd! And if nobody else will dance with me, Kent will take all the dances."

Old Lizzie followed in. She looked sharply at Lydia, then said, "You folks come out in the dining room and let Lydia have a little nap."

"No, I guess I'll go home," Margery answered, "Mother's not very well today."

"I'll take you along in my chug-chug." Kent crossed over to the couch and took Lydia's hand, while Margery went for her wraps. "Good-bye, dear," he whispered, "get well fast for me."

Lydia smiled at him over the bunch of violets.

Billy was the next caller. "I left Dad and Amos saving the Nation through Free Trade," he said. "Gee, Lydia, but you do look better! You don't suppose you could possibly go to the Prom., just for one or two dances, do you?"

Lydia shook her head. "No clothes," she said, briefly. "Ask some other girl."

"There isn't any other girl," replied Billy. "If I can't go with you, I'll be hanged if I go at all! Lydia, I don't see why a sensible girl like you lays such stress on clothes. Honestly, it's not like you. Come on, be a sport and go in your usual dress."

Lydia looked at Billy's steady grey eyes, and a faint glow of comfort began to surround her heart. Sometimes she felt as if Billy understood her almost as well as John Levine did.

"Now, look here," he said, argumentatively, "you and I had better talk this clothes question out, once and for all."

Lydia giggled. "Billy, you don't know women! It can't be talked out!"

"I know you," replied the young man, stretching out his long legs to the base-burner, and looking at Lydia, "and I want you to stop worrying about your duds. I want you to let me lend you the money to get a complete party outfit with."

"Billy Norton, you know I wouldn't borrow money from a man!" exclaimed Lydia.

"Well, then, I'll give it to Mother and you borrow it from her."

"Of course, I won't," replied Lydia. "Besides, I've got enough money I earned myself!"

"You have! Then what's all the worry about? How'd you earn it, Lyd? I thought your father —"

Lydia dug the little pocketbook from under the sofa pillow and spread the money proudly on her shawl. "There it is and it's the root of all my troubles."

Billy looked at her suspiciously. "Young woman, how'd you earn that money?" he demanded.

"Socks! Bushels of socks, mostly," answered Lydia with a chuckle that ended in a groan. She looked at Billy whimsically and then as the sureness of his understanding came to her again, she told him the story of her little midnight sweatshop.

"Oh, dearest!" Billy burst forth with a groan when she had finished, "how could you be such a little idiot! Oh, Lydia, Lydia, I can't tell you how you wring my heart."

It seemed for a moment as if he must gather the slight little figure to his heart, but he set his teeth.

"If that darned Prom. means as much as that to you —" he began, but Lydia interrupted him.

"It doesn't anymore, Billy. I've learned a lot of things since I've been sick. I was a little idiot to work so hard for clothes! But I don't think it was all clothes. I wanted to be like other girls. I wanted to have the man that took me proud of my appearance."

She paused and Billy would have spoken, but Lydia began again.

"You see, I was never sick before, so I never realized that a sickness is a serious thing in more ways than one. I mean you can't go down to death's door and ever be quite the same afterward. I've been thinking about myself a great deal. Billy, and I'm feeling pretty small. Isn't it queer how hard it is to learn just the simplest things about living! Seems as though I learn everything with my elbows."

The two young people sat in silence, Lydia watching the snowflakes settle on the already overladen boughs of the pine. Billy watching the sensitive lines in Lydia's face change with each passing thought.

"I've made up my mind," Lydia began again, "that I've been poor too long, ever really to outgrow the effects of poverty. I suppose I'd always worry about money, even if I were taken suddenly rich! Anyhow, lots of nice people have liked me poor and I'm just not going to worry about having lovely clothes, with soft colors and — and graceful lines, anymore. I'm going to take care of our lovely old mahogany furniture and try to make the cottage an attractive place for people with brains. After all, the real thinkers of the country were poor — Emerson and his circle, how simply they lived! You see, Billy, if I clutter up my mind with furniture and clothes, I won't have time to think."

Lizzie came in at this moment with a bowl of broth. "I'll hold it for you, Lydia," said Billy. "Never mind pulling the little table up, Lizzie, she's too weak to fuss with a table."

There was a remote twinkle in Lizzie's old eyes, but she gave the bowl over to Billy, and tactfully withdrew to the kitchen, where she sat down with her feet in the oven. "Drat Kent!" she said to herself.

Billy moved over to sit on the edge of the couch, and Lydia began to sip the broth, spoonful by spoonful. "It's such fun to be weak and a little helpless and have people waiting on you," she said. "It's the first time it ever happened to me."

As she spoke she was thinking how Billy had improved. How immaculate he was and how well his blue suit fitted him. There was no barnyard odor about him now! Only a whiff of the good cigars he smoked.

"Billy," she said, "what would you say if next year I took the short course in agriculture?"

Billy almost dropped the bowl. "I'd be speechless!" he exclaimed.

"I hate to think of teaching," Lydia went on, "and I'm crazy about the country and farming and so is Dad. And there's more than that to it."

What more there was to it, she did not say then, for Ma Norton came bustling in. She made no comment on Billy's posing as a table! Ma was wise and she was almost as devoted to Lydia as Billy himself.

"It's nice to see the pink coming back in your cheeks, Lydia," she said. "I just ran over to say I was going into town to do some shopping, early in the morning, and if there was anything I could do for you — ?"

"No, thank you," said Lydia. "I've begun to save up now to buy a cow!"

And Ma looked on with a puzzled smile as Lydia and Billy burst into sudden shrieks of laughter.

Chapter XVIII

THE END OF A GREAT SEARCH

"Abiding love! Those humans who know it, become an essential part of nature's scheme."

*L*ydia returned to her college work the Monday after the Junior Prom, a little thinner, and her color not quite so bright as usual, but in a most cheerful frame of mind. She was feeling, somehow, a new sense of maturity and contentment. Even tales of the wonders of the Prom did not disturb her much. She made up her lost classroom work, then took on an extra course in English Essayists with Professor Willis, just to satisfy her general sense of superiority to the ordinary temptations that should have disturbed a young female with fifteen idle dollars in her pocket!

Kent was devoting a good deal of attention to Lydia but this did not prevent his taking Margery about. He was, he explained to Lydia, so sorry for her!

"You don't have to explain to me," protested Lydia. "I want you to go with all the girls you like. I intend to see all I want of as many men as care to see me. I told you this was my playtime."

Kent's reply to this was a non-committal grunt.

It was late in May that he told Lydia what John Levine had finally accomplished, in his silent months of work in Washington. The morning after he told Lydia, Lake City was ringing with the news. The Indians on the reservation were to be removed bodily to a reservation in the Southwest. The reservation was then to be thrown open to white settlement.

"What will poor Charlie Jackson say?" were Lydia's first words.

Kent shrugged his shoulders. "Poor old scout! He'll have to make a new start in the West. But isn't it glorious news, Lyd! The land reverts to the Government and the Land Office opens it, just as in pioneer days. Everybody who's title's in question now can reenter under settlement laws. Isn't Levine a wizard! Why don't you say something, Lydia?"

"I don't know what to say," said Lydia. "I'm sick at heart for the Indians. But I'm glad that the awful temptation of the pines is going to be taken away from Lake City. Though how good can come out of a wrong, I'm not sure. I don't understand Mr. Levine. Oh, dear! It's all wrong. When do the Indians go?"

"The last of June. It's funny, Lydia, that you don't have more sympathy with my work," replied Kent, gloomily.

"Oh, Kent!" cried Lydia, "I want to believe that everything you do is right but something's the matter with my mind, I seem to have to decide matters of right and wrong for myself. When will Mr. Levine come home?"

"Next month. Well, there's one consolation. You've always been crazy about Levine and you don't approve of him, either."

Lydia flushed. "Oh, I don't say that I don't approve of him. I just don't understand him. Maybe he really believes the end justifies the means."

"Huh! Isn't that just what I believe?" demanded Kent. He looked at her so happily, his boyish eyes so appealing, his square chin so belligerent, that Lydia suddenly laughed and gave his ear a tweak.

"Poor old vanity! Did he want all the ladies to adore him? Well, they do, so cheer up!"

Kent grinned. "Lyd, you're a goose and a good old pal! Hang it, I'm glad you've got brain enough to stick to your own opinions!"

On a Sunday afternoon, late in June, John Levine turned in at the gate as casually as though he had left but the day before. Lydia was inspecting the garden with her father, when she heard Adam bark and whine a welcome to someone.

"Oh, there he is, Daddy!" she cried, and she dashed down the rows of young peas, her white skirts fluttering, both hands extended.

John seized her hands and for a moment the two stood smiling and looking into each other's face. Except that he was greyer, Levine was unchanged. He broke the silence to say, "Well! Well! young Lydia, you are grown up. I don't see how you manage to look so grown up, when your face remains unchanged."

"It's my hair," said Lydia, "and my skirts."

"Of course," growled Amos, "I realize that I count only as Lydia's father. Still I think you ought to recognize me, anyhow."

The two men clasped hands. "Well, Amos?"

"It's been a long time between drinks, John."

"I know it, Amos, but my chore's done. Now, I'll stay home and enjoy life. Lydia, is it too hot for waffles and coffee, for supper? Lord, I've dreamed of those old days and of this meeting for nine months."

"It's not too hot for anything on earth you can ask for," returned Lydia, beginning to roll up her sleeves. "I'll go right in and start them now."

John looked after her, at the lengthened skirts, at the gold braids wrapped round her head. "She doesn't change except in size, thank God," he said.

"Oh, she gets prettier," said Amos, carelessly. "She's sort of grown up to her mouth, and the way she wears her hair shows the fine set of her head. She's improved a lot."

"She has *not!* Amos, you never did appreciate her. She couldn't be anymore charming now than she was as a kiddie."

Amos put an affectionate hand on his friend's shoulder. "You always were an old fool, John. Come up and peel your coat, then take a look at the garden. There's Lizzie, dying to speak to you."

Levine looked around the living room, complacently. "Jove, isn't it fine! Most homelike place in America. Lydia's been fixing up the old mahogany, eh?"

"Yes! One of the professors told her it was O. K., so she got a book out of the library on old furniture and now we are contented and strictly up to date. These damned rugs though, I can't get her to tack 'em down. They're just like so many rags on the floor! I never had a chance to tell you what she did to my mahogany armchair, did I?"

He retailed the story of Willis' first call and John roared though he murmured, "Poor kiddie," as he did so.

"She's given me over to my sins, though, lately," Amos went on, with the faint twinkle in his eyes that Lydia had inherited. "She brought me up by hand, for a long time, hid my pipes, wanted me to manicure my nails, wouldn't let me eat in my shirt sleeves or drink my coffee out of the saucer. But her friend, Willis, likes me, as is, — so she's let me backslide without a murmur."

Amos paused and looked out at the shimmering lake. "John, I wish I had five daughters. There's nothing like 'em in the world."

Levine did not answer for a moment, while his gaze followed Amos' out over the familiar outline of blue water and far green hills.

"Sometimes, Amos," he muttered, finally, "I feel as if my whole life had been wasted."

It was an extraordinarily pleasant supper. John and Amos, in their shirt sleeves, ate waffles till Lydia declared that both the batter and her strength were exhausted. Indians were not mentioned. Levine was in a reminiscent mood and told stories of his boyhood on a Northern Vermont farm and old Lizzie for the first time in Lydia's remembrance told of some of the beaux she had had when her father was the richest farmer round Lake City.

After the dishes were washed, Levine asked Lydia to stroll up the road with him while Amos did his evening chores. It was dusk when they turned out the gate to the road, Lydia clinging to John's arm. A June dusk, with the fresh smell of the lake mingling with the heavy scent of syringa and alder bloom, and of all the world of leafage at the high tide of freshness. June dusk, with the steady croak of frogs from the meadows and the faint call of whippoorwills from the woods.

John put a long, hard hand over the small thin one on his arm. "Have you missed me, young Lydia?" he asked.

"Yes," she answered, "especially as you never came near us after the hearing."

"How could I come?" asked the man, simply. "You had weighed me and found me wanting. There was nothing for me to do but to go ahead and finish my job, as I still saw the right of it. Have you forgiven me, Lydia?"

"It wasn't a matter between you and me," replied the girl, slowly. "It was between you and your conscience and if your conscience approves, what's the use of asking me to forgive you?"

"Because, I can't stand not having your approval," said Levine.

They strolled on in silence, while Lydia considered her reply. "No matter if the destroying of the Indians were right, that wouldn't exonerate the whites for having been cruel and crooked in doing it. People will always remember it of us."

Levine gave a laugh that had no mirth in it. "Lord, who'll say the New England spirit is dead! You're as cold in judging me as one of your ancestors was when he sentenced a witch to be burned."

"Oh, no!" cried Lydia. "Dear John Levine, I couldn't be cold to you. Nothing could make me love you less. And you yourself told me to be true to myself."

John sighed, then said abruptly, "Let's never discuss it again. What are you reading now, Lydia?"

"English essayists and Emerson. I'm crazy about Emerson. He seems so much more human than Leigh Hunt and De Quincey and the rest of them. Maybe it's because he's an American, so I understand him better. I think I like Compensation and Friendship the best so far. I learned one thing from Friendship to quote to you. It's like you and me."

With both hands clasping his arm, her sweet face upturned to his in the dusk, and with the rich notes in her voice that were reminiscent of little Patience, she quoted:

"'Friendship — that select and sacred relationship that is a kind of absolute and which even leaves the language of love suspicious and common so much is this purer; and nothing is so much divine.'"

John stopped and taking Lydia's face in both his hands, he exclaimed huskily. "Oh, my dear, this is my real welcome home! Oh, Lydia, Lydia, if you were ten years older and I were ten years younger —"

Lydia laughed. "Then we'd travel — to all the happy places of the world. We must turn back. Daddy'll be waiting."

Levine turned obediently, saying as he did so, "Just one thing more, then the year's absence will be spanned. How does the Great Search go on? Do you ever have bad dreams at night, now?"

"Sometimes," replied Lydia. "Just the other night I woke up with the old fear and then — it was very curious — I heard the lap-lapping of the lake, and the little murmur of the wind in the pine and the frogs cheeping and the steady chirp of the crickets, and, Mr. Levine, the queerest sense of comfort came to me. I can't put it into words. Somehow it was as if Something behind all those little voices spoke to me and told me things were — were right."

"Lydia," said Levine, quickly, "you've struck the right trail. I'll follow it with you. What a long way you've come alone, little girl. Give me your hand, dear. I like to feel it on my arm. Oh, Lydia! Lydia!"

"What are you two mooning about," said Amos' voice, as he loomed on them through the dusk.

"Enterprises of great pith and moment," replied Levine. "Got any tobacco with you, Amos?"

"No! We'd better go in the house, anyhow. The mosquitoes will eat us up. Lydia, Margery's looking for you."

And as far as Lydia was concerned, the evening was ended.

Levine was very busy with the details of the Indian removal for the next week or two. The exodus was accomplished in a businesslike manner. A steady line of busses brought the Indians from the reservation to the outskirts of Lake City, where rough barracks had been erected to care for the government wards while they were being concentrated. The state militia was on guard here, at intervals along the road and upon the reservation. There were some disturbances on the reservation, but for the most part, the Indians were dazed and unprotesting. Before the concentration began, the precaution was taken of sending Charlie Jackson under guard to the new reservation in the Southwest. Lydia had never seen him after her day at the hearing. She always was to carry in her memory, his handsome bronze face, too early marked with lines of despair, as she saw it while she uttered her protest to the commissioners. And it was a hauntingly sad memory to carry.

She went with Billy to see the embarking of the Indians in the special trains provided for them. The streets along the line of march were lined with whites, silent but triumphant. It was a beautiful day, clear and hot. Two by two, the Indians moved along the fine old elm-shadowed streets, old Wolf at the head, shambling and decrepit, but with his splendid old head held high. Two by two, in utter silence, their moccasined feet soundless, old Indians in buckskins, and young Indians in store clothes, then squaws, in calico "mother-hubbards," great bundles strapped to their backs, and children in their arms or clinging to their skirts. A long, slow moving line, in a silence that even the children did not break.

It took until well in the evening to get the pathetic exiles into the trains. Lydia did not stay after dark. Profoundly depressed, she made Billy take her home.

In the evening she sat with her Emerson open before her, but with her unseeing eyes fastened on the open door. It was a little after nine when the chug-chug of Kent's car stopped at the gate and in a moment Kent, white faced, appeared in the door.

"John Levine's been shot. He wants Lydia!"

Without a sound Lydia started after Kent down the path, Amos following. Kent packed them into the little car and started back toward town at breakneck speed.

"How bad off is he?" asked Amos.

"Can't live," answered Kent.

Still Lydia made no sound though Amos held her firmly in the vain attempt to still her trembling.

"How'd it happen?" Amos' voice broke a little.

"That damned sister of Charlie Jackson and old Susie both took a shot at him, just as the last car-load was finished. The police and the militia got 'em right off. Shot 'em all to pieces. It looked as though there'd be a wholesale fight for a minute but the militia closed in and the last train got off."

"Where is John?" asked Amos.

"In Doc Fulton's office. They can't move him."

No one spoke again. Kent brought the automobile up with a bang before the doctor's house and Lydia, followed closely by the two men, ran up to the door, through the outer office to the inner, where a nurse and Doc Fulton stood beside a cot.

Levine lay with his face turned toward the door. When he saw Lydia he smiled faintly. She was quite calm, except for her trembling. She walked quickly to his side and took his hand.

"Looks like I was going to start traveling alone, young Lydia," he said feebly. "I just wanted to tell you — that Great Search — is ending all right — don't worry —"

"I won't," said Lydia.

"Only I hate to go alone — my mother — gimme something, Doc."

The doctor held a glass to his lips. After a moment, Levine said again, "My mother used to hold me —" his voice trailed off and Lydia said suddenly, "You mean you want me to comfort you like I used to comfort little Patience?"

"Yes! Yes!" whispered Levine. "It's going to sleep alone I — Mother —"

Lydia knelt and sliding her arm under Levine's neck, she pulled his head over gently to rest on her shoulder. Then she began with infinite softness the little songs she had not uttered for so many years.

"'Wreathe me no gaudy chaplet;
  Make it from simple flowers
  Plucked from the lowly valleys
  After the summer showers.'"

"'Sweet and low, sweet and low, wind of the western sea . . . '"

"'I've reached the land of corn and wine
  And all its riches surely mine.
  I've reached that heavenly, shining shore
  My heaven, my home, forevermore.'"

Suddenly the nurse shifted John's head and Doc Fulton lifted Lydia to her feet. "Take her home, Amos," he said.

John Levine had finished the Great Search.

Curiously enough, nothing could have done so much toward reinstating Lake City in the good opinion of the country at large as did Levine's tragic death. There was felt to be a divine justice in the manner of his taking off that partook largely of the nature of atonement. He had led the whites in the despoiling of the Indians. For this the Indians had killed him.

That a white life extinguished for a tribe destroyed might not be full compensation in the eyes of that Larger Justice which, after all, rules the Universe, did not seriously influence the reaction of public opinion toward thinking better of Lake City. And John Levine, known in life as an Indian Graft politician, became in his death a Statesman of far vision.

Levine's will was not found at first. Distant cousins in Vermont would be his heirs, if indeed after his estate was settled, it was found that there was left anything to inherit.

Kent for a month or so after the tragedy was extremely busy helping to disentangle Levine's complicated real estate holdings. It was found that he held heavily mortgaged second growth timber lands in the northern part of the State and Kent spent a month superintending a re-survey of them. He was very much broken up by Levine's death, and welcomed the heavy work.

In spite of Lydia's deep affection for Levine, she did not feel his death as much as Amos did. For after all, Lydia was young, gloriously young, and with a forward-turned face. Amos had lost in John his only real friend, the only human being who in some ways had helped to fill in the hopeless gap left by his wife's death. And Amos, though still a young man, kept his face turned backward.

After her first wild grief had expended itself, Lydia found that, after all, Levine's tragic death had not surprised her. She realized that ever since she had known Charlie Jackson, she had been vaguely haunted by a fear of just such an ending.

July slipped into a breathless, dusty August. Lydia worked very hard, making herself tasks when necessary work was done. She put up fruit. She worked in the garden. She took up the dining room carpet and oiled the floor and made rugs. After she had had her swim in the late afternoon, she would take up her old position on the front doorstep, to sew or read or to dream with her eyes on the pine.

How silently, how broodingly it had stood there, month in, month out, year after year! What did it feel, Lydia wondered, now that the Indians were gone? Was it glad that Levine had been punished?

Billy, trundling up the dusty road from the law office on his bicycle, late each afternoon, would stop for a moment or two. Since the tragedy, not a day had gone by that Lydia had not seen him.

"The drought is something frightful," he said to Lydia one afternoon in late August, wiping the sweat and dust from his face. "This is the ninth week without rain. The corn is ruined. I never knew anything like this and Dad says he hasn't either."

"Our garden died weeks ago," said Lydia, listlessly.

Billy looked at her keenly. "Are you feeling anymore cheerful, Lyd?"

Lydia turned her gaze from the burning brown meadows to Billy's tanned, rugged face.

"I shall always have a gap in my life, where he went out," she said, slowly. "I shall never get over missing him. Oh, he was so dear to me! And yet, Billy, it isn't at all like little Patience's death. He didn't depend on me and I didn't live with him so that everything doesn't cry his absence to me. And I've got more resources than I had then —"

She laid her hand on the open book in her lap.

"What're you reading?" asked Billy.

"Emerson — Compensation. Listen, Billy — 'We cannot part with our friends. We cannot let our angels go. We do not see that they only go out that archangels may come in.'

"And so," Lydia's voice trembled, but she went on bravely, "I'm trying to understand — trying to see how I can make something good come out of his poor lost life. Somehow I feel as if that were my job. And — and the idea helps me. Oh, my dear John Levine!"

Billy cleared his throat. "Let's see that passage, Lyd." He took the book and read on: "'The death of a dear friend — wife, lover, brother — terminates an epoch of infancy or of youth that was waiting to be closed, breaks up a wonted occupation or style of living and allows the formation of new ones more friendly to the growth of character.'"

The two young people sat staring at the distant hills.

"Don't you see," Lydia burst out, "that I've got to do something, be something, to make all the loss and trouble of my life worth while?"

"I understand," answered Billy. "What are you going to do?"

"I'm not quite sure, yet," replied Lydia, "but I'll tell you as soon as I've made up my mind. Billy, ask your father to come over this evening. Dad is so desperately blue."

Billy rose to go. "One thing I will tell you, Billy," Lydia went on, "I'm going to take the short dairy course this winter, besides my other work."

Billy looked at the sweet, resolute face curiously, then he chuckled.

"Whenever you deign to unravel the workings of the mystery you call your mind, I'll be crazy to listen," he said.

Early in September, John Levine's will was found. He had left his entire property, unconditionally, to Lydia.

Amos, at first, was frantic with delight. Lydia was appalled.

"All my life," she half sobbed to her father, "I've been fighting to get away from Indian lands. And Mr. Levine knew how I felt. Oh, how could he do this to me!"

"Don't talk like a fool, Lydia!" roared Amos.

Lydia turned to Kent, who was sitting on the back steps with them. He leaned over and patted her hand.

"Why worry about it, Lyd? Your father and I'll look out for it all."

"Do I *have* to keep it?" asked Lydia, tensely. "Will the law make me?"

"I should say not! You can give it to me, if you want to," laughed Kent.

"But don't you see how I feel?" cried Lydia. "Don't you see that all John Levine's lands up there are haunted by death — his own — and all the starving Indians? Oh, why did he do this to me!"

"I suppose you feel the same way about the cottage," said Amos, sarcastically.

"I don't either," contradicted Lydia. "I'm as happy as I can be that we've got that. But all the rest! I won't have it, I tell you! I'd rather be poverty stricken all my life."

"Well, don't worry too much about that," said Kent. "Dave Marshall thinks there won't be anything left after the estate is settled, but the Indian lands."

"Oh, Kent, you aren't having anything to do with Dave Marshall, are you?" exclaimed Lydia.

Kent flushed a little. "Well, his advice can't hurt me. If it's bad, I don't have to take it. You ought to go out and see his farm, Lydia. They're getting the house all fitted with modern conveniences. Dave's going to make a model stock farm."

"Bought with money earned by the Last Chance!" said Lydia.

"You can't be so darned squeamish about where a man gets his money these days, Lyd. Of course, there was no excuse for the Last Chance. But Dave's done what he could about it."

Lydia made no reply and Kent looked at her quizzically. "A New England conscience must be something awful to own, eh, Lyd?"

Lydia chuckled. "It's pretty bad," she admitted, then she went on soberly, "but I won't take those Indian lands."

"You can give them to me," reiterated Kent, cheerfully.

"She'll keep them," said Amos, shortly, "or Lydia and I'll have our first real row."

"Well, save up the fight till the estate's settled," said Kent, soothingly. "And then you'll know what you're fighting about. That will take some months."

Lydia sighed with relief. And again Kent laughed. "Oh, Lyd! You haven't any idea how funny you are! Come to, old lady! This is the twentieth century! And twentieth century business ethics don't belong to town meeting days. The best fellow gets the boodle!"

"Then Dave Marshall is the best fellow in our community, I suppose," said Lydia.

"Oh, Gee, Lyd! After all, he's Margery's father!"

Lydia looked at Kent thoughtfully. Since the day under the willows, he had not made love to her, yet she had the feeling that Kent was devoted to her and she wondered sometimes why he liked to spend as much time with Margery as with herself. Then she gave herself a mental shake.

"I'm going to tell you right now, that until I *have* to I'm not going to worry. I'm going to try to be happy in my senior year."

Chapter XIX

CAP AND GOWN

"Nature never pretends. She gives her secrets only to the unpretending."

— *The Murmuring Pine*

*T*he fifteen dollars, after all, were disposed of in a highly satisfactory manner. They paid for Lydia's senior cap and gown. Perhaps there were other members of the class to whom their senior insignia meant as much as they did to Lydia, but that is to be doubted.

Although, ever since her illness, she had firmly resolved never to worry again over her meager wardrobe, she almost wept with joy when she first beheld herself in cap and gown. For she looked exactly like other girls! It didn't matter at all, this year, whether or not she had a new suit or a new overcoat. The gown was all-concealing. Donning it was like turning from caterpillar to butterfly with a single wave of the hand.

Amos and Lizzie were as much impressed as Lydia, but for different reasons. Lizzie was sure that the gown was proof and evidence that Lydia had compassed all human knowledge.

"Land, Lydia," she murmured, walking slowly around the slender figure, "it makes you look terrible dignified and I'm glad of that. No one could look at you now and not feel that you know an awful lot."

Amos was unimpressed by Lydia's stores of wisdom but it seemed to him that there never was such a lovely face as that which looked out at him from under the mortar-board cap. There was a depth to the clear blue eyes, a sweetness to the red lips, that moved him so that for a moment he could not speak.

"It's an awful pretty idea, wearing the cap and gown, isn't it!" he said, finally. "Somewhere, back East, there's a picture of one of your ancestors who taught in an English college. You look something like him."

"Did I have that kind of an ancestor?" asked Lydia with interest. "Isn't it too bad that we Americans don't know anything about our forebears. I wonder what the old duck would say if he could see me!"

It was the rainiest Fall within Lydia's recollection. It seemed, after the drought was once broken, as if nature would never leave off trying to compensate for the burning summer. The dark weather had a very depressing effect on Amos and instead of growing more resigned to his friend's death, he seemed to Lydia to become daily more morose and irritable.

In a way, Lydia's conscience smote her. She knew that her father was worrying over her attitude on her inheritance, but she continued to avoid the issue with him while the estate was being settled. Lydia was doing heavy work in college. She actually had entered all the classes in dairying possible, while carrying her other college work. And she enjoyed the new work amazingly.

She had not mentioned her purpose to anyone of her friends but Billy. Therefore when Professor Willis, showing some Eastern visitors through the dairy building, came upon her washing cream bottles one afternoon, he was rendered entirely speechless for a moment.

Lydia, in a huge white dairy apron and cap, was sluicing the bottles happily, the only girl in a class of a dozen men, when Willis came in, followed by two tall men in eyeglasses.

"Queer, I admit, to find this sort of thing in a college," he was saying, "but decidedly interesting, nevertheless. Well, Miss Dudley, are you — I didn't know — I beg your pardon."

The class, which was working without an instructor, looked up in astonishment. Lydia blushed furiously and the two visitors looked on with obvious interest.

"It's a class in bottle sterilizing," she explained. "It just happens to be my turn."

The look of relief on Willis' face made Lydia angry. She turned her back on him and proceeded to let a cloud of steam envelop her and her bottles.

"The idiot! He thought I was dish-washing for a living, I suppose," she murmured to herself. "What business is it of his, anyhow?"

How Willis got rid of his two guests, he did not say, but half an hour later, when Lydia emerged from the dairy building, he was waiting for her. There was a quiet drizzle of rain, as was usual this Fall, and Lydia was wearing her old coat, with her mortar-board. But it was clear that the professor of Shakespeare did not know what she wore. It was a half mile through the University farm to the street-car and he wanted to re-establish himself with Lydia before some other swain appeared.

"Tell me what this means, Miss Dudley!" he said eagerly as he raised his umbrella to hold it carefully over the mortar-board.

"It looks as though it meant rain, to me," replied Lydia, shortly.

Willis gave a little gasp. "Oh! I beg your pardon!"

His chagrin made Lydia ashamed of herself. "I don't see why you should be so shocked at my trying to learn something useful," she said.

"Oh, but I'm not! Nothing that you could do would shock me! You've got a good reason, for you're the most sensible girl I ever met. And that's what I'm keen about, the reason."

"The reason?" Lydia stared at the dripping woodland through which they were making their way. "I'm not just sure I had a reason. I don't want to teach. I do love farming. I don't see why a woman can't learn dairy work as well as a man."

"You're the only girl doing it, aren't you?"

"Yes, but what difference does that make? The boys are fine to me."

"I don't know that that surprises me any," Willis smiled down at the pink profile at his shoulder. "Well, and then what?"

"Then a dairy farm, if Dad and I can rent the makings of one."

"But you have plenty of land, haven't you? Levine left all his property to you, I understand."

Lydia looked quickly up into Willis' face. "If you were I would you keep that property?"

The professor's eyes widened. "I? Oh! I don't know. It would be an awful temptation, I'm afraid."

"I'd rather be poor all my life," said Lydia. "I'm not afraid of poverty. I've lived with it always and I know it's a sheep in wolf's clothing."

"You mean you've got the courage to give the pine land up?" asked Willis, quickly.

"It isn't courage. It's being afraid of my conscience. I — I feel as if I were finishing out John Levine's life for him — doing what he ought to have done."

"I wonder if you have any idea what you mean to me!" Willis suddenly burst forth. "You embody for me all the things my puritan grandmothers stood for. By Jove, if the New England men have failed, perhaps the Western women will renew their spirit."

Lydia flushed. "I — I wish you wouldn't talk that way," she protested. "I'm not really wise nor very good. I just feel my way along — and there's no one to advise me."

"That's the penalty of growing up, my dear," said Willis. "We no longer have anyone to tell us what to do. Here comes your car. I'm afraid I let the umbrella drip on your cap."

"It doesn't matter," said Lydia, valiantly.

"Miss Dudley —" as he signaled the car, "I'm coming to see you, just as often as you'll let me, this winter," and he walked off before Lydia could reply. She sank into a car seat, her cheeks burning, her heart thudding.

Early in December, the settlement of the Levine estate was completed. John's method of "shoestringing" his property was disastrous as far as the size of Lydia's heritage went. Her father tried to make her understand the statement of the Second National Bank, which was acting as executor. And as nearly as Lydia could understand, one portion of the estate was used to pay up the indebtedness of another portion, until all that was left was the cottage, with a mortgage on it, and three hundred and twenty acres of land on the reservation.

The three hundred and twenty acres on the reservation was under a cloud. Part of it was land he had gotten from Charlie's sister. All of it he had obtained from alleged full bloods.

"Then," said Lydia, in a relieved manner, "I really haven't any Indian lands at all!"

"Oh, yes, you have," replied Amos. "The court will take the oath of a number of people that the land was obtained from mixed bloods. Dave Marshall has fixed that up."

"Dave Marshall!" gasped Lydia.

Amos nodded. "He's strong with the Whiskey Trust. And the Whiskey Trust is extra strong wherever there's a reservation."

"Oh, Daddy!" cried Lydia, "we can't take it? Don't you see we can't?"

It was just after supper and they were in the familiar old living room. Adam was snoring with his head under the base burner, and Lizzie was clattering the dishes in the kitchen. Amos stood by the table, filling his pipe, and Lydia with her pile of text books had prepared for her evening of study. Amos' work-blunted fingers trembled as he tamped the tobacco into the bowl and Lydia knew that the long dreaded battle was on.

"I can't understand why you act so like a fool," began Amos, querulously. "And I can't see why you set your judgment up as better than mine. I swan — even your Mother never did that, except on borrowing money."

"It isn't judgment. It's conviction, Daddy. And John Levine told me to stand by my own convictions, even when they were against his. Oh, how can you be willing to take land stolen in the first place and then the theft legalized by the Whiskey Trust! Why, you don't want me even to speak to Dave Marshall now, yet you're willing to take this dirty favor from him."

"We won't keep the land. We'll sell it and have the money to clear up the mortgage on the cottage. I'd take a favor from the devil in hell to get this place clear," replied Amos slowly. He took a turn up and down the room. "I can't see what's happened to children nowadays. In my day we obeyed. Lydia, I'm not going to discuss this any longer. *You've got to take that land.*"

Lydia sat with her thin hands clasped before her on the table, her clear eyes fastened on her father's face.

"I'm not a child, Daddy," she said in a low voice, "I'm a woman, grown. And if you'd wanted me to grow up without any convictions, you should have given me different ancestors and then you shouldn't have brought me up in a town like Lake City."

Amos looked down at his daughter grimly. The Daniel Webster picture in its black carved frame was just behind him and the somber vision in the living and the pictured eyes was identical.

"Can't you see what a fool you are!" he shouted. "The land can never go back to the Indians. John took good care of that. If you don't take it, somebody else will. Can't you see!"

Lydia's lips tightened. "That's not the point. It's the way we're getting it and the way John Levine got it."

"And yet you pretended that you loved and admired Levine!" sneered Amos.

Lydia sprang to her feet. She was white to her lips. "Don't repeat that remark," she said in a choked voice. "What do you know about the feeling John Levine and I had for each other? He was the one friend of my life."

"Nice way you have of showing it, now he's gone," roared Amos. "Just about the way you show your affection for me. Will nothing satisfy you? Norton and I never squealed when you and Billy got our claims taken away from us. Doesn't it occur to you it's about time you sacrificed something to me!"

Lydia had never seen her father so angry before. He had often worked himself into a tantrum on the subject of money but there was an aspect to his anger now that was new to her. She was trembling but cool.

"I'll do anything you want but this, Dad," she said.

"But this is all I want. It's what I've wanted for years, this little bit of land. And you haven't any idea what that feeling is."

Like a flash Lydia saw again long aisles of pines, smelled again the odor of the needles, heard again the murmuring call of the wind.

"Good God!" cried Amos, tossing his pipe on the table, "poverty's hounded me all my life — poverty and death. The only two people who cared about me, Patience and Levine're gone. Yet here's the chance for me to be independent. Here's a chance for me to make up for the failure I've made of life. A man with a little piece of property like this and a little bank account is somebody in the community. What do I care how I get it, as long's I can hold it? What's a lot of dirty Indians to stand between me and my future? But what do you care?"

"O Daddy! O Daddy! How can you talk so to me!" groaned Lydia. She put her hands over her eyes for a moment, swallowed a sob and then started for the outer door. She caught her coat from the nail and closed the door behind her.

An irresistible impulse had carried her from the house. She wanted to see Billy. It was still early and a lantern flickered in the Norton barnyard. She ran along the snowy road and down the drive of the Norton yard, pausing beside a lilac bush to see whether it was Billy or his father just entering the cowshed. It was Billy and she ran across the barnyard to the shed door. Billy was whistling to himself as he began to bed down the cattle for the night. Lydia looked at him eagerly in the dim light. How big and strong he was!

"Billy!" she said, softly.

The young man dropped his pitchfork and came toward her. "What's the matter, Lydia!" he exclaimed.

"Dad and I've been having an awful quarrel."

"About the land?" asked Billy quickly.

Lydia nodded. "Oh, I don't know what to do!" And then, not having meant to do so at all, she suddenly began to cry.

"Why can't they let you alone, damn 'em!" exclaimed Billy, furiously. "Come away from that cold doorway, dear." And he led her into the warm stable and over to a harness box. "There," pulling her down beside him on the box, and putting his arm about her, "don't cry, Lydia. I can't stand it. I'm liable to go over and say things to your father and Kent."

There was an edge to his voice as he said this that vaguely alarmed Lydia. She wiped her eyes.

"Kent wasn't there," she said.

"No, but he's behind your father in this. I'll tell 'em both, sometime, what I think of their bullying you this way."

"Kent hasn't bullied me," insisted Lydia.

"No? Well, give him time! Poor little girl! Don't tremble so. You don't have to talk anymore about it to anyone. Just send 'em to me."

Lydia smiled through her tears. "I can't send my own father to you. And you and Kent would come to blows."

"We probably would," replied Billy. "Want my hanky or haven't you wept yours full yet?"

"I'm not going to cry anymore," said Lydia, raising her head. Billy still held her warmly in the circle of his arm. The stable was dim and quiet and fragrant with clover. "You're such a comfort, Billy. Now that John Levine's gone, there's no one understands me as you do. How can I reconcile Dad to giving up the land?"

"You can't, Lydia. You'll just have to reconcile yourself to a misunderstanding with him."

"But I can't live that way!" wailed Lydia.

"Well, you have the cottage. He used to think he'd be perfectly happy if he owned that."

"Oh, there's a mortgage on the cottage!" exclaimed Lydia. "Poor Daddy! He wants to pay the mortgage with the lands."

"It's tough luck! But there's nothing for you to do, Lydia, but to stick to it. Don't weaken and things will come out all right. See if they don't. And you've always got me. And if I see they're worrying you too much, I'll make trouble for 'em."

A vague, warm sense of comfort and protection was stilling Lydia's trembling. She rose and looked up into his face gratefully. "I don't see why you're so good to me," she said.

"Do you want me to tell you?" began the young man eagerly.

"No! No!" Lydia began to move hastily toward the door. "Don't come home with me, Billy. I'll just run back alone."

Billy's face in the lantern light was inscrutable. "I'll obey tonight, Lydia," he said, "but the time's coming, when I won't," and he picked up the pitchfork he had dropped.

With the sense of comfort and protection sustaining her, Lydia went homeward under the winter stars. Kent's automobile was standing before the gate and Lydia's heart sank. It was the first time in her life she ever had been sorry at the thought of seeing Kent.

He was sitting before the base burner with her father and jumped up to help her take her coat off. He greeted her soberly.

"Your father's been telling me about your discussion, Lyd," he said. "You can't mean to stick by your decision!"

Lydia sat down wearily. "Oh, Kent, don't *you* begin at me, too."

"But I think I ought to, Lydia," replied Kent, his voice dangerously eager. "I don't think any of your friends have a right to be quiet when you're letting a silly scruple ruin your and your father's future."

"It certainly won't ruin my future," said Lydia. "And I won't let it ruin Dad's."

"Now look here, Lydia," began Kent, "let's begin at the beginning and sift this thing out."

"But why?" groaned Lydia. "You know exactly how I feel and why I feel it. And I know how you feel. We've been debating it for years."

"Yes, but listen," persisted Kent, and once more he began his arguments on the Indian question.

Kent had a certain eloquence of speech, yet Lydia, knowing all that he would say, gave little heed to his words while she watched his glowing face.

"Don't you see?" he ended finally.

"I see how you feel, yes," replied Lydia. "But just because you can list what you call average American business deals that are crooked, you aren't justified in being crooked, are you?"

Kent threw out his hand helplessly, and for a moment there was stance in the room, then he said,

"Well, after all, there's nothing so selfish as your Puritans. Of course, everyone but yourselves is wrong. And, of course, it doesn't occur to you that it might be a decent thing of you to sacrifice your own scruples to do a thing that would mean so much to your father."

Lydia looked at Kent quickly. This was a new angle. He would have followed this opening at once had not Amos spoken for the first time.

"Hold up, Kent," he said in a tired voice. "Don't heckle her anymore. After all, I'm getting on toward fifty and I guess it's too late for me to begin over, anyhow. I'll plod along as I always have."

"Oh, Daddy!" cried Lydia, "don't talk that way! You aren't a bit old. You make me feel like a beast, between you."

"Well, we don't mean to," Amos went on, "but I guess we have been pretty hard on you."

Amos' weariness and gentleness moved Lydia as no threats could. Her eyes filled with tears and she crossed over quickly to the window and looked out on the starlit splendor of the lake. In how many, many crises of her life she had gazed on this self-same scene and found decision and comfort there!

Was she selfish? Was she putting her own desire for an easy conscience ahead of her father's happiness? Amos went into the kitchen for a drink and Kent followed her to the window and took both her hands.

"Lydia," he said, "I'm awful sorry to press you so, but you're being unfair and foolish, honestly you are. You used to let me look out for you in the old days — the old days when I used to pull little Patience's carriage with my bicycle — why can't you trust me now? Come, dearest, — and next year we'll be married and live happy ever after."

Lydia's lips quivered. All Kent's charm of manhood, all the memories of their childhood together, of his boyhood love for her and her baby sister, spoke together to win her to his desires. And after all, what could matter so much to her as her father's and Kent's happiness?

"Kent!" she cried with the breathlessness of a new idea, "if I should give in and agree to take the land, would you go up there with me and turn it into a farm?"

Kent smiled at her pityingly. "Why, Lyd, there's nothing in that! Why should we try to farm it? The money is in speculating with it. I could clear up a mint of money for you in a couple of years, if you'll give me the handling of it."

But Lydia's eyes were shining now. "Oh, but listen! You don't understand. Mr. Levine drove the Indians out, by fraud and murder. Yes, he did, Kent. And yet, he had big dreams about it. He must have had. He was that kind of a man. And if we should go up there and turn those acres into a great farm, and – and make it stand for something big and right – perhaps that would make up for everything!"

"Lord, what a dreamer you are, Lyd," groaned Kent. "Mr. Dudley, do you hear this?"

Amos grunted. "Nothing looks good to me but this cottage. I'd have a cow and a few pigs and some bees and the whole world could go to the devil for all of me."

"Lydia," said Kent, "be sensible. Don't talk impossibilities."

"What is there impossible about it?" demanded Lydia.

"Gee, easy money on one side, and a lifetime of hard work on the other! Yet you act as if there was a choice."

"Kent, can't you understand how I feel?" pleaded Lydia. "Have you got a blind spot in your mind where money is concerned? Are all the men in America money crazy like the men in Lake City?"

"Sure," replied Kent cheerfully. "Oh, Lydia, honey, don't be so hard! Look at your poor old Dad! Think what it would mean to him. Don't be so doggone sanctimonious!"

Instead of looking at her father, Lydia looked at Kent, long and wistfully. How dear he was to her! What an inalienable part of her life he was! What was the use of always struggling against her heart. Kent smiled into her face. Her lips trembled and she turned to look at Amos. He was standing by the table, filling his pipe. Suddenly Lydia realized how grey and broken he looked, how bent his shoulders were with work, and there swept over her anew an understanding of his utter loneliness since her mother's and Levine's death.

With a little inarticulate murmur, she ran across the room and threw her arms about his neck. "Oh, Daddy," she cried, "I'll do it! I'll agree to it! If only you'll promise me to be happy!"

Amos dropped his pipe. "Lydia! You don't mean it! Why, my little girl! Lord, Kent! Isn't she just all right! Make me happy! Why, Lydia, you've made a young man of me — I swan — !"

Kent was holding one hand now, Amos the other. Both looked at Lydia with radiant faces. And she could but feel an answering glow.

"We'll make this up to you, Lyd, old lady," cried Kent. "See if we don't." There was a little pause during which the ice boomed. Then,

"Well, what happens next, now you've settled me?" asked Lydia.

"Something to eat," exclaimed Amos. "I didn't eat any supper. I swear I haven't eaten for months with any relish. Lydia, make us some chocolate or something."

As Lydia passed through the dining room with her steaming tray, a little later, Lizzie called from her bed and Lydia set down the tray and went to her.

"Did they win you over, Lydia?" she asked. "I went to bed so's not to interrupt."

"Yes, they won me," said Lydia.

"Poor child! I never wished harder'n I have tonight that your mother hadn't died. But never mind! I guess it's just as well you gave in. Kent could win the heart of a bronze image. Drat him! Run along with the supper, Lydia."

"Now," said Kent, as he sipped his chocolate, "let's lay our plans."

"Not before me," exclaimed Lydia. "My one stipulation is that you don't tell me any of the details."

"All right," said Amos, hastily. "We'll do anything she wants, now, eh, Kent?"

"You bet," replied the young man.

That night, after Kent had gone, Lydia stood long at the living room window which gave on the front gate. The pine, its boughs powdered with snow, kept its lonely vigil over the cottage.

"Yes," whispered Lydia, finally, "your last friend has deserted you, but I guess I'm keeping faith with Kent and Dad, anyhow."

Then she went to bed.

For a day or so Lydia avoided Billy Norton. But she was restless and unhappy and found it difficult to keep her mind on her college work. Finally, she timed her return from the dairy school, one afternoon, to coincide with Billy's home-coming from his office and she overtook him Just beyond the end of the street-car line. The sun was sinking and the wind was rising.

"Billy!" called Lydia.

He turned and waited for her with a broad smile.

"Billy," she said without preliminaries, "I gave in!"

"*Lydia!*" he gasped.

"I couldn't stand their pleading. I gave in. I hate myself, but Dad looks ten years younger!"

"You actually mean you're letting yourself get mixed up with the Whiskey Trust and that pup of a Dave Marshall?"

Lydia plodded doggedly through the snow. "Of course, Kent's tending to all that, I refuse to be told the details."

"Lydia!" cried Billy again and there was such a note of pain in his voice that she turned her face to his with the same dogged look in her eyes that had been expressed in her walk.

"Why," he said, "what am I going to do without you to look up to – to live up to? You can't mean it!"

"But I do mean it. I fought and fought and I have for years till I'm sick of it. Now, at least, there'll be no more poverty for Dad to complain of."

"'Just for a handful of silver he left us,
 Just for a ribband to wear in his coat,'"

quoted Billy bitterly. "Lydia, I can't believe it!"

"It's true," repeated Lydia. "I couldn't stand Kent and Dad both. And partly I did it for John Levine's memory. I'm not trying to justify myself Billy. I know that I'm doing something wrong, but I've definitely made up my mind to sacrifice my own ease of conscience to Dad's happiness."

"You can't do it! You aren't built that way," exclaimed Billy.

"But I *am* doing it," reiterated Lydia.

"Look here," he cried, eagerly, "do you expect to keep my respect and yet go on with this?"

Lydia did not reply for some time. They were nearing the cottage, and she could see the pine, black against the afterglow, when she said,

"Well, I'm not keeping my own self-respect and yet, I'm glad I'm making Dad and Kent happy."

"Kent! Wait till I see him!"

"You can't change Kent, if I couldn't," replied Lydia.

"I'll not try to change him," said Billy grimly. "I'll tell him what I think of him, though."

They paused by the gate. Billy looked down at Lydia with a puzzled frown.

"How about 'Ducit Amor Patriae' now, Lydia?" he asked.

"Oh, I don't know," she sighed. "Good night, Billy."

"Good-bye, Lydia," said the young man heavily and he turned away, leaving her standing at the gate.

But though she had maintained a calm front with Billy, Lydia went over and over their conversation that night feverishly before she went to sleep. She tossed and turned and then long after the old living room clock had struck midnight, she slipped out of bed and crouched on her knees, her hands clasped across her pillow, her eyes on the quiet stars that glowed through the window.

"O God," she prayed, "O God, if You do exist, help me now! Don't let me lose Billy's respect for I don't know how I can get along without it. God! God! Make me believe in You, for I must have Some One to turn to! You have taken mother and little Patience and John Levine from me! Oh, let me keep Billy! Let me keep him, God, and make me strong enough to keep on accepting that three hundred and twenty acres. Amen."

Shivering, but somehow quieted, she crept into bed and fell asleep.

Chapter XX

THE YOUNGEST SCHOLAR

"The Indians knew no home, and so they died."
— *The Murmuring Pine*

*I*f Amos was not happy after Lydia's concession, at least she never had seen him so interested in life as he was now. Nor had Kent ever been more considerate of Lydia. They went to a number of dances and skated together frequently in spite of the fact that Kent was very busy with his real estate work.

All this, Lydia told herself, should have made her happy, and yet, she was not. Even when Professor Willis took her to a Military hop and brought her home in a hack, she was conscious of the feverish sense of loss and uncertainty that had become a part of her daily living. Several times she had an almost overwhelming desire to tell him what she had done. But she could not bear to destroy the ideal she knew he had of her, even for the relief of receiving his sympathy, of which she was very sure.

Billy came to see her as usual, and took her to an occasional dance. But he was not the friend of old. And the change was not in any neglect of things done, it was in his way of looking at her; in his long silences when he studied her face with a grieved, puzzled look that made her frantic; in his ceasing to talk over his work with her with any air of comradeship, and most of all in his ceasing to bully her — that inalienable earmark of the attitude of the lover toward the beloved.

Lydia's nerves began to feel the strain before spring came in. She was pale in the morning and fever-flushed in the afternoon and her hands were uncertain. March was long and bleak, that year, but April came in as sweetly as a silver bugle call. The first week in April the ice went out of the lake with a crash and boom and mighty upheaval, leaving a pellucid calm of blue waters that brought a new light to Lydia's face. She heard the first robin call on her way home from college, the day that the ice went out.

She had walked up the road ahead of Billy, her black scholar's gown fluttering. Once, he would have run to overtake her, but now he plodded along a block behind, without a sound. Lydia did not pause at the cottage gate. The call of the robin was in her blood and she swung on up the road, past the Norton place, and into the woods.

Young April was there, with its silence a-tiptoe, and its warmth and chill. Lydia drew a deep breath and paused where through the trunks of the white birches she caught the glimmer of the lake. There was a log at hand and she sat down, threw her mortar-board on the ground and rested, chin cupped in her hands, lips parted, eyes tear dimmed. She was weary of thought. She only knew that the spiritual rightness with which she had sustained her mind and body through all the hard years of her youth, had gone wrong. She only knew that a loneliness of soul she could not seem to endure was robbing her of a youth that as yet she had scarcely tasted.

She sat without stirring. The blue of the lake began to turn orange. The robin's note grew fainter. Suddenly there was the sound of hasty footsteps through the dead leaves. Lydia looked up. Billy was striding toward her. She did not speak, nor did he. It seemed to her that she never had noticed before how mature Billy's face was in its new gaunt-ness, nor how deep and direct was his gaze.

He strode up to the log, stooped, and drew Lydia to her feet. Then he lifted her, scholar's gown and all, in his arms and kissed her full on the lips, kissed her long and passionately, then looked deep into her eyes and held her to him until she could feel his heart beating full and quick.

For just a moment, Lydia did not stir, then she threw her arms around his neck, hid her face against his shoulder and clung to him with an intensity that made him tremble.

The robin's note grew sweeter, fainter. The lake lap-lapped beyond the birches. Billy slipped his hand under Lydia's cheek and turned her face so that he could look into her eyes. At what he saw there, his own firm lips quivered.

"Lydia!" he whispered.

Then he kissed her again.

Lydia freed herself from his arms, though he kept both of her hands in his.

"Now," he said gently, with a smile of a quality Lydia never had seen on his lips before, "now, sweetheart, are you going to be good?"

"Yes," murmured Lydia, with the contralto lilt in her voice. "What do you want me to do. Billy?"

"I want what you want, dearest. I want the old Lydia with the vision. Has she come back, or shall I have to look for her again?"

He started as if to take Lydia in his arms once more, but with a sudden rich little laugh, she stepped away from him.

"She's here – Oh, Billy, *dearest!* How could you let her wander around alone so long."

"It didn't hurt my cause any for her to miss me," answered Billy, grimly, "though I didn't realize that till a moment ago. Stop your trembling, Lydia. I'm here to look out for you, for the rest of time."

"I can hear Adam barking," said Lydia. "Dad must have come home. Take me back, Billy."

"All right," replied Billy. "I will just as soon as you tell me something."

Lydia looked up into his face. "Not that just yet, please, Billy. I must make things right with Dad and Kent."

Billy seized her shoulders. "Is there anything between you and Kent, Lydia?" he said, jealously.

"Not in words," she answered, "but of course he's gone ahead with my land deal, with the idea he'd share in it."

Billy's hands tightened on her shoulders. "Dear," Lydia went on pleadingly, "don't spoil this perfect moment. We must have this, always, no matter what comes."

"Nothing can come," replied Billy sternly. "Give me your hand, little girl. It's getting cold in these woods."

They walked back to the cottage in silence, hand in hand. They paused at the gate and Lydia pointed through the dusk at the new moon.

"Let's wish on it," she said. "Close your eyes, and wish."

Billy closed his eyes. A kiss as soft as the robin's note fell on his lips and the gate clicked. He opened his eyes and stood looking up the path long after the door closed, his hat in his hand.

Lydia wandered into the dining room quite casually.

"For heaven's sake, Lydia!" cried Amos. "I was just going to start on a hunt for you!"

"I took a walk in the woods," explained Lydia, "and was gone longer than I realized."

"Supper's ready. Sit right down," said Lizzie, looking at Lydia, intently.

Amos was absorbed in his own thoughts during the meal. He and Kent had both been worried and absent minded, lately. He paid no heed to the fact that Lydia only played with her food and that during the meal she smiled at nothing. But old Lizzie, who had worried herself half sick over Lydia, watched her with growing curiosity.

"Seen Kent, today, Lydia?" she asked.

After a moment — "Did you speak to me, Lizzie?" Lydia inquired.

"Yes, I did. I asked if you'd seen Kent today."

"I? No, I haven't seen Kent. We had a quiz in chemistry, today."

"What's that got to do with anything?" grunted Lizzie. But she asked no more questions.

Ma Norton came over during the evening to borrow some yeast. Amos was working over some figures on a bit of paper. Lydia was sitting with a text book in front of her. She had not turned a leaf in twenty minutes, to Lizzie's actual count.

"Spring's here," said Ma. "Though there's still a bite in the air. Not that Billy seems to notice it. I found him sitting on the front steps with his cigar, as if it was June."

Lizzie gave Lydia a quick look and wondered if she only imagined that her cheeks were turning pinker.

"I can't sit down," Ma went on, "I've got to set this sponge to rise."

"I'll walk home with you, Mrs. Norton," said Lydia, suddenly. "It seems as if one couldn't get enough of this first spring day."

"Do!" Ma's voice was always extra cordial when she spoke to Lydia.

Lizzie watched the door close behind the two. "I knew it," she exclaimed.

"Knew what?" inquired Amos, looking up from his figures.

"That there was a new moon," answered the old lady, shortly, trudging off to her bedroom.

"Liz is getting childish," thought Amos, returning to his work.

"Bill's still on the front porch," said Ma Norton as they reached the Norton driveway. "Do go speak to him, Lydia. He's amiable tonight, but he's been like a bear for months."

Billy's mother went on into the kitchen entrance and Lydia went over to the dim figure on the steps.

"Your mother told me to speak to you," she said meekly.

"I heard her." Billy gave a low laugh. "Come up here in the shadow, sweetheart, and tell me if you ever saw such a moonlit and starlit night."

But Lydia did not stir. "Honestly, I don't dare look at the sky any longer. I have a quiz in rhetoric tomorrow and I've *got* to get my mind on it."

Billy came down the steps. "Then I'll walk home with you."

"No, you won't. I — I just came over to see if it's all real. Just to touch you and then run back. I'd rather you didn't walk back with me."

The night was brilliant and Billy, responding to some little petitioning note in Lydia's voice, did not offer to touch her but stood looking down at the sweet dim face turned up to his. She lifted her hand, that thin hand with the work calluses on it, and ran it over his cheeks, brushed her cheek against his shoulder, and then ran away.

She finished her studying and went to bed early, only to lie awake for hours. At last, she crept out of bed and as once before, she clasped her hands and lifted her face to the heavens. "Thank you, God!" she whispered. Then she went to sleep.

The next night, Kent came out to the cottage. Lydia dreaded his coming so little that she was surprised. Yet this day had been one of continual surprise to her. She had wakened to a dawn of robin songs, and had dressed with an answering song in her own heart. She was as one who had never known sorrow or anxiety. Her whole future lay before her, a clear and unobstructed pathway.

For Lydia had found herself. She was a creature to whom a great love and devotion were essential as motive forces. In turn she had given this, in childish form, to her mother, to little Patience and to Levine. One by one these had been taken from her and she had struggled to give this devotion to Kent, but she could not give where there was no understanding.

And now she saw that for years it had been Billy. Billy who combined all the best of what her mother, her baby sister, and Levine had meant to her, with something greatly more — the divinity of passion — a thing she could not understand, yet that had created a new world for her.

Kent tossed his hat on the couch and shook his head at Amos. "Dave's not going to get away with it. He's got some kind of a row going with the Whiskey people and he says we might as well count him out. I don't know what to do now."

Amos groaned. "Lord, what luck!"

"Don't let it worry you," said Lydia calmly. "I made up my mind today that I'd go ahead and enter on that land just as other folks are doing, in the good old way. I'm going to make a farm up there, that will blot out all memory of what Mr. Levine did. But I'm going to work for it as a homesteader has to and not take any advantage through Mr. Levine's graft."

Kent looked up crossly. "Oh, Lydia, for heaven's sake, don't begin that again!"

Lydia crossed the room and put her hand on Kent's shoulder as he sat on the couch.

"Kent, look at me," she said, then, very quietly, "I'm going to homestead that land." There was no escaping the note of finality in her decision.

Kent's face whitened. He looked up steadily at Lydia. Amos and Lizzie sensed that they were spectators of a deeper crisis than they understood and they watched breathlessly. Kent rose slowly. The sweat stood on his forehead.

"You know what that means, as far as I'm concerned," he said.

Lydia, chin up, gaze never more clearly blue, nodded.

"Yes, Kent, but we never would have been happy. You and Margery were meant for each other, anyhow."

"Lydia! Lydia!" exclaimed Kent hoarsely, half angrily, half pleadingly.

"No, you won't feel badly, when you think it over. Go to Margery now and tell her, Kent."

Kent picked up his cap. "I — I don't understand," he said. Then, angrily, "You aren't treating me right, Lydia. I'll talk to you when I'm not so sore," and he walked out of the house.

Lydia turned to Amos and Lizzie. "There," she said, happily, "I've got Kent settled for life!"

Amos sank into his armchair. "Lydia, have you lost your mind!" he groaned.

"No, I've found it, Daddy. Poor Dad, don't look as if you'd fathered a lunatic!"

Amos shook his head.

"Daddy, let's homestead that land! Let's quit this idea of getting something by graft. Let's do like our forefathers did. Let's homestead that land! Let's earn it by farming it."

Lydia's father looked at her, long and meditatively. He was pretty well discouraged about the probability of ever getting a clear title to the land through Kent or Marshall. And the longer he looked at Lydia, the more his mind reverted to New England, to old tales of the farm on which he and his ancestors had been bred.

"A man with three hundred and twenty acres of land is a power in the community," he said, suddenly.

"Oh, yes, Dad!" cried Lydia.

"You never know what a feeling of independence is," said Lizzie, "till you own land and raise wheat."

Amos stared out the door into the darkness. Little by little Lydia saw creeping into his face new lines of determination, a new sort of pride that the thought of the selling of the lands had not put there. He cleared his throat.

"Hang it, Lydia, I'm not as hard as you think I am. I want you to be happy. And I'm not so damned old as you think I am. I'm good for homesteading, if you and Liz are. A farmer with three hundred and twenty acres! God!"

Lydia nodded. Amos began to walk the floor. "I'm still a young man. If I had the backing that land gives a man, I could clean out a lot of rottenness in the State. Even if I only did it by showing what a man with a clean record could make of himself."

"That's just the point," cried Lydia eagerly, "and your record wouldn't have been clean, if you'd gotten it through Marshall."

"What young men need nowadays," Amos went on, "is to get back to the old idea of land ownership. Three hundred and twenty acres! Lydia, why can't I enter on it tomorrow?"

"Why not?" asked Lydia.

"If I take Brown's offer for the cottage, it would leave us enough to get a team and I bet I could hire a tractor to get to the cleared portion of it, this Fall. A hundred acres are clear, you know. I might as well quit the factory now, eh, Lydia?"

With a laugh that had a sob in it, Lydia kissed her father and whirled out the door. Billy was coming in at the gate. She flew down to seize his hand and turn him toward the road.

"Let's walk! I've such quantities to tell you!"

Billy turned obediently, but paused in the shadow of the pine. "Lydia, I can't tell you what it means to me. No matter what bigger things may seem to happen to me, nothing can equal the things I've felt and dreamed today."

Then he put his arms about Lydia and kissed her, and she put her arms about his neck and laid her head against his shoulder. They stood thus motionless while the pine whispered above them. And in the intensity of that embrace all the griefs of Lydia's life were hallowed and made purposeful.

"Lydia," said Billy, "I want to tell Mother and Dad. Will you come over home with me, now?"

"Yes," replied Lydia, "and then we must tell my father and Lizzie. Oh, Billy, I forgot," as they started down the road, "I've decided to homestead that land."

"But — why, Lydia dear, you're going to be a lawyer's wife. For heaven's sake, let that beastly land go."

"No, I'm going to be a pioneer's wife!"

There was a little pause, then Billy laughed uncertainly. "Well, I'm not going to talk about it tonight. I'm in a frame of mind tonight where I'd promise you to be an Indian chief if you ask it. Mother and Dad are in the kitchen."

They opened the kitchen door and stepped in. Pa Norton was sitting in his stocking feet, reading the evening paper. Ma was putting away the day's baking. She paused with a loaf of bread in her hand as the two came in and Pa looked over his glasses.

"Mother and Dad," said Billy, uncertainly, "I — I've brought Lydia home to you! Look at her, Dad! Isn't she a peach!"

Lydia stood with her back against the door, cheeks scarlet, golden head held high, but her lips quivering.

Ma dropped her loaf of bread. "Oh, Lydia," she cried, "I thought that numskull of a Billy never would see daylight! I've prayed for this for years. Come straight over here to your mother, love."

But Pa Norton had dropped his paper when Ma dropped her bread and had not paused for comments. He made three strides to Lydia, and gave her a great hug and a kiss. Then he said, "First time I saw you carrying that milk for Billy's books, I said, there's the wife Billy ought to have. Ma, wasn't she the dearest —"

But Ma shoved him aside contemptuously. "Get over and talk to Billy. This is a woman's affair. Who cares about reminiscences now. Oh, Billy, do you remember I used to worry because she didn't keep the back of her neck clean!"

"Who's reminiscencing now?" asked Pa belligerently.

Everybody laughed. Then Pa sighed. "Well, I feel almost reconciled now to Bill's giving up farming. When're you going to be married?"

Lydia blushed. "Oh, not for a long time. Now, let's go and tell my people, Billy."

Out in the night again! Curious how long the short walk to the cottage could be made! Curious how near the stars were — heaven just over the road where the lovers strolled. Not strange that such ecstasy cannot last forever. The human mind could not bear that heaven-born rapture too long.

Lizzie was mending. Amos was sitting in his armchair, with a bit of paper on which he was figuring. Lydia flew across the room and dropped on her knees beside him.

"Oh, Daddy dear, look at me! Billy's here and he's always going to be here. Tell us you're glad."

Amos looked up with a jerk. First at Billy standing stalwart and grave by the table, his deep eyes as steady as the hand he held out to Lizzie. Then at his daughter, with her transformed face.

"But," protested Amos, "I thought it was to be Kent."

"Oh, it couldn't have been Kent," exclaimed Lydia. "We never would have understood each other. Kent was for Margery."

A frown gathered on Amos' face. He did not really want Lydia to marry anyone. All that had reconciled him to the thought of Kent had been Kent's relation to the Indian lands. And now, he discovered that he didn't want to give his daughter to anyone. He threw a jealous arm about her.

"No, you can't have her, Billy," he said. "Nobody shall have her. She's too good for the best man living."

"Yes, she is," agreed Billy. "But that isn't the point. The point is that Lydia actually wants me. I don't understand it myself, but she does and I know I can make her happy."

"I can make her happy myself," said Amos, gruffly.

"But you haven't," retorted Billy. "Look at the way you've acted about this land matter. And God knows, she deserves to be happy at any cost. Good heavens, when I think of her, it seems to me that nothing could be too much for her. I think of her trudging those miles in her patched old clothes to buy her schoolbooks — what a thin, big-eyed kiddie she was. Why, even as a cub, I used to appreciate her. And then when she stood up before the hearing, the bravest man among us, and when she got sick trying to earn those silly Prom clothes — My God, Amos, if Lydia wants me, or the moon, or a town lot in South Africa, it's up to you to give it to her."

Amos did not reply for a moment. Down through the years he was watching a thin little figure trudge with such patience and sweetness and determination as he seemed never before to have appreciated. Slowly his hold loosened on Lydia's shoulders and he looked into her face.

"Do you want to marry Billy?" he asked.

"Oh, Daddy, yes," whispered Lydia.

Amos looked up at the young man, who stood returning his gaze. "Take her, Billy, and heaven help you if you're not good to her, for John Levine's spirit will haunt you with a curse."

Billy raised Lydia to her feet and the extraordinary smile was on his face.

"What do you think about it, Lizzie?" he asked. Lizzie, who had been crying comfortably, wiped her eyes with the sock she was darning.

"I'm thinking that anyone that can bring the look to Lydia's face she's been wearing for twenty-four hours, deserves her. Rheumatism or no, down I get on my old knees tonight and give thanks — just for the look in that child's eyes."

And now for a while, Lydia was content to live absolutely in the present, as was Billy. Surely there never was such an April. And surely no April ever melted so softly into so glorious a May. Apple blossoms, lilac blooms, violets and wind flowers and through them, Lydia in her scholar's gown, hanging to Billy's arm, after the day's work was done.

She seemed singularly uninterested in the preparations for Commencement, though she went through her final examinations with credit. But the week before Commencement she came home one afternoon with blazing cheeks. Billy was at the cottage for supper and when they had begun the meal, she exploded her bomb.

"Dad! Billy! Lizzie! They've elected me a member of the Scholars' Club!"

"For the love of heaven!" exclaimed Amos, dropping his fork.

"Why not?" asked Lizzie.

"Lydia, dear, but I'm proud of you," breathed Billy.

"Professor Willis told me, this afternoon," Lydia went on, "and I laughed at him at first. I thought he was teasing me. Why only highbrows belong to the Scholars' Club! Prexy belongs and the best of the professors and only a few of the post-graduate pupils. But he says I was elected. I told him lots of students had higher standings than I, and he only laughed and said he knew it. And I've got to go to that banquet of theirs next week!"

"Fine!" said Billy.

"Fine! Why, Billy Norton, I never went to a banquet in my life. I don't know what forks to use, and I *never saw a finger bowl!*"

Amos grinned. "What's the use of being a scholar, if that sort of thing bothers you?"

"I might get a book on etiquette and polish up," said Lydia, thoughtfully. "I'll get one tomorrow, and practice on the family."

Amos groaned, but to no avail. Lydia borrowed a book on etiquette from the library and for a week Amos ate his supper with an array of silver and kitchenware before him that took his appetite away. He rebelled utterly at using the finger bowls, which at breakfast were porridge dishes. Lizzie, however, was apt and read the book so diligently while Lydia was in class that she was able to correct Lydia as well as Amos at night.

Ma Norton had insisted on making Lydia a white mull graduation dress. She would not let either Lizzie or Lydia help her. She had been daughter-hungry all her life and since she made her own wedding gown, no bit of sewing had given her the satisfaction that this did.

So it was that Lydia, wearing the mull under her scholar's gown, and with the precepts of the book on etiquette in her mind, attended the Scholars' banquet, timidly but not with the self-consciousness that she might otherwise have felt.

Billy left her at the door of the hall and Professor Willis took her in to dinner. There were only two other women there, but Lydia did not mind.

"You never told me," said Willis, after Lydia had safely chosen her salad fork, "what you've done about the three hundred and twenty acres."

Lydia looked up at him quickly. She had been dreading this moment for some time.

"I'm going to give up John Levine's claim on it, and enter on it as a homesteader."

"But what an undertaking!" exclaimed Willis.

"I'll not go alone," said Lydia gently. "Billy Norton will go with me."

Willis turned white, and laid down his salad fork. Lydia turned her head away, then looked back, her eyes a little tear dimmed.

"I'm sorry," she said.

"Don't be," he answered, after a moment. "You never did a kinder thing than to tell me this now — before — not but what it would have been too late, had you told me two years ago."

"Oh, I am so sorry," repeated Lydia miserably.

"But you mustn't be! Besides, you and I are both scholars and scholars are always philosophers!"

He was silent for the rest of the banquet, in spite of his philosophy. But when he was called on for his toast, which was the last one, he rose coolly enough, and began steadily,

"My toast is to all scholars, everywhere, but also to one scholar in particular. It is to one who was born with a love of books, to one who made books — good books — so intimate a part of her life that she made poverty a blessing, who combined books and living so deeply that she read her community aright, when others failed to do so, to one who is a scholar in the truest sense of the word — a book lover with a vision. I drink to the youngest and sweetest scholar of us all!" and he bowed to Lydia.

How she got through the congratulations and out to Billy, patiently waiting at the main campus gate, Lydia was not sure, for she was quite drunk with surprise and pleasure. After she had told it all to Billy, and once more they were standing under the pine at the gate, she said,

"Billy, will you go up with Father and Lizzie and me to open up the three hundred and twenty acres?"

Billy answered slowly. "There's nothing I'd like better. I was born to be a farmer. But, Lydia, it looks to me as if, as a lawyer, I'd be a more useful citizen, the way things are now in the country."

Lydia shook her head. "We've got too many lawyers in America. What I think America needs is real love of America. And it seems to me the best way to get it is to identify oneself with the actual soil of the community. What I want is this. That you and I, upon the ground where poor John Levine did such wrongs, build us a home. I don't mean a home as Americans usually mean the word. I mean we'll try to found a family there. We'll send the roots of our roof tree so deep into the ground that for generations to come our children's children will be found there and our family name will stand for old American ideals in the community. I don't see how else we Americans can make up to the world for the way we've exploited America."

Billy stood with his arm about the slender "scholar." Suddenly there flooded in upon him the old, old call, the call that had brought his Pilgrim forefathers across the Atlantic, the call that was as old as the yearning for freedom of the soil.

"Lord!" he cried, "how glad I'll be to go up there! Think of beginning our life together with such a dream!"

"I believe John Levine would be glad, if he knew," said Lydia, wistfully.

"I know he'd be glad. . . . Lydia, do you love me, dear?"

"Love you! Oh, more than all the world! You know it, don't you?"

"I know it, but I can't believe it." His arm tightened around Lydia and as on just such an evening, four years before, he said,

"What a wonderful night!"

A wonderful night, indeed! Sound and scent of bursting summer. Syringas coming as lilacs went. The lake, lap-lapping on the shore. The lazy croak of frogs and the moon sinking low over the cottage. Above them the pine, murmuring as of old. Life and the year at the full. A wonderful night, indeed!

THE END